THE DRIFTER

THE DRIFTER

A NOVEL

CHRISTINE LENNON

wm

WILLIAM MORROW

An Imprint of HarperCollins*Publishers*

Grateful acknowledgment is made for the use of text from *I'll Take You There* by Joyce Carol Oates.

P.S.™ is a trademark of HarperCollins Publishers.

FIRST EDITION

Designed by Diahann Sturge

Library of Congress Cataloging-in-Publication Data has been applied for.

ISBN 978-0-06-245757-8

17 18 19 20 21 LSC 10 9 8 7 6 5 4 3 2 1

For Louis and Millie,
who really love stories,
but who won't read this one until 2023

I could not tell myself the old story *Once upon a time* because the time was now; the story was now; I'd believed I was causing the story to take place, but in fact the story was taking place around me, as a tide rises, brackish and muddy and filthy and filled with debris. My Kappa sisters were fascinating to me as giant, brightly feathered predator birds would be fascinating to a small songbird hiding in the brush. Or trying to hide in the brush.

—Joyce Carol Oates

THE DRIFTER

PROLOGUE

September 9, 2010

From her perch on the brownstone stoop, Elizabeth lifts up her sunglasses, runs her ring finger along her lower lashes to flick away the welling tears, and glances at her phone to check the time. *9:25*. She shifts her weight to her left hip and stretches out her other leg to let the blood circulate to her toes, then sits backs against the iron railing and scans the street.

As nonchalantly as possible, doing her best impression of a person who isn't entirely unhinged, she scrolls through her emails, keeping her peripheral vision trained on the front door of the tan brick building across the street. Several times a minute, her eyes dart back to the entrance.

By now, she knows the morning rhythms of the block by heart. The middle-aged silver fox in Italian loafers who catches a cab on the corner of Fifth Avenue. The pair of Caribbean nurses who swap comic insults as they walk to the radiology clinic down the street. The twentysomething who stumbles out of her apartment in pricey yoga wear at the same time every morning but never makes it further than the corner for a coffee. Their familiarity has become a comfort to Elizabeth. It's the new faces, like the driver of the black sedan who seemed to stare at her from behind his mirrored glasses while he waited for his fare, that unnerve her.

Today, a quick study of the scene reveals a FedEx delivery truck, two tattooed bike messengers, a few flustered parents dragging their children to school. Elizabeth eyes these women with a bit of envy and suspicion; perversely, she wishes that her own daughter would put up more of a fight each morning at drop-off. Back in July, on the first day of the weeklong "transition" period, Remi was the child in her classroom to wander over, tug at her mother's hand, and say, "Mommy? It's OK if you want to go now." Elizabeth had tried not to look as stricken as she felt. "Alright, sweetie," she said, forcing a smile. She'd lingered for a while in the other room, out of her daughter's sight, sipping weak coffee from a thin paper cup, waiting for the school's beatific director, Elodie, a woman whose chipper condescension she found impossibly irritating, to come in, pull her aside, and whisper gravely, "*Elizabeth, can you come back in for a minute? Remi* needs *you.*" It never happened.

"I guess that's the one good thing about waiting to send your child to preschool until she's *nearly five years old*!" Elodie had said to Elizabeth on the morning of Remi's first full day of school. Elodie rarely missed an opportunity to remind Elizabeth that her daughter was starting preschool unusually late for a sophisticated city kid. "Is Remi ever ready to be here with us!" Elodie would say in front of the other moms at drop-off. "It's like she was shot out of a cannon."

ELIZABETH KNEW SHE had started off on the wrong foot with Elodie during the parent interview many months ago. Things started heading south right in the middle of Elizabeth's grand inquisition about teacher background checks. She grilled Elodie about how frequently the school changed the code to the keypad at the door, whether the strike plates on the door locks were kick resistant, and what the school's disaster preparedness plans were. But then, just as Elodie looked really disturbed and on the verge of showing them the door, Elizabeth's husband, Gavin, leaped to her rescue. He put his arm around his wife, flashed the preschool director his trademark grin, and saved the day with his relaxed charm, as he so often did whenever Elizabeth got carried away.

"Well, when I was about Remi's age, I found an alligator paddling around in our pool, and my mom came out to take a picture before she called the fish and game department," he said, using his best syrupy drawl. "So I guess danger is fairly relative." They all laughed. The ice broken, the conversation turned more benign, to childhoods spent in Florida and the weather. Crisis averted.

Still, before they left, Elodie had asked offhandedly if there had been anything unusual about Remi's birth or infancy, anything at all that would impact her ability to thrive in a new environment. Elizabeth and Gavin had avoided each other's eyes as Elizabeth explained that Remi came more than a month early and had stayed in the NICU for two weeks.

"We can be a bit . . . overprotective, as a result, I guess," Gavin said. "She was just so . . . fragile for so long." Elizabeth blinked hard and pretended to examine her wedding ring, a simple, gold band they'd bought in the men's section at Cartier. There was so much more to the story than Elodie could ever guess. The real story was something she would never begin to understand.

"I'm sure Remi will be just fine," Elodie said as she stood up to escort them out to the school's cheerful foyer. "Children are so much more resilient than we are."

JUST AS ELODIE predicted, every morning since school started, Remi bounds in as if she is on the payroll, and Elodie has to shepherd Elizabeth out the front door.

"Elizabeth, your daughter is not the least bit fragile anymore. Look at that happy smile. You have to relax," Elodie insisted earlier that morning, not unkindly. "Let her go."

Let her go. Elizabeth shuddered. *I'll never be able to do that.*

Elizabeth had knelt down in the doorway to the classroom so Remi could wrap her arms around her neck. "Have a great day, sweet girl," Elizabeth whispered, smoothing Remi's unruly hair behind her ears. Remi gave her mother a quick air peck near her cheek, then hurried across the room to study the "jobs" that lined the wall. She picked up a small bowl of plastic animals and carried it to a mat on the floor. Watching as her daughter lined up the figurines by size, Elizabeth arranged her face into a smile. Elodie was right, her daughter was fine. Look at her, so happy to be out in the world, making friends. Elizabeth was holding her back.

"Remi has been very interested in sifting the flour," said Elodie, peering cautiously at Elizabeth over her glasses. "You should ask her about it later."

"Well, what can I say? She's a natural-born sifter, from a long line of accomplished sifters," Elizabeth said.

Elodie took Elizabeth's arm and guided her out to the school entrance like a reluctant child. "Trust me, Elizabeth. She's really thriving here."

Elizabeth nodded and mumbled while fumbling through her bag for her black sunglasses that would obscure the tears welling in her eyes again. She hurried past the parents who were still peeling their toddlers off their pant legs, nodding at a few, but too paranoid about botching a name to say hello.

Outside on the sidewalk, away from the waxy smell of crayons and the astringent sting of hand sanitizer, she inhaled deeply. She wondered how she must look to passersby in her studied urban gear—the discus-sized sunglasses under her razor sharp bangs, platform wedge heels, a giant tote bag with hardware too heavy to be practical, and a shapeless sleeveless dress in an arty print that was cooler than it was flattering, which she'd smarten up with a blazer once she got to the office. If she ever got to the office. If she could ever lift herself up from the purgatory of the brownstone stoop.

IT'S NOW 9:43. Elizabeth checks her email and starts to reply to the forty-two unread messages that show up in her in-box, tapping quick replies with her thumbs. The clock is ticking on the biggest project of her career, an estate sale of more than 350 lots, including rare prints and lithographs from Picasso, Magritte, Kandinsky, Munch, and Mary Cassatt, that is less than two months away. She is dangerously behind schedule. Her assistant, Nina, sent her a message the night before at around midnight to remind her that the public relations department needed some answers about promoting the auction in *The New York Times*, and there were still contracts from the heirs that needed to be finalized and signed. The auction catalogue is due at the printer in a week, and she is going to have to work overtime to finish it. But she can't manage to peel herself away. She clicks on an email from Jessica, her closest friend in New York, asking her to lunch next week. She starts to write back, and then stops. She's been avoiding Jessica, too.

At 9:57 the phone rings. A picture of Remi as a wrinkly faced newborn, wearing a cap with tiny brown bear ears knitted onto the sides, pops up on her screen. She panics, considers letting the call go to voice mail, then decides it's best to answer or he might call the office instead.

"Hey, Gav," she says as breezily as possible. "What's up?"

"Nothin' much. Whatcha doing?" he asks. Gavin never rushes his speech, but a pace this slow is deliberate, and suspiciously casual. He is crunching something, loudly, in her ear.

"Not much, sweetie." She eyes the ragged cuticle of her left thumb, and the deep navy polish that is starting to lose its sheen. "Just finished my coffee outside, getting a last blast of fresh air before work, you know. Sort of makes me miss smoking. I don't get to linger on the sidewalk on a nice day anymore."

"Oh, really. That's weird . . ."

She listens as he takes another bite and munches in her ear.

"Because Elodie just called. She tells me that you're camped in front of the school," he says. "Again."

Elizabeth's eyes dart across the street to the window on the left of the front door. The blinds are raised and there is Elodie, peering over her hateful little glasses with pursed lips. Elizabeth offers a smile and a limp wave. Elodie does not wave back.

"Honey, what's going on? You're starting to freak everyone out. Remi's fine, she's safe. What is it?"

"I don't know," she says, even though it's a lie. The tears reappear on cue and this time she uses the heel of her palm to swipe them away. She checks her hand for black streaks before she remembers that she stopped wearing mascara for this very reason. "It's awful. God, Gavin, I'm so fucked-up. And I'm late for work again. Everyone probably thinks I'm a total nutjob."

Gavin takes another bite in her ear. "Well, I mean, you *are* stalking the preschool."

"What are you eating, anyway?" she asks. "It sounds like you're chomping on gravel."

"Oh just one of your extremely undelicious granola bars," he says, with a lilt of sarcasm. To assuage her working-mom guilt, Elizabeth spent last weekend making corn-syrup-free snacks for her daughter.

"Oh God, sorry. They're so gross. You might want to chase it down with some milk or something," she says, grimly. Remi had taken one bite and spit out the chewed mush into Elizabeth's palm, then asked for cheddar bunnies instead.

"Look, honey, Remi is *safe*. She really is. We wouldn't have sent her there if we thought she wasn't. And by the way, a little corn syrup isn't going to hurt her either."

They pause for a minute, letting the silence and the weight of all that they never need to say settle between them. He knows that her nightmares are back. "You were talking in your sleep," Gavin had said to her when she awoke in a daze on Friday morning, and Elizabeth blew it off, pretended not to remember how she'd bolted up in the middle of the night, a spasm of dread in her chest. She could hide it from everyone else, but not Gavin.

For years, the fear has come like this, in waves that pound

over her and then recede. Her mind was calm for most of the summer. She was fine, happy even. She left Remi with their nanny, Flavia (who had been background checked within an inch of her life), each day; at work she was focused and productive. Then, last month, an email out of the blue brought it all rushing back. She knew what would happen as soon as she saw the name in her in-box, Leslie Portner, an old acquaintance from her college sorority days. Elizabeth dithered over whether to open the message for a few minutes, peered out of her office window to see if anyone was approaching, and angled her monitor to be sure no one walking down the hall could see. She considered deleting it. Perhaps she could look at it later. But then, her heart hammering, she clicked, and the past opened up on her screen.

"Look how young we were!!!" the email exclaimed. Attached was an invitation to a sorority reunion, scheduled on the weekend of the Tennessee football game, written in bold orange letters over a grainy photo. "Bygones," Elizabeth mumbled to herself, as she scanned the image, five rows of beaming college girls in sundresses on Bid Day. Once you were in, even if you strain against it and resign in a huff, they never really let you go. She zoomed in with her mouse to scan their blurred faces. First she found her own—soft angles, her long honey-colored hair curled for the occasion.

Then she saw them. To her left was Caroline, and Ginny was wedged between them, seated on Caroline's lap, her slender tanned arms draped around their shoulders. That's how it always was. Ginny was the bridge between them, filling the empty space. Elizabeth went over their features again and again, suddenly aware of how long it had been since she had seen this photo, and that she could no longer recall their faces precisely from memory. All of the photos she had from that time were out of sight, stored away in her mother's attic. Faces that had once been as familiar to her as her own had become hazy in her mind, until now.

Now they are all she sees.

Gavin's voice shakes her back to the present. "Honey, listen. You've got to let her go."

"Let who go, Gav?" she whispers into the phone, leaning her head down and pressing her thumb and forefinger against her brow bones to try to stop the tears. They both know she no longer means Remi. "That's the question, isn't it? And I can't. She's with me every day."

Elizabeth has tried to move on, for years and years. Sometimes, on good days, she feels like she has. But the memories come nightly now. In her sleep, she walks into a dark apartment and notices a light burning in the bedroom, the door left slightly ajar. Sometimes there is a dark puddle of blood on the old hardwood floor. Sometimes he's there, his face turned away from her, but she knows who it is. She wakes up in a sweat, runs into Remi's room, feels the covers for her warm little body, watches the sheets move up and down with her breath.

"I can't let her go, Gavin." She sits on the stoop. She is shaking now.

"I'm coming, Betsy, don't move." And those words, hearing Gavin say her real name, sends her hurtling back. She is not Elizabeth anymore. She never was. She is Betsy, she will always be Betsy. Betsy, who left her friend alone to die. Betsy, who will never be able to move on, who will never deserve the beautiful life she has made. She sits on the stoop, warm now from the bright sunlight, and cries.

PART 1

CHAPTER 1
THE DRIFTERS

August 22, 1990

In another world before New York, before Remi, before the nightmares, Elizabeth was called Betsy, and she rode a bicycle to work. The pedals were leaden under the soles of her Converse, which were worn paper-thin. And, as always, the last stretch of the steep hill she climbed to get to campus was slow and brutal, through air that clung to her skin like jeans snatched impatiently out of the dryer: damp, hot, sticky. It was seventy-four degrees at 5:30 in the morning, the coolest it would be all day.

The one obvious con about Betsy's job at Bagelville was that people ate bagels in the morning, sometimes desperately early. They'd had a lock on the market until the culty Krispy Kreme doughnut shop opened down the street and challenged their dominance in the round, pre-noon food category. Regardless, business remained steady as long as refills were free, and Betsy, for the moment, was employed.

The upside of the job was that the coffee was decent and the place was derelict enough to be acceptably dingy to all of the cool kids in town who avoided anything too shiny. Betsy's battered cutoffs and last night's T-shirt were considered an acceptable uniform. Plus, there was ample fresh-squeezed orange juice to slip to her friends, who'd shuffle in dry-mouthed with bloodshot eyes around ten. If she was in at six, she was out by noon and sufficiently caffeinated for a class or two, her backpack loaded with remarkably versatile day-olds to stow in the freezer for times when money was tight, and it always was.

She hung a left to cut a diagonal line through the Plaza of the Americas, past a handful of drifters. They usually ended up in Gainesville after wandering off the interstate, growing impatient in their search for the mythical Florida orange groves. Inside the pastel halls of the sorority, it had been easy enough to ignore the seedier side of Gainesville, but outside those walls, it was impossible. It's the first sizable city intersected by I-75, the freeway that begins in Michigan. It starts north of Detroit at the Canadian border and snakes down to Ohio past Toledo and Dayton, further south to Lexington, Kentucky, before it passes through the depressed west Tennessee mountain towns into Atlanta and Macon until it crosses the state line into absolutely empty, impossibly green space. The verdant wasteland of low trees and fields punctuated by the occasional cow is an epic disappointment for kids who expect an eight-foot Mickey Mouse to greet them upon entering the Promised Land, not realizing that they still had nearly four Disney-free hours in the car ahead of them. In the fall, it's the migratory path for Midwestern snowbirds who flee the cold en route to their slumped, one-story cinder block homes in sixty-plus communities. Then, after Easter they do the reverse trip "up north" in understated, gold four-door sedans. Gainesville was brimming with Last-Stop Larrys of the world—sad sacks who just want to see one palm tree before they die, and anyone who'd given up on the rust belt cities and decided to try their luck in the Sunshine State. During the school year, the young, tan coeds were the center of attention in town. In August, before the semester started and the stream of returning students clogged the three exits into town, the people trickling in off the highway more likely stuck out their thumbs somewhere north of there and hitched a ride. It wasn't unusual for bad news to tag along with them.

When people realized they'd stopped short of their destination by a hundred miles, they'd typically stay awhile, sleep it off in the grass. They never wanted for company.

Betsy picked up speed through the flat quad, enjoying the movement in the air it created, and then caught a flash of her reflection in the vast windows of Emerson Hall. The seat on the pink Schwinn she was riding, which she'd lifted from her friends Ginny and Caroline's place, was at least three inches too low for her spindly frame, so her knees grazed the handlebars, and it made her look hunched and twisted, like an ampersand. Since she had cut her dark blonde hair to just below her chin, a trace of sunny highlights still clinging to the ends, it had started sticking to her face and neck in little, sweat-damp hanks. She was so startled by her reflection that she let out a little gasp. She knew how different she felt lately, but hadn't realized that the transformation was apparent on the surface, too.

She made it to work with a chocolate glazed in hand (has anyone ever spotted an illuminated neon Hot Doughnuts sign moments before sunrise and resisted its pull?) and five minutes to spare. The windows were steamed from the boil-

and-bake operation in back, which started every day at about 3:00 a.m. She tapped on the glass and peered through the fog to get Tom the manager's attention. When he looked up from the industrial-sized vat of dough he was mixing and saw her fuzzy silhouette through the condensation on the windows, she motioned to the midget bike.

"No lock," she shouted through the glass to Tom, the son of the Filipino owners, Tammy and Agapito Castillo, miming a gesture that might look significantly cruder than "U-lock" if anyone were passing by the store. Tom motioned to the back door with an impatient wave and Betsy wheeled herself around.

"Nice breakfast, asshole," he said. "You can bring in the bike today, but next time I'll let someone steal that piece of shit. Again."

Betsy had lost her third bike of the year just a few days before. It wasn't stolen, exactly. She'd left it locked on a rack downtown in front of a bar and hitched a ride home when she was too buzzed to pedal it home.

Later, when Betsy returned to the street sign where she locked it, the bike was missing its seat and front tire and she was too lazy and embarrassed to unlock the hulking mess and have it repaired.

Betsy stuffed the last half of the doughnut into her mouth, now frosted in the corners where last night's lipstick lingered. She squeezed the bike through the door. "Just one more time. I really appreciate it."

Tom was even crankier than usual, and Betsy doubted it was just about the doughnut.

"Is everything OK?" she asked him. "I would say that it looks like you woke up on the wrong side of the bed, but I know you sleep standing up."

"There is some seriously crazy shit going down in this town right now, Betsy," he said, opening the oven to let a blast of heat fill the room. She was washing her hands in back, examining her distorted reflection, this time in the paper towel dispenser. Maybe the blurry image in the stainless steel and her plate-glass-window reflection were lying to her, but it looked like the edge of her jaw was sharper, there was the slightest hollow under her cheekbone. She wondered if maybe Ginny's summer popcorn with soy sauce diet actually worked, while Tom slid out a tray of everythings and the scent of charred garlic stung her sinuses.

"And by crazy, I mean *weird*. Even by Gainesville standards. So just be careful."

"How weird is weird?" she asked, grabbing a wire basket from under the counter to fill with cooling sesames, unconvinced.

"I don't know exactly, but the cops came to the back door for coffee not long ago and they'd seen some grisly stuff," he said. "Just don't do anything stupid. Or maybe do stuff that's less stupid than your typical bullshit."

"And when you say grisly, you mean . . . ?"

"I don't think I'm supposed to say until they notify the family. That kind of grisly," he said. "I don't think you're supposed to be talking so much while you're on the clock, either."

TOM HANDLED ALL of the staffing for Bagelville's two locations, the original here in the student ghetto and the far less desirable (cleaner, newer, friendlier) annex in a strip mall near the highway, because his parents hated students after twenty years in a college town. Though Tom would shake his head in empathetic disgust when his mom ranted about the mysterious juice deficit ("Taga*long* is a Girl Scout cookie," he barked, when Betsy asked him to translate and help her defend herself when Tammy accused her of giving it away, "Taga*log* is a language. What the fuck are they teaching you here?"), he was mildly entertained by the antics of his employees, a scruffy lot of pretty young women who tried hard not to look like they were trying, and knew they were good for business. English Lit TAs and bored fifth-year seniors didn't come here and stay for hours, past breakfast into the less satisfying pizza bagel territory, just for free coffee refills.

When Betsy was arrested for using a fake I.D., Tom gave her an advance on her paycheck to cover the fine so she wouldn't have to tell her mom. She was grateful, and she trusted him. And though he would never admit it, she knew he liked her. She was routinely fifteen minutes late, critical of customer's orders—when Betsy's favorite professor, Dr. Loman, a patient man who taught Shakespeare to auditoriums full of sunburned students in flip-flops and tank tops, would order his "usual" tuna melt on a cinnamon raisin bagel, she made a gagging sound as she placed it in a waxed-paper-lined plastic basket more than once—and had a murmured, smart-ass retort for every one of Tom's requests. But she worked hard without too much complaint, and she was grateful for the job. Over the year and a half she'd been there, Tom teased her for being a flake and she mocked him for his complete lack of a social life and terrible taste in music, all while making $5.25 an hour.

Once, as she fed handfuls of oranges into the gaping maw of the industrial juicer, Betsy tried to explain the local employment hierarchy to Tom.

"Your job is like your shoes," she said. Tom was about to

hire a very tan sophomore from Fort Lauderdale who wore slouchy socks pushed down over white Reebok high-tops. "Like those girls over at Armando's next door? They have tattoos, like a marine does, hearts with thorns and anchors and stuff. You know, they're brunettes. They're Doc Martens. They're more like us, the Bagelville crowd, not into Rob Base or pastels. But we're Converse, Chuck Taylors. Low- or high-top, it doesn't matter."

There was an unspoken allegiance between the women of Armando's Pizza and the Bagelville employees. At least once a week, a sixteen inch veggie and a pitcher of lite beer was bartered for a half-dozen sesames, a pint of lox spread, and a quart of fresh-squeezed liquid gold in the alley that connected the two buildings, and no one was the wiser.

"That girl with the big socks?" she continued. "Maybe she could iron her pleated khakis and work at Blockbuster? Or if she bought a pair of Birks she could try Joffrey's, that overpriced vegetarian place in the old Victorian house on the corner? Her calves are tan enough. She might need to wrap her hair in a bandana, though, maybe a patchouli-scented bandana? And she could pick up some of those dangly Indian earrings from the kiosk at the natural foods store."

"This is profound, Betsy, truly. Real senior thesis shit here," he said. "Thank you for sharing your insights on microeconomics."

What she didn't bother theorizing about was the universally accepted notion that anyone who paid for their share of the $700 rent for a two-bedroom in an off-campus complex with a decent pool by working, those who were still stuck with a shoe box full of cassettes in a shiny CD world, were considered poor, and all other things being equal, not as fabulous. Betsy was sure that there were more people like her on campus than she realized, meaning that there were more people who were relatively broke and anonymous, but because she had thrown herself into the specious Greek life during her very first week of college, she didn't socialize much with many of them. It seemed like everyone in Betsy's social circle had fathers who were alumni with deep, golfer's tans, exaggerated drawls, and an oversized parking space reserved for their game day RVs. They'd show up with four-foot-long sport fisherman coolers full of free booze for their daughter's friends wearing tiny khaki shorts. Just before game time it was a long-standing tradition for students to fill Ziploc baggies with bourbon and smuggle them into the stadium in their shorts with the "zip" part tucked over the waistband of their underwear. Inside, they'd use it to spike their Cokes when security looked the other way. Somehow, parents found this charming. Like most big state schools, the football culture prevailed, and even Betsy would catch herself feeling intoxicating pride about the team's winning streak, or the latest Heisman contender on the team. Florida was known for its sports team, being a host of the world's largest tailgate party in Jacksonville, and for the fresh-scrubbed athletic wholesomeness of its well-tanned student body. Most of her classmates there were completely fine with that reputation, riding on the fumes of the Reagan era, delighted by Jell-O shots and Day-Glo parties, where they'd ruin perfectly good J.Crew T-shirts with splatters of fluorescent paint, and dance all night in front of a black light, marveling at the blue-whiteness of their teeth.

Betsy had reservations about all of it. She had a vague notion that they were on the tail end of a cultural moment. She knew that elsewhere in the world, kids her age were literally tearing down the Berlin Wall and risking their lives in Tiananmen Square. Yet Betsy still had to wear a dress to enter her sorority's dining hall on Monday nights. She was chastised for standing on the bar and screaming her lungs out, for smoking, for drinking too much, for her occasional flirtation with drugs. There was no room in that world for the anger that was stirring inside her. Betsy often wondered when her life would stop resembling a 1980s movie, if the still-warm corpse of that decade would stop haunting her at night.

Until recently, Betsy had made her best effort to fit in. She'd lived at the sorority house among the quilted bulletin boards and photo collages, the afternoon soaps in the TV room, the baby-faced busboys that cleared her dinner plates, and the estrogen-charged pranks. There were some highlights, she'd admit. The brownies baked with a carton of ex-lax and tagged with a Do Not Eat! Post-it in the communal fridge in an attempt to nab a notoriously hungry food stealer were vicious and brilliant. She would miss the late-night-study snack runs that somehow led to Jäcgermeister shots, and the incredibly loud singing of the *Annie* soundtrack at all hours of the night. None of those moments were enough to cancel out how terrible she felt during the annual cattle call known as sorority rush.

HER SIX-HOUR WORK shift seemed desperately long today, given the fact that the second summer session had just ended and classes weren't due to start for almost a week. Bagelville, like the rest of town, was practically empty. At noon, finally, Betsy slid on her red JanSport backpack and rode into campus to sell back her textbooks at the University Bookstore before they had a chance to collect dust. Once the contents of her backpack were unloaded, twenty-eight dollars suddenly burned a hole in her pocket. Betsy decided to splurge on a cheap bike lock and a three-dollar loose meat sandwich at Steamer's. She'd had a dream about the vinegary ground beef on the soft onion roll the night before, which prompted the book sale, since it was often the first thing she bought when she had extra cash. Then she planned to ignore the heat and venture downtown toward the Duckpond. She loved to ride through that neighborhood under shady oaks past Gainesville's historic homes with their wide Victorian porches, admiring the houses whose owners were smart enough not to rent to undergrads. She took the stately plaques forged with long-ago dates next to the front doors as a reassuring sign that there might be something about this place and this experience that was worth preserving and protecting. Sometimes, she would find a bench at the Thomas Center, a former hotel that had been converted into a gallery and arts center, and sit down to smoke a rare daylight cigarette. She hated the taste, but she would take her time, ashing into an empty Coke can and imagining that she lived somewhere else important, in a city that took up more space on a map, where interesting daytime smokers might live. It was all so pleasant and placid and downright boring that she couldn't imagine that anything as grisly as what Tom mentioned earlier could happen there. Her other favorite spot was the new art museum on the opposite side of town, where she started spending time after she decided to minor in art history. It was a relief to lose herself in the gleaming white space after the tedious time she spent in the classroom. It was a long ride across the vast campus sprawl to get there, but whenever she made the trek, she would stand in the cool, spare room in front of her favorite image, a gelatin silver print by Todd Walker, and stare at it until her skin was studded with goose bumps from the turbocharged air-conditioning. The photo was of what looked like a woman, lying on the floor on her side and curled into a ball under a sheet or a blanket, hiding. It had the murky, underwater quality of an ultrasound image, and there was no real evidence that the form was a person, let alone female, but Betsy felt she knew instinctively what it was. The image filled her with a curious despair.

"Is there anything more frustrating than the title, *Untitled*? Don't you want to know what happened to her?" she once asked her favorite guard, who just shook his head and left her to wonder on her own.

From the Duckpond she looped downtown past the Hippodrome and bumped along the old brick streets in front of it. Betsy propped the bike against a brick wall in front of a dusty vintage shop, locked it, and wandered in. It was a closet-sized space stocked with square-heeled shoes for tiny, pre–WWII feet and stiff dresses decorated with decaying lace. She found a pair of black, cat's-eye sunglasses and stuck a felt bowler hat on her head, then studied her reflection in the swivel mirror that stood on the counter.

"Nice hat," said a voice behind her. Betsy turned around to see a woman hidden by giant black vintage sunglasses, her skin the blue-white color of glacial ice. She wore a Metallica T-shirt modified with a pair of dull scissors into a tank top, which was half-covered with a cascade of dyed black hair.

"Betsy, right? From the bagel place?"

"Oh hey, yeah." She recognized her as one of the pizza-swappers from Armando's.

"What're you up to?"

"Just, uh, buying a hat," said Betsy, gesturing to her head

with one hand, then immediately feeling silly for doing so. She fished four dollars out of her pocket with the other.

Another Armando's employee with a Louise Brooks bob and a shock of brick red lipstick emerged from the dressing room with an armful of 1940s print dresses. Betsy wasn't sure who Louise Brooks was, but she had read about her hair in one of Caroline's magazines and was pleased that she used the phrase "Louise Brooks bob," even if it was only to herself.

"We're off to find AC and cheap drinks at Diggers," said the shorter of the two. Betsy realized her window of opportunity for asking their names, and thereby admitting that she'd forgotten them, was closing rapidly. "You in?"

After a suffocating fifteen-minute ride, she locked the bike onto a street sign in front of Diggers, the cave-like lounge at the Holiday Inn on University. Once inside, she squinted in the dark to find her companions, who had saved her a stool at the bar. Betsy shared her philosophy about day-drinking while she waited for the bartender to shuffle over and take their order: If there was a substantial serving of fruit (strawberry, pineapple, coconut, etc.) and/or vegetables (celery, olive) in a cocktail, it could be consumed pre-sundown without remorse.

"I'm partial to the Bloody Mary," Not-Louise said. "It's like a salad in a glass. You can argue that tomato is a fruit until you pass out, but I will still think that's bullshit."

Betsy settled on a five-dollar Digger daiquiri, a caloric, high school drink that she would never have dared to order in front of Caroline, but her judgmental friend wasn't back from summer break yet, and wasn't there to witness her transgression. It had what tasted like at least a serving of canned peaches in it, so it qualified as a drink and a snack. The first few sips were so cold and smooth that her buzz rode in on the back of an ice cream headache. The frozen drink and the blast of recirculated, sixty-five-degree air was enough of a reprieve from the heat that she didn't mind the dull, chemical sweetness of the Schnapps floater. For the next round, because two-for-one almost always equals four-for-two, she would switch to rum and Diet Coke. Betsy liked to plan ahead.

She peeled her bare forearm off of the wood bar, which was covered in a thick layer of milky-looking lacquer, which itself was coated with a thin film of something that the bartender's mildewed rag couldn't remove with a perfunctory swipe. She sniffed the soft, pale skin below her wrist for clues about what could have dried down to the tacky consistency of packing tape and pasted her arm to the bar. She narrowed it down to either Midori or margarita mix.

It made Betsy think that she and Ginny needed to go back to the Copper Monkey, a relatively quiet pub on the second floor of a shopping center off of University that was Ginny's favorite spot. It had rust-colored carpet, spindly wooden stools, and old-timey bar mirrors and reminded them of the Regal Beagle on *Three's Company*. On a slow night, when nothing else was happening in town and they had a little extra cash, Ginny and Caroline would hide out in a booth, order stuffed mushrooms, and vow that they would grow old together, get bad perms, and wear caftans like Mrs. Roper. Despite the depressing staleness of the bar, Betsy felt a warmth bloom inside of her, a feeling of contentment verging on happiness. She was happy to be there and, after a long, lazy summer with Ginny, swimming in the pool at her apartment complex and lying on the lounge chairs, feeling the sun braise their skin in the humid heat, she was happy in general.

Over the last year, Betsy found herself composing a sort of Dear John letter to the campus, the entire city of Gainesville, really, citing all of the reasons they weren't right for each other. Their time together was nearly over, and she felt like she had to explain why she had to leave a semester early. *It's not you, Gainesville, it's me*, she thought. The school was too big, with all of those auditorium-sized classrooms full of faceless students, and the city was too small, without much of the charm she expected from a sleepy town. The novelty of their first months together, when Betsy was giddy with her hard-earned freedom and breathless about her new friends and the alien excitement of a keg party attended by no-longer-teenaged boys, was over. It had taken three full years, but she had finally decided who and what she wanted to be, and that was on her own, for the most part, without anyone tallying up her many social faux pas with hash marks, adding up her demerits, and scolding her with fines and sideways glances over chicken Cordon Bleu in the sorority dining room. She wanted to work hard and go to school and see and hear music as much as possible. She wanted to spend a half hour in the university museum at night before it closed, wandering its halls, alone in the clean, white, open space, and to drive out to Cedar Key on Sundays to listen to reggae at Frog's Landing. She would be happy to scrape together spare change and eat fried okra at Grandy's for dinner for a few more months. And she wanted to spend more days like that one, biking around the Duckpond and having spontaneous drinks with people she only sort of knew. Her relationship with Gainesville wasn't perfect, but it had its perks. Gainesville was where she found Ginny, Tom, and Melissa at Bagelville, and the handful of people she looked forward to seeing at parties. It's where she'd met Caroline. However complex their friendship was, they had their fun together. Betsy made a silent vow to make their remaining months together—with her friends, the town, even the school—count.

No amount of optimism could make Diggers appealing for more than two hours, so she grabbed her backpack, pulled nine dollars out of her pocket, suspecting that it wouldn't cover her share of the bill, excavated a dime encrusted with lint from another pocket, and set off into the lobby to find a pay phone.

"I'll be right back . . . you guys," she said, knowing it was a lie.

GINNY PICKED UP the call off of the answering machine, which played the chorus of the Smiths's "Stop Me If You Think You've Heard This One Before" before it beeped.

"Gin, pick up. Pick up pick up pick up pick up pick up," she shouted. "Giinnnny. I know you're there. It's *Oprah* time. Half-past *O'prahclock*!"

"Betsy? What's going on? Where are you?" Ginny fumbled with the phone.

"I'm at Diggers. You know, at the Holiday *Inn*."

"Uh, no, actually. I do not know Diggers at the Holiday Inn."

"It's the sad place. On University. I'm here with Louise and Not-*Louise*."

"Of course you are."

"I got here on the pink bike, but now I'm unfit to *ride*."

"Of course you are."

"Oh, Gin, please. Come get me. Don't make me *beg*."

Betsy's eternal carelessness made her feel like one of the

stragglers she rode past on the way to work that morning. Most of the time, Ginny was a surprisingly tolerant chauffeur.

"Fine," she said, "I'm leaving now."

Betsy slipped past the vending machines and out through the depressing lobby without saying goodbye. When she caught her reflection in the mirror behind the front desk, for the third time that day, it shocked her. This time, she was surprised to see that she was still wearing the hat from the vintage shop, which looked roguish and charming in the store, but now made her look insane. To her relief, the Schwinn was still locked to the pole. When Ginny finally pulled into the parking lot, Betsy was sitting near the curb in front of the hotel, curled up around her duct-taped backpack like a pillow.

"Nice hat," said Ginny as she pulled over to the curb. "You are such a pretty girl, Betsy Young, despite all of your efforts not to be."

"Oh thank God for you," said Betsy. She hoisted the bike into the back of the Rabbit convertible, flung the passenger door open, and jumped inside. "We need to get to Taco Bell fast before I hurl frozen peaches with a Schnapps *floater.*"

She knew she had only about three dollars and change left, but Ginny had never passed through a drive-thru window without wrangling free food. People were always tossing in something extra for Ginny, making it a baker's dozen, giving her an extension on her paper or the benefit of the doubt that she was, in fact, thirty-one-year-old Raquel Schuler from Alachua, Florida, as the fake I.D. in her hand indicated. She'd flirt with the pimply Little Caesars employee in exchange for a free pizza as a kind of exercise, a small social experiment. There was always a spare Nachos BellGrande to be had when Ginny was around.

"So, who is this Louise friend I've never heard of?" Ginny asked.

"Not her real name, by the way. I only sort of knew Not-Louise from Armando's. Not Louise—the other one. Oh God, anyway, it doesn't matter because I do not remember their *names*." Betsy had a habit of drawing out the last syllable of any sentence whenever she'd had too much to drink: "I can't find my *shoes*," "I lost my *keys*," "What is your prob*lem*?"

"So you had two-for-one drinks with strangers, at Diggers, starting at 3:00."

"Four-for-two, technically, and yes. I *did*."

Ginny laughed and shook her head, which made Betsy weirdly proud, in a perverse kind of way, that she could still surprise her best friend. Betsy leaned back against the headrest and noticed that the day was almost tolerable now since the sun was starting to dip beneath the tree line. The light was fading, casting a golden, nearly amber glow on everything around them, including Ginny, which made her dark eyes glow hazel.

BACK IN MAY, Betsy heard the Sundays for the first time and dug into her emergency cash fund to buy Ginny the tape. Ginny had only two cassettes in her car. One was the Violent Femmes, which someone in her high school car pool left in the deck. The other was her favorite, 'Til Tuesday. Both of them were warped and distorted from overuse. So Betsy convinced Ginny that the eleven dollars she should have spent on something else was actually an investment in her own sanity, since she spent nearly as much time in that car as Ginny did. But it was more than that. Something about the layered, angelic songs about breakups and the miserably cold, cloudy weather of a distant place felt like the soundtrack to being young in the spring of 1990 with a best friend to whom she felt she owed the world, and "Here's Where the Story Ends" became their theme song. The two of them spent nearly every night driving around, rewinding and replaying it, singing loudest at the end, shouting "*Surprise . . .*" over and over again, their voices trailing behind them in the wind.

The memories made Betsy ache with a weird longing for that simpler time, just a couple of months ago. That evening, still woozy from the rum and Schnapps, Betsy kept her head from spinning by looking up at the coral pink clouds as "Hideous Towns" filled the air around them.

"Oh, Bets, I completely forgot: Your mom called earlier. She was looking for you," Ginny said.

Ginny and Caroline's number was the only one Kathy had written in her address book in ink. Her most persistent complaint about her daughter, and at that point in time there were many, was that she lived like a "gypsy." Kathy never knew where to find her and threatened, more than once, to look under "Bars" in the Gainesville Yellow Pages and call every number on the list, beginning with the A's. But Betsy suspected that the real reason Kathy called the apartment was because she liked talking to Ginny. In fact, the only thing Betsy didn't like about Ginny was that Kathy clearly adored her.

"Did she ask you to keep tabs on me again? Keep me on the straight and *narrow*? Emphasis on the *narrow*?"

"She's a mom. She called because she loves you. And because she worries about you," said Ginny. "Did it ever occur to you that she likes to talk to me because I'm nice to her? You should try it."

"Ha!" Betsy scoffed. "She likes to talk to you because she thinks you're a good Christian girl who can keep me out of the *bars*. She doesn't see that you're playing the long *con*. And besides, she has to start being nice to me *first*."

When they circled around the parking lot to order into the drive-thru speaker, Betsy shouted from the passenger seat.

"We'll take two of everything that costs ninety-nine cents, and three of everything that costs seventy-nine cents."

"Oh Christ, Betsy, will you shut up?"

"I'm sorry . . . Welcome to Taco Bell . . . Could you repeat that order, please?"

"Let me handle this, Betsy. I promise you're not as funny as you think you are right now."

"Oh Dorothy, you are absolutely no *fuunn.*" Even sober, Betsy's Blanche Devereaux was awful. They had been on a *Golden Girls* watching spree that summer, and Betsy, who memorized every episode, quoted the show with alarming frequency. Ginny rolled her eyes.

"Fine," she said, pretending to be exasperated, though Betsy could tell that she was secretly thrilled. "Uh, sorry about that, sweetheart, scratch that first order. What we really want is three of everything that costs seventy-nine cents. And two of everything that costs ninety-nine cents."

"Excuse me?"

"You heard the lady," said Betsy, peering ahead at the guy leaning out of the glass enclosure to see who was taunting him, straining the cord attached to his headset. "My mistake. I thought that since you look like Yoda you were also *wise.*"

"Enough," Ginny said, in a pleading whisper. "He is obviously not a fan."

"Next window, please."

"Uh-oh," Betsy whispered. "Somebody is *pissed.*"

Of course, they had to reach the second window in order for Ginny to work her magic. After some profuse apologies and deft negotiation, they left with two orders of Nachos

BellGrande, which they paid for, and three crispy beef tacos and two large Cokes, on the house.

"Oh see how handsome he is when he smiles?" Ginny said as she collected her change. "I could tell you had a generous heart."

"Works every time," said Betsy, digging into the bag. "Like a *charm*."

"My days of taco swindling are over," said Ginny with a laugh. "From now on, you're on your own."

As she pulled away from the drive-thru window, Ginny waved goodbye and grabbed a messy handful of tortilla chips. Then, when she dropped a glob of hot fake cheese on her bare thigh, she was squealing and laughing in pain when her car inched forward toward the sidewalk. Betsy was searching through the bag for a napkin and didn't notice that the car was rolling slowly forward. Ginny looked up just in time to see the bike pulling in front of the car, from out of nowhere, and she slammed on the brakes with a quick chirp of rubber tires on hot asphalt. The nachos slid off Betsy's lap onto the dirty floorboards.

"Holy *shit*!" Betsy shouted without looking up to see who or what was in front of them. "Don't mind this big metal thing on wheels, jack*ass*. It's just a car. That could kill *you*."

"Jesus, Betsy, it was my fault," Ginny said, as she put the car in Park and jumped out. A man on a bicycle scrambled to his feet and stood silently, staring at them. "I'm so sorry, sir. Oh my God, are you OK?"

"Yes, sir. Sorry, sir," added Betsy with a salute, still in the passenger seat. "It won't happen again, sir."

Betsy looked up to find him staring at her and returned his gaze, which was oddly unsettling. He wasn't outraged, shouting at them, or threatening to call the cops.

He was eerily calm and studied both of their faces. It was hard to guess his age. Could he be a graduate student? He was a little over six feet, shabbily dressed in dirty jeans and work boots, but that didn't mean anything. Maybe he was just poor, like Betsy, scraping to pay tuition and stay afloat, but didn't try to hide it. He had shaggy sandy-brown hair, glasses with cheap wire frames, a blue duffel bag, and a beat-up guitar case slung over his back. His clothes were too warm for the weather. And whether he was intimidated or resentful, or both, he didn't treat them like peers. He was tense, and you could see it in the small, animal-like movements he made, like an actual, twitching deer in the headlights. Betsy sensed in her gut that there was no way this guy was a student.

"Don't you have to get going? Aren't you late for class?" Betsy said.

"Rude!" said Ginny, glaring at her, head cocked to the side in disbelief, knowing exactly what Betsy was implying. He didn't belong there. He was a drifter, a hanger-on. "That is so unlike you, Betsy. Sir, I'm sorry about my friend's bad manners. Rum makes her mean. I didn't hurt you, did I?"

His eyes darted between hers and Ginny's. He had a strong jaw and a delicate nose, but his pale eyes were sunken.

"I'm fine," he said, shaking his head, pushing his hair off of his forehead and shoving his cap back on. He pushed the bike for a few feet, hopped back on, and rode away. He was the kind of man who vanished almost as soon as he appeared.

"That was odd," said Ginny, getting back into the car. "Don't you think that was odd?"

"At least he's not dead," said Betsy, tossing the chips tainted with dirt from the floorboards onto the sidewalk. "I mean, you didn't kill him, which is a good thing."

"God, Betsy. Please promise me that a return trip to Diggers is not in your future."

They pulled out of the parking lot and drove toward home. Betsy took a huge bite of her taco, which she could already tell wasn't working the magic she had anticipated. Ginny turned down the music.

"You know Caroline will be back in a few days, right?"

"*Right.*" Betsy nodded, mouth still full.

"I'm sure she won't mind if you stay at our place until Kari is back in town and gets her furniture out of storage. You can just sleep on the couch."

"Right, *right.*" They drove for a few blocks in silence, considering what their lives might be like once Caroline came home. Things had been rocky between Betsy and Caroline for a while and then took a dramatic dive last May.

"I mean, you can't let one dumb guy ruin everything," said Ginny, sounding unconvinced that what she was saying was true.

"It wasn't just about a guy," Betsy insisted. "John was as lame as they come. It was the rest of it. The three-way calling? The lying? She tormented me. Tell me you remember that part. You didn't conveniently *forget.*"

"Betsy, it's your last semester here. I just want things to be fun again, like they used to be. Will you promise that you'll try?"

Betsy wrapped up her half-eaten taco and put it back in the bag. Her stomach seized.

"Bets? You OK?"

"You've got to pull over, *now.*"

Ginny pulled the car to the curb so Betsy could open the passenger door, hang her head out of the side, and launch a river of orange ick into the gutter off of Archer Road.

CHAPTER 2
DIRTY RUSHERS

August 23, 1990

On her way home from work, Betsy took the pink bike on a detour along the southern edge of campus, past Norman Hall, which was directly behind Sorority Row. She stopped in the parking lot under a shady tree, a couple of hundred yards away from the rear entrance of her former sorority house. She felt an urgent, morbid curiosity, and wanted proof that the world continued to revolve without her. She watched from a distance as people hurried up and down the back stairwell, shuttling suitcases and boxes. She'd lost touch with most of the friends she'd made during her two and a half years there, though their faces were all still so familiar. Ginny was the only one who didn't stop calling after she turned in her pin. Caroline stuck around, but Betsy was convinced it was only for the entertainment value. She liked to watch Betsy suffer.

It was the last Friday in August, and fifteen hundred freshmen girls in linen sundresses were about to emerge from their newly assigned dorm rooms, with their stiff sheets just out of the package and freshly stocked mini-fridges, to participate in the ritual of sorority rush, which had been happening on campus since 1948. In Florida, securing a bid from one of the university's sixteen houses also involved wrestling with a perpetually sweaty upper lip, oppressive humidity, and a caste system so complicated that it left everyone involved baffled and a little bruised.

For ten days leading up to rush, before the semester began, sisters returned to Gainesville early to put in mandatory fourteen-hour days rehearsing songs and skits and building sets for the song-and-dance numbers they'd put on during rush "parties," crafting a convincingly ridiculous front to conceal the evil-genius mechanism at work behind it. This is what Betsy had come to witness now, to see the evidence that it was real, and was all still happening without her.

It was impossible to watch them file into the house and not let a flood of memories come rushing back.

Betsy first met Ginny and Caroline on Bid Day, the afternoon when rushees learned which house they pledged and then sprinted to the sorority with mascara-stained tears of joy streaming down their faces. The three of them had run down the sidewalk to the steps in front of the house searching for the signs with their names. Betsy had noticed both of them during rush and marveled at how confident they were, how entirely at ease. Only later did she learn that Ginny had been visiting her older sister, M.J., who graduated in 1987, at the house since she'd been an awkward seventh-grader in a Snoopy T-shirt and braces. Caroline also knew the security code on the front door before rush even started. Her mother, Viv Finnerty, pledge class of 1968, was a successful real estate agent in Miami and, because of her gold Kieselstein-Cord belts, St. John jackets, and icy blonde bob, Viv was the most glamorous woman Betsy had ever met. Ginny and Caroline were both "legacies," which meant that they had a family member, a sister, mother, or even grandmother, who was a member of the sorority. Viv left school to get married in the middle of her sophomore year and had Caroline six months later. But the sorority was nothing if not loyal. Once you were in, you were in for as long as you wanted to be, as long as you paid your dues and you weren't asked to resign. So Viv rarely missed an alumni weekend, and a stack of recommendations from her most socially prominent peers were stapled to Caroline's rush application.

During those first weeks, when they took Betsy under their wings and showed her the ropes, the two of them together were pure magic. Ginny was the sparkly, impish sidekick to the deviously charming Caroline. Betsy soon learned that they could talk their way into any party, walk past the velvet rope to the front of any line, or drive past security guards onto restricted areas of campus with a wink and a wave. Their appeal went beyond that of a pretty girl who could cry her way out of a speeding ticket. On that first night out, after Caroline introduced Betsy to every guy at the bar as her cousin Ruta from Latvia, Betsy would follow them anywhere.

"She barely speaks English," Caroline said, shaking her head. "I mean, the accent is impossible to understand. I get, like, every fifth word on a good day."

Betsy fumbled with a bad impression of Count von Count from Sesame Street.

"I said Latvia, not Transylvania," Caroline said, as they stumbled out of the bar. "Five! Five stupid boys, ah ah ah."

Ginny showed both of them M.J.'s secret spot where you could scale the wall of the football stadium for a midnight sprint down the fifty-yard line. They made it across and back and halfway over the fence before they heard the security guard shouting after them. When they made it to the car, Caroline waved at him and shout-sang the school fight song as they sped away. Just riding in their wake was enough to erase all of the infinite times Betsy didn't feel special. She basked in their attention, their invincibility, their reflected glow, until she didn't.

Physically, Caroline and Betsy were more similar than Betsy and Ginny were. They were roughly the same height, with light hair and eyes, born just a few months apart. That's where their similarities ended. Betsy was tall and lanky with dirty blonde hair. Objectively, she was pretty, but she did everything she could to not draw attention to it. She tried to fold herself like an origami bird into a smaller body to avoid standing above the crowd. She was funny and wry if you were standing close enough to hear the sly remarks. She noticed everything, examining her surroundings so carefully, paying special attention to the flaws that no one else caught. The fact that she *noticed* things proved problematic at times. At the most basic level, the whole social framework of sorority life hinged on the idea that everyone bought into it, that they sang the songs, and held hands, and flashed beaming smiles in photos with a total commitment to their sisterhood. Betsy had questions and doubts, and that made her more threatening than she realized.

Caroline, on the other hand, was imperious. She had the strong, tan shoulders, sharp clavicles and perfectly streaked blonde hair of a girl who'd grown up playing country club sports, and a quicksilver quality that lent her humor, which was sharp and unrelenting, a kind of menacing, unpredictable edge. One minute, you were in on the joke and the next, you were stunned silent when you realized you *were* the joke.

Ginny was petite and dark-haired with a gentler kind of confidence. Life was fantastically easy for her. Even the way she drove struck Betsy as simultaneously careless and graceful, her brown doe-like eyes saw everything but the road in front of her. Betsy would grip the sides of the passenger seat and wince, tensing her body for the impending car wrecks that somehow never materialized. Betsy had had close girlfriends before, but Ginny was her favorite. She saved her from Caroline's mean streak, from a lonely summer, from herself.

She felt a tinge of sympathy for the incoming sophomores, who were showing up newly SlimFasted and wide-eyed with anticipation. Since they'd been initiated only a semester earlier, this was their first glimpse behind the scenes at the production that had seduced them so completely just a year before. She guessed it wouldn't take many of them long to connect the dots and realize how they'd all been duped, that their fate had practically been sealed before they even walked in the door. Betsy noticed a few people from her pledge class, who were entering their senior year, as the stragglers who were filing in last. They'd put in their time for three years and their numbers had dwindled, gradually. A few girls had transferred, a couple had been kicked out for not meeting the minimum grade-point average or for unbecoming behavior, and a handful just stopped showing up entirely and no one seemed to notice or care. All active members needed to be present for rush, and every day of pre-rush a sister missed there was a hefty fifty-dollar fine. Caroline wasn't due to be back for two days, four days late in total. No one dared complain about her missing so much time because Caroline was a master at recruiting pledges, blinding the truly clueless with her singular magnetism. She was what they call a closer, in that *Glengarry Glen Ross* kind of way, and would do whatever it took to seal the deal and get the girl. Being rushed by Caroline was to experience the art of seduction at its best. She was a sly manipulator, skilled at reading people, matching the tone and volume of their voices; Betsy had watched as she focused that laser beam charm on any guileless girl they'd place in front of her, intuiting what she wanted to hear with stunning precision. Betsy saw what happened to the girls who had Caroline's eyes locked on them. Her glow was as warm as the sun.

AT FIRST, THE group of fifteen hundred is divided into ten groups of one hundred fifty, all organized alphabetically under the white tents pitched on the front lawns of the street known as Sorority Row. The five-day round robin started with each group spending twenty minutes at all of the sixteen prospective houses over two days. They'd arrive at their designated starting point, fanning themselves with the rush catalogue, which was printed with pictures of each of the houses carefully selected to convey the subtly coded messages of the communal "personality" of the house. The sisters of one house are studious, from good families with good reputations but—truth be told—a little staid. Theirs is a reputable house that a fraternity would partner with for homecoming if they had been especially naughty and needed to tidy their reputation with the school administration. The girls in the neighboring house are beautiful, but with slightly looser morals. They are game for not just a toga party, but a *wet* toga party, where entire rooms were sandbagged and filled with a foot of fetid water and spraying hoses for the occasion. The only discernible clues that tipped you off to this distinction were that, in the pictures, their shorts were an inch shorter, their hair a little bigger. There is a sorority for the party girls, one for the Jewish girls who iron their T-shirts, and another for the Jewish girls who follow the Dead, worship Jerry, and hang tie-dyed tapestries on their dorm room walls. There are two black sororities, and a sort of unspoken assumption that the Asian girls are too focused on premed for such useless distractions. The process is surprisingly efficient. There is a sorority for the conservative Southern girls, the ones with tight bows tied to their ponytails who give blow jobs by the dozen but refuse to give up their virginity before marriage. The top three houses duked it out for the 10 percent at the highest end of the food chain and then would fill in the remaining slots with legacies and some dark horses who'd make it past the finish line by a nose. Once Betsy made it to the other side of the curtain, she'd determined she had been one of those.

The idea that Betsy would pledge sort of began with her mom. While she didn't actually come right out and tell her daughter that she wanted her to be a part of the Greek system, because Kathy didn't come right out and say anything directly, it was strongly implied over the years that Kathy craved a kind of social acceptance for her only daughter, her only child, that she herself had never experienced. Kathy never went to college. She was popular and pretty and met Betsy's father in high school in Connecticut. She took a job in a typing pool after graduation, passing her time while he was away at Amherst. They married in the summer after his senior year and Betsy was born in the spring. Betsy was barely a year old when Kathy discovered that her husband was having an affair with a girl he'd met in school. Threats were made. Plates were thrown. It went on for years, until Betsy's durable memory was intact, until he finally made a decision. Later, when Betsy struggled to imagine what had happened between her parents, it occurred to her that he bailed when he realized the "other woman" wouldn't wait forever. Kathy packed their suitcases, scraped together whatever cash she could, and let Betsy play on the floor of the backseat of their Oldsmobile during their long drive down I-95 to Florida, the land of eternal sunshine and fresh starts. She got a job as an office manager for a hotel chain. It was made clear that Kathy was filled with remorse about her choices, and that, deep down beneath all of that anger, she felt that Betsy's father had chosen the better woman, the kind of woman who went to college and, she could only assume, was in a sorority. Kathy was the kind of woman who collected the September issues of *Vogue* and dreamed of a better life. She beamed when Betsy's rush application arrived in the mail from the National Pan-Hellenic Council. It was a life she wanted her daughter to be a part of, and what Betsy wanted was beside the point.

Yet the more Betsy discovered about herself, the more she found the myth of the only child baffling. Betsy's experience was different. She was supposed to be competent, self-reliant, and possess life skills acquired from attentive parents that her peers with siblings did not. But she couldn't shake the loneliness, the connection she was missing with her own detached mother, and the mystery of her father, who would reappear for awkward annual visits during her childhood, but vanished altogether by the time she was fourteen. Betsy understood that the reason she had attached herself to the sorority was because she'd never had a sister. At first, she wanted to be a part of it to please her mother, to prove that she belonged somewhere, that she had a hundred sisters, despite the fact that, even from the beginning, she felt like a fraud.

Once you were inside the system and assigned to one of the three houses you selected as your favorites, ranked in order—assuming that at least one of the three houses wanted you back—the Greek letters you wore emblazoned on your chest determined your entire life. At first, it was just where and with whom you partied and which fraternity socials you would attend, and which ones you considered beneath you. The letters were social shorthand, a way of communicating to everyone else on campus that you had been deemed the most beautiful, the most popular, the most desirable. Betsy didn't realize it until she was on the other side of the wizard's curtain, but she learned soon enough that a great many of these women would forever identify themselves by which sorority they'd joined when they were eighteen or nineteen, like Viv, or Ginny's sister, M.J. When they stood up for the first time to introduce themselves at a school committee or a local charity board, they wouldn't say, "I'm a marketing manager" or "I'm passionate about ocean conservancy." They'd say, "I was an ADPi at Florida State," or a "Tri Delt at Bama," or a "Kappa at Georgia," or a "Pi Phi at UT." That said it all.

But in that moment, the future is unthinkable. As these unsuspecting girls are shuttled through plush, carpeted halls amid all of those beaming smiles, all anyone can worry about is whether she has lipstick on her teeth.

When the ceremonies began, a row of perfectly coiffed smiling girls would trot out on the long sidewalks that led to the imposing front doors to line up and greet their pretty prey with a song, typically a show tune with the words altered slightly to reflect their near-maniacal enthusiasm for their bonds of sisterhood. They'd laugh and wink, because everyone knew it was embarrassing schlock. And when they were finished singing, the sisters would lock eyes with one girl under the tent, make introductions, and offer her a glimpse into her future, showing her the possibilities of what may be awaiting them behind door number one, two, or three, if only they came up with the right answer before the buzzer sounded.

Someone blonde and smiling would lead Jenn (two Ns, recently dropped Y) from Tuscaloosa into the great room and kneel on the pale peach carpet beside her. Jenn would tuck her hands into the folds of her Laura Ashley dress and listen, as Ginny or Betsy or Caroline or any of the other sisters would start the mind-blender, nimbly steering the conversation to a topic, like a recent family vacation to Paris and a visit to the Louvre, that felt like an eerily familiar, nearly Psychic Friends moment.

"That's so strange," Jenn would say, astonished, "because I plan to double major in French and Art History!" She never suspected, of course, that the sisters had seen her photo at least a dozen times. It was flashed against a white sheet tacked to the wall in a slideshow of this year's pledge class dream team, also known as "board girls," so named because their photos were also glue-sticked onto poster boards hung around the house. All of the rushees had been vetted by their application, which always included a photo, a brief bio, their high school GPA, and three references, or "recs." The rush committee would spend hours sifting through the paperwork and select the fifty most desirable incoming freshmen for that year. Then they'd run lunchtime drills, quizzing everyone about the details of Jenn's high school résumé over salads drowned in ranch dressing. Her picture would appear on the screen in the chapter room. "Jenn! Alabama! Dance team captain! Volleyball! French! Painter!"

In the back of the room, lying under the piano and flipping through a fashion magazine written in a language she couldn't read, Caroline nudged Betsy and said, "Oh my God, did you notice? Man hands."

It didn't matter what Caroline actually thought of the board girls. She would captivate them. What made her particularly ruthless was that she'd also bond with the unsuspecting anonymous ones, the ones who didn't stand a chance, in an expertly insouciant "isn't this all just a waste of time?" way. After Caroline deposited her victim back under the tent, she'd turn away, maybe she'd roll her eyes just the tiniest bit, and then grab a red felt-tip marker to cross the name off of the list, swiftly, when she was barely through the door. "Spotters," sisters in charge of identifying the MVPs under the crowded tent through parted blinds, had the job of procuring the rarest specimens and getting them into the hands of the sister they'd relate to the most. By the third round, Caroline had worked her magic on Jenn. She'd grabbed her vascular man hand, even when rush guidelines strictly forbade any physical contact, and led her into her room upstairs for a lip gloss touch-up. Meeting behind closed doors in a private room was an even more egregiously illegal maneuver than touching. Then, she invited her to a keg party later that night, and made a "you *completely* know that your picture's going to be on that wall next year" well-outside-the-guidelines confession. Caroline was a dirty rusher, and she'd been reported to the "authorities" that monitor these proceedings and reprimanded more than once. Never in the long history of sororities and sorority rush had anyone given less of a shit about that.

The way Betsy's former sisters saw it, there were three top sororities (though theirs was the best, of course) and four respectable second-tier houses. There was always serious attrition after the first round, dropouts who were either smart enough to rise above it or to realize they were about to be eaten alive. The ones who stuck it out were divvied out to the remaining nine houses.

Rush got particularly ugly during the debates about who among the young women who attended the "parties" that day would be invited back for the next round, thus narrowing the field from fifteen hundred to five hundred to one hundred fifty and then the final fifty, who'd receive bids. Names were brought up individually for discussion, and the process was agonizing and endless. Sisters would flee the room in tears so the rest of the house could discuss the fate of their *biological,* as in *genetic* sister, who was criticized for wearing pleather flats, or who made the mistake of admitting she slept at her boyfriend's house the night before. Officially, the sorority discouraged catty comments of all kinds, so there was a shorthand among the most ruthless sisters to avoid being reprimanded. To be fair, Betsy knew that other people struggled with the process, but they seemed content just to keep their heads down and stay out of it. But that was the part that Betsy remembered most vividly, as she stood straddling that bike in the parking lot. She couldn't ignore it.

"Y'all, I just think she'd *be happier elsewhere,*" someone would say, a handily coded euphemism for "not a chance." The chapter president would call a name and open the floor for discussion and if the "scary balloon"—a helium balloon that Margie, a mean girl from Vero Beach, had scrawled a scowl on with a black Sharpie marker—rose above their heads like the

Bat-Signal, they were doomed. Not everyone was in on the joke, but there were enough sisters who knew what it meant that their votes would add up, and, just like that, they tallied the raised hands and she was "happier elsewhere." Margie once made a tearful speech at 2:00 a.m., after a blistering day of singing and talking trash about people, that revealed how her big-shot Daddy would not pay her annual dues if he knew that the biracial girl (Betsy would never forget: Shannon. Salutatorian. Macon.) had been offered a spot in his sweet angel's sorority. Betsy was shocked by her own reaction, which was stunned silence by intimidation, and never forgave herself for not speaking up. Shannon eventually pledged a black sorority, and Betsy would find herself scanning the crowds between classes, searching for her face as she pedaled through campus, unsure of what she would say, if she'd say anything at all, if she found her. Their paths never crossed again.

Betsy couldn't explain why she'd endured rush in the first place, and she often ran through every possible excuse she could think of to justify it. She had some kind of bizarre obligation to her competitive streak. She'd never been able to resist wanting something that was perceived as hard to get, whether it was an A, or a cute guy, or a position on the drill team, or one of fifty coveted spots in a sorority pledge class. She wanted to make her mother proud. The school itself was so immense that she figured she'd need a way to shrink it in order to find a manageable circle of friends. She wanted people to think she was OK, that she was likable and popular, even though most of the time she felt anything but. She wanted a little of the magic, of the Ginnys and the Carolines with their surplus of charm. By surrounding herself with so many rows of perfect teeth, a hundred overachieving young women with respectable GPAs in cotton floral sundresses, Betsy felt special by proxy. Befriending Ginny cemented her status and made her think, for a little while at least, that all of those feelings of acceptance were true and real. When she followed Ginny and Caroline at a party, Betsy would catch the looks that were first cast on them and then lingered on her, the way people would pause to remember her face, to wonder who she was or if they'd ever seen her somewhere before. Betsy noticed how everyone, busy bartenders, campus traffic cops, even the guy at the Taco Bell drive-thru, treated her differently when she was with them.

BUT DESPITE ALL of that, it wasn't long before Betsy decided she wanted out. Like all secret societies, when a person is inducted into a fraternity or a sorority there is an unspoken agreement that comes along with the tiny gold pin. The system relies on people not looking too closely for flaws and, more specifically, not sharing the unsavory elements they may see with anyone on the outside. But it was obvious to anyone who was paying attention that Betsy wasn't buying it, and that made her a sort of threat, someone who couldn't be entirely trusted, despite her allegiance to Ginny and Caroline, who often dismissed the flaws that Betsy would point out with a shrug.

"It's just how it is," Ginny would say, when Betsy pointed out the complicated social hierarchy, the strange double standards. "You take the good with the bad, I guess." Betsy realized it was the sorority that created her friendship with Ginny and Caroline in the first place, and that it felt wrong to doubt the very institution that shored her self-esteem enough to give her the nerve to walk out on it. But the whole situation was causing her more pain than pleasure, piling layers onto what was surely an existential crisis in the way that Joan Didion wrote about, that the beauty, and the torture, of being young is that you think that you're the only one who'd ever felt those feelings or asked those questions or lived that life. Or something like that, since Betsy was never much good with quotes.

The fact was that once she got behind the scenes, there wasn't much magic left at all. It just felt like one, big long obligation and an endless litany of fines, weekly fraternity mixers with sagging card tables covered with gallon bottles of Popov vodka and Ocean Spray cranberry juice, trashcans full of ominous grain alcohol and Kool-Aid hunch punch, and then the battery of chastising looks from the sisters when any female guest dared to drink it. There was only one Ginny, but there were ten others like Dana—a scowling senior from the Panhandle who paced the house holding a plastic pitcher of water and a cup, which she would fill and drink obsessively in an effort to lose weight while she barked at pledges to answer the phone. Caroline's wicked but hysterical humor was drowned out by earnest Amy and snobby Shelly, who turned and left the room if they walked in and saw that Betsy, a known troublemaker, was in it. Betsy was used to feeling uneasy in her surroundings, like she was never quite of the place where she was from, but in that world, it was the stifling scrutiny that broke her. She decided that she wanted out. For one deluded instant, she thought maybe Ginny would leave the sorority with her. She was wrong.

Finally, by the end of summer, she felt settled in her new ostracized life. She'd had enough of Caroline, though Ginny would not give up her efforts to make peace between them. Betsy had one more semester, then she could put all of this behind her for good. In the blazing afternoon sun, her eyes stung with sweat and bad memories as she got back on the bike and rode to Ginny's, undetected, to wait for the storm.

CHAPTER 3
WELCOME BACK

August 24–25, 1990

When Betsy walked into Ginny and Caroline's dark apartment after work, she could smell the familiar mix of cigarettes and Quelques Fleurs before she even saw her, which gave her a funny pang of fondness wrapped in nausea. She climbed the stairs and poked her head around the doorframe of Caroline's room, the one Betsy had occupied all summer, and saw her in silhouette, standing in a sea of half-exploded suitcases and L.L. Bean boat and tote bags that spewed their contents on the floor like preppy, disemboweled Tauntauns. Even though the air-conditioning was on full blast, Caroline's window was open about six inches beneath its heavy shade, and her left hand was dangling out of it, tapping a cigarette into a stolen Howard Johnson's ashtray on the sill.

"There you are," Caroline said, flatly.

"Jesus, it's pitch-black in here." Betsy's eyes hadn't adjusted from the glare outside so she reached for the light switch.

"If you turn that on, I will fucking kill you. How many times do I have to tell you? Overhead lighting is for peasants." Caroline clicked on a small, porcelain lamp on her bedside table. In the light, Betsy could see her deep tan, the streaks of sun-bleached blonde in her hair. Caroline reached into one of the canvas bags with her free hand and produced a carton of Gauloises Blondes, which she tossed to Betsy with an expert flip of the wrist. "Bonjour, freeloader."

"Thanks, Car," said Betsy, catching the smokes and flopping down on the bed. "How was France?"

"It was French," she said with a shrug. "Viv loved it, of course. I think she hooked up with one of the bellboys in Nice. *I* finally got to touch an uncircumcised penis. Not the bellboy's. We're sick, but we're not that sick."

"Nice," said Betsy. "You can check that one off the list."

"We made a deal. Viv let me chain-smoke as long as I didn't call her Mom. She thought it made her seem old. You know, just your typical family vacation. How were things here?"

"You know, the usual. *Le popcorn dans l'apres-midi*. Wait, is it feminine or masculine?"

"It's sort of androgynous," Caroline said. "It's like the hermaphrodite of snacks."

"Thanks for letting me stay here. I washed the sheets," said Betsy, and she slowly traced a perfect navy stripe on an Agnes B. T-shirt that Caroline tossed on the bed. The fondness she felt just minutes before faded. Only the nausea was left.

"How generous of you," Caroline said. "Now you can sleep on that beast of a couch downstairs or return to your cave."

"Thirty-six hours, max, and I'm out," said Betsy, throwing her hands up in surrender. "I'll be invisible. Like a ghost." She picked up the cigarettes and started to leave the room.

"I'm just giving you shit, Bets," Caroline said, but if she regretted picking the fight, it wasn't obvious. "Hey, I'm not going to show up for rush till tomorrow morning so we're going out tonight, right? Old times?"

"Right. Old times."

Ginny was the one who suggested that the three of them go out, like nothing had ever happened. They started out at CJ's, the kind of dive with sawdust on the floor that in a month or two, when football season was in full swing, would be crowded with alumni drinking stale beer and trying to relive their glory days. The first whiff of the place made Betsy worry that she'd one day remember it fondly, and that life was all downhill from there, even though "there" felt close to the bottom. The plan was to celebrate Caroline's end-of-summer homecoming with hot wings and a dozen oysters, though Ginny preferred the cocktail sauce straight up on saltines, hold the shellfish.

None of them mentioned the real reason they chose the place, which was because last fall Caroline had had a brief thing with the bartender, Justin something-or-other from Miami. For three weeks, it was their evening hangout. Caroline would toy with Justin in exchange for free drinks and a basket of fries for herself and her friends. Nobody said she wasn't generous. On their final night as regulars, Betsy and Caroline had shut the place down at 2:00 a.m., doing one last shot of Jäegermeister with Justin and an unremarkable waiter. It was Betsy's idea to head to Lake Alice, an oversized pond on the southwest corner of campus, for a drunken, adrenaline-fueled trail run. Lake Alice was an alligator habitat, fenced off from the public with fairly explicit signs depicting open-mouthed reptiles under words like Danger and clearly marked orders to Keep Out. If the presence of live alligators wasn't enough to scare any sensible person shitless, there was the university's Bat House, a tall, eerie-looking structure that was built to house a giant, displaced colony of Brazilian bats, diverting it from the tennis stadium, where it had taken up residence and was routinely covering the courts with guano. By the time the foursome arrived near 2:30, the sky was swarming with them. Adrenaline was hard to get in that town, and Betsy found herself coming up with increasingly outrageous ways to coax it out of thin air. Once, she convinced Ginny and Caroline to wander a pasture near town in search of hallucinogenic mushrooms, which grew on cow manure. Even in the moonlight, they couldn't make out what was growing out of where, and the three of them made such a racket that they woke up the rancher, who chased them out of his field with a flashlight and a loaded shotgun.

"Betsy Young, you almost got us killed," shouted Caroline as they sped away in Ginny's car. "I love it!"

On another night, Betsy commandeered Krystal, the fast-food burger place, jumping over the counter and putting on a spare apron to pass out free French fries to a hungry late-night crowd, until the manager called the police and they ran out the back door. The bats and alligator obstacle course was by far the scariest distraction of them all, and therefore Betsy's favorite.

They made it around the lake, running wild-eyed and howling, amazingly unharmed. But back at Caroline and Ginny's apartment, Ginny and the waiter passed out in her room, and Betsy was the only one to notice the smoke filling the air. Justin removed a forgotten Gino's pizza from the oven and tried to slice it by pressing a knife into it with the palm of his hand, blade side *up*. Caroline, who was laughing uncontrollably, could not be convinced that the inch-deep gash in Justin's hand needed stitches. So Betsy took his keys and drove him to the hospital, leaving Caroline, Ginny, and the waiter back at the apartment. After that, Justin decided that no sociopath was hot enough to endure the utter lack of compassion that came with the deal. He stopped calling Caroline, and she generally avoided CJ's. On the evening of her summer homecoming, however, the memory of that evening seemed foggy, and she wanted to start the new school year off right: with a reminder that she still owned that town and a round of free drinks. So CJ's it was.

When the cracker basket was empty and the two free rounds of Sea Breezes drained, the three of them waved goodbye to Justin, who nodded with visible relief as they filed through the door to leave. Then they piled into Ginny's car, pretending like no time had passed, like no feelings had been hurt, and Betsy was furious at herself for backing down and giving in to Caroline once again. As usual, they had no real destination in mind. Even though it was after midnight, they were restless and eager to see who'd made it back to town from summer break. They wanted to replace the stories they'd heard a hundred times before with new ones, and they needed a distraction from the building tension. They ended up in the back room of the Porpoise, a too-dark bar with pool tables and three-for-one drink specials inked on black mirrors with neon paint pens. The place was largely empty, except for a dully handsome trio from Ginny's high school whose names Betsy didn't catch over the frantic, grating chorus of R.E.M.'s "Pop Song 89" and didn't care enough about to ask them to repeat. Ginny had legs that dissolved beneath her after two glasses of syrupy Chardonnay, but that didn't slow her down. She and Betsy managed, mostly, to stay out of trouble, which is to say more sober than not, for weeks.

Technically, Betsy lived in a small two-bedroom apartment in a fourplex near Bagelville with a roommate, Kari, a junior from Ocala whom she had met in Masterpieces of Modern Drama. She signed the lease in June and Ginny helped her move in her meager belongings: a secondhand floor lamp, some crates of books, a couple of boxes of clothes, and a mattress without a box spring or frame. Once Kari came back into town, she would move her furniture out of mini-storage. Until then, it was grim and lonely, and Betsy loved Ginny even more for giving her the spare key to their apartment without making her ask for it. Betsy had been staying with Ginny all summer, feeling safe and cozy watching TV on the overstuffed couch, surrounded by grown-up furniture and dainty table lamps that added to the "bridge club" vibe of the place, and the popcorn popper they fired up every day at 3:30 when the clouds would open up and dump a couple of hours' worth of summer rain. There was something oddly comforting about the riotous mess of clothes around Ginny, the Stein Mart shopping bags giving at the seams from the strain of untouched purchases, tags revealing 75 percent off of the retail price.

So the arrangement worked perfectly—Ginny, who hated to be alone, got company while Caroline was away, and Betsy got furniture—until Caroline returned.

Instead of the wide, soft bed and crisp sheets monogrammed with Caroline's initials, Betsy had the couch for another night. Then, she'd move into her last apartment in Gainesville with her own lower thread count linens for four more months, one more long semester.

By the end of the year she'd be gone for good, ahead of schedule and not soon enough. Not that she had any particular plan. Even if she did have a specific goal, or the beginnings of a dream about what her life would look like in ten, five, or even two years from that moment, she wouldn't dare admit it to anyone. Ambition felt sort of awkward and pointless to her in that place, where looking for work typically involved browsing bulletin boards. Some people she knew showed up at the university's job fair in their cheap suits, half hoping to miss a shot at an entry-level gig at the First Union Bank, or as a manager of an Enterprise rental car outpost, and some of them got the job. They moved to Atlanta or Charlotte or even Orlando. English majors with an Art History minor weren't in high demand in that marketplace. Anyway, most of the people Betsy knew were going through the motions; technically, they were open to the idea of full-time employment, in case careers jumped out of the bushes and attacked them. So they polished their résumés, but that was where the go-getting ended.

The *Time* magazine article about useless, entitled twenty-somethings that her mother ripped out and sent her that summer with the words "hazy sense of their own identity" underlined in shaky ballpoint ink did nothing to convince her that opportunity would come knocking. Betsy was surprised to learn she was part of a generation of any kind, even one so dubiously described. All she knew for sure was that she'd have to put as much distance between herself and Gainesville as possible if she wanted to make something of her dismal life.

None of the answers to those haunting *What Color Is Your Parachute?* questions were likely to be answered the night the three of them piled into Ginny's car and drove to the Porpoise.

People had grown accustomed to seeing the three of them together. They were a unit, and from the outside looking in, Betsy realized that the strain between them was barely perceptible. At the beginning of their friendship, it didn't bother Betsy that Caroline and Ginny were flashier and more conventionally pretty. She learned that traveling in a pack of beautiful women is a powerful thing, that each head that turned to notice them fired a tiny spike of adrenaline. But lately, Betsy was growing increasingly paranoid that she was the sensible Charlie's Angel, the tall, pantsuit-wearing Sabrina to Ginny's beautiful but slightly dim Kelly, and Caroline's sun-kissed Kris, if behind Cheryl Ladd's gleaming blonde hair, straight patrician nose, and flawless smile lurked the shrewdest manipulator you'd ever met.

At the bar Caroline broke out her thick, mint-green Amex and bought the first round of shots.

"Five lemon drops and one tequila, no lime, for my angry friend over there," she said, snickering conspiratorially with the bartender. She pointed across the room at Betsy, who produced a middle finger on cue. "She's too cool for fruit."

An hour later, Betsy was desperate to leave. Caroline had disappeared into the front room. Betsy watched as Ginny walked over to the booth Caroline was hidden in to try to convince her to leave, and she squinted to focus on their exchange. Caroline stood up on the banquette and shooed her away, like she was swatting a fly.

"Just go already," Caroline shouted across the bar at Betsy, swaying slightly, trying to right her balance to prove she was capable of making sound decisions. "I'll find a ride home."

Ginny walked back toward Betsy, rolling her eyes.

"She's huddled in that booth with some guy," Ginny said,

rolling her eyes. "He looks like a real prize. Let's just get out of here."

Ginny and Betsy drove home in silence. It wasn't the first time they'd left Caroline to fend for herself with a new guy at a bar. Caroline was proud, almost defensive, of her independence, since it had been cultivated over the years she spent as the only child of a single, working mom. She was walking home from school and letting herself into an empty house for as long as she could remember. Caroline was afraid of nothing.

"Which do you think is scarier?" she often joked. "Riding home with a strange guy, or getting into a car with Ginny behind the wheel?"

They stumbled into the apartment, ears ringing from the noisy bar and thirsty as hell. Betsy went to the fridge for a glass of water. In a messy collage of ticket stubs and party pictures, she spotted one from the sorority hayride last January, the scandalous smoking event that would transform her life into something she'd barely recognize, stuck to the door with a cheeseburger magnet. Betsy looked like a jerk in a cheap straw cowboy hat, with that dumbstruck, desperate look that she was beginning to notice was the watermark of her college photos. She was obviously smitten with her friends, the sinister Caroline, who, at the time, was claiming not to drink but had Betsy sneak Solo cups full of grain alcohol punch to her in the bathroom at parties, and beautiful Ginny, with her head slumped on Betsy's shoulder. To her left was her ex, a snarky Georgia boy named Mack who had so clearly lost interest in her that he didn't bother to look at her or the camera. She had always found him to be intermittently petulant, prone to irrational outbursts of anger over botched restaurant orders or people who didn't understand his jam band obsession, and dull. He was considered desirable, by consensus, though, and Betsy felt desperate to hold his interest. In that sad fraction of a second preserved on film it was clear that she'd lost it a while ago. He broke up with her in the back of the hay-strewn wagon minutes after the shot was taken, while a lone piece of straw dangled from her bangs over her right temple. She knew Caroline was the one to deem the picture worthy of a spot on the fridge, as a souvenir of Betsy's pain. She'd been tempted to take it down all summer, but she wanted to at least appear too cool to care enough to throw it out. Betsy moved the burger magnet to obscure Mack's bloated, self-satisfied face.

Betsy gulped down her own water and filled another glass, which she took with her when she climbed the stairs to where the bedrooms were. She put it on Ginny's nightstand. Then she opened the linen closet in the hall to grab a quilt and an extra pillow for the night. Ginny leaned against the doorframe of her room wearing a boxy, oversized T-shirt from a Sigma Chi party that they decided to tie-dye a deep shade of rusty orange, which, Betsy suddenly realized, looked like bloodstains.

"Why don't you just crash with me?" Ginny asked. "You don't have to sleep on the lumpy sofa."

They got into bed, eyelids heavy with exhaustion and booze.

"Why are you so nice to me?" Betsy asked Ginny, as she drifted off to sleep. "Why haven't you kicked me out yet?"

Ginny shifted her head on the pillow.

"Bets, I swear you're the only one who doesn't understand why people like having you around. How many times do I have to tell you? You're good enough. You're smart enough. And people like you."

They fell asleep with the light on.

Betsy woke with a start to see Caroline hovering at the end of the bed, swaying ominously over her sleeping friends.

"Jesus, Caroline, you scared the shit out of me," Betsy said, rubbing her eye with her knuckles. "Why are you standing there? Who drove you home? Are you alright?"

"I didn't know you were awake," Caroline slurred; the neck of her T-shirt was stretched to expose one of her shoulders. Her eyeliner was smeared and sooty, and the back of her hair was rough with tangles. Betsy could smell the alcohol and sour mix across the room and wondered how anyone could think that vodka was odorless.

"What time is it?" Betsy asked, propping herself up on her elbows.

"I don't know," Caroline said, a smile widening across her face. "Time to make the doughnuts?"

"Very funny," mumbled Ginny, with her head still on the pillow. "This is why you barged into my room to wake us up, hovering over my bed like a total psycho. To make terrible jokes."

"God, Caroline, what happened to your knees?" Betsy asked. "Do you even know you're bleeding?" Caroline's knees were scraped raw and a thin trickle of blood traveled down her left shin. Betsy looked at the red numbers on Ginny's alarm clock. It was 4:21. There was no point in going back to sleep.

"Great. Rug-burned knees. Keep it classy, Caroline," said Ginny, her voice muffled from the down.

"Maybe it's time for you to get your own apartment, Betsy? Maybe that's what time it is," said Caroline. She shuffled into the bathroom and sat down hard on the toilet seat. Betsy got up out of Ginny's bed, went into the bathroom, opened the medicine cabinet, took out some cotton balls and Bactine, and placed them on the side of the sink.

"Do you want me to help you clean those off?" she asked.

"I've got it. I can handle it," Caroline said. With eyes half-closed, she crouched on the edge of the tub and rinsed her knees under the faucet. Still dripping wet, she picked up her noisy, electric Waterpik toothbrush and jabbed it around in her mouth in an almost violent way.

"Hey, Caroline, maybe it's time to take that picture of fat-face Mack off of the fridge? Maybe that's what time it is?" Betsy said.

"Yeah, Caroline, that guy put the 'ick' in 'dick,'" said Ginny.

"He put the 'ew' in 'screw,'" said Caroline, through a mouthful of water.

"Hey, I know! We should burn it, like in a voodoo shrine," added Ginny, who sat up suddenly in bed, inspired.

"Sure, but maybe we wait until all of us are sober to start striking matches," said Betsy.

"I'm going to miss you, fake roomie," said Ginny, making an exaggerated frown with her already rubbery face. "Who's going to convince me to go on those crazy late-night dare-devil adventures? Who's going to deliver my water before bed? Who's going to make me put butter on my popcorn?"

"Yeah, Orville Redenbacher, we're all sad to see you go so soon," added Caroline, in her best, nasal deadpan, as she hobbled past Betsy in the hall, thoughtlessly stripped down to her bra and underpants.

"Oh Christ, Caroline, will you just shut up already?" said Ginny. "You are ruining the moment."

"Don't waste your time, Gin," said Betsy, who had turned her back and started down the stairs to find her shoes and then ride to work, her voice trailing behind her. "It's been over for a while. Caroline, you know, you put the 'end' in 'friend.' The very bitter end."

CHAPTER 4
CRAZY SHIT

August 25, 1990: Early Morning

The fact that she slept in Ginny's bed with the light on and was woken up by a hostile drunk should have made her stiff and cranky. But at twenty, she could still crash for a few hours in someone else's bed and get to work before 6:00 a.m. without much fallout.

She brushed her teeth quietly in the kitchen sink, dug through her duffel bag for some clean shorts, cutoffs that were over-bleached and worn at the edges, and slipped on her Converse. She felt for the spare key on the small table in the hall, which was piled with unopened mail, and slid her arms through the straps of her backpack. Betsy closed the door behind her carefully and jumped when she noticed their neighbor's cat on the stoop. It seemed just as irritated to be awake at this hour as she was. It snarled at her before it slunk away into the shadows. She unlocked the Schwinn, impressed that she remembered the new combination so early, and pedaled off into the muddy, orange light of dawn.

Hungover but still, miraculously, ahead of schedule, she reached the top of the hill, thighs burning as she strained at the pedals. The streets were empty, for the most part, but in the near distance she saw the red flashing lights of a police car approaching. As it got closer, she realized that pedaling away from the sound, which was now echoing off of the imposing brick buildings of the campus, was no use. She hopped off of the bike and covered her ears as her shoulders crept up the sides of her neck. The wail of the siren pierced through to the center of her headache, which had been impressive even before that little cops-and-robbers interlude.

What's with the fuss? she thought, certain that nothing could be happening in that town at that hour that was worthy of such a production, and that it had been way too long since she'd seen anyone in a hurry of any kind. She remembered Tom talking about the police, that they had discovered something grisly a day or two ago, but she hadn't heard much since. Betsy made a point of avoiding any police officers that came in for free coffee after her fake I.D. arrest, and what Caroline referred to as the "ecstasy episode." During their sophomore year, Betsy and Caroline tried MDMA at a fraternity party, giggling wildly as they swallowed the tiny capsules with a swig of warm beer. About forty-five minutes later, Betsy started having chest pains and her pulse was racing. She was convinced she was dying of a heart attack. Caroline, whose pupils were wide with wonder, tried to take her outside for a walk to try to calm her down, but Betsy panicked. Eventually, Caroline grew tired of her friend's anxiety and was drawn back inside by the thumping music, leaving Betsy alone in the grass. When the pains refused to fade, Betsy found the nearest pay phone and called 911. Minutes later, an ambulance, a police car, and a fire engine were parked on Fraternity Row, red lights blaring. Betsy was alone, lying on the gurney, watching the scene around her flash in frames as the drugs kicked in for a second wave. What seemed like every male on the entire campus poured out of the frat houses that lined the street to see what was happening. As the onlookers gawked, the medics took her vitals and determined that Betsy was, no surprise, not in cardiac arrest. She was having a panic attack. They took her to the hospital anyway to check her blood levels for alcohol poisoning. She got a stern lecture from the emergency room physician about the dangers of illegal drugs, how she had no idea what she was taking—it could have been cyanide for all Betsy knew—and how she was taking precious time away from people who really needed a doctor's care.

Even though the police let her off with a warning, word quickly spread to everyone in the house, and when she was finally brave enough to show her face in the dining room, there was a wave of snickers and whispers that followed her to the salad bar. When she finished her lunch, she checked her mail cubby and found the small strip of paper requesting her presence at Standards. Standards was the secretive meeting held every Sunday night in a small, somber library off of the foyer. The purpose of the gathering was for the house alumni advisor, the house president, and the "chaplain" (the biggest prude they could find who was willing to discuss the amoral conduct of her friends) to reprimand members for their disreputable behavior—to their faces for a change. Betsy was lectured in Standards about unbecoming conduct and the dangers of alcohol abuse (she never admitted to the drugs, despite their leading questions), which struck Betsy as confusing and hypocritical, since alcohol and underage drinking was assumed, and, the way she saw it, practically expected, at every Greek party on campus. She was advised to be more careful and let off with a warning.

The following year, Standards was a regular Sunday night appointment for Betsy, which made her realize that things may not be working out for her there. The final straw, or her epiphany, as Betsy called it, came during a single week when she'd been accused of three offenses: smoking weed on the sun porch (True.), dropping "roaches" between the wooden slats of the porch deck (False. She liked to get high but she was not an arsonist.), and smoking (cigarettes) at a sorority function (True.).

The behavior in question occurred during the annual hayride, which was essentially an excuse to get drunk outside, in the woods, in front of an enormous bonfire. She'd shown up promptly at 7:00 ready to face the music. The vague unrest that had been percolating inside Betsy for months was coming into sharper focus.

"Were the people huddled around that twenty-foot stack of flaming timber offended when I smoked a single cigarette?" Betsy asked the group.

"It's just that, Betsy, you know how it goes," said Holly, their president, the very same Holly who'd been busted for a DUI (at 4:21 p.m. on a Friday, according to the police report) during her first month on campus just three short years earlier. Her gaze was trained on the tiny silver cross on Betsy's necklace so she could avoid eye contact. "It just looks bad."

The sorority bylaws, which were likely written in the 1950s, specified that sisters were only allowed to smoke indoors while seated. Betsy knew it was a stupid habit and bad for her, but she was being chastised for being tacky, not endangering her health.

"OK, got it. Smoke inhaled from the giant fire: OK," said Betsy. Her voice began to break. "Smoke inhaled courtesy of Philip Morris: not OK."

"The cigarettes are just . . . unbecoming," stuttered Leslie, the chaplain. "But the pot thing? Well, it's an illegal drug, for one. Plus, we're going down in flames, 'Burning Bed' style, if you keep dropping the butts into the deck."

"This isn't the first time you've been called in here for this," said Laurie, the alumni advisor, who was on the university's music faculty. Laurie had pledged somewhere in the Midwest back in the 1970s when sororities were out of favor, and made a point of telling all of the active sisters that she would never have made the cut had she rushed in Gainesville today. No one argued with her. "Betsy, if it happens again, measures will be taken. This isn't a joke."

"Are you sure about that?" said Betsy, forcing her voice to be steady. "It feels a lot like a joke to me."

The weed accusations she flatly denied. The last time someone admitted to doing drugs in that room it was sweet Kelly from West Palm who had a small cocaine problem. She was coaxed into confessing to a few lines under the guise of the sorority board's goal to "get her help." She was kicked out the following day. Her parents were called. Tears were shed. She moved home and spent the next two years commuting to Florida Atlantic University. To that, Betsy said, "No thanks." Straight-up denial was the only way to go. Betsy could pretend not to care in that suffocating room, but she was barely out the back door before she burst into tears, vowing never to return again.

Over the following week, she'd had her chrysalis moment: She quit, moved out of the house, dropped her pin in the president's mail cubby, and moved in with her coworker Melissa, despite her surly roommates' protests, until she could find a place of her own.

On a whim, she lopped her long, wavy hair to just below her chin, and stuffed the dozen or so floral dresses she owned into a black Hefty bag, which she dropped at Goodwill. Then, just like that, it was over. She rode her bike to class, slept at Melissa's, showed up for work, studied at the library, and went back to being unspecial, save for her moments with Ginny, just like before.

The following Saturday, Ginny came by the bagel store to pick her up after her shift, as usual, and the next day the two of them drove out to Cedar Key to drink dollar Red Stripes, watch the sun reflect off of the Gulf, and listen to a mediocre reggae band with the regular sweaty mob like nothing ever happened.

There was no way any of the officers in town remembered her from the ecstasy episode, and she knew that, but she kept her head down anyway. She was determined to make it to the end of her college career without another incident. One more semester, just four more months, and it would be over. She felt the excitement of a new school year stirring inside of her. After a long, quiet summer, students were finally starting to trickle back into town. She wondered who would show up that day and order their first breakfast of the new school year. Would she ever run into John again, or would he just disappear into the business quad, be absorbed into the masses like everyone else? If nothing else, with people coming back to campus, things would start to get interesting.

When Betsy rounded the corner on her bike and Bagelville came into view, she saw two police officers get into their cruiser in front of the store and drive away. When she got to the back door, it was unlocked, and she walked in to see Tom sitting at his small desk in the corner, holding his head in his hands.

"Hey, Tom, what's going on?" Betsy said, warily, worried about what he might say.

"It's the crazy shit I was telling you about," he said, lifting his eyes up to meet hers. "We'll talk about it once you're done with the juice. There's work to do."

A MOUNTAIN OF overripe citrus beckoned. It was her job to toss all of it into the industrial juicer, sacrifice the fruit into the humming, pulp-covered abyss, and then empty the hollow peels into the Dumpster out back.

There was no way Betsy could have known that on the opposite side of 34th Street just hours before she struggled to climb the hill, swerving down the slope that made her fight for air that morning, was a man in a stolen car, struggling to focus on the road through the tears streaming across his temples, blown by the air coming in through the window. Betsy would later read that man had cried tears of confusion, remorse for the girl he'd slaughtered in her room. The victim, his second in a week, had just returned from the gym with plans to shower and head to work, the graveyard shift manning the switchboard at the sheriff's office, of all places. But he was waiting for her in a closet, having pried the sliding-glass door open with a screwdriver. When she didn't show up to work by midnight, an hour after her shift started, or answer the phone at her house, a patrol car drove out to her apartment to see if she was OK. She was found on her bed, stabbed in the back five times with a foot-long blade, and wiped clean of her own blood. She was his second victim in the eight days since he'd rolled into town.

All Betsy knew was that there were a shitload of oranges to squeeze by 7:00 a.m., and that this was the year her life would change. Later, she thought, she'd smear veggie spread on a toasted sesame and try to swap it for a slice out back.

CHAPTER 5

GAVIN

August 25, 1990: Morning

Hey, do y'all have any fresh-squeezed juice?"

Betsy heard the smug, raspy giggle. Even with her back turned she knew it was the moron. It had been three solid months since she'd heard that drawl, the smoker's cough, the relentless sarcasm she once mistook for humor. There was a time when she found that rebellious but still preppy Southern thing—the fraying Izod, the ball cap pulled low, the hard pack of Camels in the back pocket, the flattened Reef flip-flops, the easy smile, the giant Chevy Suburban with Georgia plates that smelled, eternally, of gasoline—irresistible. But she quickly realized that these guys came with a package deal, and the package included a habit of traveling for jam band shows and playing endless rounds of golf. As a bonus, they also came with frequent visits from a condescending, plastic-nosed mother and/or sister, regular lost magic-mushroom weekends, and a baffling number of out-of-town fishing trips (the latter two were often concurrent events).

"Hey, Mack, no freebies today," she said without looking up. "Tom's onto my ways and he's started counting the cups." The morning rush had vanished, along with her caffeine high, and she was in no mood for assholes.

"I'm a paying customer today. Semester's just started and I'm flush." He laughed. "So I guess we'll take two."

It was the "we" that got her attention. She turned around to see Mack, tan and lean from a summer caddying on Hilton Head, standing next to Gavin.

LAST SPRING AT the Dish, a gritty club downtown, American Music Club was in town to play to a packed house of about forty-three people. Betsy had pleaded with Ginny to go with her, even bartered joining her on a drive to Ocala to visit her grandmother, Nana Jean, the following day. By 11:00, the band still hadn't made it onto the stage. Ginny, with her shiny brown hair and royal blue miniskirt, beamed like a distress signal.

"So this is where you go," Ginny said, glancing around at the sparse groups of filthy T-shirt-clad guys, "when you're not with us?"

"You mean when I'm not drinking three-dollar pitchers at a bar called Balls?" she said. "Honestly, Gin, is that the best they could do? Balls? At least at Hooters they're going for a somewhat veiled innuendo with the owl thing. But a sports bar called Balls is just lazy and, frankly, a little gross."

"Um, three-dollar pitchers?" Ginny leaned in to whisper in her ear, "They could call it Scrotum and I would still show up every Thursday."

"And who is the 'us' you're referring to, anyway? You and Caroline?" said Betsy.

"Well, yeah, me and Caroline. Plus every other person we know," said Ginny.

A guy wearing giant black glasses and a faded Kool-Aid T-shirt walked by, nodded, and offered a barely audible "What's up, Bets?"

"Or at least everyone *I* know," Ginny said, pausing to see if that was a good moment to bring up what she'd been avoiding for weeks. "You know, you could tell Caroline you're sorry and just move on. It would be so easy. You wouldn't even have to mean it."

"Sorry for what? What do I have to be sorry about?" Betsy barked at her.

At that point, to Betsy's relief, the band took the stage, albeit with the bombast and dynamism of a slug. Sullen and exhausted, they were met with a single woot and some limp applause. After what seemed like endless tuning, Mark Eitzel, the lead singer, had a bit of a meltdown onstage, though calling it that lent it more drama than it deserved. He looked around at the sparse crowd, which must have seemed pathetic to someone who'd been somewhere else, anywhere else, but seemed perfectly fine to anyone who hadn't, made a kind of condescending harrumphing sound into the mic and stormed off the stage. It was more like a minor tantrum than a breakdown. The band must have been used to his antics because after the drummer and bass player exchanged a weary glance, they shrugged and kept playing. Within a few minutes, when it was clear Eitzel would not return, a guy from the audience hopped on the stage, shook the guitarist's hand, whispered something to him, and lumbered over to the mic stand.

"I'm taking requests," he said, pointing at the audience with one finger and wrapping the others around a Rolling Rock. "And no fucking Skynyrd."

It was Gavin. She knew his name from hearing Mack say it, and seeing him around at parties and shows. He'd caught her eye once or twice. And last year, she drove out to his house with Caroline one night, but she hadn't paid much attention until that moment.

Twenty minutes later, midway through a more shouted than sung version of "Sweet Home Alabama," Betsy had a new crush. Ginny had had enough.

"I feel like Strawberry Shortcake, or what's her name, the blueberry scented one, in this place," she said, glancing at her crisp T-shirt and handing an empty can of PBR to Betsy. "And I either need to do a shot or go home."

They slipped out the back door into the alley without saying hello or goodbye to Gavin. And there he was, looming before her at Bagelville, taller than she remembered.

"Hey, Gavin," she said, nodding at him, looking past Mack's shoulder.

"Hey, Betsy."

He knew her name. He *admitted* he knew it. This might be easier than she thought.

"Y'all know each other?" Mack asked. "I mean, well enough for you to serve him a bagel?"

"Yeah, I've seen him around."

"You, too."

"That was quite a performance at the Dish last spring," she said, wondering if she'd brushed her teeth that day as she tucked an unwashed strand of hair behind one ear. She ran her tongue behind her upper lip to check and hoped he wouldn't notice. "How long did you stay up there?"

"I ran out of songs I knew by heart pretty fast," he said. "Some asshole kept shouting 'Tom Sawyer' but I haven't been able to sing high like Geddy Lee since seventh grade."

"Um, I'll have a large coffee and a sesame, toasted with chive cream cheese, thanks for asking," said Mack, sliding a ten-dollar bill across the counter. Betsy moved to the counter to slice his bagel and put it in the toaster.

"We have light cream cheese now," said Betsy. "I just thought you should know."

Mack clenched his teeth.

"It looks like you leaned out over the summer. You don't want to get, what's that word?" She motioned vaguely to the underside of his unshaven chin.

"Jowly," said Gavin.

"Yeah, that's it! Jowly. You don't want to get jowly. Again."

Mack brushed his jawbone reflexively and grunted something obscene.

"I'll just have coffee, no juice for me," said Gavin.

Tom barged through the swinging doors from the back with a brown paper sack full of cinnamon raisins. Steam carried out the yeasty, sweet smell of bread baked with fruit.

"It's $2.75 for the juice," Tom said, looking dead straight at Mack. "I know you don't pay, Newland."

"There's a murderer on the loose and all you care about is money," said Mack. "I don't want any of that shit anyway."

"I'd charge the killer double," said Tom.

"What killer?" said Betsy, trying not to seem alarmed as she spread a thick layer of green-flecked cream cheese and watched it melt into the warm bagel.

"Two girls were found dead in two different apartments in the last week. They think they're connected. That's what I was talking about earlier," said Tom. "By the way, Newland, where have *you* been the last couple of nights?"

"Ah, hilarious," he said. "Who knew you had to be funny to make my breakfast for a living?"

Gavin took his coffee. Mack grabbed his bagel and wandered over to a table in the corner near the window. Betsy tried to look busy, slicing tomatoes, refilling the cream cheese bin, straightening the refrigerator case, sweeping up the relentless downpour of poppy seeds on the floor, but her eyes kept darting to the corner. Melissa, a bird-like blonde from South Carolina, came in to help with the morning rush. She washed her hands in the steel sink and wiped them on her paint spattered Duck Head cutoffs.

"Hey, so did you hear about the dead girls?" Melissa said, slicing and scooping a salt bagel with her fingers for an impatient and bleary-eyed med school resident in hospital scrubs on the other side of the counter.

"Somebody mentioned something," Betsy said, thinking *If that guy's going to be a doctor one day, he should know better than to ask a stranger to dig her fingernails into his bread, even if it meant a few extra calories.* "Some lunatic was ranting about a murder a few minutes ago." She glanced over at Mack and Gavin's table, where they were, without question, talking about her. "But I thought it was the usual bullshit. So it's true? Two girls are dead?"

"Yeah, they found a girl dead at her apartment out by the highway or something. Then another one this morning. They think it's related. One of them worked as a dispatch at the sheriff's office. It was all over the police radio," said Melissa. "I ran into my landlord and he told me. That crazy bastard has a scanner, like a police radio. What a cliché. Anyway, that's how he heard. The cheap asshole was replacing all of the broken locks in our complex today so it must be serious."

"Jesus," said Betsy, thinking of her pre-dawn bike ride, trying to remember if she'd locked the door at Caroline and Ginny's behind her. She thought about leaving Caroline at the bar.

Eventually Betsy's curiosity got the better of her and she wandered over to Mack and Gavin's table with a fresh pot of coffee under the guise of refills.

"So, you're talking shit about me, obviously," she said, filling Gavin's cup first.

"Always, Young, always," said Mack, balling up his napkin and tossing it on the table.

"What do you know about this so-called murderer?" she asked them, hoping Gavin would answer.

"What I hear is that some girl was sliced from her chin down. Never saw it coming," said Mack, shoving the last bite of bagel into his mouth. "Alright. Gotta go get unpacked. I got some speakers to attend to. See you back at the house."

"Ah, so you're roommates now?" she said, trying not to let her disappointment show. "When's the first rager?"

"No, not roommates," said Gavin, quickly. "Just neighbors. Mack moved into the house next door to mine."

"But there will be a rager. And don't act like you need an invitation, Betsy. You'll just follow the scent of beer. Kinda like a drunk, desperate dog, like, like, more like a bloodhound," Mack said.

"You can bite me, Mack."

"Been there, Betsy, believe me. Not going back," he said, pausing a moment to let a dumb, slow grin spread across his face.

"You know, it would suck if you were the next one to get hacked to bits," he said, turning to look at Gavin. "Later, Gav."

"Later."

She stood there holding the rapidly cooling coffeepot, noticing her hangover again for the first time in hours. Mack was one of the latest in a long line of bad decisions. Freshman year, there was George, her first mistake in town, which lasted forty-eight hours before she found out he had broken up with Heather, a senior in her sorority, a week before they met. George had given her a ride to the stadium for her first football game on the handlebars of his bike. Later, after he treated her to her first sushi dinner at a bad Japanese place by the highway, they had sex in a way that made Betsy think George was used to getting what he wanted without asking for it. Though what happened between them was just a degree or two from date rape, consensual in only that she didn't ever exactly say "no," she still went to his house the next day to play Spades with his roommates. She didn't yet understand that what she wanted, or didn't want, counted for something. Heather tracked Betsy down at dinner on Monday and gave her a loud, demeaning lecture about what happened to slutty pledges, and it was over. George left one weak message on her answering machine ("Hey, Betsy. Gimme a call.") and was never heard from again. Betsy had a few deeply average make-out sessions here and there, a handful of forgettable flings, then, during her sophomore year, she had a monthslong flirtation with Andrew, her Geology TA, with whom she'd spend hours talking in the corner of a microbrew pub over warm, hoppy beer to no avail. The relationship culminated with a Friday afternoon trip to Devil's Millhopper, a sinkhole about twenty minutes outside of town. He'd mentioned it in a lecture about local natural landmarks and Betsy expressed an interest, more in his chronic scruff and the way he blushed when he spoke to her than in a hole in the ground. But once they parked in the empty lot and took the long, wooden boardwalk 212 steps down into the funnel-shaped depression in the earth, she was mesmerized. Each layer of soil beneath the surface, every scrambling vine and tree that stretched its branches skyward for sunlight, told a story. There were bones of long-forgotten mammals buried within the dirt, fossilized marine life from the time when the ocean stretched across the peninsula, which was now covered with only a tangle of highways and subdivisions. The deeper you descended, the more alien it all became. At the bottom, it was cool and shady even when the surface was suffocating, and mild and balmy even on the chilliest January day. The boardwalk ended in a mysterious little rain forest of electric green ferns and odd plants that somehow survived beneath the gnarled oaks, conifers, and evergreens on the surface. They didn't belong there in that deciduous forest. But they'd found a way to thrive by burrowing deep, staying low and out of sight, and the metaphor felt eerily familiar. *That is how I will survive in Gainesville*, she thought. It was silent down there, except for the waterfalls that trickled down its sides, carving a path through the rocks and moss, which then disappeared under the ground below. Andrew explained that a local grain farmer at the end of the nineteenth century had found human remains, bone fragments, and teeth, at the bottom of the depression, which was shaped like a grain funnel into hell, and since then the spot had acquired its share of creepy folklore.

"There's an Alachua Indian legend about this place," he said, stopping to catch his breath halfway back up the steps. "The story is that the devil fell in love with a beautiful, young princess and captured her near here. When the bravest members of the tribe tried to come rescue her, the devil created this hole. The warriors set off to find her and bring her home, and each one would fall in the sinkhole to his death. No one could save her, or bring her back. The waterfalls were said to be rivers of tears her friends and family shed over their loss."

By the time they were back above ground, Betsy was so transfixed by what she'd seen that she forgot all about her crush and she and Andrew parted with a firm handshake.

During her junior year, she met Mack, and the roller coaster of their relationship lasted for five months, her longest to date. After she was dumped, unceremoniously, on the hayride, there was the doomed attempt to go out with an absurdly preppy tennis player named John who supposedly had a girlfriend up north. That didn't keep him from going out with Caroline less than a month later, which caused the rift that tore them apart. There'd been no one special since she noticed Gavin last year and circled around him until he left for summer break. And there he was, sitting before her in awkward silence. *"How long have I been standing here?"* she wondered.

"Mack can be a real asshole," he said, finally, avoiding eye contact. "Sorry about that."

"Oh believe me, I know. We have sort of a history," she said. "But obviously that's over. Really over. It's been a while now, actually."

He rose to leave and they stood there, both searching for another witty comment but coming up empty. The early lunch crowd was starting to stream in and Melissa was shooting Betsy pleading looks from behind the counter.

"Well, look. I've got to get back to work," she said, nodding to the line. "Enjoy the big-screen TV. The only good thing about living near Mack is that he comes with a lot of electronics.

"OK, so, I'll see you around?" said Betsy.

"Alright," he said

She started to walk back toward the counter, her heart rising through her chest to choke her, worried that whatever chance she had with Gavin was slipping away.

"Hey, Betsy," he said. She stopped to look back.

"Uh, a few of us are going out to J.D.'s today, you know, at the lake?"

"Uh-huh."

"You in?"

"Do you mean do I want to go?" she asked.

"Yes." He laughed. "I mean do you want to go."

"Sure," she said, with a shrug. "I'm out of here pretty soon."

"Tell you what. I'm going to do a few things and then hit Schoolhouse Records. You know where it is, right? You can come meet me over there about one. Deal?"

"Deal."

Back in the corner behind the counter, Melissa was poking at the industrial toaster with a rubber spatula. Betsy picked up some red plastic baskets and tossed a mound of crumpled napkins in the trash on her way back to the counter.

"Well, something smells delicious," said Betsy, washing her hands again in the metal sink.

"Oh, this is just hilarious, isn't it, Bets," said Melissa, scraping blackened mozzarella from the rack with a rubber spatula. "You could at least pretend to not be enjoying my hangover so much."

"What? Do I look like I'm enjoying myself?" she said, fighting the smile that had suddenly, unexpectedly, returned to her face. The acrid smell of scorched cheese filled the air.

CHAPTER 6
SHARPIES

August 25, 1990: Midday

Betsy squeezed the juice, toasted the bagels, and made the coffee, and the rest of the morning passed in a slow, predictable way. At about 11:00, Dr. Loman wandered in, looking as distracted as ever, with several crumpled sections of various newspapers tucked under one arm. Betsy made him his usual tuna melt without a single rude comment, since she herself was distracted, thinking about Gavin, about the news on campus, about the sirens she heard on her way to work that morning. Just before her shift ended, she wandered over to his table to refill his coffee.

"What's happening in the real world today?" Betsy asked, nodding to the stack of papers, now spotted with grease and coffee stains. "I want to hear about anywhere but here."

"Let me ask you: Do you know what's happening in Kuwait? Or even where it is?" he said, raising an eyebrow in a quizzical way.

"Yes," said Betsy. "It's in the Middle East, I think. And the Iraqis have invaded it, for oil, right? Am I close?"

"You *think*." he said. "Are you close?"

He folded the section he was reading and placed it on the pile.

"You know the answer, but you feel obligated to act like you know absolutely nothing at all. Why?"

She stood there blushing, holding the coffeepot.

"It's early, I guess?" she said. The vocal fry, the timbre at the end of Betsy's sentence that lilted up into an eternal question, was an irritating habit, even to her.

"Betsy, you're a bright girl. Your brain likes to think for itself," he said. Then he drank the remains of his coffee and stood up to leave. "You've just got to get out of your own way."

She shifted her weight from one leg to the other, still holding the coffee, uncomfortable with his attention.

"Alas, I have hope," he said, placing a hand on her shoulder. "For a while, I was worried that you were going to become one of *them*."

He pretended to shiver to emphasize *them* and Betsy had to laugh.

"Hell is empty," he said, looking at her deliberately, more serious now, "and all the devils are here."

"Let me guess," said Betsy, "that's Shakespeare."

"Right again," he nodded, clicked his heels, and left.

AFTER SPLASHING WATER on her face in the sink in the back—a blatant violation of Bagelville policy—and borrowing some wild cherry ChapStick from Melissa, Betsy walked out the front door into the punishing sunlight. It was noon, and she had an hour to kill before she met Gavin at the record store two blocks away. She stood on the sidewalk, shielding her eyes, considering what to do next when she spotted Ginny's beater Rabbit speeding down 2nd Street with Caroline in the passenger seat.

"Where's my midget bike, bitch?" shouted Caroline, as Ginny pulled up to the curb beside her. Ginny didn't drive the newer, more sophisticated Cabriolet (which Betsy thought must be French or German slang for "rich white girl"). It was a straight-up, mud-splattered Rabbit. Her Nana had offered to buy her a new car, but Ginny wasn't interested.

"Hey, friends," said Betsy, preparing for the worst. "Sprung from prison camp for the afternoon?"

"There was a poster board and snack emergency at the house," said Ginny, whose T-shirt and cutoffs were speckled with paint from building sets for rush. Caroline was spotless as always. "We volunteered to make a run. It's rush stuff, but you know that."

"How noble of you," said Betsy.

"Completely selfless, as always," said Caroline, squinting hard at her.

"I came by to see if you needed a ride. It's too hot to be out on a bike," said Ginny.

"I guess I could leave the dwarfcycle here until later. But, hey, Caroline, I promise that I'll get it back to you tomorrow," Betsy said.

"Oh please, that piece of crap? Someone left it at our place last year. Like I would ever ride that thing," she said.

Ginny shot Caroline a hard look and punched her in the thigh.

"So get in. Come to Walmart. We're making a frozen yogurt run, too."

Betsy weighed her options. It was ninety-six degrees and

anyone who knew better was inside. Until classes started again and she could scurry across campus and into a classroom, and let her perspiration evaporate into the air-conditioned ether, she didn't have anyplace to go. In that moment, getting in the backseat of Ginny's car seemed like her only option.

"Alright, I'll come. But I've got to be back here in an hour."

She climbed in without opening the door, Ginny hit the gas, and the car sputtered around the corner onto University Boulevard. Caroline craned her neck around to look at Betsy over the top of her Ray-Bans.

"So I am assuming you've heard about the dead girls, right?"

"Uh-huh," said Betsy, trying to be nonchalant, not to show Caroline any fear.

"As I am sure you can imagine, everyone at the house is losing their shit. The rumor is that there's a killer on the loose, and he's dressing up like a pizza delivery guy so people let him into their houses."

"I heard that he was pretending to be from the department of water and power," said Ginny. "He says that the landlord sent him and then once he's inside he pulls out a gun."

"Wait, weren't they stabbed?" asked Caroline, who was now checking her manicure.

"You seem really concerned, Car," said Betsy. "I mean, concerned that you've chipped a nail. Not that people are being stabbed to death."

"Oh please, you know how this town is. How much of this shit are you going to believe? Also, honestly, the numbers are in my favor. How many female students are on this campus? Say, fifteen thousand? I have a one in fifteen thousand chance of being murdered this week."

"Um, I don't think that's exactly how it works. Am I right?" asked Ginny, taking her eyes off of the road for a dangerously long time to look back at Betsy. "I mean, I don't remember much from Probability and Statistics, but I am almost positive that's not how it works."

"You're so cute when you're dumb," said Betsy, reaching over the back of her seat to squeeze Ginny's shoulder.

"The exact number doesn't even matter, Gin. You're always so *literal*," said Caroline. "Besides, I took Self-Defense for two credits! That guy comes at me, and I could kill his sorry ass with a rolled-up newspaper. You roll it up so tight you can stab someone with it! I could rip his ear off with my hand. All it takes is twenty pounds of pressure. Or thirty. I can't remember."

"That is just gross," said Ginny. "So you just pull on it till it rips off, and you're just standing there with another person's ear in your hand? What about you, Betsy? Could you rip someone's ear off?"

"You're ripping mine off right now with all of this yammering," said Betsy, who couldn't help but crack a smile. Then she and Ginny and even Caroline were laughing, that kind of nervous, appalling laughter that sneaks out at the least appropriate times.

Ginny steered into the last parking spot on one of several long, empty aisles in a largely vacant parking lot of a strip mall. What was the hurry? The longer they stayed away from estrogen camp, the frantic panic of pre-rush preparations, the better. She and Caroline had been in stale air, filled with raspberry-body-wash smells and bad karma, all day. What the three of them needed was arctic AC, frozen yogurt, a trial-sized hair spray, a long peruse down the aisles of Walmart, and the reason for their furlough, poster boards and markers.

"Primo spot, Gin," said Caroline. "Honestly, we could have walked and gotten here faster."

"Think of the thirty-five-second walk to the door as a chance to work on your tan," she said. "Let's get yogurt first."

Inside the TCBY—"This Can't Be Yogurt" or "The Country's Best Yogurt," depending on which side of the lawsuit you landed—a melancholy post–Go-Go's Belinda Carlisle song was playing from an enormous boom box on the shelf next to the cake cone dispenser. The girl behind the counter had deeply tanned, nearly purple skin and a cascade of Aussie Sprunch–sprayed curls tumbling over the side of her white visor.

"Welcome to my nightmare, how can I help you?" said Caroline, looking over her shoulder at Ginny and Betsy. Caroline had mastered speaking at a range that was not quite loud enough for her victim to hear, but left the subject of her scrutiny with a vague feeling of unease nonetheless. Turning to expressionless Tracy, according to the nametag pinned to the blaze orange sweatshirt she was wearing despite the ninety-five-degree day, she said, "My friend here will have a medium strawberry in a cup with whatever kind of crap cereal you're selling today. What's your poison, Betsy?"

"Fruity Pebbles OK?" Tracy asked, getting a better look at Caroline. There was a faint glimmer of recognition in her flat, blue eyes, which then narrowed into tiny, accusatory slits.

"No frogurt for me today, I'm good," said Betsy, noticing Tracy notice Caroline for the first time.

"Are Fruity Pebbles OK? I don't know, depends on who you ask," said Caroline. "I'll take a sample of chocolate. But just a sample."

"You look familiar," said Tracy, who'd grabbed a foam cup

and turned her back to them as she depressed the cold handle of the thrumming, metal machine and dumped a long, oozy rope of frozen ick into it.

"Who me?" asked Ginny, suddenly panicked. She searched Betsy's face for clues, but Betsy just shrugged. Betsy had started to notice that this happened to Ginny more than it should, and was an unfortunate reminder of her boozy camaraderie and regular blackouts at bars and parties across town. Everyone remembered Ginny, but she remembered no one. She confessed to Betsy once that she started plastering a smile on her face and nodding at everyone she passed as a precaution. But the summer had been uneventful. Betsy and Ginny burned through the new releases at Blockbuster and not much else. They'd shut down the Porpoise only once all summer. Ginny picked up a couple of cute law students, whose names she couldn't recall, if she ever knew them. It didn't take much effort. Guys loved Ginny. She was quick to laugh, a gifted flirt, and the one voted "Best All Around" her senior year when people couldn't describe her with just one superlative.

"How is it that I've never let you buy me a drink before?" she'd said to the guys at the bar, by way of introduction. Betsy rolled her eyes. It was a Tuesday night so boring and oppressively humid that they had to get out of the house. Three pitchers later, the law students gave them a ride home in a vintage Chevy Impala, but not before the four of them dismantled a Pepsi pyramid in front of a gas station, howling with laughter as they loaded the trunk with as many of the two-liter bottles as they could. It was a classic Ginny night.

Ginny squinted at Tracy, trying to place her face, but Betsy saw that Tracy's eyes were locked on Caroline, and she saw Ginny's face relax.

"No, your friend here. It's Caroline, right?" she said. Caroline was steely, calm, but Betsy thought she saw an almost imperceptible twitch of panic pulse under her left eye. "You rushed me last year."

"Oh shit, sorry, yeah. I remember now, Tracy," said Caroline, who was linking together words that might have formed an apology if they were delivered in a more sympathetic tone.

"I dropped out of rush after that," she said, slamming the yogurt on the counter, stabbing it with a plastic spoon and extending a limp hand for the money. "It's $2.49."

"Hope it wasn't something I said," replied Caroline flatly, never averting her eyes from Tracy's glare.

Hell is empty, Betsy thought. *All the devils are here.*

Ginny dug four crumpled bills out of her pocket and dropped them in a wad on the counter.

"Keep the change, Tracy. Thanks! Great to see you again," said Ginny, with forced brightness, as she grabbed her friend's arms and exited the store so quickly that the blast of heat outside greeted them like a punch in the face. Once they were safely beyond the plate glass window, beyond their new nemesis's sight line, Betsy stopped and turned to Caroline, who was chuckling and checking the cuticle on her thumbnail again.

"It's like once Belinda realized she was hot it all went to shit," Caroline said.

"What are you talking about?" asked Ginny.

"Belinda Carlisle. She's like 'I've got an idea. I'm going to lose twenty pounds, abandon my totally bitchin' band and become the most aggressively mediocre pop star of my generation,'" said Caroline.

"You have no remorse, do you?" asked Betsy.

"I love the Go-Go's. I am not ashamed."

"I'm not kidding, Car," she said. "This Tracy person seems to blame you for ruining her life. And you've got no remorse."

"Remorse?" she said, stopping on the sidewalk, shielding her eyes from the sun. "About what? I was nice to her during rush, or nice enough. I may have made a comment about her white shoes. Do you want me to apologize for not leading on the yogurt girl with Kentucky Fried hair? Did you see her cold sore? She's totally got herpes. She put the 'itch' in 'bitch.'"

"Come on!" said Betsy, losing patience.

"Car, I get what you're saying. You didn't have to lead her on exactly, but . . ."

"But what? What, Ginny?" she said, with a fury igniting inside of her. "You should be *thanking* me. You think that everything just happens this way? That you get to live in this perfect little world where all of your friends are smart and cute with perfect hair by some kind of luck of the draw? You *need* me. I'm the *heavy*. You sure as hell aren't going to do it. Are you willing to tell Tracy that she'd be 'happier elsewhere'? Would you say it to her face or just talk shit about her after she slumped down the sidewalk in her white pleather heels?"

Ginny looked down at her own shoes, gleaming white Tretorns. Betsy, who couldn't think of a single response, felt the heat from the pavement seep through her sneakers to the sticky soles of her feet.

"There are over a thousand girls who want one of fifty spots. What are you going to do?" said Caroline, calmer now, back to picking at her nails. "She didn't even give me my sample. And she shorted your Pebbles by about half."

They walked for a minute without saying a word, past the

Fantastic Sams, past the Chinese restaurant with the coal black tinted windows, past the Dollar Tree, where Ginny, Betsy, and Caroline used to go when they were bored and high to look for paint-by-number kits. Betsy would badger the surly old lady at the cash register by picking up a series of items, a dishcloth with a map of the state on it, a bunch of drooping silk lilies, asking, "How much is this?" while Caroline and Ginny hid near the greeting cards trying in vain to stifle their giggles.

"It's a dollar. All of it," the cashier would snap. "And you damn well know it by now, Betsy."

Afterward, they would watch Betsy squirm with regret. She would try to make amends by chatting about football or when she thought the heat might relent.

"She always breaks first. No fun. No commitment," Betsy would hear Caroline whisper, while she jammed a birthday card back into a graduation card slot on purpose. Caroline never broke first.

"It's life," said Caroline, letting her intensity fade. "If everybody won a blue ribbon, blue ribbons wouldn't be worth winning."

Ginny dragged her spoon through the yogurt, which was melting into a weirdly clear liquid faster than she could eat it, so she pitched the remainder in the trash.

"Let's get going," said Betsy, desperate to erase Tracy's scowl from her short-term memory and get on with it. "I've got to get back downtown by one."

"What's the rush? Is it a *boy*?" Ginny chided, elated to change the subject. Betsy gave her a warning look.

"Oh my God, you are meeting a boy, aren't you? How can you think about guys *at a time like this, with a campus in crisis,*" said Caroline, in mock newscaster mode.

"I'm just going to J.D.'s with some guy," Betsy said, trying her best to seem unimpressed with herself.

The exact location of J.D.'s, a bait shack that served beer off of a lake approximately forty minutes outside of town in one direction or another, was a closely guarded secret. Even if one could find J.D.'s—which wasn't listed in the phonebook because they'd need a phone for that—one wouldn't just show up. The regulars arranged it so that there would have to be an invitation. Arrive without one, without an escort to show you the way, and even if you'd seen the eight or ten people sprawled out on the dock or the picnic tables shaded by a giant wisteria around town for the last three years, you might find yourself sitting alone until your beer lost its chill, wishing you hadn't wasted the gas money. J.D.'s was for fifth-year seniors, burn-outs, and guys like Gavin who were too cool, or too high, to let on that they cared that they knew the way to J.D.'s. It was for members of local bands who may have realized that their days of relative fame were dwindling, but wouldn't let on they were counting. It was for guys like Weird Bobby, who wore ironic striped tube socks and enormous, black-framed glasses and claimed "Frisbee golfer" as his profession. It was for a handful of girls who stopped talking whenever Betsy would walk by them at a party, with what she sensed as a predetermined hatred for the sorority girl trying to pass as someone else in their midst. Betsy was, not surprisingly, obsessively curious about anyone who didn't talk to her, so she knew all of their names and identifying details though she was sure she was invisible to them, like she was watching through a two-way mirror.

"J.D.'s? Have you been holding out on us?" asked Ginny.

"No, I've never been there. Mack came in for breakfast

today with Gavin Davis, the guy from the Dish. Do you remember, Gin?"

"Heeey, Mr. Skynyrd himself," said Ginny.

"I know who he is," said Caroline in a way that made Betsy panic in advance of the story that would surely follow. *Please God,* she thought, *don't tell me she got here first.*

"You remember when I bought weed from him earlier this year?" she said. "At least we know he's industrious."

Betsy suddenly remembered the three of them driving to a house on the west side of town one night when she was fighting with Mack. She was wasted, in the back of the Rabbit listening to him yammer about Reaganomics. Ginny was driving. Caroline and Mack got out of the car and walked to the back door of a squat brown house that was nearly hidden under a canopy of drooping oak trees. Mack went inside, without looking back to say goodbye. She could hear *AmeriKKKa's Most Wanted* from the open windows before they'd even pulled in the gravel driveway. Through the back door, they could see that there were people inside, two guys and a couple of girls. One of them was Gavin.

"Oh shit, there are pledges in there," said Ginny. "Caroline's gonna eat them alive if they're high. I'd sort of hate to miss that."

Betsy could see straight into the house from the backseat of the car. When she noticed the pledges spot Caroline under the porch light, they both leaped off of the couch and smoothed their clothes, trying unsuccessfully to appear sober. Ginny snorted a little laugh.

"Don't you worry, ladies," she heard Gavin say to the girls, who were clearly scared shitless. "Caroline here can keep her mouth shut. Can't you, Caroline?"

"I didn't see a thing," she said.

"*Huh?*" said Betsy.

"She's letting them off the hook," said Ginny.

"Who knew you two were such big Ice Cube fans?" Caroline asked. "I'm just going to wait outside."

Caroline made her way back to the car, glaring at Betsy and Ginny.

"What?" she said, as she walked back to them across the gravel, silhouetted by the porch light, which was swarming with moths the size of hummingbirds. "I can't be nice?"

A minute later, Gavin shuffled out to the car. He leaned against the driver's door. Caroline handed him some cash and he passed her a small Ziploc filled with crumbly green buds.

"Ziploc must make a killing in this town, right?" asked Betsy.

Gavin chuckled.

"Do you ladies care to join in the fun, or are you above getting high with a couple of dim freshman girls?" he asked. Betsy was convinced that Caroline and Ginny would go inside and either force her to join or make her sleep in the car until dawn. Under normal circumstances, she knew that was when Caroline would have made her move, shocked him with her spot-on recitation of the lyrics to "Once Upon a Time in the Projects," flirted with the roommate to make him jealous. But even this late, even from the backseat of a car after half a dozen beers, it was clear that Gavin saw straight through Caroline's bullshit.

"Tell Mack that we're giving Betsy a ride home, not that he seems that concerned," said Caroline.

Betsy suspected that the truth was that Caroline noticed him long before that. He was tall, hard to miss. And she could tell that he wasn't much like the other guys hanging around, ready to eat out of Caroline's hand on command.

Since then, she hadn't thought about it. But that day outside of Walmart, she realized Caroline had been watching and waiting for a second round, a decent chance to change his mind. It looked like Betsy had gotten there ahead of her this time, and she smiled to herself at the thought.

"I think he's cute," Ginny said. "Betsy, I just don't know if, you know, you're dark and mysterious enough for him."

"Mysterious?" laughed Caroline. "If you're looking for mystery, you're in the wrong town."

Inside the store, Caroline and Ginny both grabbed a shopping basket off of the stack. Betsy wandered the aisles behind Caroline, enjoying the frigid air, and watched her pluck a *Baywatch*-themed air freshener, Tucks medicated pads, and lip waxing strips from the shelves. When they made it to the school supply section, Caroline passed the basket to Ginny.

"I got you a few things," she said, and picked up six or seven pieces of the biggest poster board she could find. "I'll grab these. You get the markers."

"Now that I'm here I can't tell if I want markers or poster paint," said Ginny, studying the selection of art supplies. "Betsy, what do you think?"

Betsy was already bored with the day, the yogurt drama, Caroline's dumb pranks, and the heat. She glanced at her Timex. It was 12:40.

"Definitely markers. You won't have time for the paint to dry. Now let's get out of here."

"Oh fine, you're in a hurry to go drink beer by a lake. You know what I'm going back to. I'm taking my time."

Caroline decided to speed up the operation considerably.

"Oh Ginny, I know you like the giant black ones," she said, waving a marker in front of Ginny's face, exaggerating her volume. "Forget all of these skinny pale ones. Didn't you tell me you liked the feel of the big black ones in your hand? It gives you something to hold on to, right?"

"Oh my God, would you just shut *up*?" Ginny hissed at Caroline, accidentally knocking a box of permanent markers to the floor, which then scattered like toothpicks into the aisle.

"Spaz," Caroline said. Ginny and Betsy put down the baskets and the unwieldy poster boards and knelt on the cold, gray-flecked linoleum to collect the pens.

"I need a new mascara and some Tic Tacs. You like spearmint, right?" Caroline said, to no one in particular, and left them to clean up the mess. "I'll see you at the cash registers."

"If you have someone announce 'Clean up on aisle six' I swear on my life, Caroline, I'm leaving your ass here," Ginny called after her, but Caroline was already out of earshot. Betsy caught a glimpse of a mud-spattered work boot from the corner of her eye.

"Ladies, you missed one," said a man with a thick Southern accent, who crouched down to pick up a stray pen and handed it to Betsy.

"Oh, thanks, but that's hers, not mine," she said, passing the marker to Ginny. Betsy registered the intensity of his gaze, the way his eye traced the ragged edge of her cutoff shorts, and glared back at him.

"Thanks, and sorry about that," said Ginny, blushing, as she took the marker from his dirty hand. Betsy recognized the faint whiff of second-day alcohol. She scanned his face, which looked vaguely familiar, but she couldn't place it. He had a youngish, angular profile, high, sharp cheekbones, and fair eyes. His skin was tan and freckled from the sun. He had deep pale creases in his forehead and around his eyes where he squinted. His hair, brown and long, was shaggy around the collar, and he was filthy, in a plaid shirt with the sleeves rolled up to reveal strong forearms and inky dark fingernails. His jeans were withered and creased like a note that had been folded and refolded and passed between classes. Whether he was dirty in a studio-art way, a "working on my motorcycle" way, or a vagrant way was hard to say. His tan suggested a lot of time spent outdoors, not necessarily poolside. Regardless, he was making Ginny nervous. Her eyes returned to the boots. She had seen them somewhere before, but where? "She can be a handful sometimes."

"I bet she can," he said. "Is this yours, too?" he said and passed Ginny the basket with the facial wax, the car freshener, and the hemorrhoid pads Caroline had assembled. Ginny looked at Betsy, pleading.

"Oh God, no, well, it's sort of mine," Betsy said, trying to help. "It's our friend. She thinks she's really funny. I don't, uh, well *we* don't really need this stuff."

Ginny grabbed a handful of Sharpies, tossed them in the basket, and dumped the Tucks and the Sally Hansen strips on a low shelf. Betsy could see the color burning in her cheeks.

"Well, you ladies have a nice afternoon."

Ginny paid for the art supplies with the petty cash she'd taken from the house, crammed the change into her pocket, and stormed back out into the parking lot. Caroline and Betsy followed. The car was blurry in the distance from the infrared waves of rubber-melting heat rising from the blacktop.

"Why didn't I park closer?" she said with a hiss.

"Hey, Gin," said Betsy. "That guy. Did he look familiar?"

"Oh good Lord, Betsy, how would I remember that?" Ginny said.

"Yeah, she can barely recognize her own mother," Caroline laughed.

Ginny tossed the bag in the back of the convertible and sat hard in the driver's seat and slammed the door. Betsy climbed into the back and Caroline slid into the passenger seat. She handed Ginny a Diet Dr Pepper and offered some Tic Tacs. Ginny shot Caroline an angry look.

"Jesus, I got cherry passion. Sue me! Who knew that you would have a complete hissy fit if you didn't get spearmint, for once?"

The ignition started on the third try and soon they were back in traffic on 34th Street. Ginny's warped Violent Femmes cassette was back in rotation, and it crackled and hissed through the tape deck. Hot late-summer air blew Ginny's long ponytail into knots. Betsy shielded her eyes from the sun, wishing she'd remembered her sunglasses. The vanilla-scented Hasselhoff flapped wildly at his new post under the rearview mirror. The three of them were too distracted, or too irritated, to notice that the stranger in the boots, the one who grazed Ginny's hand with his when he picked up the marker from the floor, was trailing a few cars behind them on his bike.

CHAPTER 7

J.D.'S

August 25, 1990: Afternoon

Ginny pulled over in front of Schoolhouse with a clumsy jerk and halted.

"Y'all have a good time!" she said. Caroline stared straight ahead, silent. Ginny clamped her hand down on Caroline's leg with enough force to make her leap an inch off of her seat.

"Yeah, sure. Looks like you forgot your fishin' pole," Caroline said with an exaggerated drawl, "but I'm sure you'll find something to do."

Betsy paused to take a look at her friends, feeling uncertain, a little scared, and a little more alone than she would ever admit.

"Alright, well, since you two are staying at the house later, I guess I'll try to settle in to my hovel. It could use a little sprucing, you know." Betsy forced a laugh.

"Bets, I mean . . . you should . . ." Ginny fumbled for words before Caroline interrupted her.

"Hey," Caroline said. "Look, come to the house later if you don't want to be alone. We'll be there all night. The plan is for everyone to crash there, bring sleeping bags and all. Really, you should. I mean it."

"I know you do," Betsy said. She climbed over the back of the convertible and hopped out onto the sidewalk in front of the record store.

She would have paused there for a bit, trying her best to pretend not to notice the forlorn expression on Ginny's face, but before she could say goodbye, Ginny gave her a sad little wave and pulled away. Caroline extended her right hand to the sky and shot her the bird as they disappeared into traffic.

She stood at the window in front of Schoolhouse for a moment, watching Gavin glide through the aisles. She remembered that he worked there for a while last year. The record store was a place Betsy was curious about, but mostly avoided. She was self-conscious about her limited knowledge of music and certain that the smug employees were judging her as a dumb sorority girl with Top 40 taste. She'd sneak in for a glimpse of the bulletin board to see who was playing at the Dish, or the Florida Theatre, avoiding eye contact so no one would ask her a question she couldn't answer. It was hard to come up with excuses to stay there if she could never afford to actually buy anything. It didn't occur to her that the place was teeming with freeloaders, sticky fingers, hangers-on angling for ways to get on the list when a Sub Pop band dared dip south of Athens, Georgia, or east of Pensacola. She hesitated outside, feeling her skin sear in the reflected sun from the plate glass window. She would have to go inside if she wanted to go to J.D.'s.

Gavin was tall, maybe six foot three, but in certain situations he appeared much smaller. As it turns out, this skill was especially useful when he was stealing something. Betsy saw the cashier lean down to answer the phone while Gavin slid a CD, with its giant plastic theft-deterrent brace around it, out of the bin and into the back of his shorts. Quickly, he pulled his T-shirt over to cover it. Betsy turned away with an anxious jolt. She would have run down the sidewalk were she not paralyzed with a kind of naive shock, but her sudden movement caught his attention and he turned to the window to give her the subtlest, remarkably unself-conscious wave. Had she really never seen anyone steal something before? She'd swiped a lipstick tester herself last spring, as a kind of dare, to see if she had it in her. But something about her petty crime moment was oddly innocent. She needed the lipstick. She didn't have the fifteen dollars to pay for it. It had already been *used*, for God's sake. This felt different somehow, like walking in on a stranger with his pants down in a public bathroom.

So he steals CDs and sells them for beer money, she thought. *Nobody's perfect.*

She walked over to the door and the bell attached let out a pained little jangle as she took the handle and yanked it from its swollen, rotting frame.

"Hey, that was fast," he said, glancing over his shoulder. "Let's get out of here."

"Hey, Betsy," said the girl behind the counter. They took a Studio Drawing class together the year before, but it took a minute for Betsy to register her face, given the randomly executed green hair that she dyed, judging by the blonde roots, about three months ago. Betsy remembered sitting on the plaza sketching moss-covered trees and badgering her with all sorts of questions about her nose piercing, which was a ring like a bull's that spanned her nostrils. (How much did it hurt? "A lot." What was her inspiration? "Dunno.") She searched for a name and came up empty-handed, then smiled and offered an awkward half wave.

"Hey," she said. Better to say as little as possible in these situations, she thought, though she'd never been in one of these situations before.

"Later, Gavin."

"Later, Wendy. Good to see you back in town," he said. *Wendy,* that's it. Betsy wondered what the parents of cute Wendy, with a sprinkle of freckles on her nose, thought when she came home, post-bull's-ring, post–Manic Panic, for summer break. "Don't sweat the hair. It grows, right?"

"Screw you, Davis," she offered limply before the door jangled shut and cast a small shower of leaded paint chips on the sidewalk.

"Did you drive here?" he asked, scooting sideways past the window to conceal the bulge in the back of his T-shirt.

"No car," she said, remembering the tiny pink bike at Bagelville and not caring enough to retrieve it. They'd reached his bike, an anonymous, matte black cruiser with five pounds worth of heavy link chain wrapped around it and a bulky, rusted padlock.

"I'll give you a tow back to my place so we can take mine," he said, and she perched herself on the center of the wide, flat handlebars, placing her feet on the pegs on either side of his front tire, quietly thrilled. She wished she'd washed her hair that morning so he'd catch a faint whiff of grapefruit or fresh cut grass as it blew back near his face and be forever smitten.

They took a slightly longer route to pass through the shady, oak-lined streets behind the stadium, a cooler, possibly more romantic detour and an oddly chivalrous move for someone with stolen goods crammed in his pants. Whether it was the shade, or the breeze from the ride without the burden of actually pedalling, or the petty thief making small talk behind her, she felt lighter than she had in weeks.

When they got to the squat, beige cinder block house surrounded by patchy grass and a wide, gravel driveway, Betsy noticed Mack's truck parked in back. She looked into the large window and saw him standing in a tangle of cables, his fingers buried in his hair. She ducked behind a tree. Mack must have spotted Gavin because she saw him raise his hand in a two-finger wave. She tiptoed around the other side of the house and met Gavin by the back porch.

"So how much do you feel like explaining to Mack what we're doing today?" he whispered, as he quietly chained his bike to a tree.

"Not much. Not much at all," Betsy said, as she pressed herself against the side of the house. "He may need some help with the manual, though. I'm not sure that he can read."

They bolted across the yard toward the carport.

"He'll have a heart attack by dinner," said Gavin. "The guy's a hothead."

"He's *your* friend," whispered Betsy, ducking low to hide behind his Honda Accord. "For reasons unknown."

"So you two . . ."

"Biggest mistake of my life."

He unlocked the car door and sank into the driver's seat, his head clearing the roof by maybe an inch, and heard the crunch of plastic under his weight. He reached around to pull the CD out of his waistband and tossed it in the backseat. Betsy got into the car, unused to using the handle to open the door.

"Have you heard this Sonic Youth record?" he asked, entirely unfazed by being exposed as a small-time crook. "It's so good."

"So you already own it?" she asked. "But you stole another one for fun?"

"I was going to sell it back used to Schoolhouse for lunch money when Wendy wasn't around." He backed out of the driveway in a hurry. "Don't worry. I'll buy you lunch, too. Maybe even a beer."

He squeezed her knee hard and she laughed.

"But you can take it if you want," he said. "Consider it a gift."

"You knew just what I wanted."

Ten minutes outside of town, the buildings disappeared and the scrub and low trees, the endless tangle of green, started to take over. Betsy knew she should have been paying attention to where they were going, but the signs—to Micanopy, Alachua, High Springs, Waldo—meant nothing to her. They listened to Neil Young with the windows down and pulled over to buy boiled peanuts from a man who served them from a rusty oil drum. Though she couldn't have possibly known that this moment would happen today, she felt like she expected it, like it had been something she knew would happen for a while, and she enjoyed the odd, buzzy déjà vu head trick of an experience that was foreign and familiar at the same time. Every once in a while, Gavin would look at her and smile, a glance that revealed his own satisfied shock over what was happening this day, too, and she was relieved.

When they pulled into the parking lot with another crunch of gravel, the building before them looked all but abandoned, with nothing but a couple of cardboard boxes green with mildew to be seen. But once they walked around the busted planks of the boardwalk, there was a small, flat, teal lake surrounded by an infinitely soggy, lush, green landscape. To the right, there was a guy, presumably J.D., who sold a carton of worms for a buck, bags of chips for fifty cents, and cold beers from a cooler for two dollars each. Three guys were sitting silently at a picnic table in the shade: Weird Bobby; Jacob, who played guitar and sang for a local band, Boba Fett and the Bounty Hunters, which had been gratefully shortened to the Bounty; and Teddy, who lived with George, the first of Betsy's many mistakes back in 1988, and was one of the only truly decent guys she knew on campus. Teddy taught her how to play Spades when she was hanging out at their house. At least Betsy got something out of it other than a bad reputation.

Weird Bobby was in his late twenties, thirties tops, but he was considered an elder statesman in town. He wore an Orioles hat pulled low over a mass of curly hair and his signature tube socks up to his knees under threadbare Converse high-tops. Jacob, with dirty blonde hair, a dirty red T-shirt, dirty, shredded Levi's, and dirty work boots, was gorgeous in the filthiest possible way. Once, she caught him sneaking out of Ginny's room at 5:00 a.m., but his then-girlfriend, a beatific Deadhead named Marion who wore long, Indian print skirts with bells stitched around the waist, was none the wiser. Marion had disappeared earlier that summer after a Dead show in Atlanta and no one expected to see her back anytime soon.

Teddy's equally dirty blonde hair was snarled in the back of his head like a toddler's. His glasses, sort of round and square at the same time, a mottled tortoise, slipped off of his nose, and his tattered blue oxford shirt, Duck Head cutoffs, and leather flip-flops hinted at a preppy past that was getting little upkeep. He played with a bottle cap, absentmindedly, listening to Weird Bobby's nonsense.

"I bet he's some total psycho, like Jason, with a, a hockey mask or something. Maybe a chain saw! Or a sickle," said Weird Bobby, who punctuated every sentence with a silent, body-shaking giggle. The conversation had steered toward the murders, since the news had spread slowly across town and eventually made it here, a place that seemed immune to current events of any kind. Nobody seemed to have any new information, but that didn't stop them from repeating it.

"I heard the cops were tracking down all of the first victim's old boyfriends, like it was some kind of lover's spat gone batshit crazy," said Jacob, taking a long drag from a cigarette. Betsy spotted his soft pack of Camels on the table, and he offered her one.

"What do you think, Betsy? Psychokiller on the loose?" asked Teddy with a smirk. No one had bothered to introduce her, and this seemed like the closest she'd get.

"I don't know," she said, blushing from the focus suddenly trained on her. "I'm thinking it's a good idea not to go to sleep tonight so I can make sure I don't, you know, never wake up again."

She was dead serious, but it got a big laugh nevertheless.

"We can arrange for that," said Weird Bobby, shaking again. "Who wants another?" And he walked over to the bar to replace the empty steel bucket full of longnecks with a full one.

Gavin and Betsy took their beers to the end of the dock and sat with their legs dangling over the water. In the distance, there was a small Boston Whaler on the move, its engine buzzing like a lawn mower. Otherwise, the lake was silent.

"So this is J.D.'s," she said, leaning down to graze the water with her fingers.

"Ah, first-timer, are we?" he said. "Not much to it."

"Nah, but it's great. I'd keep it a secret, too."

"How do you know Teddy, anyway?" he asked. She suspected that he feared another failed fling with a friend, which would make her officially un-datable, according to unspoken guy protocol.

"We played cards together once awhile back and he was in this Nineteenth-Century Lit class I took last year," she said. "He's a friend."

She paused.

"I've seen Jacob play a few times. He may have hooked up with a friend of mine," she said. "But I'm told he left before dawn. I guess he snuck out in the middle of the night? I took that as a very subtle but bad sign."

"Yeah, that's subtle alright."

"Weird Bobby, is, uh, interesting?"

"Yeah, it's a well-deserved nickname," he said. "The story goes that he inherited a little money when his grandparents died a few years back and just decided to stay here, never graduate." He shrugged. "The guy's a professional Frisbee golfer. And by pro I mean he's won a couple of fifty-dollar Little Caesars pizza gift certificates. He's harmless, but he's fucking crazy. The thing is, he always has parties, and so he always has friends."

"Huh. Seems like he's goal-oriented," she said.

"What about your crew? Ginny and Caroline? They're real sweethearts," he said, his tone confirming that he knew them better than she thought he did.

"Ginny's a drunk, but she *is* a sweetheart, no joke. Caroline is complicated."

"So you three were tight?" he asked her. "And now, it seems, maybe not."

"Yeah, something like that," Betsy said, first describing Ginny, how close they were, but she explained that when she left the sorority it put a strain on their friendship. Ginny interpreted Betsy's criticism of the way things worked at the house as a criticism of her, which it was, in a way, but she knew they could get past it. Caroline was less understanding, and started mocking Betsy's "new life/new look" approach to starting over, telling her that her wardrobe downgrade made her look like a homeless twelve-year-old boy. Things between them were limping along until just after spring break, when Betsy met John. Caroline knew that Betsy had a thing for a tennis player from New Jersey named John, despite the fact that he was a business major and had a girlfriend from back home who went to a real college in New England. Betsy met him at a party and she fell for him, hard. They made plans to study a couple of times, but Betsy was too subtle for John, and unwilling to ruin the long-distance girlfriend's life, so they became friends, as a consolation prize. Caroline, who met him with Betsy once in the stacks of East library, was more aggressive. That the two of them started hooking up on the sly shouldn't have come as a surprise, but that she was so mean about it to Betsy was shocking, even for Caroline. Betsy showed up at Caroline and Ginny's apartment on a Tuesday night, unannounced, with her well-worn *Seventh Sign* videotape in hand (she found the combination of late-1980s Demi Moore and clumsy religious apocalypse imagery irresistible). She found John the tennis player in Caroline's room, on the bed, cramming for an Econ midterm. When he saw her, he stuffed his book in his backpack, grabbed his shoes, and squeezed awkwardly past Betsy in the hall, as she stood there mute, filled with rage. Never had she felt so stupid and betrayed.

"Nothing happened between you two. Nada," said Caroline, jumping to defend herself before Betsy could speak. "What's the big offense? Did you pass him a note and ask him to check the box? This isn't seventh grade, Betsy. You may have liked him, but you never touched him, so he's totally fair game."

Betsy stormed out of the apartment, humiliated, feeling more naive than ever. It wasn't the first time she had been angry with Caroline, but it was the first time they stopped speaking.

Three-way calling was a novelty, and Caroline used it prodigiously in her schemes. When she got bored and mean at night, she'd put mortal enemies and venomous exes on the phone together while she sat holding the mute button, giggling wildly.

"Hello," said Betsy.

"Hello," said John.

"Who's this?" asked Betsy, fearing the worst. Melissa had her own phone line at the house, and only Caroline and Ginny knew she was staying there and had the number.

"What do you mean who's this? You called me."

"I didn't call you. You called me."

"Is this Betsy Young?" he'd asked, his tone growing hostile.

"Holy shit, it's John, isn't it?" Only Ginny and Caroline knew she was staying at Melissa's. Only they knew the number.

"You should know since you just called me."

"Listen, I didn't call you. It's Caroline. She three-wayed us just to torture me."

Of course, he didn't believe her. He was too stupid to suspect anyone of such bizarre and pointless mischief. After the third time it happened in a week, he called her a psycho and a stalker, threatened a restraining order, and slammed down the phone. When Betsy confronted Caroline and suggested, just a suggestion, that she may have a problem, like a sociopathic problem, Ginny was the mediator.

"Caroline, what is your deal?" shouted Betsy. "Jesus, you have no mercy. Zero. You're like a serial killer or something."

"Oh my God, you have completely lost your sense of humor," she replied. "John the limp-dicked jock with the virginal girlfriend in New Hampshire is a waste of my time and yours. If you weren't so earnest all of a sudden you'd play along."

"Guys," Ginny pleaded, "can we please just stop? You can't throw away our friendship over some guy in madras shorts. He is way too impossibly boring for that."

Caroline's total lack of remorse confirmed that Betsy was now on the wrong side of a ruthless bitch, and their trips to the drive-thru liquor store in Ginny's car to bat their eyelashes for free bottles of cheap wine were over, maybe forever. This all happened in early May. By the time spring semester ended three weeks later, Caroline and Betsy were speaking again, but just barely.

Then Betsy told Gavin about Godzilla. Caroline and Betsy crashed a party near campus sophomore year. They just happened to be walking by after studying in the library one night. Betsy would never have thought to go in to a party on her own, uninvited, with total strangers. But Caroline couldn't resist. They walked in the front door and went straight for the keg, where Betsy grabbed two Solo cups and waited in line, feeling more than a little conspicuous. When the host of the party, a sweaty, pale engineering major named Rich, who was smart and nice, and therefore no one she would have met otherwise, introduced himself, Caroline disappeared to the back bedrooms. Rich and Betsy chatted about how massive their school was, how they'd both been there for so long and neither face triggered a flicker of recognition. Betsy had started to feel good about the night. Maybe she'd meet some new people, branch out a little bit? Maybe she'd finally learn what an engineer did? But she had barely filled the second cup when Caroline appeared in the doorway, motioning to her to leave.

"Right now?" she mouthed across the room, but Caroline was out the door.

"Thanks for the beer, Rich," she said. "My friend has to go. Guess I'll see you around?"

"Yeah, sure, no problem," he said, confused by the sudden departure.

"I hate to tear you away from your new boyfriend," Caroline said, once they were back on the sidewalk, downing her beer. "Geek much?"

She took out a cigarette and lit it with a flame shot from a tiny dragon monster's mouth and then tossed the perfectly weighted specimen into Betsy's hands.

"I got this for you," she said. "Courtesy of Rich."

That he had collected these lighters, painstakingly, at flea markets, from mail-order catalogues in the back of *Mad* magazine or wherever you'd find something this strange, and that

Caroline had plucked one from its mates on the shelf of his bedroom at his own party, which she was allowed to enter only on the remotest chance that nerdy Rich would get some action that night, was of little consequence to her. She'd also cleaned out his medicine cabinet of an expired Percocet prescription and some Tylenol with codeine.

"Thank God for wisdom teeth," said Caroline, shaking the bottle like a maraca, a little demonic glint in her eye.

Had Betsy told him her last name? Had she mentioned where she worked? Had it not been for the crashed keg party, she would have survived her entire undergraduate experience without seeing Rich once. Now, thanks to Caroline, she was sure she'd pass him weekly on the way home from work and she could already feel the searing hatred of his eyes boring into her skull. She remembered the feel of the lighter, which was hard and cold and fit perfectly in her palm.

"That," said Gavin, squinting in the sun, rubbing the back of his head, "is one malicious bitch."

They were quiet for a minute. She had never told anyone that story.

"You've got some pretty selective morals, Gav," she said, sitting up, suddenly defensive of her onetime friend, sensing his judgment of Caroline, and of her by proxy, even though she agreed wholeheartedly with his assessment.

"That's totally different. I took a CD from a record store. I didn't cock tease some stranger at a party and then lift his prized possession," he said.

"I wasn't teasing him. And I didn't steal it."

"So you brought it back, right? The lighter?" he asked. Until then, the thought hadn't occurred to her. She mumbled some kind of excuse.

"Oh shit, Bets. You're just as bad as she is if you don't," he said.

"He probably doesn't even live there anymore," she said, raising her voice a little. "Rich is off engineering somewhere with other engineers and has forgotten all about it."

"But, really? You kept it?" he said.

She was quiet again.

"I know. You're right."

She leaned back and rested her elbows on the dock, letting the sun hit her face. Before, she would have defended her friend. She would have rolled her eyes, told him he didn't understand, maybe even walked away. This time, she felt the warm wood under her forearms and the backs of her legs, and she let the quiet rest between them for a while.

They sat in the sun for far too long, chatting about their classes, about post-graduation plans. It turned out that he was only slightly less aimless than she was. He was a fifth-year senior, squeezing some forgotten credits into one last semester, and would graduate in December, like Betsy, as a Broadcast Journalism major. She was English with an Art History minor. Given the size and sprawl of the school, they'd never had a class together. They talked about what they did when they should have been studying. Betsy had discovered Joan Didion's *The White Album* at a used bookstore downtown and was desperate to talk about it with someone, anyone, even if it was only to say how much it affirmed her hatred for the Doors. She told him about the photograph in the museum that she liked to visit and promised to take him there. Gavin talked about Raymond Chandler in an emphatic whisper, like what he wanted to say about Philip Marlowe, and had no one to say it to, had built up inside him like steam in a kettle. Betsy ate it up like a hungry little fish just beneath the surface of the water that leaped at a tiny crumb or the buzz of a gnat.

"Maybe I'll teach?" he said. "I don't know what the hell else to do. Definitely not law school like every other dickhead around here."

"My mom thought that maybe I should be a flight attendant," she said, forcing back a smile. It was a pop quiz she was praying he'd pass.

"Because you're clearly such an asset to the service industry," he said.

"Hey, I am employee of the freaking decade," she said. Her faced burned red with pleasure. He knew her. He thought about her enough to know her. He was in it as much as she was, already. "But you're right. Never in a million. I don't even like planes."

With that, she stood up, took off her shorts and her Hanes T-shirt, and jumped in the lake, hoping the cool water would calm her skin, flushed and blotchy with excitement, not bothering to remember which bra and underwear she had put on in the dark that morning, and not caring that much. In the cool lake, she could forget about psychokillers and dead girls, about Caroline and even Ginny. All of that would be waiting for her back in town.

CHAPTER 8
SERIAL, AS IN MORE THAN ONE

August 25, 1990: Night

By the time Betsy and Gavin were driving back from that first trip to the lake, both with sunburned cheeks, itchy, bitten ankles, and the remnants of a buzz, Betsy was in deep. Neil Young had been replaced by the Feelies in the CD player. As they sped through the long, tree-lined roads she thought the humming of the locusts, hidden among the leaves, sounded like backup singers, their low, vibrating buzz in perfect rhythm with *Only Life*. The cool lake water, the sunbaked dock under her skin, the lazy drowsiness of the day, the weird yearning she was feeling for what was happening, even while it was happening, made her think that if she could peer inside her brain she would see the memory forming. At one point, she caught herself staring at the way Gavin's tattered T-shirt hung over the top of his shoulder and had to talk herself into getting her shit together. From the passenger seat, she could see that his Wayfarers were smudged with greasy fingerprints and that the scruff on his chin was sparse and, from certain angles, a little seedy. But she decided she was fine with it—all of it.

As soon as they were back within city limits, reality was there to greet them. Gavin pulled into Pete's Chevron to fill up the tank and they ran into Danny, a gangly, perma-grin stoner who wore nubby gray socks with his flip-flops as a sort of signature, the strap that separated the big toe from its companions cramming the fabric between the two digits in the most unfortunate way.

"What up, Gav?" said Danny, as he let the snack-shop door slam behind him with a jangle. He had a pack of sunflower seeds in one hand and a plastic cup for the newly vacant shells shoved into the pocket of his vintage checked shorts.

"Danny," Gavin announced, in that ambiguous name-shout greeting that didn't reveal the intentions behind it, no happy "How you doin', brother" or subtly hostile "Where you been, fucker?" Just *Danny*.

"What's your theory on this serial killer thing?" he asked.

"What do you mean, serial?" Gavin said, glancing at Betsy in profile, still in the passenger seat, to see if she could hear him. She could.

"As in, *more than one*," said Danny. "It's confirmed. They found a third body. The first one they found they thought was a fluke, some pissed-off boyfriend who lost his mind. Then they found two more girls early this morning, same weird bite marks on their bodies."

Danny lifted the empty cup to his lips and launched a shell into it.

"And dude, get this. One of their heads was on the bookshelf."

"Bullshit," said Gavin. "You are so full of shit."

"Ask the guys inside. Cops were in here earlier and they all but confirmed what they'd heard on the police radio. They got some kind of scanner and shit," he said. "Hey, you don't have to believe me. But you'll read it in the paper soon enough. There are three victims. That crazy fucker cut off a girl's head and put it on a bookshelf. He stabbed all of them something like ten times, in the chest, with, like, a machete or something. I mean, they're saying that he cut off their tits and . . ."

"Whoa, whoa, we've got it. I got the picture," Gavin said, as he glanced back at Betsy, whose eyes were trained on Danny.

"Fine. Like I said, don't believe me if you don't want to."

"What's surprising is that you're still believing everything you hear. In this town?" said Gavin. "Bored-ass people making up stories is all that is."

"I speak the truth, brother," he said, shuffling through the parking lot, head shaking. "Why don't you ask Phil Donahue what he thinks? He's setting up cameras in the Plaza right now. They think the killer might be dressing up like a cop, or a deliveryman, since there's no sign of forced entry. It could be anybody."

"Good idea, Danny. I'll ask Phil Donahue if he thinks you're full of shit," said Gavin.

"Seems like he's targeting young girls, maybe brunettes? That's all they can guess about his pattern so far," continued Danny, despite Gavin's skepticism, his raised eyebrow. "Not Phil Donahue, dickhead. That murderous lunatic on the loose."

"Uh-huh."

"Just you wait," he said, scuffing across the hot asphalt, in no particular rush. "You'll see it in the papers, and think, 'Ole Danny knew all the news that's fit to print.'"

Gavin and Betsy drove the rest of the way into campus and neither of them dared to say a word. Betsy had a rare moment of absolute clarity. She was still a kid, selfish as hell, and she couldn't shake the feeling that these dead girls were ruining their moment. During her entire time at college, she imagined the threat came from the young women around her, casting judgment, chastising her for being different, mocking her behind her back. And now there was a threat so visceral and real that she could barely process what was happening around her. It occurred to Betsy, suddenly, that she should feel sympathy for the parents of the victims, or consider their families in some way. She thought, *Why wasn't that my first instinct?*

"I wonder if we knew them," Gavin said at last, when they were stopped at a traffic light. "Like, did I sit next to one of them in class? Were those girls in that room full of five hundred strangers, nodding off to a lecture nobody remembers?"

"I know," she said. "I was thinking the same thing."

Gavin offered to drop her off at "home," a first-floor apartment in an old, stucco fourplex behind Norman Hall, and he walked her to the door.

"So, my new roommate?" she said, with one hand placed on the doorknob, as she hesitated to let him in. Her words lilted at the end, a tick that was exaggerated when she was nervous or drunk, and she was a little of both. "She's not back in town with her furniture yet. I just want to warn you, it's *spare* in here." *Here* came out like a squeak.

She unlocked the door and surveyed the mess, the lonely lamp on the floor, the milk crates full of books, a cardboard U-Haul box spilling over with clothes, the dusty Matisse *Harmony in Red* poster in a cheap frame leaning against the scuffed wall, and a double mattress on the floor of one of the bedrooms in back. The message light blinked on her answering machine. Melissa had called with the same news that stoner Danny had shared at the gas station, saying that all of the sorority girls were camping out at the houses because no one wanted to go home alone. Betsy and Gavin had escaped to the lake for a few hours, and in that time the fear on campus had grown from something vague and unsettling to something sharper, more menacing.

"You think I'm going to say 'I love what you've done with the place,'" he said, coming out of her empty room. She wondered if he had overheard the message.

"But that would be too predictable."

"Yes, indeed."

"I've been staying with Ginny, at her place over in Williamsburg Village on 16th. I slept in Caroline's room while she was away, but she's back," she said.

He nodded.

"Anyway, I'd crash on their couch, but I just heard that they're all camping out at the house until they catch this guy, you know . . ." She trailed off.

"The psychokiller."

"Yep, that one."

They stood there for a bit, under the bright overhead light in the kitchenette, and she was suddenly aware of her own pulse, every creak in the building, the tiny bugs circling the lightbulb above their heads.

"I tell you what. You grab some clothes and you come to my place for a night or two, just until the roomie arrives," he said.

"What?"

"I'm serious," he said. "My roommate, Jeff, isn't back for

fall semester yet. We'll sneak you in the back door. Mack won't notice a thing. You're at work a good three hours before he wakes up anyway, right?"

"But, Gavin, I'm not, I mean . . ."

"You're not having sex with me. I get it. Totally fair."

"It is?"

"Of course, I wouldn't mind if you . . . wanted to. Believe me. But I get it."

They stood in silence and made the only truly awkward moment of the day last for longer than it should have. While the prospect of premeditated sleeping at a semistrange guy's house was terrifying, it was not as terrifying as the idea of being decapitated in her sleep, or worse. Despite her serious doubts about the merits of the idea, she grabbed whatever clothes she found on top of the box and shoved them into a grungy, monogrammed boat and tote. *It's just a night, two, tops,* she thought. If it got ugly, she'd beg Melissa and her grouchy roommates to let her come back, or she'd call Ginny and crawl back to the sorority house to beg for mercy.

Despite the apartment's utter lack of anything worth stealing, she left the hall light on and locked the door and the dead bolt behind them.

"So, nothing weird," she said, back in the car. "No middle of the night groggy, maybe she won't remember it date-rape situation?"

"Jesus, Betsy, who have you been hanging out with? Oh, scratch that. My classy friend Mack, right?" he said, opening her car door. She slid into the passenger seat and he leaned down to kiss her. Betsy felt a strange tightness around her lungs, a warmth creeping across her face from her neck. She imagined it was a little like a heart attack, maybe slightly better.

"Just getting that out of the way," he said, his mouth close to her ear.

Back at Gavin's place every interior light was on and the back door was unlocked. "Went to Joe's. Fuck you," read a note scrawled on the top of a half-full pizza box on the counter in Mack's handwriting.

"Guess I should remember to lock that door," Gavin said. "But look, Mack bought us dinner!" He turned off the lights and took the box and a six-pack of Rolling Rock into his room, which had a bed, a desk, columns of paperbacks neatly stacked on the floor, a guitar propped in one corner, and a turntable with speakers on a piece of plywood between two wooden boxes. When they finished eating, Gavin pulled out crates of albums from the closet.

"We've got nothing but time, right?"

He started with the Velvet Underground.

"That's Nico. I know this," she said, nodding eagerly, relieved to not be a complete idiot.

The Pixies she also knew, albeit vaguely, plus a little pre–*Combat Rock* Clash. Then he moved on to Fugazi, Hüsker Dü, Dinosaur Jr. Years later, when she remembered that night, she felt the sort of nostalgia that would have made her twenty-year-old self cringe. When you lived in Florida in the 1980s, and every shitty Buffalo wing–slinging dive posing as a family restaurant dished out sanitized 1960s hits from a jukebox to sunburned middle-aged tourists, nostalgia was the weakest, most pathetic thing in the world. Slurring through "Louie Louie" in a rayon floral shirt over a plate of mushy peel 'n' eat shrimp was life at its worst, the way Betsy saw it. She was drowning in a sea of oldies, watching needle-thin speedboats barrel through the turquoise water blasting the Steve Miller

Band. She'd seen enough too-tan old men in golf shirts, driving their pastel Cadillacs with the windows down, singing along to "Under the Boardwalk," the Drifters song that was nearly as ubiquitous and irritating as "Cheeseburger in Paradise." For decades to come, any time she'd catch the sound of Jimmy Buffett's twangy, vapid lyrics about shellfish and frozen drinks, her eyes would cloud with a murderous rage. John from New Jersey liked Jimmy Buffett. She bet his lame girlfriend did, too.

On that night with Gavin, she felt like she'd found the secret door in the library, the one where if you'd lifted a dog-eared copy of *The Stranger* out of its place on the dusty shelf, it would open up and reveal a passageway to the place where the other people lived. She'd seen every decent band that had made its way to Gainesville in the last year. She devoured as many of the music magazines as she could find to read about new CD releases that she couldn't afford to buy. Somehow, with any other guy, she'd have resented the seminar. She would have squirmed with discomfort, annoyed that a guy had to explain it to her, embarrassed by her cluelessness. She would have left. With Gavin, it was different. He wanted her to listen to hear what she thought, not to prove what she didn't know. That he was showing off for her, trying to impress her, didn't occur to Betsy. And she was desperate to hear it.

Betsy went so far as to join a Baptist church youth group in the ninth grade on the promise that the associate pastor would chaperone a group to the U2 concert at the Sun Dome in Tampa. Otherwise, she would have never been allowed to go. Ten kids crammed in a white van with four rows of seats, singing along to "The Unforgettable Fire" in the tape deck, made the hour drive north on a blistering May afternoon. They parked in the last row of the vast parking lot, and walked past legions of guys in stonewashed jean shorts, their dates in brief white skirts and neon tank tops swigging from Malibu Rum bottles, ducking next to their Camaros to shotgun cans of Busch beer. Once inside the small arena, Betsy broke off from the group to wind her way to the front of the general admission crowd on the floor in front of the stage. Someone passed her a flask, and she took a long swig of something strong and terrible. Halfway through "A Sort of Homecoming," she was transfixed, convinced that Bono was singing directly to her. She wept, surrounded by total strangers trying to console her. Somehow, she'd been jostled around enough in the fray to lose one of her Keds. After the show, when she eventually hobbled back to the church van on one purple sneaker, the accusatory looks on the faces in the group made it clear that she would not be invited back for Stryper the following month. No surprise, she got the last seat in the very back row of the van, which was particularly claustrophobic once the windows fogged up with the evaporated sweat of multiple, irritatingly sober teenagers. She smiled to herself thinking that Bono didn't look any of those other chumps dead straight in the eyes and sing about running on a borderland. Betsy also knew for once without a doubt, that there were other people like her, people who understood the supreme awfulness of Night Ranger. Since then, she'd been on a mission to learn about music, driven by the desperate feeling that she had years of catching up to do.

Just a few years later, she was in Gavin's bedroom, fully clothed but asleep at 3:00 a.m. When the needle of the record player scratched along the inner edge of Dinosaur Jr.'s *Bug*, she woke up with a start. *I'm safe,* she thought, as she looked around the strange room and at Gavin's sleeping form. *I think.*

CHAPTER 9

WEIRD BOBBY'S PARTY

August 26, 1990

At 5:20 the next morning, Gavin gave Betsy a ride to Bagelville, with the promise of meeting her for a burrito later. She stood in the low, muddy light, since dawn was just starting to creep over the trees, and watched him drive away. Just yesterday morning, she didn't really know Gavin. Then he wandered in out of nowhere. She smiled to herself as she replayed the last twenty-four hours in her head. This was the Gainesville she would miss. It was a place where time stretched out into long, lazy hours, which were oddly boring and unpredictable at the same time. All it took to change your life was one person coming in to order a cup of coffee. Betsy wondered what strange new development this day would bring as she made her way down the side alley to the back door. Somehow, even the muggy morning didn't bother her. There was a faint breeze in the air that hinted at the promise of autumn. She rounded the corner to the back parking lot, dreamy and distracted, thinking of how it felt to wake up in Gavin's bed, hoping she would get to do it again.

Then she heard something move near the Dumpster, a rustle of boxes, and in less than a second there was a flood of adrenaline that filled her brain with a roar in her ears. Instinctively, she looked around for something that she could use to protect herself and knocked into a metal trashcan, which made a harsh metallic sound as it scraped the cinder block wall and hit the ground. The reality of her surroundings came rushing back. She wouldn't remember it as the day she fell in love with Gavin. It was the day that police learned that someone was hunting and slaughtering students, women like her, the day when people stopped feeling safe. She wanted to run, but then she'd be late to work.

"Betsy, is that you?" said Tom, who was now standing at the back door. One of the night-shift bakers peeked out from around the Dumpster, where he was breaking down boxes.

Betsy felt the blood drain from her face. *There's a serial killer stalking this place and I'm still worried about punching the clock,* she thought. *Pathetic.*

"Jesus, you see a ghost or something?" he asked.

"No, I was just a little absentminded, and then I heard . . . I don't know," she said, shaking her head. "It's nothing. I should have known it was nothing."

Tom studied her face carefully.

"Nah, don't worry about it," he said. "Everybody's on edge. Come and get some coffee while it's hot."

"You mean before it boils down into that sludge we serve our customers?" she said, feeling her pulse level off.

"Exactly."

Betsy spent her shift pretending not to eavesdrop on the

conversations among the customers about the Gainesville PD and what, if any, leads they had. She scanned a copy of *The Gainesville Sun* that someone left behind on a table. According to the paper, the details at the three crime scenes were shocking, and though facts were scarce while the investigation was under way, everyone somehow knew the specifics of the violence, the taped wrists, the nipples that had been sliced off of the bodies, and passed the information through conspiratorial whispers.

WHEN GAVIN SHOWED up where he said he would on campus, only two minutes late, Betsy reacted like it was a minor miracle. She would have spent more time worrying about her lowered expectations from life if she hadn't been so preoccupied thinking about everything else happening around her. When she went to the registrar's office to pick up her fall schedule, Betsy was given a notice from the administration that, because of the "situation" with the "tragic loss of innocent lives," they were informing students that the semester wouldn't begin in earnest until the chaos had died down, or until they had a suspect in custody. Classes were postponed for a week and it was implied that the police department would step up to the challenge of catching the perpetrator in that designated time frame, even though it was a case well outside of their usual beat.

News vans had begun showing up and were parked along 8th Street. Reporters, popping up on the lawns skirting the perimeters of campus in their pastel skirt suits, lined up to talk to eager viewers at home about sporty students with ". . . Colgate smiles . . . feeling stalked by a madman." No one on campus had any experience with publicity that wasn't focused on the aggressive and corrupt habits of recruiters wooing promising athletes, or the lawless behavior of the athletes themselves, so the town felt quieter and more somber than usual, and more than a little stunned.

Gavin and Betsy made the long walk through campus, past Fletcher Hall, a Gothic dorm built during the Depression as part of the Public Works program that, despite its beauty, was the last to fill up because it was without modern conveniences—or just the most critical one: air-conditioning. Gavin mentioned that some friends left town when they heard the news, considering it an extension of their summer vacation, since the seasons blended together without much distinction anyway. At Burrito Brothers, they picked up two bean and cheese and ate them on a concrete bench near the business quad. After lunch, the rest of the day played out a lot like the one before, only with less talking. Betsy wondered whether the silence was about the dead students or about her, or if they'd said enough the day before for a week. They drove to the lake, went for a swim, which they followed with a couple of beers, under the shade tree, this time on the far side of the parking lot.

On their way back to the car, Weird Bobby spotted them and called them over to his usual spot next to Jacob at his designated picnic table. This time they were joined by a girl with delicate blonde dreads falling past her shoulder blades, grazing the top of her Indian cotton halter, sitting with her back toward them. Betsy didn't need to see her face to recognize that this was Channing Williams. She had noticed her a hundred times before, the way she could wear a scarf wrapped around her head and manage to not look like she was wearing a fortune-teller costume, or how she always found an electric green tuft of grass to sit on and look irritatingly perfect and mellow between classes. She'd seen her at the bars downtown, at the occasional show at the Dish. And even though she danced like a creepy Deadhead, in a sort of rhythmless hop with palms outstretched, Betsy thought that her own life would be better if it were a little bit more like Channing's.

"Here we go," said Gavin, under his breath, making his way across the grass to where they sat. Betsy followed her gut and trailed a few feet behind.

"So, Gav, I'm having a little jam tonight at my place and would hate for you two lovebirds to miss it," said Bobby, with a tremor.

"Oh, he's a looovebird now, is he?" said Channing, turning around to show her enormous blue eyes crinkled at the edges, her voice slow and raspy, a pack of Marlboro reds on the table before her. She grabbed Gavin's hand. "That's so cute."

"Yeah, real cute, Chan," he said, pulling his hand away.

"And you're the lucky lady. It's Betty, right?" she said, turning to take in all of Betsy, the baggy 501 cutoffs, the T-shirt she'd swiped from Gavin that morning, the dirty bare feet, and ratty Chucks in hand.

"Betsy," she said. Suddenly, the dots connected. "My name's Betsy."

"You hang out at Bagelville, right?"

"Yeah, it's sort of like hanging out except that I put things in the toaster and make coffee and throw away your trash," she said. Weird Bobby thought Betsy was hysterical and the entire table shook with his approval.

"Well, watch out, Betty Bagelville, this one's a real heartbreaker," she said, hooking her finger into one of Gavin's belt loops. "Aren't you, Gavvy?" He turned quickly to leave.

"Thanks for the tip," said Betsy.

"We'll see y'all later, then?" said Bobby.

"Yeah, later," said Gavin, scratching the back of his head, which she was starting to notice was something he did when things got tense, a kind of nervous tic.

Betsy didn't mention Channing during the drive home, and it fit in well with the pervasive silence. Ribbons of pale orange light filtered through the canopy of trees, and it was so beautiful that Betsy thought she might cry. She was tired, desperate to hang on to the moment and trying not to ruin it, any more than it had already been ruined—by Channing, or Caroline, or the murders. When they pulled onto Gavin's street and saw Mack's Suburban coming from the opposite direction, Betsy knew that her private idyll was about to be destroyed in a more aggressive way. Through the driver's window, Betsy saw Mack raise his hand to wave at Gavin. Then, Mack noticed someone next to him and did a cartoonish double take when he recognized Betsy in the passenger seat. She watched his smile shift to fury in dramatically slow motion and her own jaw clenched in panic. Gavin lifted two fingers off of the steering wheel and nodded briefly, but he kept driving. When they noticed Mack's brake lights burn fast and red in the rearview mirror Betsy held her breath and Gavin slowed to a stop. After a few seconds, in that odd game of backward chicken, Mack broke first, hit the gas, and sped out of sight.

"Cat's outta the bag, all around," Gavin said, turning to look at her straight on, a devious smile on his face. He grabbed her hand and they burst into a fit of laughter, letting the icy AC blow away all of that tension. For the second time that day, for very different reasons, Betsy wanted to cry.

"Maybe he left us some fried chicken this time."

Betsy showered in Gavin's bathroom, which reeked so heavily of mildew that she shampooed twice and hoped the scent of concentrated Prell would mask the sour-towel stench. She pulled on the 501s she'd been breaking in since the ninth grade, a white tank, and a gray men's suit vest she'd picked up for a dollar at a thrift shop during her last visit to her mom's house over a year ago. She'd cinched the silk strap and buckle in the back to make it less boxy around her waist, all the while thinking of Channing and her tawny, angular back. She parted her wet hair down the middle and patted Cherries in the Snow, her one tube of lipstick, worn down to a flat nub, onto her lips with her ring finger. Ginny had talked her into some bronzer once or twice, chided her disinterest in makeup, and even talked her into a visit to the Lancôme counter, but Betsy resisted. Channing or no Channing, that was the most effort she'd ever made for a guy.

Her friends would be barricaded in the upstairs TV room watching slasher flicks in a kind of distasteful nod to current events. But Betsy didn't want any surprises, or to run into anyone unexpectedly, least of all Caroline. She had no desire to field their questions about her temporary living arrangement, so she checked her answering machine to be sure. There was one hurried message from Kari, her delinquent roommate, saying that her parents wouldn't let her come back until classes started again and the murder mayhem subsided. The second one was from Ginny.

"So Kim drove by the Chevron today on a snack run and saw you with Gaaavin," she sang into the tape. "I need every last detail. Promise me you'll remember the way to J.D.'s. We have to go once rush is over. Nana Jean told me that we should just come stay with her until this all blows over. She sends her love."

Ginny and Betsy would often drive to Ocala on a Sunday with trash bags stuffed with laundry filling the backseat under the auspices of "helping" Ginny's grandmother Nana Jean. They'd take her to Grace church, walk her dog, and make a stop at the market. Then they'd swim in her pool and beg her to make lemon bars. For breakfast, they'd eat Jean's famous sausage gravy with the fluffiest biscuits imaginable. Ginny and Betsy spent quiet afternoons on the wide screened-in porch of her rambling old house, under the fan, napping or reading and not saying much at all. Betsy felt a deep ache of longing for all of it. She could taste the iced sweet tea and feel the fan cool her skin.

"Anyway, Caroline called Holly's cousin from Vero fat and the s-h-i-t is hitting the fan. I've got a killer headache and I want to go home to sleep it off, but I'm trapped. Also, I'm beginning to think you had the right idea about bailing on this whole thing. My spirit is officially crushed." She sighed. "It's just not worth it. That's all. Call me later."

The last message was from Caroline.

"Hey, it's me," she said. "Just checking in from hell."

She paused so long that Betsy thought the message was over, and she waited for the beep. Then she started again.

"I guess, I, I don't know. Ginny said she hadn't heard from you this afternoon. Just want to make sure you're good, that you made it back from J.D.'s. If you're staying in your dungeon apartment then you're either really brave or completely stupid. Uh, my money's on stupid. I am tempted to bail on the slasher movie marathon and go home to sleep it off. I'm still so hung from last night. Oh, and you better remember the fucking directions to J.D.'s. You and me, we're going when this is over."

"EVERYTHING OK?" GAVIN asked after she hung up.

"Yep, totally fine," she said, clearing her throat, choosing to wait until the next day to discuss her indefinitely delayed move-in date.

It was 10:30 by the time they got to Weird Bobby's, and things were just getting started. The house, which was off of University Boulevard down the hill from the stadium, was a neglected split-level at the end of a long, downward-sloping driveway. Inside, instead of furniture, he had a full studio set up in his gray-carpeted living room. There were a couple of guitars leaning on stands, some amps, a drum kit, a keyboard, a bass, and a mic for backup singers next to a stack of tambourines. To the left, stained, carpeted stairs led to the bedrooms, and the fluorescent-lit kitchen was separated from the main room by a low Formica counter. A thick haze of smoke filled the room, which was wall-to-wall people, none of whom Betsy recognized. Urge Overkill's "God Flintstone" was playing loud enough to imprint itself instantly in the darkest crevice of her brain, and she knew that she would never forget Weird Bobby's house, with its fluorescent green, algae-filled pool and bong-water stained rug. Gavin took her hand and led her through to the backyard, where the crowd thinned a bit. Jacob and Teddy were sitting at a glass patio table, which was covered with empty bottles and a quarter-inch layer of leaves with dust beneath it. Across from them with his back toward the house was Weird Bobby, who was holding court by packing sticky hash into a metal pipe with nicotine-stained fingers. A small pile of joints rested next to a Rolling Rock. In the grass nearby, a guy in a black trench coat was already passed out, facedown, and a couple of partygoers were launching empty beer cans at his head in a twisted version of horseshoes. It had been years since Betsy had been at a party where she barely knew anyone, or where she couldn't ride on Caroline and Ginny's wake through a crowd of strangers and not give a shit. Tonight she felt out of place and adrift. Out of the corner of her eye, she saw Channing huddled with Anna Johnson, a Miami girl who'd pledged the sorority the same year as Betsy, but she didn't dare look in their direction. Anna had shown up to mandatory study hall in a tiny stretchy miniskirt and oversized tank top that kept slipping off of her shoulders and passed out in a massive pile of her own hair one too many times. She was given the boot by the end of freshman year for not making her grades, and became the first casualty of their pledge class. She'd since become a punch line when any of them got woozy in a bar.

"You're not going to pull an Anna on me tonight, are you?" Caroline would bark at Ginny, as she slid off of a bar stool. "Nobody's going to go Anna-sane this evening, ladies."

Back when they were freshmen, Betsy remembered how intimidated she felt when Anna was around, floored by her perceived ability to not give a fuck about what anyone thought and general badass posture. But over the last couple of years when Betsy spotted her on campus, face covered in giant plastic sunglasses, hair curtain pulled around her features, perpetually hungover, she realized Anna was attempting to hide from her. Betsy was one of "them" according to Anna, and Anna wasn't about to give her a chance to prove otherwise. So Betsy stopped trying to say hello after she was ignored at least a dozen times. That she and Channing were friends should have come as no surprise.

"Lovebird, we need you on drums later," Weird Bobby said to Gavin, body shaking, hands oddly still, now rolling a joint with one and fishing for a lighter in his pocket with the other.

"Yeah, we'll see."

"Jacob's been practicing 'Psycho Killer' all day and I think he's finally got it right," Teddy said. "*Qu'est-ce que c'est* . . . Fa fa fa FA fa, fa fa fa FA far, better . . ."

"Y'all are hilarious," Gavin said. "Truly."

"We spent the whole afternoon thinking of dead girl songs. Hey, is Newland coming?" asked Jacob, slumped so far down in the chair, with broken plastic straps hanging out of the bottom, that his head was barely visible over the bottles clustered on the table.

"Doubt it," said Gavin, glancing at Betsy to see her reaction. She was looking at Channing, who Gavin noticed for the first time. Bobby passed the pipe to Betsy first and she took a drag and stifled a cough, surprised by its tarry thickness. She passed it on to Gavin. Bobby lit a joint and passed it in the other direction.

"I'm going in for beers," Betsy said, as she noticed Channing and Anna making their way across the patio. "Teddy, show me where the kitchen is?"

"It's the room with the stove in it," he said. "Hard to miss."

Betsy stared hard at him across the table until he took the hint.

"Alright. Now I'm going to the kitchen," he said.

Inside, she shouted over the noise.

"You've got thirty seconds to tell me what's up with Channing and Gavin," she said, pressing herself against the wall of a long hallway to squeeze past the crowd.

"They had a thing last year," said Teddy, shaking his head. "But she's crazy. I mean legitimately nuts. Her parents are super loaded but they are never around. She flew Gavin to their house in the Bahamas after their first hookup. She's clingy as hell, and he tried to end it, but she kept breaking into his house. She put her hand through the glass of his bedroom window and he had to take her to the emergency room. Twenty stitches. He's just trying not to piss her off so she'll leave him alone. Hopefully without drawing *his* blood next time."

In the kitchen, Teddy opened the cabinet under the sink and pulled out a hidden bottle of Jack Daniels. Betsy grabbed four nearly warm Coronas from the sink.

"So I should probably stay away?" she asked Teddy.

"From her? Yes," he said. "From Gavin? No. He's alright. No joke."

By the time they got back to the table, Channing and Anna were each sitting on one of Jacob's knees.

"Hey, look who's here! It's Betty Bagelville," said Channing, raising her Red Stripe in the air. Anna just glowered.

"It's Betsy," she said, weakly, starting to feel her heart beat a little faster, her tongue getting heavier.

"You two know each other, right?" Channing gestured to Anna.

"Yeah, we go waaay back," said Anna, laughing without smiling, staring her down, waiting for Betsy to break first and look away. "Betty Bagelville was my *sorority* sister."

Jacob coughed out a half laugh.

"*You* were in a sorority?" he asked Anna. "The slutty one, right?"

Anna pinched his knee hard and threw her head back with another sardonic laugh. Betsy looked at Teddy first, and then Gavin. *Are all men too terrified of these kinds of female inter-*

actions to intervene, she thought, *or just so deeply oblivious to the manipulative shit that's going down that they sit wordlessly and limply?* Teddy passed her a joint and, deeply aware of Channing's and Anna's eyes on her, she smoked the rest.

"Yeah, hey, Anna," Betsy said, finally, choking on her exhale. "It's been a while."

Betsy checked to see if Gavin had noticed that the sharks smelled blood in the water and were circling in. If he did, he wasn't letting on. He and Teddy were talking football. Bobby and Jacob were running down a list of songs: "Down by the River," "Chain Saw" by the Ramones, the Stones's "Paint It Black," "Pink Turns to Blue" by Hüsker Dü. Anna was whispering into Channing's ear, never taking her eyes off of Betsy for a second.

Betsy's limbs suddenly felt heavy, which complicated her urge to flee.

"So why aren't you at rush, Betty?" asked Anna. "It's hell week, right? Shouldn't you be singing show tunes with the rest of the stick-in-the-ass bitches?"

"I quit, actually," she said, wondering if this would somehow change the tenor of the conversation, make them members of the same club and align them against the stick-in-the-ass bitches of the world. "I turned in my pin last year."

"So that explains the makeover," said Channing. Anna barked a kind of harsh, halting laugh this time. The revelation that Channing had noticed Betsy, too, even if it was to take inventory of her somewhat embarrassing style evolution, made Betsy believe that the fight wasn't over yet.

"I was wondering why you were slumming over here," said Channing, taking a swig of her beer.

"Sometimes, if you aim too high, you miss the target. But you should know that, right?" Betsy said. *So this is just how it works.* Bitches were everywhere. Channing was the Caroline of her domain, but Betsy could take her. "Felt like coming down from my shiny mountaintop tonight."

"Excuse me, ladies," said Jacob, as Channing and Anna slid off of his lap. "Bets, you up for singing backup later?"

"Uh, sure," she said, tucking her hair behind her ear self-consciously, her old friend paranoia back in her head, telling her that Jacob only asked in order to make fun of her later, in front of them. When Betsy was high, it was like thinking in an echo chamber. Any of the insignificant, insecure inklings she'd have when she was sober would be amplified, played back to her a few times, louder and louder, until it became more important and dire than it was or funnier than it should be. Nothing was funny about that night, though, and she struggled with the "they're laughing with me" vs. "they're laughing at me" mind fuck. The fear around her, the sense that any one of the derelicts at the party could be the killer, made the feeling infinitely worse. She scanned the crowd for faces, trying to remember details. Would she recognize any of them in a police lineup? Even though she wanted to beg Gavin to leave, to go back to his house and disappear into his room, all she could think to say was, "Maybe."

"You alright?" asked Gavin, touching her elbow. She turned to look at him and, in a half-second flash, realized that she was practically living with a total stranger. *Who is this guy?* Was he in on the joke with Channing and Weird Bobby, out to humiliate the sorority girl as some kind of game?

"I'm fine. Why do you care?" she said.

"Why do I *care*?" He laughed, guiding her away from the table. "Because Channing is into blood sports and she is totally after you."

"Oh you actually noticed that?" she said. "I thought you were just tossing me in the water to bloody it up like chum." She didn't know if she'd made the shark analogy out loud.

"What the fuck are you talking about?" he said.

She hadn't said it out loud.

"Look, I would lay off the weed if I were you. That's serious shit. Weird Bobby doesn't mess around."

"What, so now you're my chaperone? You think Betty Bagelville can't handle it?"

"What are you talking about?" he said. "Weird Bobby's shit is strong. Period. Sorry if you're some kind of expert hash-smoker and I didn't know it."

"Yeah, well there are a lot of things you don't know about me." *Ugh,* she thought, *Really? That's the best you could do?*

"Hey, Gav, you in?" asked Jacob. "Weird Bobby's on bass. We need you on drums."

"Yeah, one sec," he called back, and then turned to Betsy as he reached up to scratch the back of his head. "Are you going to be OK if I go in there? Bets, you're acting weird."

"I can handle myself," she said. "As of forty-eight hours ago, I was totally capable of living without you."

Neither one of them knew what to do or say next. They stood there for a minute. Gavin tried to make eye contact, but Betsy wouldn't do it. The words were out. Maybe that's all it took to crush something that was so soft and new that it hadn't formed a protective shell yet.

"Alright, if that's the way it's gonna be," he said, at last. "I'm going to go inside that house and play some brutally insensitive songs right now, and when I come back I expect you to be normal again. Got it?"

She didn't reply.

"We'll leave when this is over?" he said, stuttering, noticing the gaffe. "I mean, when we're finished, if that's what you want."

"Sure. When it's *over.* Whatever. That's fine," she said, deliberately obtuse, not completely understanding why. *It was easier to hate him, to drive him away,* she thought, *than to find out he'd been fucking with her.* She hated how dramatic she was being, but couldn't stop. They made their way back through the crowd into the house to the sound of Jacob doing his best sullen Morrissey impression out of the crackly speaker: "There are times when I could have muuuurdered heeerrrr." Betsy found a spot on the stairs so she could look out over the crowd and hide at the same time. She wondered if they could actually play or if they would just tune the instruments until people gave up and left or fell asleep.

She glanced at the thermostat on the wall. The air-conditioning was set at sixty-five, but the room was airless and suffocating. The crowd was a raggedy mix of hippies, skaters, punks, and general-purpose slackers. They were people who, if they lived in a real city, would have the luxury of avoiding one another, even hating each other. Here, the population that qualified as bohemian or, that new word, alternative, or marginal in any way, was so small that they had to band together as kindred, disaffected youth. Though in Weird Bobby's case, calling him "youth" of any kind was a stretch. It was Gainesville, summer of 1990, and less than a mile down the street there were a dozen steroid-addled assholes sitting on a fire truck permanently parked in the front yard of their frat house, draining a day-old, half-empty keg of Bud Light and rating women as they walked by on the traditional scale of one to ten. So from Betsy's angle, Weird Bobby's party, full of wasted, misfit strangers, and the ironic and wildly inappropriate song set Jacob put together, was better than her other options. She sat on her perch and watched. Across the room, she spotted Louise and Not-Louise huddled against the wall, laughing conspiratorially. Betsy watched as Anna slinked through the crowd and let her shirt slip off of her shoulder like she didn't notice, and Channing stumbled her way across the room in a long skirt that hung low on her jutting hips, scarf wrapped just so. Eventually, Teddy climbed the stairs and took a seat next to her.

"You know, people can actually see you here," he said.

"They can?" she asked. "I thought that weed that strong must give you superpowers. I was praying that mine was invisibility."

"Good one," Teddy said, as he reached out and clinked his beer bottle against hers. "I'm always torn between X-ray vision and the power of flight."

They sat together for a while and listened to Jacob's Neil Young whine, howling "*shot her dead, I shot her dead*" over and over. Betsy felt relieved to be partially hidden on the stairs, safe with Teddy, that internal voice, the one that was out to destroy her, silenced for the time being.

"I thought you would have graduated by now?" said Betsy.

"Nah, I'm on the five-year plan," he said. He had to shout to be heard over the music.

"I'm out of here in December," said Betsy. "No idea where to, though."

"I say just pick a spot on the map and go. Get out of here. I hear Seattle's cool? Maybe Chicago? Where else?" he said.

"Maybe New York? All of those places feel way too far away. Way too cold. But you never know. Right now, I'd be happy just to go to a place where a shirt and shoes are required for service. I'd be happy to be in a town that wasn't turned upside down by a serial killer, too," she said.

Predictably, Channing made her way over to the percussion section and was shaking a tambourine in time to a messy cover of "Dig It Up" by the Hoodoo Gurus. *"My girlfriend lives in the ground,"* growled Jacob. She did a kind of spinning dance move that made Betsy feel nauseous just watching. Then, as if the party wasn't a complete disaster already, the front door opened and in stumbled Mack, clearly smashed, with a ball cap pulled low over his eyes. He searched the room from the doorway and when he saw Betsy on the stairs next to Teddy he pointed at her hard and shouted, "Outside!" which was barely audible over the music. Gavin didn't see anything.

"Shit," said Teddy. "You can just ignore him, you know."

"I've tried it before. Doesn't work," she said, and steadied herself on the stair rail as she stood up. If Channing's spinning got the pukey feeling started, Mack's grand appearance sealed the deal. Betsy tottered down the stairs and ran out of the front door to throw up in what was left of the landscaping on the far side of the driveway near a woody patch that separated Weird Bobby's place from the house next door. She rinsed out her mouth with the remains of her Corona and spit, as delicately as possible, fearing any stragglers outside who saw her in the bushes might not find the whole situation very refined. By the time she looked up, the front yard was empty. She was alone, except for Mack, who was looming in front of her. Even in silhouette, backlit by the porch light, it was clear that he wasn't merely wasted. He was belligerently, blindly wasted. She steadied herself against a tree, ready for the fight.

"Is this some kind of joke?" he shouted. "You and Gavin?"

"As of this morning, I didn't think so. Now I'm reconsidering."

"How long has this been going on?"

"There's nothing going on," she said.

"It looks like you're staying in his house, Betsy. There's something going on or you're a bigger whore than I thought."

Teddy walked out onto the front porch.

"You kids playing nice?" he asked.

"Fuck off, Teddy," said Mack, flinging a near-empty Solo cup at him, which hit the front door and sent a spray of booze over the back of Teddy's shirt and shorts when he ducked to shield his head. "This has nothing to do with you."

"Christ, settle down!" he said. "Betsy, are you OK?"

"I'm fine," she said, straining her voice to be heard over the music. "Just give us a minute." *Am I fine?*

"Why don't we all calm down and come back inside," Teddy said. The music blasted behind him.

"This has nothing to do with you, Teddy," Mack shouted.

Teddy paused. *Don't leave,* Betsy thought.

"OK. If you're not back in the house in five minutes, I'm coming back out here." Teddy went back into the party.

"Why do you care, anyway?" Betsy said, turning to Mack, shouting in his face. "It's been over for so many months now. You want me to die, right? Isn't that what you said at Bagelville over your morning coffee? You hated me even when we were together."

"I wanted you to die *before* you started fucking one of my best friends," he said, so close now that she could smell the bourbon on his breath.

"I'm not fucking Gavin," she said.

"*Yet.* You are not fucking Gavin *yet,*" he shouted, and he reached out and shoved her against the tree, pressing his body against hers, his rage turning suddenly to a condescending stage whisper. "But if I were you, I'd wait till he was finished with Channing first."

"What do you mean? You're so full of shit," she said, trying to push him away.

"I mean that she was over at his house the night before we saw you at Bagelville." He was spitting as he spoke. Betsy managed to push him off of her and stumbled backward, further into the woods. Mack followed. "Her car was outside. I unpacked some boxes and looked back out there two hours later. It was still there."

His words were slurred, but the message was clear. Betsy was stunned. She'd never even thought to ask if he was with anybody. It didn't occur to her. What right did she have to be mad about it, really? If there was something she needed to know, he'd tell her, right? They'd been together for a couple of days, and what did he owe her? She wondered why Channing had played along with Bobby's lovebird bit at J.D.'s. The wheels had already started to spin, and once that started, with Weird Bobby's drugs added to the mix, there was no stopping. *It was a lie,* she thought, *all of it.* Gavin was messing with her. It would be over before classes started again. Betsy's mind raced, and she started to see the darkness in Gavin. He was just like the rest of them, like Mack, like Channing and Anna, like Caroline . . . even Ginny. *Where is she now, when I really need her? Hiding in the sorority house behind those letters, behind a crowd of hollow girls.* Betsy had been afraid of this ominous killer, of the unknown, but what if the real threat was right in front of her? *Could Mack actually hurt me?* Betsy wondered. She remembered what he'd said that morning.

It would be a shame if you were next.

"You're a joke and a fucking slut, Betsy," he said, lunging for her. She turned to run, but she tripped on a tree root and fell to the damp, spongy ground. She looked up through the trees toward the door. *Where was Teddy? Was he in on it, too? Was she completely alone?* Going back inside was not an option. Betsy wanted out, to get away from there, to go anywhere else. So she struggled to her feet, turned, and ran up the driveway, down the long empty residential street into the dark, muggy night.

Mack's voice trailed after her.

"The way I see it, both of you are getting sloppy seconds."

WHEN SHE FINALLY made it to University Boulevard, the headlights of the cars came as a shock. It had to have been after 1:00 a.m., but there were still people on the road. And as she walked along the sidewalk toward campus, occasionally someone would roll down the window to heckle her. Two guys in a pickup truck slowed down to her pace and drove beside her for a minute or two. When Betsy declined their offer of a ride, she just shook her head. If she opened her mouth, she was afraid of what would come out.

"Nice night for a walk, you moron," shouted the drunk from the passenger seat. Once she made it to the stadium, she decided to take a shortcut and make her way through the all but abandoned campus, down Stadium Way, past Weil Hall through the North Lawn, past McCarty Hall to 8th Street. The news crews that had been swarming the campus had retreated to the Residence Inn or the University Hilton for nachos and hot wings at the hotel bar and an early bedtime, counting the minutes before they caught the killer, if only so they could return to civilization. Without the beaming sunlight, students milling about, gaudily decked in orange and blue, there was no story. It was just another small town in Florida with derelicts hiding in the crawl space. Serial killers were good for ratings. Mix in college-age female victims in an "idyllic campus setting" no less, and you've got a solid national headline. Betsy thought of her friends hunkered down on Sorority Row nearby. "You think you're safe there?" she muttered to herself, happy to be alone at last. "What would Ted Bundy have to say about that?"

The recent killing spree was like gory icing on the sketchy cake for Gainesville, a place that wasn't as safe as the university claimed. She'd read an article in *The Sun* not long before that dubbed the town the shadiest in Florida, referring to the number of mature trees per square mile within city limits.

"You better believe it's the shadiest," said Melissa, scanning the paper someone had left on a table at Bagelville. "And it doesn't have a thing to do with leafy glens."

It's like the Millhopper, Betsy thought, as she plodded along silently, eyes scanning the shadows for lurking things of any kind. Just below the surface, there's the stuff that doesn't belong, the bits of bones and teeth, the unusual things, completely out of place, that thrive under the cover of darkness and neglect. At first, she found that image comforting, that something could thrive below the surface, unnoticed, but now it felt threatening.

Even under normal circumstances a late-night, solo campus stroll was a terrible idea, and she blamed her rash decision on the drugs. *What was I thinking,* she wondered, picturing Anna and Channing back at the party, laughing at her. *How could I have let my guard down so completely?* She made it to Beatty Towers, a high-rise dorm made famous by Tom

Petty when rumors about his song "American Girl" claimed that he was singing about a girl who threw herself off of her eighth-floor balcony, even though it wasn't true. She spotted the crammed bike rack in front of the building and said a tiny prayer, out loud.

"If there's just one unlocked bike somewhere in this rack, God, I swear to You that I will never steal another object, wheeled or otherwise, for the rest of my life." She paused. "And I will resume believing in You."

Betsy worked fast, trying to wrestle each front tire out of its place, sandwiched between the metal bars. A beat-up ten-speed with a wobbly front tire sprang free, she swung her leg around the back of it, and, just like that, she was out of sight.

At the intersection, she paused again. If she took a left, she was back to her dusty, empty apartment with a mattress on the floor. If she went straight, that road led her to the sorority house, where Ginny and Caroline were staying the night. To the right was their apartment, with its feather beds and freshly laundered sheets. The key to their front door was still in her front pocket. Betsy followed her gut and took a right, partly because it was a downhill ride, and partly because she needed to be alone, but not alone enough to face her own grim life and apartment, both of which felt empty, both of which were a mess. She coasted down 13th Street on her last stolen bike, vowing to remind herself about the God stuff tomorrow.

At the bottom of the long hill, she hung another right at the Steak 'n Shake, where three graveyard-shift employees were forced into the meat freezer at gunpoint by one lunatic last year while his crack buddy emptied the till. That prompted Caroline to announce "I'd *kill* for a steak burger!" every time they drove by and howl with laughter. It didn't seem funny anymore. In this section of town, a few miles away from the nearest bar, the streets were entirely empty, and Betsy somehow felt safest riding in the dead center on the double yellow line. The slope of the hill, the arch of the tree branches that grew over it, were all so familiar to Betsy. Ginny and Caroline had been in their apartment in Williamsburg Village for three years, starting their day, every day, to a state-of-the-art CD alarm clock set to play "Superman" by R.E.M. at 7:30 a.m. sharp, the most optimistic song Ginny could find to rouse her for another day. Even though Ginny and Caroline wouldn't be there, she needed to smell that faint popcorn scent mixed with Caroline's Quelques Fleurs and feel the musty, deep, chintz sofa that practically grew arms to embrace her. So when she coasted into the parking lot, she ditched the bike between a couple of parked cars under a streetlight, just in case, and jogged toward the building, up the front stairs. With the building's 1970s-era fake-colonial facade there to greet her like an old friend, she'd nearly forgotten about Weird Bobby and Channing, Mack's apoplectic freak-out, attacking her in the woods, and Gavin—well, almost Gavin. She just wanted to sleep it off and wake up tomorrow with clearer eyes and start all over again. She would clean up her new apartment. She would buy a dresser at Goodwill and unpack her boxes. She would add a few more lines to her letter to Gainesville. She would start over, again.

Betsy was halfway up the steps when she felt something crunch underfoot, followed by the hissing and snarling of the neighbor's cat, whose tail she'd apparently stepped on. She fell hard against the stair rail, heart racing with another adrenaline surge. A blur of matted gray fur disappeared into the darkness under the stairwell in a flash. She was still breathing hard from the last leg of her journey on the stolen bike and that hadn't helped matters.

"It's just me," she hissed back, "you big, fat grouch."

Once she was sure the cat wasn't coming back for revenge, and that she hadn't had a hash-fueled heart attack, she fished the key out of her front pocket and put it in the lock.

Betsy sensed that something was off immediately. There was a faint warm glow from the upstairs hallway casting a half circle of dim light on the floor at the bottom of the stairs. It was the light. She was definitely still high, almost certainly still drunk, but she knew that light shouldn't be on. Caroline would have removed the bulb from the ceiling fixture, her profound hatred for overhead lighting capping the list of her many idiosyncrasies, if she hadn't been too lazy to borrow a stepladder. *You're high, Bets,* she told herself. *Don't freak out on me. Ginny left it on to make it seem like someone was home, and awake, and definitely not into being murdered.* Still, her heart thumped against her sternum and she closed the door quietly behind her. She had taken about eight quiet steps down the long hall when she first heard the music, playing faintly, and started to panic in earnest. Standing in the dark, eyes trained on the soft light coming from the top of the stairs, her mind riffled through all of the possible sources of the music: an insomniac next-door neighbor, a party in the adjacent building, a clock radio alarm set for the wrong hour belonging to someone who decided to shack up elsewhere for the night. *He's in the house,* the voice in her head told her. She remembered Caroline's comment in the car. *What are the chances? One in fifteen thousand?* Then, when she heard what sounded like a footstep on a creaky floorboard, the reliable, slow, crackly groan of wood from the noisy spot at the foot of

Ginny's bed, she was convinced. *He's here. Get out. Get out. Get out.* He, whoever he was, *the* he was in the apartment, waiting for her. Betsy turned so fast to head for the door that she ran into the wooden side chair they kept in the front hall and sent a stack of junk mail scattering to the floor and then fell to the ground on top of it. She scrambled to get to her feet, slipping on mailers and phone bills and delivery menus, and out of the apartment, reaching for the doorknob to help her up. She flung the door open and slammed it behind her, shot down the stairwell, past the parked cars, struggling for breath, too terrified to stop or turn around or find the bike that she'd abandoned just minutes before. She rounded the corner onto 16th Street and nearly lunged headfirst into the hood of an oncoming car, which screeched to a stop. She froze in the headlights, shielding her eyes from the beam, until she heard her name.

"Betsy? What the fuck?" It was Gavin. She hurried to the passenger side, sat hard in the seat, and slammed the door.

"Go! Go, go, Gavin, get out of here, now. I'm serious! We've got to go."

CHAPTER 10

NEW ORLEANS

August 27, 1990

Once Gavin was a couple of blocks away from Williamsburg Village in the parking lot of the Steak 'n Shake, and Betsy calmed down enough to talk, she told him what had happened.

"I don't know. I can't know for sure. But I swear to God it felt like someone was in that apartment, Gavin," she said, sensing his doubt about the details.

"Well, you said that there was a pissed-off cat on the stairs, Betsy. You don't think that it could have made some of those noises? It's not unheard of for people to be up listening to music at this hour, either. It could have been coming from a neighbor's place."

"I don't know." She shook her head. "It didn't sound like it was from a neighbor's place, but maybe you're right. My brain hurts."

"I mean, we could go to the cops. But you're underage, right? When do you turn twenty-one?"

"In November," Betsy said, feeling as small as a child.

"And you're high as shit," he said. "And your blood alcohol level is likely pretty impressive." He reached over to touch her forehead.

"How did you get mud on your face?" he asked.

She had almost forgotten about Mack.

"I fell in the woods near Weird Bobby's," she said. "With Mack."

"That guy . . ." Gavin trailed off, gritting his teeth.

"I've already forgotten about him. I think the adrenaline took care of that," she said, feeling dumb and paranoid about being so paranoid.

"You've had a rough night, Betsy. Who can blame you for thinking the worst?"

"You're probably right. I don't know. I'm just scared. I hate it here right now. The place is crawling with news crews. Class is canceled. I saw Phil fucking Donahue on campus today. I just want to go. I've got a little cash. Let's just go."

Betsy turned her face away from his and looked out the window. *He thinks I'm crazy,* she thought, *and he's still sleeping with Channing.* On the white stucco wall in front of her was a pay phone.

"I'll be right back," she said, and jumped out of the car. Betsy picked up the receiver, took a breath. She was going to call 911.

"Gainesville nine-one-one. What's the location of your emergency?"

"Um, I'm at a pay phone now," Betsy's voice started to tremble. She remembered the humiliation she felt on Fraternity Row. The firemen stood in a line, wearing their giant helmets, arms crossed, staring at her with clear condescension.

"What's going on down there?"

"Well," she said, reviewing her story in her head, trying to avoid any scenario in which the police found her drunk, high, and underage. She pictured her mom in bed at home in Venice, fumbling for the phone when the police would inevitably call. *What am I supposed to say,* she thought, *I think I heard something suspicious? The floor creaked? A light was on that shouldn't be on. And music was playing.*

Oh shit.

"Ma'am, are you there?"

Betsy's story, and her confidence, started to crumble. Her eyes were trained on the wall next to the phone. Someone had scratched "slut" into the paint with a car key.

"Hello?" The operator's tone was short, obviously tired, and completely over stoned college kids flipping out about a tree branch grazing their bedroom window. She imagined how weary a 911 operator in a college town besieged by the media must be at 3:00 a.m., and suspected that she was one of many panicked students making calls about sinister-looking pizza deliverymen and creepy sounds. Betsy could hear herself breathing in the receiver.

"Sorry. False alarm."

She hung up. Betsy glanced back at Gavin, who was covering his face with his hands. She remembered the party, Channing and Anna, Mack pouncing on her in the driveway. For a second, she could see herself in the parking lot, the bluish glow of the Steak 'n Shake sign on her face, like she was hovering over the building and peering down. From up there, she looked impossibly small.

"How'd that go?" Gavin said, once she was back in the car.

"Not well. I'd say that wasn't good at all," she said.

AFTER SOME CONVINCING, Gavin agreed to leave for forty-eight hours. Once they decided to leave Gainesville, Betsy started breathing again.

They'd settled on their destination, New Orleans, an hour into the drive. It was an unusual approach, sure, but neither of them had been thinking very clearly. They drove back to Gavin's so he could scavenge enough clothes for a night or two, careful to avoid his raging bull neighbor. Betsy had already packed a bag to stay at Gavin's. Then they made one stop, at Bagelville, to get an early payday from Tom. They'd pulled up to the store and saw the light in the kitchen was on, steam already clouding the windows, and Betsy pounded on the back door with the palm of her hand. Tom cleared the glass with his sleeve and peered out the window before he opened the door.

"Jesus Christ, Bets, you scared me," said Tom, talking through the wrought-iron gate covering the door, glancing at his watch while he turned the dead bolt and let her in. "And you're more than two hours early, which does not make up for the eight times you were fifteen minutes late. Just so we're clear."

"Tom, I'm not here for work. I can't do it today," she said, looking at his shoes so he wouldn't see how wasted she was. "I . . . I was just wondering. Can you . . . just . . . pay me now? Is that OK?"

It occurred to her how hard she was trying to act sober, and she felt the judgment behind his concerned expression. "I need to get out of here for a couple of days. And I can't come in tomorrow. Or I guess it's today now."

"You seem a little spooked. You OK?" he asked, stepping outside to look over at Gavin's car to see who was inside. "If you're in some kind of situation . . . I . . . I don't know. Can I help you out in some way?"

"I'm fine, Tom," she said. "Honest to God. It's just with the reporters crawling all over the place, and classes being canceled, and you know, a guy on the loose who is murdering young women . . . I . . . I have to go. Now. So the only thing you can do to help me right now, if you want to help like you say you do, is to pay me a couple of days early, and give me today and tomorrow off."

He stood there for a moment, leaning on the doorframe, still suspicious of the car. He pulled a handful of bills from his wallet.

"I've got a hundred on me. We can figure out your hours when you get back, OK?"

"Thanks, Tom," she said, shrinking a little with gratitude. When she reached to take the money, he took her hand.

"But, Betsy, be careful. I'm serious," he said. She nodded, fighting her tears. "If you need anything, for real, let me know."

Back in the car, Gavin attempted a joke.

"What, no fresh-baked sesames?" he said. She didn't laugh.

"I've got to tell you something, and I think now is the perfect time," he said.

"What?" asked Betsy, her stomach knotting again. "What is it?"

"I hate bagels," he said. "Hate 'em. They're gummy and thick, and generally disgusting. Nobody needs that much bread. I'm more of a toast guy."

"Can I ask you a question?" she said. "I mean, two questions?"

"Shoot."

"How did you know where to find me?"

"Well, I didn't realize you'd left for a while," he said. "I saw Newland stumble in and Teddy confront him, and before I knew what was what he dove over the drum kit swinging at me, I mean, like a lunatic. It got pretty ugly."

"Oh God."

"They finally pulled him off of me, but not until he trashed Bobby's drums. He was pissed."

"Jesus, are you serious? I'm so sorry."

"Don't be sorry. It was my fault. I should have said something to him about it, about you," he said. "But you know what a hothead he is. I was just waiting for the right time. I never imagined he would snap like that. No offense, but he told me he hated you. I didn't think he'd care if we were together."

"No offense taken," she said. *Gavin said they were together.*

"By the time he settled down and Teddy told me what happened, you were long gone. I went to your place first, but you clearly weren't there. Then I went back to my place for a minute thinking you might show up. But then I remembered you told me about staying with Ginny over at Williamsburg, and I took a guess."

Before they left town, Betsy requested one more stop. They made a right turn on 10th Street and she directed Gavin to pull into a dark driveway nearly overgrown with an ornery, untamed hedge.

"Give me a second," she said. She got out of the car and crossed through the headlights, stepped lightly onto the sagging front porch of Rich the Geek's house, reached into her pocket to retrieve Godzilla, still deep green and bumpy like an avocado and warm from her pocket, and placed it near the door.

"What's going on?" asked Gavin.

"Just something I forgot to do before."

BACK IN THE car, they started on the eight-hour drive to New Orleans. Gavin had friends there who they could stay with for a day or two. Once they were on I-75, she drifted in and out of sleep. When she was awake, she circled the events of the night in her head in a deep panic, convinced one minute that the worst of her suspicions were true, and then the next that she'd let her fear get the best of her. She'd barely noticed that she was in a moving car, let alone that Gavin, heretofore known as the guy from the record store, a friend of her psycho-ex-boyfriend, was in it with her. They'd known each other, formally, for less than three days. It seemed like so much longer.

But there they were, at the Circle K near Live Oak. They stopped for gas, gas station coffee in a foam cup, and original Corn Nuts at a convenience store in such a desolate place, even the dimmest lights drew hordes of moths and flying roaches as big as a toddler's hand. As she was shaking the last clotted flecks of Coffee-mate into her cup it occurred to her that it was the kind of place where one might not be entirely surprised to bump into people who were fleeing a possible crime scene.

"You should get some rest," she said, her voice dry and cracked from booze and adrenaline. "I'm OK to drive for an hour or two. It's the Corn Nuts. Tough on the dental work, but they keep me awake."

"You sure?" he asked, putting his hands on her shoulders.

She nodded, staring at the asphalt, inspecting a splatter of thick red ooze that she hoped was day-old Slurpee.

"Wake me up in an hour," he said, as he moved his palm to the side of her face.

"I know this is weird—all of it," he said, not in an unkind way. "Everybody's leaving town. Classes were canceled, remember? We're just changing the scenery. Getting a little distance. You're gonna love these guys we're staying with in New Orleans. It'll be OK."

"I know," she said. "I think I know."

The last time she made this drive north was when she was ten. She and her dad made a mostly silent journey north to Connecticut, in his off-white Buick LeSabre with brown velour interior, for his mother's, her Grandma Young's, funeral. *Why did people have to die in order for her to leave Florida?*

Betsy made it across most of the Panhandle before she couldn't take the silence and the swarm of her own thoughts for another minute. She'd been memorizing the lyrics to the Afghan Whigs's "You My Flower," on repeat for an hour, astonished by Gavin's ability to sleep through her "singing." So she woke him up with a doughnut, a pint of Tropicana, and an airplane bottle of vodka in a parking lot near Mobile.

The original thought was that they'd stay with two of Gavin's friends from Jacksonville, Tulane guys who worked at a bar near campus. When they arrived unannounced at their crumbling house off of St. Charles, the last address Gavin had written in his book, the place was empty. There was no sign of anyone, anywhere. In front of the house there was a wide porch with enough half-assembled bikes to make even Betsy wince, and a withering, yellowed pile of *The Times-Picayune* in the corner. Gavin left a message on an answering machine from the pay phone down the street, saying that they were in town and they'd swing back by again later.

"I didn't recognize the voice on the recording," he said. "I'm hoping it's a roommate. Otherwise, they moved."

They stopped for more coffee, better this time, but the heat of the day was mounting, pressing down on their hangovers, and they needed a place to sleep it off. They wandered around looking for a room. When they stumbled onto a sloping, defeated Victorian bed-and-breakfast with a vacancy sign in the window, they climbed the creaking steps before Betsy paused on the shady porch.

"I'm sure that you think I'm an unbelievable moron right now, and possibly a little crazy," she said. "But thank you, you know, for getting me out of there."

"You're cute when you're crazy. Plus, I've got nothing better to do," he said in a way that made her think that maybe he meant it.

For sixty dollars cash, up front, they got a room from an ancient, round woman wearing a long, purple knit vest with long pockets weighed down by rings of more keys than she could ever identify. Check-in time wasn't until three, she said, peering over the top of her red-framed reading glasses, taking a long look at Betsy's drawn, delicate face before she decided to show some mercy. At the top of a dark, narrow staircase, down a long hall of unmarked doors, they dropped their duffel bags in a room with dark green walls and a simple iron bed made up with an old flour sack quilt and pushed up against a large window with its heavy, brocade tasseled shade pulled low. Across from the bed was a small desk with a reading lamp and a ladder-back chair. A slice of sun crept in from under the shade and made the dust particles in the air look like tiny, floating, electric snowflakes.

"Bath's third door on ya left," she said. "Drinks on the porch at six. You're buying. Come down for breakfast. Not before eight. Big key's for the front door. It's locked after ten. Little one's for the room."

"Thank you, um . . . ," Betsy asked.

"Miss June," she said, turning sideways to pass through the narrow door. "Get some rest. You two look like you saw the wrong side of dawn. Keep the noise down and you'll make me happy."

Betsy barely remembered taking her shoes off, but five hours later, she peeled her face off of the crocheted pillowcase and pushed her hair off of her forehead. It was the kind of dreamless, heavy sleep that left her drenched in sweat and feeling oddly weightless. It took a minute for her to remember where she was. The light had dimmed. The sun was so low in the sky that it made the tiny room glow a deep shade of amber. Gavin was still asleep but she didn't dare look at him, afraid he might wake up to find her staring at him like some kind of psychotic house cat. She cracked the window, letting in some of that early evening summer breeze. Then she grabbed a towel and a change of clothes and padded out the door to the shower down the hall. She closed her eyes to let the water rinse the soap from her face and thought again about the night before. *Maybe it was the upstairs neighbor, opening the sliding door*, she thought. There have to be at least a dozen explanations for that noise, the creak of the wood, the music, but she kept going back to the first one, over and over again.

She remembered the time, early in their freshman year, when Caroline convinced her that the cops were in front of that same apartment, ready to arrest them for smoking pot. Caroline saw a neighbor's brake lights through the curtains in the living room and suddenly hit the floor, inspired to mess with her new friends' heads.

"Get *down*," she'd hissed. "What are you? Idiots? Can't

you see there's a cruiser out front? Shit! Our neighbors must have smelled the smoke."

Betsy, who was panic-stricken, turned around to see Ginny in the kitchen, clutching her middle, doubled over with laughter. Their pledge-sister Holly was with them, and she hit the floor to crouch between the sofa and the coffee table, eyes wide, so impossibly high that she'd believed every word that Caroline fed her about their impending arrest for possession.

"Poor Ginny," said Caroline, still in a husky whisper, never once breaking character. "She is so high that she doesn't know she's about to spend the night in jail with a fifty-year-old hooker."

Ginny had fallen for it before and was giddy to be on the other side of the joke. But Betsy and Holly were the new girls who still believed, wholesale, that Len Bias let his guard down *just one time*, snorted a solitary line of coke, and that was all it took to stop his heart on the spot. Fear of sudden death by mild drug use was enough to keep Betsy straight through all of high school. So the first time she let herself go in her friends' apartment, no curfew, no one to notice or care, pulse feeling strong, inhaling the weed smoke through a cored apple pipe, her only misstep was to fall for the old "cops outside the window" routine.

"My mom is going to kill me" was the only thing Betsy could think of to say. When Caroline saw that she had succeeded in terrifying her latest subjects, she flopped on the couch and said, "I'm completely fucking with you," through a sinister, self-satisfied grin.

After that, Betsy's paranoia became the stuff of legend. And Caroline's performance cemented her status as a devious but, if you squint a little, entirely awesome superhero in Betsy's eyes, once she realized what was happening and laughed at her own expense. Holly wasn't so forgiving.

"You're an insane cow, Caroline. Really twisted," she said, before she grabbed her Dooney & Burke bag and stormed out of the door, past the neighbor's idling car outside.

After that, the three of them started what was to become a regular, GPA-destroying thing: Betsy in the backseat, Ginny behind the wheel, and Caroline shotgun, making their first stop of the night at the drive-thru liquor store so Ginny could flirt with the guys who worked there until they handed over three bottles of Asti Spumante to underage girls who would never, ever pay. It would become their routine. That's how it all began. Later, the John incident would be how it ended. But in that moment, Betsy still basked in the reflected glow of her slightly demonic friend and Ginny's sweet but devilish smile, the glint in her eyes, which Betsy could see reflected in the rearview mirror.

BETSY STEPPED OVER the edge of the claw-foot tub, wrapped herself in a stiff yellow towel, and cleared the steam from the mirror with her palm. Even after the shower, the crochet imprint was embedded on her cheek. She combed her fingers through her hair, pulled on her last pair of clean underpants, fresh Levi's, and a threadbare black V-neck T-shirt and crept down the stairs with her army surplus boots in one hand, steadying herself on the railing with the other.

Miss June was in what appeared to be the library, though the shelves that lined the walls were deeper and bowed in the middle from the weight of vinyl. Betsy had never seen a record collection so immense, or a turntable quite so old. June sat in an overstuffed chair that was bulging at the seams, exposing the cotton stuffing beneath, making something out of variegated yarn that appeared to have three sleeves. She was listening to jazz.

"Thought you children might be dead up there, heh heh," she said, not bothering to look up.

"Hate to disappoint you," said Betsy, forcing a smile. Dead girls. Always hilarious. "If I don't eat soon, I might be."

"Got some biscuits in the kitchen left over from this morning," she said. "There's a place on the corner that'll fix you up with some dinner. Cheap and good, the best kind."

Betsy ate the stale biscuit with honey on a chipped saucer in the dark kitchen and, newly fortified, walked the two blocks to the nearest liquor store. She bought a six-pack of Shiner—the cashier didn't ask for her I.D. and Betsy assumed that it was because the last two days had aged her ten years—and a bag of Lay's. Back on the wide porch of Miss June's house, Betsy took a seat in a crackly rocking chair to watch cars rolling by and people strolling on the sidewalk making their way to somewhere in no particular rush. She breathed in the weighty, unfamiliar air and Miss June's music, which drifted through the screen door. Betsy would never learn to love jazz, but that night she came close. She felt a little ragged, uncertain, raw in the strangest way, and the music mirrored that. She heard Gavin's low, slow voice greeting Miss June inside and the creaking of the front door.

"There you are," he said, taking the chair next to hers. The scent of Camay soap had followed him from the shower. Betsy handed him a beer and a biscuit wrapped in a paper towel.

"Yep, and I'm never leaving," she said. "Miss June is making me an ankle-length vest that matches hers and I'm going to stay here forever."

"Just skip the finding a job and having a life part and head straight for retirement," he said. "It's a half-decent plan. But I couldn't handle the jazz. Way too annoying."

I have to call my mom, let her know I'm OK, Betsy thought, feeling a familiar tightness in her chest. *She'll be worried.* But the fact that she'd left town with a strange new guy, someone she'd barely known, to escape a serial killer might not soothe her mother's nerves. It could wait until morning.

"Do you want to call Adam and Brett again?" she asked. "Or we could go back by the house? Somebody's got to be there by now."

"Nah, maybe later," he said, leaning forward to put his elbows on his knees, his leg brushing against hers. "I think we could probably entertain ourselves for a while."

Miss June was right. At the end of the block, they got a deep bowl of beans and rice with corn bread and a couple of beers for fifteen dollars. They walked aimlessly through the warm night, her arm around his waist, his across her shoulders, and she felt safer there, with him, on the street in New Orleans, than she had in some time. She decided not to press him for Channing details. That would keep for a while. On the way into town that day, they passed a billboard painted black with Thou Shalt Not Kill written across it in all caps. Of all of the commandments, Gavin had said, surely that was the easiest to remember, not recognizing the irony of the situation until it was behind them. It's an odd place to go if you're fleeing danger. Betsy had always heard how crime-ridden the city was. But the threat there seemed to be out in the open, recognized, hanging in the breeze like a shingle hung in front of a bar—a handbag dangling from a shoulder, ready to be snatched, a fight in the streets that spilled out from a crowded bar. You knew that bad guys were supposed to be there, so you wouldn't be surprised to run into one.

That night, the only thing that seemed to run wild in that town was music, and small bands played everywhere, in the backs of bars, on the sidewalks, even in the middle of the street sometimes. For a few hours, Betsy felt normal, maybe even a little happy, and deeply aware of the fact that it wasn't going to last.

When they got back to Miss June's, well after ten, they fumbled noisily with the key out front. Every single step in the stairwell squealed under their weight, and they'd fully forgotten which one of the unmarked doors along the hall was theirs. They wondered, *Are we the only guests*? The key fit into the third door that they tried.

"If you don't stop with the laughing Miss June's going to have to crochet you a ball gag," he said, pulling her inside the room.

"It'll go nicely with my straitjacket," she said, reaching up to put her arms around his neck. "You know I'm not crazy, right?"

"Oh I *know* you're crazy," he said. "Because if you think I'm having sex with you in that ancient, broken bed you are out of your mind."

"Come on! It'll hold up for one more night," she said, grateful that he couldn't see her face, flushed like a radish in the dark. "It's built to last. Just think of how many times it's been given a good workout over the years."

"Holy hell, now there is no *way* that's happening. We could be the latest of thousands of people to be naked in that bed," he laughed, and then stopped abruptly. "Actually, I might vomit."

"Sexy," she said, using her big toe to pry off her boots. She lifted her face to kiss him.

Betsy was used to the fumbling, the clumsy grasping for zippers and buttons, racing through the motions to speed through what felt like the humiliation of her own desire. Somehow, she still thought of that yearning as improper, unladylike. She was deeply aware of balancing her longing with her need to keep her *number* in the acceptable, if not exactly prudent, five-to-ten range until she graduated from college. Even if no one else was counting, she would remember the Georges of her life. With Gavin, it was different. She let him peel the T-shirt away from her torso, easing it past her shoulders and over her head. She moved her hands across his lower back. To him, she was already exposed. Her weaknesses, all of her doubts, had been splashed across the last couple of days.

"I've thought about this at least a hundred times," he said, burying his face in her neck. "I'd see you out somewhere, lurking in the back so no one would notice you, and I'd think, 'How the hell does *that girl* think she's invisible?' I would look at you until I was sure you could feel me staring, but you never did."

"You're so full of shit," she said, turning her face so her mouth was near his ear.

"Usually, yeah, but not about this," he said, softly. "I said to Newland, 'You know that Betsy girl, the one who works at the bagel place? What's her story?' He was like, 'Nah, man. No idea.' Next thing I knew, he was all over you."

He kissed the curve of her shoulder and sat down on the bed as Betsy stood before him, his hands around her waist. She pulled his shirt over his head and smoothed out his hair, the dim glow of the streetlight making the outline of his features just visible.

"What about the rickety bed?" she said, letting her jeans drop to her ankles.

"One more round won't seal its fate."

IN THE MORNING, they were surprised to see three or four older couples seated at two crowded dining tables, draped with extra large doilies, talking about jazz over pastries and coffee in still more chipped porcelain cups. The two of them ate their biscuits, fresh this time, bleary-eyed and sheepish, with a mug of strong coffee on the porch and prayed that no one had heard them stumble through the cramped hallway, or the tired springs of the seventy-five-year-old bed. Betsy went to the hallway to call her mom with her calling card. She was an adult, after all, mostly. She could handle the interrogation.

"Hey, Gavin, check the paper for news about Gainesville, will you?" The story was by now making headlines everywhere. She was sure there'd be something written about it.

Miss June held the screen door open for Betsy and then walked out to see Gavin.

"Y'all from Florida you said, right?"

"Right, we drove here from Gainesville," said Gavin. "Some crazy shit happening down there."

"You better believe it," she said. "Some more of that crazy shit in that paper today."

Gavin scanned the headlines and found the story on the second page. Two more bodies found. He dropped the paper and ran inside, just as he heard Betsy let out a long, low wail.

"He was in the house. I knew it. She's gone," she said through tears. She closed her eyes and covered her face with her hands. *She's gone.*

PART 2

CHAPTER 11
EVERGREEN

August 31, 1990

Betsy's eyes kept closing. She'd focus all of her effort to force them open, straining against the Valium, the Percocet she took an hour after the Valium, and the sandpaper texture her inner lids had acquired after forty-eight hours of sobbing. In a matter of seconds, they closed again. In the brief moments when they were open, her view was strangely menacing. From the passenger seat of Gavin's car, which she'd reclined to a nearly horizontal position, the mid-morning light was diffused through a giant, old cypress tree. Spanish moss hung from its branches like tattered lace, or decaying flesh decomposing from spindly bones. She would open her eyes, shudder slightly, and then they'd close again. How long she'd been repeating that cycle, she didn't know. Finally, Gavin spoke, and Betsy was startled. She kept forgetting that he was sitting next to her.

"We should probably go inside, I mean, eventually," he

said. Betsy didn't know exactly how long they'd been parked. It could have been a few minutes, or an hour. She couldn't say. They found a spot two blocks away from the church, hoping they wouldn't be noticed. In the time since they arrived, the streets had filled with cars, and dozens of people had walked past their car, dressed in mourning clothes. Betsy wore the only black clothes she owned, a cotton knee-length T-shirt dress that was still wrinkled from the box, the thrift store sunglasses, and some oxfords she bought at the Army/Navy Surplus. She spotted a group of Ginny's high school friends piling out of a white BMW, each in double strands of pearls and prim, somber cocktail dresses. Caroline's mom, Viv, in a black suit and an enormous pair of sunglasses, walked toward the church with her head down and her arms folded. Betsy slunk further in the seat.

"That church looks pretty small. And I don't know if they chartered a bus or two, but it seems like all of Gainesville is here," he said. "I just want you to be prepared."

"OK, I'm good. I'm ready," she said. She slid on the glasses she'd bought with Louise and Not-Louise just days before, though it felt like months, years, a lifetime ago.

Betsy looked over at Gavin, who was wearing a navy blazer, a white shirt, and a burgundy striped tie, articles of clothing she couldn't believe he owned. None of it was pressed, of course, and he still looked like a rumpled mess. But the fact that he had ever been within a hundred yards of a Brooks Brothers shocked her.

They walked down to the church, avoiding eye contact with everyone. It was easier for Betsy than she thought, through the fog of the pills. She had been ready to shirk away from hugs, to fend off anyone who approached her to offer condolences, but everyone must have known to stay away from her. Betsy kept her head down and grabbed Gavin's hand, and the two of them winnowed their way through the crowd gathering in the back of the church to the center aisle and squeezed into the end of the second to last pew. At the front of the church, behind the pulpit next to the priest, she spotted her: Caroline.

Once everyone was seated, Ginny's parents, Robert and Martha, made their way in from the steps of the church, puffy-eyed and exhausted. Ginny's older sister, M.J., stood behind them holding a writhing, wailing infant. Ginny hated M.J., who married a pompous young lawyer from Charleston named Griff, or Gruff, or something absurd that Betsy could never remember, and had a baby in the whirlwind eighteen months after graduating. The sisters were lifelong rivals, and since M.J. had gotten married, her newly religious, deeply conservative ways made Ginny look like a Riot Grrrl by comparison. M.J. spotted Betsy on the end of the pew and eyeballed Betsy's men's shoes and the faded, wrinkled dress before she realized Betsy was watching her, and then offered a sympathetic nod and a quick, forced smile. When Martha saw Betsy, her tears welled. She reached over to put her hand on Betsy's stiff, frozen shoulder.

"I'm so sorry," Betsy said. It came out in a dry, throaty voice that Betsy didn't recognize. Gavin squeezed her hand.

"I know you are, sweetheart. Ginny loved you so," she said. Betsy wouldn't look at Ginny's father. What would he, what would any of them, have said if Betsy told them the truth? She was in the apartment when it happened. Through the haze of the pills, Betsy remembered that night like it was a distant dream. She could have stopped it. Gavin reached over to shake Mr. Harrington's hand briskly and wordlessly.

The service was a blur. The priest, who had known Ginny her entire life, but apparently not at all, delivered a service that felt like it was composed entirely from captions written in her high school yearbook. There was a forced anecdote or two, a lot of "gone too soon" rhetoric, some unfortunate allusions to heaven.

"We may find the present moment more than we can bear," he said. Father Tom was a sturdy man with ruddy cheeks and fine, coppery hair that had been arranged and sprayed with impressive precision. He found Betsy's eyes in the back of the church, which were locked on his with seething resentment, and looked away. "Jesus knows that, and so He meets us here. He offers us Himself, promising that our loved ones will rise again, and that our greatest flourishing is yet to happen."

When he finished speaking, Ginny's high school soccer coach said a few stumbling words about her spirit and dedication. One of her high school friends talked about her being the most beautiful of all of the Royal Dames at the debutante ball. And then, to Betsy's horror, Caroline took the pulpit.

She wore a simple halter-neck dress, exposing the muscles and tiny bones of her slim, strong shoulders, and pearl earrings, of course. Her hair was pulled back off of her face. Even from the back of the church, Betsy could sense her calm. Caroline had a note card in her hand, but put it down quickly and shook her head.

"Ginny was my roommate and my sorority sister for the last few years," she started, her voice clear and strong. "Some people might say that she kept me in line, maybe even made me a little nicer, but I doubt it."

There was a low grumble of muffled laughter.

"I know that she was the sweetest person I'd ever met.

And every day we were friends, I was impressed by her kindness. She was funny, too, in that beat-up convertible. Everyone in Gainesville seemed to know Ginny Harrington. She was my best friend. Ginny and Betsy Young and me, um, and I." Caroline searched the pews of the church for Betsy, who looked down at her lap immediately, intensely. She could feel Caroline's eyes scanning the crowd for her, and she tried to will herself to disappear, to condense her body or melt onto the floor of the church somehow. She felt Gavin's leg press against hers and tried to control her quickening breath. What would Caroline do if she knew that Betsy was at the apartment the night Ginny was murdered, that she heard something, anything at all, and didn't try to stop it? Betsy couldn't bear it. It was a mistake, a fuckup of colossal proportions, and she would never tell a soul what had happened. She was high and paranoid, convinced that she imagined she was hearing something: That was her excuse? She felt unforgiveable, small, pathetic, scared. "We had some of the greatest times, and you know, I thought we would have more." Caroline finally started to break, her composure dissolved, and she paused for a moment to collect her thoughts.

"I don't know if Father Tom can help any of us make sense of this, why this happened, why Ginny, why five college kids had to die in this way. I don't know if I'll ever understand. But my hope, for Ginny's sake, is that justice is served, and served quickly. I know that I won't find any peace until they catch that . . . the person who did this to my friend. But I hope Ginny does. I hope she's at peace now. At least that's what they say happens. I . . . I really don't know. I don't think any of us do."

With that, the priest put his hand lightly on Caroline's tan shoulder and she walked slowly back to her seat.

GINNY GREW UP in Winter Park, but her father was born and raised in Ocala, in the house where Nana Jean still lived. Her family had settled there back in the late nineteenth century, and the Harrington family plot at the Evergreen Cemetery was large and overgrown with vines. Ginny would be buried near her grandfather. Betsy knew Nana Jean never suspected that her lovely Virginia, the youngest of her five grandchildren would get there first.

There was a plaque at the front of the cemetery that identified it as a historic place, stating that Civil War veterans and former slaves were buried there. That may explain why the land was divided into two parts by a road, segregated even in death. There were low, crumbling walls, some of the state's only real ruins. Betsy wished that everyone she'd ever met who denied that Florida was part of "the South," the proper South of mint juleps and formal stationery, could see that place. The moss-draped trees, the decaying headstones, the constant buzzing chorus of insects that played in the background all felt as Southern as it gets. And the dark thunderheads rolling in (the Harringtons planned the service and burial for the morning, no doubt, because of the likelihood of afternoon rain, but Florida weather wasn't a system that was easily beaten), cast a heavy, damp pall on the day that made Betsy feel the presence of the past, all of those souls surrounding her, intensely.

"This place is freaking me out," whispered Gavin into Betsy's ear. They were standing on the periphery of the crowd, hanging back so far that Betsy could convince herself they were watching the service on a screen, like it was happening to someone else.

There was a small tent over the freshly excavated earth, and a circle of grieving friends and family that extended about twenty feet in every direction around it. Betsy and Gavin couldn't hear a word of the service until one of Ginny's cousins, a bartender and occasional busker in Tallahassee who Nana Jean referred to as an "aspiring musician," took out a guitar and played "Life Without You" by Stevie Ray Vaughan, who had also died on August 27th, the same day as Ginny. Betsy felt weirdly angry that more people in the world would remember that day in honor of *him* and not the most important person in her world. As the heavy raindrops started to fall, umbrellas shot up one by one, slowly at first, and then in a flurry, like popping corn. Some were tasteful, somber, and black, like you see in the movie-version of funerals, and others were Florida-style, large and garish, awning striped, emblazoned with the crests of country clubs across the state, and pulled from golf bags when the sky loomed ominous and dark.

The smell of rain was intense in the cemetery. The drops fell to the already damp earth, which was dense with decaying plants. Betsy hardly noticed she was wet until there was a low, distant growl of thunder, and Gavin touched her arm and motioned for them to leave. Then she felt someone grab her other wrist.

"There you are," said Caroline, who was holding an umbrella large enough to cover the two of them, but Betsy kept her distance.

"Hey," Betsy said, still hiding behind her sunglasses.

"I assume you spoke to the police? I know that they were looking for you," said Caroline.

"I did. I got your message. I called Officer Mendes and went in to answer his questions yesterday," Betsy said, praying her inquiry would end there.

BETSY AND GAVIN drove back from New Orleans immediately after they saw the story in the paper, after her conversation with Kathy, but Betsy was in shock, not quite believing what she had heard. They found Ginny and the other victim on the same morning, though the woman had been dead for three days. They went to Nana Jean's first, then back to Gavin's house for a bottle of emergency Valium in his medicine cabinet. Then they went straight to the police station. They had settled on a story. Betsy left the party at Weird Bobby's house after her fight with Mack, walked across campus, found a bike, and was riding toward Ginny's apartment. She didn't know Ginny had left the sorority house. As far as Betsy knew, Ginny and Caroline were staying the night there. Betsy was disoriented and scared after her argument with her ex-boyfriend, Mack, and wasn't sure why she wanted to go to that apartment instead of her own. She thought it would be more comfortable. Gavin left the party to come look for her, and spotted her on 16th Street, down the block from Williamsburg Village. Betsy ditched the bike she was riding, jumped in his car, and they made a plan to get out of town, to go visit a couple of Gavin's friends and get away from the chaos on campus. It made sense. It was clear that Betsy was not a suspect, and after a half hour of simple questions about her whereabouts, Betsy was free to go. The detectives had their hands full, trying to catch a murderer, and Betsy, who was barely responsive, wasn't much help. She apologized for stealing the bike and offered to repay the owner, if he or she ever came forward to report it stolen.

"SO THAT'S IT. That's all you have to say to me?" said Caroline.

"What do you want me to say?" said Betsy. "I can barely breathe. You can stand up in front of a church full of people and talk about her, and I can't get through a single sentence without sobbing."

"Do you think that makes me miss her less? Do you think I'm some kind of awful, insensitive person because I'm not a mess like you?" Caroline said.

Viv walked over and placed a hand on Betsy's shoulder.

"Caroline, that's enough," she said. "It's clear that you and Betsy are grieving. Ginny was important to both of you. You can help each other through this, you know. You *need* to help each other."

"I . . . I can't," said Betsy, and she rushed back to Gavin's car to make the short drive to Nana Jean's house. The wide porch that Betsy remembered so fondly was filled with people huddled in small groups, talking in low whispers. They found a corner of the dining room, ignoring a table full of Jell-O salads, casseroles, and a spiral cut ham. The day was far from over. Betsy's mom, Kathy, was driving up to Ocala for the day to offer her condolences to Ginny's family, and Betsy would have to introduce her to Gavin, which she was dreading. Betsy's face was wet again with tears which, like the rain, had started to come down in big, round drops that rolled heavily down her face, dripped off of her chin, and fell to the floor.

CHAPTER 12
THRIFT STORE CHRONICLES

November 17, 1990

Betsy stood in front of the bakery case at Publix, surveying the brightly lit confections constructed from perfect, squat circles of bleached flour, spackled smooth with whipped powdered sugar and shortening, and edged in puffy, colorful trim. In five days, she would be twenty-one. That seemed like a good enough reason to buy a slice of cake, which she planned to eat in the grocery store parking lot before she returned to work as the sole employee of Timeless Treasures, a vintage store, or junk shop, depending on whom you asked, down the street from her mom's house in Venice.

Outside of the freezing store, Betsy popped open the plastic clamshell package and scooped off a swipe of frosting with a weak plastic fork. She placed the airy sweetness—with just the right dash of salt—on her tongue, and all of the bleakness of that place disappeared. She walked slowly through the parking lot, dodging cars driven by ancient drivers barely tall enough to peer over the steering wheels of their white sedans, savoring every crumb. While she waited for the light to turn at the crosswalk, she looked around her and realized that she was the only person on the sidewalk who was actually on foot. Everyone else had wheels: rollators, walkers, electric Amigos. Betsy knew that selling the possessions of long-dead people, surrounded by the practically dying, was no way to be almost-twenty-one. For the moment, at least she had cake.

When she arrived at the door there was a woman outside waiting, impatiently, for Betsy to return from her lunch break, five minutes late. Betsy forced a smile. The woman glanced at her watch, then at the sign Betsy had taped to the window, which said Back at 1:00. Betsy opened the door and flicked on the light switch.

"It's just me today. Sally's picking up some new inventory from an estate in Sarasota," said Betsy, feeling that an explanation was more necessary than an apology. She resumed her spot on a tall stool behind the giant, 1960s cash register and pulled out a spiral notebook to continue the letter to Gavin she'd started writing that morning. Her schoolwork, which she was submitting by correspondence, was almost finished for the semester. She had two more papers to write before she was a college graduate, but the long letters she wrote to Gavin, sometimes as many as three a week, were her last ties to Gainesville. She read a few lines on the page to remember where she left off.

> *If you thought I was already a high-achieving pen pal, just wait. I'm going to be the correspondent to shame all other correspondents. I'm going to own that mailman, or mailperson (mail supervisor?) now that Ole Sally, my boss, has declared my Walkman*

headphones unprofessional. She has also claimed that my reading habit is distracting me from my work, and the customers get the wrong impression about my dedication to selling a bunch of secondhand shit. Or I should say customer, singular, because exactly one person has walked through the door so far today. So One Hundred Years of Solitude *will have to wait until I'm home, in solitude, which I suppose is for the best. And the good people of Venice, Florida, who want to come sort through the belongings of the recently deceased, a pastime sometimes referred to as "thrifting," will now see me scribbling in this spiral notebook and think that I am an industrious employee making some kind of inventory list. When in reality I will be scribbling total bullshit, which I will then put in an envelope with your address on it.*

Betsy searched the desk and her pockets for the black felt pen she had been using, but when she couldn't find it, she relented and used a blue one, even though the sight of gummy, blue ballpoint ink on lined paper made her a little queasy.

Hey, sorry for the pen change. I can already tell that you're blown away by my fancy stationery. It's going to be Mead spiral notebooks for me from now on because I am saving my scheckels (sp? shechles? shekels?) for something amazing. A M A Z I N G! Like, bubble-letter poster amazing. More on that later.

The good news is that today is Saturday and so I have the day off tomorrow. The bad news is that tomorrow is Sunday so my mom will probably read the classifieds, aloud, again. Kathy continues to scour the St. Petersburg Times *in search of my life's purpose. You'd think she would just be happy that the dark days are over. I finally got out of bed. I'm wearing something other than pajamas and I'm out the door by ten. But no. Last week she announced that First Union was hiring tellers, but she was hiding behind the paper like it was some kind of shield when she said it. When I laughed at the prospect, she launched into another one of her lectures about goals. She reminded me that I wanted to be an art teacher when I was in third grade. Who doesn't want to be an art teacher when they're nine? Except you? And look how those dreams of being the Incredible Hulk turned out for you? At least she vowed never to mention the flight attendant thing again. She said, "Oh, clearly that's beneath you." And when I pointed out that, technically, it was above me (pointing to the sky for emphasis), she chucked her toast at my head. Doesn't she know how terribly unpopular a sky waitress with crippling depression is?*

The lone customer in the shop, who now appeared to be perpetually, chronically irritated, cleared her throat to get Betsy's attention and held up a teacup.

Hold on. There's a teacup emergency.

"May I help you?" Betsy asked.

"I have a question," the woman said. "This teacup is missing its saucer."

"That's technically a statement, not a question, but you're right," said Betsy. "It is missing a saucer. That's why we're selling it on the half-price table for fifty cents."

Betsy picked up her pen and got back to the letter.

I have to do something extreme, Gavin. I don't have a choice. I know that I only have $820 and I'm still afraid to leave my house after dark, but I have to get out of here. My mom has a morbid collection of newspaper clippings that she keeps in a folder on her desk in the kitchen. (I had no idea how Goth she was.) But there are no new details. Caroline called once but I can't call her back. She's still pissed at me for spacing out at the funeral. But you know I couldn't deal. Have you seen her? I know I'm always desperate for details. Sorry. I just ate a piece of Publix cake for lunch and now I am crashing, hard, from the sugar. I hope this letter makes it to you before you get here. I have big plans for the big 2–1. We'll go to Sharky's on the pier and I will buy you a shot every time a Jimmy Buffett song plays. It's going to be huge. Then, I've got two more papers to write and I'm done. I'll get my diploma by mail. How's that for a major college graduation flameout? My professors don't know how to deal with me when I call, you know the emotionally fragile girl who lost her best friend thing. So I've just been plowing through the work and sending it in. This semester might be my best shot at straight A's, right? Right? It's a pity party but I'm putting on my best dress and going. My mom wants to see *me graduate, the whole cap and gown thing, but I am not ready to go back. Not even by next month. I know that the killer is gone, and that no one else died after Ginny. But what if he comes back? Until they catch this guy, I won't be able to sleep. And Gainesville? I'm not going back. I'm getting as far away from that place as possible.*

The customer left without buying anything, and the wooden door slammed behind her with a jangle from cheap wind chimes.

That brings me back to that amazing thing I mentioned before: I'm moving to New York. At least, I want to move to New York. And I want you to come with me. Maybe we can figure out the careers we've dreamed about all of our lives together? Are you in?

Betsy paused for a moment, considering what she was proposing. She wouldn't have the nerve to say it over the phone or ask him in person, so this was the only way.

I'm actually totally, deadly serious.

Anyway, sorry for the novella. Pretty soon I'll have to start springing for a second stamp. Write me, please! I need to know that people are out there among the living, buying things that are new or newish, not stuck among the half-dead, wondering how to feel alive again.

Lots of love,
Betsy

CHAPTER 13

THE BIG PLAN

December 31, 1990

Betsy sat cross-legged on the spot of the warped, sloping floor nearest the radiator. Everyone else in the apartment, the ten other stragglers who chose to ring in 1991 downing cheap whiskey in the railroad apartment of Gavin's high school friend Ari on 3rd Street and Avenue B, were complaining about the heat. The harsh, dusty warmth blasting from the paint-encrusted tangle of pipes felt just fine to Betsy. Even a few inches away from it she was shivering, and tempted to dig her coat out of the pile on Ari's bed to wear indoors. Only the fear of being mocked by Ari's friends, all fellow NYU students who were, collectively, quick-witted and cynical in a way that Betsy found incredibly intimidating, kept her from doing it. She was afraid to open her mouth, to utter anything at all that might reveal that she was the hick they all assumed she was, and would rather lose a toe or two to frostbite than admit she was freezing in that airless tomb of a room. She'd first noticed she was cold in South Carolina, the day before yesterday. *Or was it yesterday?* She couldn't remember. They stopped at a gas station so she could use the pay phone and she hadn't been warm since.

Betsy was outside of Charleston before she worked up the nerve to call her mom to announce that she and Gavin were moving to New York. She had rehearsed her short speech across the eastern edge of Georgia and for a few excruciating minutes her mom listened to it in silence. It wasn't until Betsy got to the part about calling with an address when she got settled that she was interrupted.

"You don't even have a warm coat," Kathy said. "Where in God's name are you going to live?"

"Gavin's got a friend in the East Village," she said. "We'll stay with her until we can find a place. Once I get a job."

Betsy pictured her scowling in the silence on the other end of the line.

"I got that leopard coat at the shop, you know with the big collar," she said, wondering why she was talking to her mom about lapels on a pay phone in the parking lot of a Waffle House off of the highway. "I can buy another one. Some gloves, you know, the usual."

"You know that I can't help you right now," said Kathy, sounding smaller, more distant than the five hundred miles between them. "If you're stuck, you're stuck. I won't be able to bail you out."

Betsy couldn't remember the last time she'd asked her mother for help, or even the last time she had told her the truth. She knew she would judge her. She knew she would use the exact tone that was vibrating through the receiver. Betsy pictured her mom standing in the tiny Venice kitchen, a kettle taking forever to boil on the electric stovetop, that low wall of 1980s-era glass blocks behind her that distorted anything you saw through it. She had never been able to talk to her mom about the ugly stuff, the complicated, gritty side of her life that would have made her look like a failure. The fact that Betsy was moving to New York to live with her boyfriend was not information Kathy would share with pride.

"I know," she said. "I can take care of myself."

"You're too scared to go back to Gainesville, but you'll move to New York on a dare? With a boy you barely know? That's taking care of yourself? Betsy, I just don't understand you."

"He's an adult, Mom, not a boy. I'm twenty-one years old. How old were you when you got married, anyway? Twenty-two? You can't call the shots for me anymore," she said, shaking with nerves and rage. New York seemed less terrifying because there was enough noise and plenty of distractions to drown out whatever was in her head, like New Orleans. Maybe there were killers there, but Betsy was convinced it would be easier to spot them or to hide from them. There were other threats back home that her mother wouldn't understand, and Betsy couldn't explain.

Their plan had been hatched after Thanksgiving. Betsy floated the idea in one of her letters, and had been shocked when Gavin asked to hear more about her fantasy life "up north." In the long, rambling letters they'd exchanged during the months she'd spent in Venice, they'd constructed the Big Plan, though all it really amounted to was a rough departure date, a AAA TripTik with driving directions from Jacksonville to Manhattan, and a forced invitation to sleep on someone's lumpy pullout sofa. There was a part of Betsy that never imagined either of them had the guts to pull the trigger.

By mid-December, she had mailed her final pa
couple of boxes with her belongings in the back of her
stashed her warmest clothes in a duffel bag, and boarded a
to Jacksonville. She told her mom that she was spending Christmas vacation with Gavin's family and then she'd decide what was next after that. Kathy stood in the parking lot of the bus station with her arms folded, certain her daughter was making a mistake of some kind but unable to pinpoint exactly why.

"You can always come back when you need to," she said, offering the most discouraging of all parental send-offs.

The day after Christmas, which was celebrated in the Davis household, with his parents and younger brother, Jay, with a cheese log and a HoneyBaked ham, Gavin and Betsy bought a bottle of Cuervo and sat on the beach, wrapped in blankets, passing it between them.

"Let's do it," Gavin said after his final swig. "Neither of us is getting any younger."

"And then I have to say, 'Or any smarter,'" Betsy added, pulling the blanket up around her shoulders. "I have to."

Five days later, she was staring at Gavin as he filled the hallway/kitchen of Ari's place, deep in a fake argument about the Clash with Ari's boyfriend. Gavin, for no reason other than to piss off this total stranger, was firm on his position that Mick Jones could kick Joe Strummer's ass. And his adversary's stuttering response made him smile wide, turn to Betsy, and wink. Betsy mimed drinking a glass of water to Gavin, hoping he'd get one for her, and then she was horrified to realize that he might not know her well enough to know what she meant.

"So Ari tells me that your best friend was murdered," said the sullen girl with deep burgundy-lined eyes, who had been chain-smoking Parliaments on the pullout couch where she

...uld later sleep. She extended the pack, with two ...cigarettes lingering in the bottom. "Want one?"

"Uh, yeah," Betsy answered, struggling to keep her voice from cracking in her throat, which was parched from heat, smoke, and exhaustion. She had kept her anxiety in check as they crawled up the coast, silent through a snowstorm near the Virginia border. Her muscles tensed as the population density increased and the traffic grew thicker until they were at the mouth of the Holland Tunnel, struck dumb by the icy lower Manhattan skyline. She could barely eat. Every couple of hours she'd look over at Gavin, when he was behind the wheel of the car, or last night when he was huddled with her on the pullout under a slick polyester sleeping bag, and freeze in terror. *What have I done?* she thought. She waved to get his attention, and motioned for him to get her a glass of water again, tipping an imaginary glass to her mouth. *Ginny would have known what I meant.*

"So you're saying that Big Audio Dynamite II is your favorite band?" She heard the poor sod plead with Gavin to use reason. "And you're totally OK with putting that information out into the world?"

"So it's true?" the Parliament girl said to Betsy, over the Love and Rockets song Ari was playing on repeat. They'd all split the handful of ecstasy tablets Gavin had offered, stolen from his brother, and driven across many state lines in his backpack, in exchange for a few nights room and board. Ari's kicked in first, and she was having her moment in the corner, vigorously petting her cat, listening to "No New Tale to Tell" over and over again. "Do you know who killed her?"

"Not yet. They had some guy in custody, but he was just some punk kid who beat up his mom," Betsy said. She flashed to the mug shot in the paper, the scarred face, the hooded eyes. She was surprised how she sounded totally unfazed, as though the information didn't sting every time she repeated it. Ginny had been dead for four months. It had already been woven into Betsy's story. Having a dead best friend was her normal. "He didn't do it. The police just needed to put somebody in jail to make the university happy, and that guy's number was up."

"That's major." The girl nodded dumbly, her jaw grinding her back molars to tiny nubs.

"Yeah, real major," said Betsy. "Hey, it's got to be close to midnight, right? Doesn't a ball drop or something? I might go get some air."

She made her way across the small apartment, stepping over bodies, now quiet and huddled in pairs together on the floor, to Gavin.

"So you never learned the international symbol for thirst," she said.

"Oh God, sorry, I saw you but I totally forgot," he said. "I was distracted by what's-his-name having a shit-fit about the Clash. I thought for a second that he was going to jump out of the window if I kept bagging on Strummer, but then I realized it was painted shut."

Betsy filled the one clean cup she could find, a ceramic mug picturing a cartoon porcupine holding a balloon, from the tap.

"Meanwhile, Wednesday Addams on the couch over there was asking me for Ginny's autopsy report," said Betsy.

"You've got to be kidding me. Ari can't keep her fucking mouth shut."

"No, it's OK. I'm alright. I just think I should grab my coat and get some air. Some frigid, lung-seizing air. I can't take that everyone in this room is talking about Ginny."

"That's not fair, Bets. Ari didn't tell everybody. You're just being pa—" Gavin stopped himself before he could finish.

"Oh, I'm being paranoid? Where have I heard that before?" Her eyes locked on his, daring him to continue.

They talked about the night Ginny was killed only twice: once on the drive back from New Orleans, when they decided what they would tell the police, and once just before Kathy came to Gainesville to collect her daughter a week after the funeral, when it was clear that Betsy wasn't going to make it through the semester and she made arrangements to finish her classwork by correspondence. They loaded her milk crates and bags in the back of Kathy's Buick Skylark. It was getting late and her mom wanted to get on the road to start the three-hour drive before dark. Gavin came out to the Embassy Suites, where Kathy was staying, to say goodbye. They were standing in the parking lot as the sun disappeared, leaning against his car.

The details of the night Ginny died were fuzzy for both of them. Betsy remembered riding a bike back to Ginny's apartment, hearing a noise, running out of the apartment and into the street, freezing in his headlights, getting into his car, confessing that she thought someone was in the apartment. She remembered feeling ashamed, nervous to reveal her anxiety. In a twisted way, it felt like narcissism. Of all the women in Gainesville, the female half of the thirty-five thousand students on campus, *she* was the one to walk in on him and live to tell the tale? It felt delusional. Her most vivid recollection was that she did not want to call the police when she was high, or more specifically, she did not want the police to call her mother and tell her that her daughter smoked hash, hallucinated about a murderer, and made a bogus call to 911. Gavin was all too eager to let her off the hook.

"I should have stayed on the line, when I called nine-one-one. I should have woken up a neighbor, used their phone, stayed there, and waited for the police, Gavin," she said, quietly, fighting tears in the hotel parking lot. "I'm such a coward. I'm such a selfish fucking coward."

"No, Bets, no," he said, pulling her closer to him. "You didn't know. You weren't thinking straight. I was fucked up. Mack was being such a psycho. You were scared to death."

"You should just say it," she said, lifting her shoulder to wipe her tears with the sleeve of her T-shirt. "You thought I was out of my mind."

"We were both out of our minds. Jesus, everybody around here was," he said. His voice lowered to a more serious whisper. "And what can we do about it now? You didn't see anything. You didn't get a look at him, or even hear his voice. Should you have told the cops when they were questioning you the other day? I don't know, maybe. Maybe not. Do we call the cops now? That's not going to change anything. Ginny will still be dead. And you will be in major fucking trouble."

"Just me, then? I'm alone in this."

"No, *we*." He shook his head. "Of course. *We* will be in major fucking trouble. It's 'we' now. We're in this together."

IT WAS THEIR secret. They drove it to New York with them like a third passenger asleep in the backseat, like an uninvited guest at the New Year's party.

Gavin checked his watch.

"It's a few minutes before midnight. You're right, we should get some air."

They shrugged on their coats and stumbled out onto the frozen street, over a smattering of smashed plastic bags full of dog shit, some dirty ice patches, shards of shattered glass, and the occasional used syringe to ring in the New Year in Tompkins Square Park. Even in that ugly coat, Betsy felt shiny and new by comparison, like the Easter Bunny, Ginny would say. She thought of Ginny at the Dish in her royal blue skirt, the night that Gavin hopped onto the stage. She thought of Caroline, who she'd been avoiding for months, who didn't even know Betsy was in New York. For some reason, she wanted her to know.

"So how does our first New Year's Eve together rate?" Gavin asked, desperate to change the subject. "Thumbs-up? Thumbs-down?"

"Our first New Year's? I think it might be our first Monday, Gavin," she said, rubbing her hands together for warmth.

"Wait, what's that supposed to mean?"

"Counting this past week, I think we've spent a total of twelve full days together," she said. "And now we're here. Doesn't that seem a little impulsive?"

"And whose idea was that?"

"That's not what I mean. I don't regret it, I just . . ."

"We could turn around and leave tomorrow. It's that easy. We're not locked into anything, but Christ, Betsy, I thought you wanted this."

"I do! God, I'm just trying to be honest, to tell you I'm scared." Her teeth chattered from the cold, from the lack of food, the cigarettes, the shots, the fear. "I don't know if you've noticed, but I've been scared since August. Now we're standing in the middle of this park, which is straight out of a zombie movie. I don't want to talk about Ginny with total strangers and pretend that having a dead best friend makes me deep and interesting. I'm cold. I have no real winter clothes. I'm tired. And I can't go to sleep because Ari's friends are probably giving each other creepy back rubs on the couch, where I currently *live . . .*"

"With me."

"Yeah, with you." She looked up at him through the vapors of her frozen breath and saw him smile.

"It's going to be great," he said. "We're going to make it great."

"How can you be so sure?" she asked.

"I just know it. I've known it since I first met you in Gainesville. You weren't like everybody else. You were into stuff. You were desperate to get out into the world and do stuff, and so was I. From that very first day at the lake," he said. "It was just something I knew was going to happen."

In the distance, someone started the countdown.

"*Ten . . . nine . . . eight . . . whoa, wait . . . six . . . five . . .*"

He kissed her at four.

"You really believe what you're saying, don't you?"

"One hundred percent," he said. "No, wait. If I'm being honest, I'd say eighty percent, minimum. Now let's walk up to Times Square and find us some morons. It'll warm us up."

Gavin swung his arm around Betsy's shoulder and pulled her tight.

"But first we have to find you some mittens," he said. "It's the city that never sleeps, right?"

"Right, but is it the city that never closes its mitten stores?" she asked, as she slid her hand through the buttons of his jacket, temporarily fearless. "That's what we need to find out."

"I'm starting to feel like a local already."

Tiny specks of icy snow began to fall as they trudged across 9th Street, crossing to avoid packs of rowdy drunks, hoping they could figure out which way was north.

CHAPTER 14

DEBRA MUST BE A PI PHI

Winter 1991

New York had been exactly the escape from reality that Betsy and Gavin wordlessly sought. They found a small one-bedroom, a sixth-floor walk-up in the East Village. Its only clear attribute was that it had huge windows that looked out onto the shabby rooftops of the neighborhood, which excited Betsy to no end. The wide-plank floors were decent, but the kitchen was sad and the bathroom was "original," meaning that the once-charming tile and porcelain sink were cracked and stained. Betsy would buy a handful of subway tokens, put them in her red backpack with a map, a banana, and extra layers, and explore the city for as long as she could stand the cold. After every snowfall, they'd wander the streets, thrilled by the crunching sound it made under their boots. And there was music: Tramps, Wetlands, Brownies, even Webster Hall. They'd scrape together enough money for two tickets and walk through the freezing night, passing a flask, to save cab fare and money they'd spend on a bar tab. Betsy would borrow Gavin's leather jacket with too-long sleeves and they would walk down the sidewalk, her shoulder tucked under his arm, her cheeks flushed from the cold, or from happiness, or from both. They would sit across from each other on the subway with dumb smiles on their faces, hardly believing the stunt they were pulling. They were together, in the city. They were so distracted by the constant motion around them that they hardly thought of Gainesville. They were in love.

That was the easy part. Finding employment was more of a challenge. It didn't help that Betsy had no idea what she really wanted to do. She had loved her English classes, but she didn't think she could write. She loved art, but the galleries she had seen downtown were so aggressively urban and cool that Betsy was too intimidated to walk in the door, let alone ask about a job. She scanned the Help Wanted section of the *Times* for something that sounded promising. Her first interview did not go well.

"How sad the sisters of, um, let's see here, Delta-*something* must be to lose you to the big city. When did your bus arrive?" said Debra, the human resources assistant at Schulman & Brown, two years out of Cornell, prematurely world-weary and a condescending shrew well before her time, as she glanced at the last line of the brief résumé on the otherwise empty desk before her. She did not even try to hide her disdain.

"Well, we—my boyfriend and I—drove here, actually? In a Honda Accord, if you're into details," Betsy said, suddenly thinking the navy "interview suit" she'd received from her mother, the one that crushed her with disappointment as she removed it from its box under their miniature Christmas tree and then hemmed in an effort to seem more fashion forward, might be, in fact, tragically short. She shifted her knees far to the left. "Oh, and I'm sure they're managing without me." *Debra must be a Pi Phi,* she thought.

"*We* drove here, did we, Betsy? Or is there another name you prefer?" asked Debra, who was practically smirking.

"Betsy's fine. That's my name," she said, punctuating her sentence with a nervous, machine-gun fire giggle.

"I'm guessing this is your college boyfriend, right? Let me guess. He was a Sigma Chi!" She laughed. "That's going to last. For, like, *ever.*"

"I'm sorry?" *Could this really be happening?* "Maybe we could just talk a little more about the assistant to the editor position? I'm eager to work. I'll do anything, really."

"It pays eighteen-five a year," she said. "But I'm just going to be honest with you, Betsy, you're not going to get it. I've seen five candidates for this position already this morning, and they're all experienced writers, or campus newspaper editors. They've had multiple internships in publishing. They know what editing *is.* You need clips, and not from the sorority newsletter."

That didn't seem like the right time to mention the sorority didn't publish a newsletter. Betsy must have looked stricken, because Debra's expression changed ever so slightly and she tilted her head with feigned concern.

"Look, *Betsy,* I'm just being honest with you. Somebody should tell you this now before you get too settled. It's not too late to go back to Florida."

Betsy focused her gaze on the false grain of the mahogany laminate on the desk between them to steady herself. She could feel her pulse in her ears. Did Debra agree to see her just for sport, or to prove some kind of point? She must have excused herself from the room, maybe even thanked Debra for her time, but she had no memory of how she made it from the office to the elevator, and later onto the sidewalk, where she thought of about a dozen choice comebacks about ten minutes too late. From the pay phone in the ladies' lounge at Saks Fifth Avenue, she called Gavin in tears.

"I'm an idiot." She sighed into the receiver, tears of frustration streaming down. "I'm just not ready for this." No one in the enormous, sixteen-stall bathroom even glanced in her direction. An elderly woman with a tight wash-and-set hairdo sat on the long, mauve pleather bench that stretched across the length of the room under a row of frosted windows, silently reapplying her coral lipstick in the mirror of a case lined with red Chinese silk. *Anonymous,* Betsy thought, feeling the pang of hope that she would one day feel completely at home in this weird city. The woman caught Betsy staring at her, and when she got up to leave, she patted Betsy gently on the arm on her way out, without saying a word.

"She's a bitch," he said. "That wasn't about you. She's stuck in HR interviewing people for the jobs *she* wants. There isn't a kid in the world who dreams about being a human resources assistant when he grows up."

"I guess you're right," said Betsy, still unconvinced.

"Or she's a Pi Phi," he said.

Betsy laughed a short, hard laugh and a stream of snot landed on her jacket. She caught sight of the shiny buttons. *Why am I wearing something with shiny buttons?* She wiped her nose with a tissue and sniffed the receiver. It reeked of Kool menthol cigarettes.

"Just forget about it," he said. "You'll get a job. You're

great at folding. Check to see if the Gap's hiring. Employee discount?"

"Ha. Ha. You're such an original," Betsy deadpanned.

"Come on. We'll go to SoHo tonight for pizza, have a shitty interview party. It's only your first one. We should start a tradition. I suspect we'll be eating plenty of pizza."

"Again, hilarious."

"I know. But we're gonna be alright, B."

Betsy suddenly recognized a perfect opportunity for total reinvention. After walking fifteen blocks in the wrong direction, she spotted a Kinko's, slid her floppy disk into the hard drive of a ten-dollar-an-hour PC, and edited her résumé. With a few clicks of the keys, she metamorphosed into Elizabeth Hammond Young, a self-possessed woman who'd never once drank a pinkish Everclear-infused beverage from a trashcan. Debra wasn't going to tell her what she could and couldn't have, what she did and didn't deserve. She moved the cursor over to the line about the sorority and pressed the delete button repeatedly until the evidence was destroyed. She printed out twenty copies and vowed to get a job before she had to make more.

After a drug test scare and a bottle and a half of Goldenseal, Gavin got a job as a camera assistant on a new cable news show. Betsy, on her way toward becoming Elizabeth, was down to her last three résumés. She spent all of her free time uptown, wandering through museums, starting at the top of the Guggenheim and winding her way down, then moving onto the Met or the Whitney. On an unusually warm and breezy March afternoon, she decided to skip the subway and head down Madison Avenue, peeking in the windows as she went. Near 71st Street, in the window of a shop filled with three-foot stacks of hand-knotted Persian carpets in every size, she noticed a small sign that read Sales Assistant Position Available. Inquire Within. She slid a résumé out of a folder in her backpack and walked inside.

"Gavin, I got a job!" Betsy shouted over the traffic noises into a pay phone at 72nd and Lexington. "It's at a fancy shop on Madison, working for a rug dealer."

"A what dealer?" he said.

"A *rug* dealer, not a drug dealer. It pays in cash, you know, under the table. The owner seems a little sketchy, but I'll just be answering phones and stuff. Now that I'm describing it to you I'm realizing I may as well be working for a drug dealer, but it's a job."

Gavin sang "Let the River Run" from *Working Girl* into the phone, and they celebrated with Indian takeout and a bottle of cheap champagne.

Three months later, she was sitting at her desk with one hand cupped around a hazelnut coffee from the deli on the corner, paging through the *New York Post* with the other, feeling as employed as she ever had. Hazelnut coffee had become her new obsession, and she had one for breakfast and lunch because it was all she could afford, even though she was almost certain it was the source of some significant gastric distress. Regardless, she lost eight pounds on her new regimen and had no plans to stop. When she looked up, she wasn't entirely surprised to see a couple of serious-looking men in dark suits walking through the door, carrying badges that identified them as IRS officers, since her boss had been dodging their increasingly persistent phone calls since the day she'd started. In a rare prescient moment, she stashed the Rolodex on the desk into her backpack. The next day when she showed up for work, the door was padlocked.

About a week later, she downed a double espresso and worked up the nerve to spin through the contact cards and start calling some of the designers she had met at the shop for job leads. One of her favorites, Kenneth Marks, a small, pinched decorator who was constantly taking $30,000 rugs out on memo and hauling them to Litchfield County for a particularly indecisive client, said he would put in a good word for her with the human resources department at an esteemed auction house.

"Wear something nice, Elizabeth," said Kenneth.

"What do you mean?" she asked, glancing down at her Levi's, realizing that she was still wearing the white, ribbed tank top she'd slept in.

"I mean, not that ratty Muppet-fur sweater that you wear every day, and those *shoes,*" he added.

Betsy looked toward the pile of shoes near the front door and found the offending footwear, black loafers with large, square block heels. She could feel her face burn hot with shame.

"Look, you're well-spoken and you're smart. You *can* be charming, when you want to be. And you're sort of blonde, which helps. I know you don't think people notice or care that you walk around with that red backpack and rotate the same three work outfits," he said, "but . . ."

"But what?" Betsy's face burned a little more, but with pride this time. That Kenneth thought she was smart came as a pleasant surprise. Ever since she arrived in New York, Betsy found herself constantly on the verge of apologizing for going to a state school, in the South no less. Whenever she would meet someone and the talk would start about where they went, usually in that coded, subtle way of naming the location of the college rather than its name (New Haven not Yale, Cambridge not Harvard, Philly not Penn), or dropped references to boarding school and summers spent in Maine or on Nantucket, Betsy would notice her pulse quickening a bit in anticipation of her end of the conversation. She would avoid talking about it, if she could. If someone pressed the issue, she would have to explain, again, why she went to school in Florida to some guy who felt superior to her because he grew up riding the train into town to chain-smoke at Moran's, or some other date-rapey bar on the Upper East Side. The truth was, when she was in high school, she didn't realize she had options. Money was tight. The guidance counselor at her high school was brain-dead. She got in, with a little scholarship money. She went. The end. "What is it? But what?"

"But people do. They notice. I think it's time for you to break out that emergency credit card and use it to buy some heels, a decent coat, and maybe even a bag. It doesn't have to be Hermès, just something spunky. Because it is. An emergency."

She took Kenneth's advice and headed to Bloomingdale's on 60th and Lexington, but even after the splurge—the slightly stumpy Charles Jourdan heels, green Coach bag, khaki blazer, and button-down shirt (which she scored for a steal in the boys' department) that she wore with a black stretchy skirt she bought in 1987 for a high school choral performance—she felt conspicuous. When she arrived at the strange little gazebo filled with stacks of catalogues off of the lobby, the three women standing behind it, each wearing a different jauntily tied silk neck scarf and a sleekly tailored navy jacket, looked at her like they had just heard the best joke ever told.

Betsy had thought that Kenneth was being charitable when he sent her in for the interview. Once she passed through the gleaming brass doors into the marble lobby, past the guard in the weird gilded cage and up the important stairs, she was struck by the swirl of officious-looking mean girls filing through the turnstiles in the lobby, and she realized that Kenneth must have detected that glint of uncertainty, even a smidge of self-hatred, in her eyes. He must have known that Betsy was hungry to prove something. He may also have suspected that Betsy had a secret, though he couldn't possibly have guessed what it was. "How may we assist you?" asked the tallest of the three, who had the curious posture of an ostrich and Princess Di hair.

"I'm here to see Cheryl, in human resources," Betsy said. "I'm here for an interview."

She heard a snicker from somewhere in the back, behind a wall paneled with gleaming mahogany.

"Certainly, miss, I'll take you back to Ms. Morgan," said the youngest-looking one of the three, who had lank blonde hair to her shoulders. Her scarf was covered with perky seashells. Once they rounded the corner to a long, carpeted hallway, her voice dropped to a hushed tone.

"Oh God, just ignore them," she said. "They're impossibly mean. There's a girl who works here who's from England and so posh. I mean, they're saying that she's a Windsor, like, she's related to the Queen. And Bea, the big one, tortures her so much that she sucks her thumb in the break room. She's twenty-two! I'm Jessica, by the way."

"I'm Bets. . . . Elizabeth. Elizabeth Young," Betsy said.

"I know who you are. Kenneth told me to look out for you," she added, glancing over her shoulder to see if anyone was within earshot. "Here's the deal: When you get into the interview they're going to ask you if you're married, and what you do on the weekends, and even though it seems like it's illegal or something you have to answer them. Just make it all sound really fabulous even if it's a big fucking lie. I live in Connecticut with my parents in my childhood room with a canopy bed, but they'd have to beat that information out of me. I'm a Catalogue girl. Most of the people in that job are just aiming to get into Client Services so they can meet a rich husband. I've got bigger plans. You're interviewing to be an assistant in one of the departments, and then maybe you'll be promoted to junior cataloguer. I think that's a better fit?" Jessica said, as her eyes scanned Betsy from head to toe.

"And listen, if you get the job, do yourself a favor and buy yourself a nice bag. It'll take you a year to pay it off but it's worth it."

She knocked on the door to Cheryl's office and mouthed "Good luck," and then slid back down the hall. Betsy clutched her new Coach saddlebag reflexively, worried that it was too late to return it.

Jessica disappeared silently down the plush carpeted hallway.

Betsy remembered nothing about the interview, aside from the fact that she thought she blew it. Later that night at Cedar Tavern on University Place, she and Gavin sat up front in the window, which, on that chilly spring night, was fogged around its perimeter like a Maxwell House commercial. She told Gavin about horrible Princess Di and about Jessica from Connecticut, and that she hoped she would get the job just so she could be her friend.

Much to her surprise, "Elizabeth" got the job, on a provisionary basis. She had three months to prove herself. When she walked into the building the first day, she had a vague idea that working there was a rite of passage for twentysomethings who spent their teen years on horseback and tennis courts and summer holidays in Europe, like Caroline, not her. And there was scarcely an hour that passed at her new job when she didn't think of her old friend. Betsy knew she didn't belong there just by eavesdropping on the women who handed out catalogues at the front desk, and the more experienced women who escorted VIPs through the auction previews. They were whispering about handsome divorcées with impressive collections of post-war art, what Yoko Ono was wearing when she came to meet with the contemporary art specialists about selling pieces in her collection. They memorized the gossip columns like they were racing forms and exchanged cookie recipes. Betsy's time was spent behind the scenes, researching and cataloguing prints, lithographs, and lesser paintings for upcoming sales. She was also out of her depth with the department specialists, all experts in their fields and haughty in their own right. She wasn't as certain of her place there as Jessica, whom Betsy quickly realized was a sort of snake charmer, fearless and smiling in the face of viciousness and capable of winning over even the most bloodless of their colleagues.

Betsy was also worried that someone would find out, at any moment, how little she remembered of the tedious art history classes she'd taken, the hours she'd spent nodding off to the sound of her professors droning on about Medicis and encaustics. Betsy loved the way the art made her feel but was lousy with details. Her only defense was preparation, so she read for hours, watched, and learned. She just wanted to press her nose against the glass and peek in for a while, never expecting to survive, there or anywhere, for long.

CHAPTER 15
CONFESSIONS

February 2, 1993

Two years later, no one had caught on to the fact that she didn't know what she was doing, and she was beginning to think that was how the whole system worked. On some level, everyone was faking it, at least a little, pretending like they knew what they were doing until they didn't have to pretend anymore. Betsy's job wasn't exactly the lowest on the food chain, but most days still involved stuffing envelopes, running out for sandwiches, or schlepping around town to pick up signed contracts from clients, who were often reluctant to put their prized possessions on the auction block. Sometimes, the sellers just grew tired of the pieces, and treated their collections as a living thing that needed to grow and change. Most were forced to liquidate out of necessity: a nasty divorce, a death in the family, bankruptcy. Betsy was oddly at ease in the midst of this kind of crisis, almost relieved, actually, to see that other people suffered, too. She was learning not to be so naive, and that even if a life looked perfect from the outside, it didn't always stand up to closer scrutiny.

Once, she waited three hours in the foyer of an apartment that belonged, at least for the moment, to a woman in the middle of a high-profile split Betsy had read about in the *Post*. She sat quietly through the woman's personal training session and an eighty-minute massage, waiting on a stiff bench near the front door, on the receiving end of some wilting stares from the domestic staff. Her supervisor instructed her to not come back until she held a signed contract to sell a coveted, million-dollar Jasper Johns painting. When the woman finally broke down and signed it, she sent Betsy out of the door with not only the contract, but the actual painting, which she then transported back to the office in the back of a cab wrapped in a packing quilt, chewing on her nails over every bump and pothole.

Another advantage was that Betsy was a fast learner without much of an ego, so she figured out which brand of black tea one of her supervisors preferred (PG Tips, never Lipton) and would raid six different delis to find the right kind of potato chips for another one. Things were relatively quiet in the Prints and Multiples department, which was nowhere near as glamorous as Jewelry, or as cutthroat as Impressionist Art, and only the tiniest bit more exciting than Watches, or the lower-priced Decorative Furniture and Interiors Sales. On occasion, she was invited to attend the pre-sale previews and then the sales of major works in the evenings, to mingle with the bidders and collectors. When the gavel dropped and a Matisse cutout sold for over $13 million, chills shot down her spine. Her gut ached with envy when a David Hockney drawing would sell for $6,000, which may as well have been

$13 million, given what she and Gavin were living on. Every piece was out of their grasp. Betsy was aware that she was granted the privilege of attending evening events only because she didn't have chubby legs, and qualified, in the most perfunctory way, as eye candy. She was a clumsy flirt, always concerned that she had nothing to say to the silver-haired men who circled her colleagues. When the pressure was on for her to make small talk with important clients, Betsy tried to channel the ballsy confidence of Caroline, who would act like she owned the place, or the full-blast charm of Ginny, who showered everyone with compliments until they loved her. Just imagining what they would do somehow soothed her.

Jessica had become the closest imitation of a best friend Betsy found at work. They'd run out for coffee and whisper about an assistant in the Rare and Collectible Wine department who was fired for sending a town car to the wrong address to pick up her boss during a snowstorm, forcing her to stand in the taxi queue at the Waldorf, shivering in her evening gown, for forty-five minutes. She was still an assistant, but Betsy was convinced that Jessica was secretly running the place, since she knew every major collector and gallery owner by name and moved with a grace that Betsy envied.

She knew what it was like for the other cataloguers who often cowered and hid from the more elitist specialists. Senior Client Services "administrators" weren't exactly open to socializing below their ranks, either. They were the ones who got to rub shoulders with the big bidders because they never threatened to expose them for not knowing much about what they were waving their paddle at. But the brains of the operation were also, oddly, expected to look the part, as if having even one employee in Payless shoes would cause the stock of the whole lot to drop. Jessica was ascending the ranks, booking cars that drove to the right addresses, using college and family connections to bring in millions in inventory, and knowing the right places to order minimal floral arrangements to thank clients with loose purse strings. At work, "Elizabeth" devoured as many books as she could about contemporary painting, printmaking, lithographs, and twentieth century art, shocked by how little she had learned in college. At home, she drank Pabst Blue Ribbon with Gavin, and scoured *The Village Voice* for every cheap event they could attend in town—free concerts, gallery openings, walking tours, even following every subway line to the very last stop just to get out and explore. Eventually, her boss handed her some actual work, researching the lots that were never worth more than a couple thousand dollars, the grunt work than no one else was interested in. She made calls to dealers and specialists, nervously scribbling and messily erasing notes until she had to print a fresh copy of her research and start again. Betsy was proud of her newfound diligence, how careful she'd become as a full-blown adult. She'd become so terrified of making a mistake, which now meant wearing the wrong shoes, missing an exhibit at the Whitney, or admitting to falling asleep during subtitled movies, and she found the perfect spot to feed and exercise that worry. After every auction that Elizabeth catalogued, she and Gavin celebrated with dinner at Great Jones Cafe, which reminded them of when they were first together, their twenty-four hours in New Orleans.

The culture at the auction house felt uncannily familiar. She was not the center of attention, but she was close enough to the spotlight to feel its warmth. Betsy was surrounded by women and a few conceited men destroying one another for sport, sort of like a redo of college with more expensive haircuts and proper handbags. The difference was that among the hallowed halls, important leather chairs, and gleaming overhead lights, there wasn't a single shadow, no place to hide.

Mostly, Betsy smiled shyly, kept her head down, and tried to stay invisible. She was almost at the end of her third winter "up north" and spent most of the coldest nights on a bar stool, nursing a whiskey, reading a book. Gavin worked most evenings, and occasionally she would get bored and antsy. One of Gavin's coworkers had given him the number of a nameless guy who would deliver weed, whatever you wanted, really, to your front door. She and Gavin were assigned a code, seventy-nine. They would dial the number to his pager, tap in seventy-nine when prompted, and he would arrive with a tackle box full of goods in about thirty minutes like a Domino's pizza delivery man. She and Gavin liked to call him Ian after Ian MacKaye. He showed up one day, on a referral from one of Gavin's late-night work buddies who managed his off hours work schedule with a speed addiction, wearing a Minor Threat T-shirt. Gavin pointed out the brilliant irony of a drug dealer wearing the T-shirt of a band led by MacKaye, a well-known proponent of the straight-edge, sober lifestyle.

"You know, it's a great decoy, the Minor Threat thing," Gavin said, chuckling. "Though I'm not sure the NYPD would totally get the reference."

Betsy scanned "Ian's" face for a reaction, but he just stared at Gavin blankly, impatient for him to stop talking to him about this amusing paradox. Betsy had become his more frequent customer, and she could always sense a relief in the kid's face when he saw that she was the one who answered the door. It was harmless, she would rationalize to herself, just a few pills and pot, and the only repercussion was that she was a little foggy at work the day after a "delivery." Which is one of the reasons she was so startled when the phone rang at work one day, mid-daydream, and taken off guard when she answered it and heard her mother's voice on the line.

"May I please speak to Betsy Young?" she asked, in her most efficient and professional voice.

"Mom?" Betsy asked, her eyes darting around her desk to see if anyone was around to hear. "It's me."

"Oh, hi, darling. Is this a good time?"

"Not really," she said, clicking the top of her Tupperware over the rest of her uneaten lunch. "But I guess I have a minute."

She covered her mouth with her hand and lowered her voice to a whisper.

"Also, I'm *Elizabeth* at work, remember?"

"Oh, darn it, hon. That's right. I've got to remember to be more official." Kathy giggled. She had had time to get used to the idea that her daughter was living in sin, and only asked when Betsy and Gavin planned to get married about once a quarter now.

"So what's up?"

"Well, I don't want to upset you, but I also didn't want you to hear it from anyone else," Kathy said.

"Hear what? What's going on? Are you OK?"

"I'm fine, Betsy, it's just that, there was a story in the paper today about Gainesville. They think they got him, the killer. And it's not that Rhodes boy, either."

The last Betsy had heard of the investigation, before she willed herself to stop obsessing over details and following it completely—not that it would have been easy in New

York, where it wasn't exactly headline news—they'd arrested Dwayne Rhodes, a violent twenty-year-old who attacked and robbed his disabled mother two days before the first body was found, and kept him in custody for longer than what was necessary. It was the only lead they had, even though it was clear to everyone that they had the wrong man. The police needed to save face with the university, which was answering to an understandably concerned student body and their anxious parents who demanded action, but it was a feeble effort.

Betsy's throat tightened. She leaned forward in her chair until her head was practically under the desk.

"Are you serious? Are you sure? What happened?"

Kathy took her time reporting the details she'd read in the local Florida papers. His name was Scottie McRae. He was twenty-nine, twenty-six at the time of the murders, but he could have passed for early twenties with his longish sandy curls and rumpled, slouchy posture. He was a drifter with a long criminal record on the run from authorities in Mississippi. He said he picked Gainesville on a whim, because voices in his head told him that something was waiting for him there when he rolled through on his journey south from his hometown, Biloxi, on the run from the police after he shot at his grandfather. Betsy pictured the bus wheezing and groaning out of the empty depot as it started its journey through the deepest South, across the Panhandle into Fort Walton, Destin, Pensacola, Tallahassee, and on to Gainesville. He bought a ticket through to Sarasota, but, mysteriously, got off two stops early. For nearly seventeen hours, half of them in darkness, McRae must have considered what awaited him in the Sunshine State. *Why Gainesville?* Betsy thought. Maybe he couldn't be still and quiet on that bus with his own thoughts any longer? Maybe he walked off of it and felt relief, with the last, pneumatic sigh of air before the doors clapped shut? With each dot on the map he passed, he widened the gap between the past and the present, between reality and the infinite possibilities of starting anew. He arrived in Gainesville on August 19, 1990.

The worst part of the story, Betsy thought, was that they didn't even arrest him for murder. They picked him up for armed robbery after he held up a convenience store near Orlando. He only confessed to the killings to brag about them to his fellow inmates. The theory was that he wanted to be recognized, to be famous in the way that serial killers, not armed robbers, are.

Scottie had been cooperative, almost docile, with the Orange County jail authorities and in court during his armed robbery trial back in 1991. It wasn't until he attacked a fellow inmate, biting his face in a fit of rage, that the warden started to believe that he was capable of any kind of real violence. Their interest in him was officially piqued, and when detectives from Mississippi started to reach out to law enforcement in states across the southeast to look for someone who fit certain behavior patterns of a man wanted for triple homicide, they started looking more closely at Scottie. Scottie, sensing the increasing scrutiny, must have loved the adrenaline rush it caused and wanted to add to the intrigue, because he started to run his mouth to fellow inmates about the women he assaulted in Gainesville. Eventually, state authorities dug out the blue duffel bag from the box of evidence they'd sealed and stowed away when they first arrested him. In it, underneath some white Reeboks and dirty clothes, were cassettes and a small tape recorder. Scottie made a habit of recording songs, his thoughts, letters he hoped to transcribe and send to his family, an attempt to finally be seen and understood by them. At the end of the one cassette still snug inside the tape deck, which was filled with long descriptions of the women he was following, was one simple but ominous warning.

"I've gotta go. There's something I've gotta do."

The attack in prison and the contents of the bag—including the disturbing tape—were grounds to bring him in for questioning. Three hours into the interrogation, he described in dispassionate detail carving the first victim with that foot-long blade. Then another, and another, until they had linked him to all five murders. The newspapers described it all. Kathy avoided the details specific to Ginny. But as she rattled off the information, Betsy closed her eyes and she was back in Gainesville, on the stolen bike, in Ginny and Caroline's dark apartment. She heard someone clear her throat and opened her eyes to see Jessica standing at her desk, staring at her. Jessica mouthed "What the fuck?" and nodded toward the end of the hall, where the department head and a handful of other supervisors were returning from lunch.

Betsy straightened up in her seat.

"Betsy, I'm sorry," said Kathy over the phone when her daughter fell silent. "But I think we should focus on the fact that he's behind bars, and he will never hurt anyone again."

Kathy agreed to fax the articles to Betsy, and she stood by the machine waiting for the slick paper to churn slowly out.

After work, Betsy raced to the newsstand to see if any of the papers ran the story, and in the following weeks she collected all the clippings she could find. Her mom sent her the manila folder filled with all of the articles she had started clipping back in 1990, and Betsy kept it in a drawer in her desk at home.

Her thoughts took another obsessive turn. Scottie McRae was all she could think about.

"Aren't you feeling at all relieved?" asked Gavin one night after work. They were sitting on the large fire escape outside of their bedroom window, wrapped in blankets, watching the sunset, sharing a six-pack of Rolling Rock. "He's behind bars. He confessed. Those rednecks on the jury are going to give him the chair. He's going to die in the Florida state pen. There's no way that guy's getting out of prison alive."

"I guess I should be relieved," she said. "But now that I've seen his face, it's all I can see, you know? I see his face and I think, *That face is the last thing Ginny saw*. It seems weirdly familiar to me, like I knew him. And I just feel like I'm there, in that apartment, all over again."

On the evenings when she decided to take a long amble home down Madison Avenue past the jewel box stores that sold precious objects to the precious people she avoided at work all day, she would walk through the canyons between towering skyscrapers manned by bored security guards whose revolving doors exhaled indistinguishable men in important suits and women in snug pencil skirts and white sneakers. She would watch them scatter off to Metro-North trains and buses at a very important pace, wondering how many of them had lost someone too soon. Whenever she wasn't distracted by work or Gavin, or Ian's pills, or long runs along the Hudson, she would try to piece together the details of what happened in Gainesville.

She was fixated on the duffel bag. Why did that detail stick with her? Betsy hated to admit it, but McRae had what people might describe as a sympathetic face, handsome even. He had a strong jaw and a delicate nose, and eyebrows that turned down at the corners, slightly, so he wasn't likely to be pegged as a murderer or an armed robber at first glance, though he was both several times over. His eyes were what gave him away eventually, though. They were hollow and haunted. The look of them made her so sick she could never stare at his picture in the newspaper for long.

Of course he found Gainesville, she thought. The town was flat enough to suit a bike without gears, easy enough to navigate, big enough to absorb strangers in its daily routine without anyone noticing. And the sun's glare hid everybody's flaws for a while. There was a revolving door of people showing up for the party. How many times had Betsy turned away random guys just like him when they stumbled into the bagel store, drunk and desperate, asking for food? Maybe he was one of them? He looked familiar, but she couldn't place him. It had been two and a half years since she left Gainesville, and she had filled her brain with new scenery, as many distractions as she could, in an effort to erase those memories. Now she was struggling to recover them and it brought out a certain recklessness in her. Every night, she fell asleep wondering how many times she could be in a room with a murderer and still make it out alive.

PART 3

CHAPTER 16

NUMBER 79

August 27, 1995

Betsy noticed the sheets first, which were dark and flannel, and completely unfamiliar. *Is that . . . plaid?* she thought, recognizing how odd it was for her to be asleep on top of a bed made with a combination that she found so offensive. She struggled to focus her one opened eye, which felt heavy and crusted at the edges.

That usually meant that the previous night involved too much bourbon and a couple of lint-covered pills that she found buried in a pocket. She scanned the room for familiar details: the IKEA school clock on the wall that she loved but Gavin hated because of its faintly perceptible ticking, the chipped, black dresser she found on the street when they first moved into their place on the Bowery, the fraying, stuffed armchair in the corner that was always piled high with their rumpled clothes. When she spotted nothing she recognized, a shot of adrenaline coursed under her skin, and it took her roughly twenty seconds to execute her quick escape. She checked to make sure she was still wearing the last article of clothing she remembered putting on (a vintage sundress, which was cheery enough to draw disapproving glances from her colleagues, even under a prim beige cardigan), scanned the bed to see if there was another occupant beside her (there wasn't), and surveyed the rest of the sad studio. Despite her panic about waking up, again, in a stranger's apartment, she couldn't stop her mind from wandering back to her favorite moment of *Wall Street*, ca. 1987. Whenever she saw an "exposed brick wall," she thought of Daryl Hannah's withering critique, and remembered what an impression that movie made on her. It was when she first realized that New York was amazing, which she now realized was not the intended moral of the story. There was no time to consider the profound impression Gordon Gekko left on her young mind, and the ripple effects that would push her toward this place, through uncertain waters, and eventually to this weird little hovel of an apartment, whose current occupant was unknown. She spotted an asymmetrical slice of light under the crooked bathroom door and knew her next moves had to be stealthy and swift. Betsy scooped up her shoes and her bag, which were dropped on the floor next to the bed, and as she stooped down she realized, to her horror, that it was actually a futon, and raced out of the battered front door down far too many flights of stairs. Betsy burst past a row of neglected mailboxes in the vestibule and out onto a sidewalk. She identified her whereabouts instantly by smell alone. In the far–West Village, one avenue from the Hudson River, the pre-dawn sounds and odors of slaughterhouses at work on a muggy summer morning were unmistakable. She checked her watch. It was nearly 5:00 a.m. She remembered it was Saturday.

As she trotted east, she raced through all of the pertinent details of the situation: Gavin was out on Long Island, fishing in Montauk with a few of his friends. It was way too early to call and check in, and if he had called the house the night before and left a message on the machine, Betsy would claim that she missed it because she was out, and she crashed at Jessica's house, again. She had stayed in town to finish the October auction catalogue before it shipped to the printer, one of a small, skeleton crew left behind while the rest of her higher-ranking colleagues scattered to other less aromatic, or more pleasantly fragrant, end-of-summer vacation spots. She imagined all of them putting distance between themselves and oppressive Manhattan, on small prop planes, or jitneys, or gleaming wooden speed boats with tiny American flags flapping at the stern. Jessica was visiting her family in Martha's Vineyard, but Gavin didn't know that. Maine and Nantucket and the homes behind-the-dunes across Long Island didn't reek of animal parts and sun-warmed garbage, or oily water stagnating in gutters. She and Gavin had ventured out to some of these places, for weddings and long weekends, and were amazed by the crispness of New England, the brisk sweater-across-the-shoulders evenings, its polished, rust-free boats, and utter lack of rowdy, beer-soaked beach bars.

Betsy had spent most of her summer-Friday evenings working on a fall sale of modern prints, poring over every book she could find about the artists. She was deep into research on a series of Frank Stella prints, dizzy from the rainbow bright optics, feeling as wonky as an irregular polygon after filling her brain with as much information as she could before her colleagues suspected that she didn't really know what she was talking about.

Thanks to a little boost from Jessica, who was now high on the chain in Client Services, where she was determined to stay even after she found a rich husband, and wasn't embarrassed to admit that her goals had been modified slightly, Betsy was promoted to a more senior position in her department. Prints was still the shabby cousin to Post-War and Contemporary Art, or any kind of painting, really. Even still, every time she discovered the price of a coveted item, the fact that it was beyond her reach, that all of it was beyond her reach—most of them more than her rent—filled her with doubt about her choices and a sense of defeat.

She left the office at around 8:30, so confused by the psychedelic midcentury time warp she had been in for the last few hours that she wasn't certain of the day, the month, or even the year. After a head-clearing stroll through the city on a sweltering summer night, she remembered. It was August 1995, almost exactly five years since Ginny died.

Like Betsy, Ginny would have been twenty-five, about to turn twenty-six, with a job of some kind. Betsy imagined her living in the South somewhere, though she couldn't place her anywhere precisely. Betsy often wondered what would have become of her friend if she had lived. When she pictured Ginny at twenty-five, she imagined her somewhere lovely, surrounded by fabric samples and paint chips, pinning images to mood boards in an interior design office, debating the merits of brushed nickel or chrome hardware. If she weren't already married, she would have been engaged, though God knows to whom. Betsy had to stop and imagine herself erasing her mind, to actually picture herself with a chalkboard eraser wiping all of her dreams about Ginny away, to push the beautiful bleakness of a life never lived out of her mind. It hurt just to think about it, so she rarely did. Better just to try to piece together her own messy life, starting with last night.

Betsy had a vague memory of wandering south on Madison Avenue, wondering which of her favorite dives she'd end up in that night: Siberia Bar in the 50th Street subway station, Smith's in Hell's Kitchen, any of the dark, depressing holes near Penn Station. Every once in a while, she and Gavin would splurge on two martinis at Bemelmans after a movie at the Paris, or order rare steaks at Les Halles, share a bowl of pasta and a bottle of red wine at Gino's and fool themselves into thinking that they'd become real New Yorkers. But when Betsy was alone, she would explore a different side of the city she was growing to love. She would buy some fancy Fantasia Lights at Nat Sherman and then scour the city to find the dankest, cheapest bars she could, park herself on a stool, and sit, hunched over a Jameson on the rocks.

Had she been to any of her favorite places the night before? She rustled through her bag as she walked to dig for clues, a receipt, a matchbook, any kind of breadcrumb she could follow that would help solve the mystery. But she came up short. She remembered a pool table, someone daring her to try to smuggle the cue out of the bar in the back of her dress, the angry bar manager asking her to leave, and finding it all hysterical. After that, she went blank.

In the hazy light of dawn, she attempted to distract herself by watching the other people milling about on a Saturday, which amounted to a couple of joggers, some small groups of two or three stumbling guys making their own messy walks home from the night before, and a single, dedicated hooker.

It had been close to six months since she had woken up on a strange couch, four months, minimum, since she was shaken back to consciousness in the backseat of a cab by a driver demanding his fare. Technically, she was only lying to Gavin about her whereabouts, not exactly cheating, though it felt to her like an equal betrayal. What's worse is that she thought, obviously incorrectly, that she had made progress.

A year or so earlier, when Gavin started working a crushing graveyard shift at a twenty-four-hour news network, their conflicting schedules took a toll. They both found themselves with many unoccupied hours, post-work, which, needless to say, they didn't always fill with sushi-making classes and gym time. While they never discussed it directly, Betsy sensed that Gavin hadn't been the poster boy for fidelity, either.

"I don't envy the single people," Betsy would say, in a not-entirely-convincing tone, as they walked past endless bars filled with their twentysomething peers casting sullen looks at each other over a feedback-heavy soundtrack of angsty alt-rock. The music on rotation on their sound system at home, pulled from stacks of CDs they piled on the floor—Portishead, Elliott Smith, and Red House Painters when Betsy chose the playlist, and Guided by Voices, Superchunk, and Teenage Fanclub when Gavin was in charge—didn't distract either of them from those feelings that having a happy, conflict-free relationship at twenty-five was incredibly uncool.

"Yeah, that looks pretty lame," he would say. "But maybe we should go check it out, have a drink, like we're performing a kind of social experiment?"

Her love for Gavin was resolute, but her curiosity also ran deep and, like many people who paired off young, Betsy had an itch to explore, or at least *observe,* her options from a semi-safe distance. Her evenings on the town without him would start innocently enough, with cheap happy-hour outings with the few colleagues with whom she'd forged some awkward friendships. She would tell people she was shy, and in return they would offer a sympathetic nod, with patronizing pursed lips and sad eyes, that suggested they understood that she was out of her depth, struggling to keep up. It surprised her how no one could tell that she wasn't actually an introvert, just an imposter using social anxiety as an excuse to stay away. She danced around making actual friends, but would pull back when she felt them get too close. Once in a while, she gave into Jessica's badgering her to go out for drinks, and would join her and a few colleagues, including a fastidious young guy named Nathan from Chicago, who was a walking, talking decorative arts catalogue, and Shana, who looked like a Parisian waif, with a jet-black pixie cut, until she opened her mouth and let Port Washington, New York, fall out with her accent. Even though Jessica's parents had the right zip code in Greenwich, they did not have the usual bankroll that accompanies it, so on the rare occasion when she had to pay for her own drinks her taste was more Pabst Blue Ribbon than Châteauneuf-du-Pape. They would venture well south of 57th Street to some of Betsy's favorite dives, and she would play nice for an hour, a couple of rounds of drinks, and then inevitably she would wander out alone. That would lead to confessional conversations with strangers (mostly male), which sometimes led to a bump of coke in a graffiti-covered bathroom, and then, to her continued horror, more than a few nights when she didn't make it home. She worried that the slept-at-a-friend's-place excuse wouldn't hold with Gavin much longer. And the guilt she felt for her behavior, that she would betray the one person whom she felt she could trust, was crushing. When Betsy tried to rationalize it, she'd say it was a reaction to her life, which was becoming more sterile and predictable than she'd expected. It wasn't just about the culture that surrounded her, the grungy, smeared lipstick, don't-give-a-shit atmosphere of New York in the mid-1990s. She still felt the stinging urge to live dangerously, to creep right along the knife's edge between her real life, the one in which she appeared to be thriving, had a respectable job, and a happy, committed relationship, and the life of punishment she thought she deserved. Betsy wondered how long she could beat the odds and stay out of harm's way when she was blackout drunk and alone in the city, or how long it would take before the world discovered she was a fraud.

No matter how hard she tried to shed her former life, to live in the present without the uncomfortable burdens of the past, she couldn't. It would inch its way back in like morning fog, and then she'd try to burn it off, by getting wasted with strangers and dabbling in drugs. With the right combination of whiskey or tequila or bourbon and Percocet or Vicodin, or whatever her "guy," the reedy, nameless punk with a backpack full of any chemical distractions said was an adequate stand-in, she could forget. And that night, she pushed it too far, and ended up on a futon covered with plaid flannel sheets.

When she got to 6th Avenue, she noticed a handful of stragglers leaving the Limelight at dawn. One woman in a filthy vintage slip and a molting stole was walking slowly along the side of the club, which was a converted church, dragging her fingers along its stone facade. Betsy noticed her slow, muddy movements and realized that she must be a heroin addict, about the same age she was. She thought, on paper, at least, how they were slightly different expressions of the same being: early twenties, white, female, damaged beyond repair by some unseeable evil. She paused on the sidewalk to watch her, wondering how alike their stories were.

"What are you looking at?" the woman slurred, shaking the scuffed metallic sandals in her hand at Betsy angrily.

"It's fox, isn't it?" said Betsy. "Your stole. I've seen plenty of fur in the last few years, and I'm guessing it's fox."

"What are you even talking about?" said the woman, struggling to bring her eyes up to meet Betsy's, though her gaze stopped at her collarbone. *"Bitch."*

The Courtney Love impersonators, the women who wore shredded vintage slips and over-the-knee stockings, smeared eyeliner, and tiaras, had either moved on to shrunken T-shirts, L'Oréal Rum Raisin lipstick, and schoolgirl skirts, or were too out of their minds to notice that the rest of the style-savvy world had left this moment behind. This one in the thrift store stole—in August—was one of the leftovers.

"So what happened to you?" Betsy asked, undeterred.

"Nothing happened to me. Nothing I didn't want to happen to me. Now will you just fuck off?"

"Well, something happened to *me*. And we might be more alike than you think," Betsy said. She thought if someone were making a bad movie about this moment, she would offer to buy the junkie coffee. And maybe they would sit in a charming diner and share their stories until she sobered up. The woman leaned against a building and examined her forearm, which she had scratched raw with her own fingernails.

"Me and you? We've got nothing in common."

Then, Betsy thought, maybe she'd reach out and touch her arm and say something like, *It's not your fault*. Betsy went on, despite the fact that she was being ignored, as the woman inched further away from her, and she raised her voice to project to this mess of a passing stranger.

"If this were a movie, now is the time I'm supposed to say 'It's not your fault,'" said Betsy. "But I have a question for you. What if it is? What if it is your fault? Or my fault? What then?"

BETSY WENT TO the diner anyway, just by herself. She took a seat at the far end of the counter at Joe Jr.'s and ordered hash browns, coffee, and a small orange juice and, newly fortified, made the trek the rest of the way home in the bright sunlight. She was grateful to be alone in their apartment. After a couple of years on the Bowery, they'd upgraded to a slightly larger one-bedroom in an elevator building on East 10th. The galley kitchen was an improvement, and the light streaming in the windows from the sixth floor was cheery enough, even midwinter. It was also close to McSorley's, which made Gavin absurdly happy. The summers, however, were rough. There was a single window air-conditioning unit in the bedroom that was on its last legs and no match for late August.

Ever predictable, Gavin had left a message for her the night before, but he would be deep into the Atlantic on a boat off of Montauk by the time she got it, so she decided to sleep it off first and call him back later. When she woke at around 2:00 with a splitting headache, the apartment was an oven. The windows were open and the traffic noises indicated a busy Saturday five floors below. She shuffled into the bathroom in search of Tylenol, but only after she checked her bag and the pockets of her favorite jeans to make sure she was completely out of anything stronger. She threw on one of Gavin's old T-shirts and some cutoffs she'd had since college, then she ventured out to the corner deli for a Diet Coke and a turkey sandwich. Afterward, for lack of anything better to do, she rearranged their sagging, homemade cinder block bookshelves, organizing the books alphabetically by title, and debated doing some laundry. She scanned the paper for movie showtimes and decided on *The Brothers McMullen* at the Angelika. But first, she thought, at about 4:45, she would page the kid.

Even after years as a loyal customer, she did not know his name, and he claimed not to know hers, though he must have scanned a pile of mail on his way out of their apartment at least once, or noticed their last names (Young/Davis) on the buzzer.

At 5:10, the buzzer rang.

"That was impressive," said Betsy, when she greeted him at the door.

"You know." He shrugged, swinging a heavy black backpack off of his shoulder. In a backward Yankees cap, a plain white oversized T-shirt, baggy khaki shorts that fell just below the knee, and a hormonal constellation of acne across his scruffy chin, this entrepreneur looked twenty, tops. "I was in the neighborhood."

He wandered over to the small table with two ladder-back chairs pushed against the living room wall, where she and Gavin ate when they weren't "dining" on the couch. He unzipped the bag and pulled out a well-used tackle box. Betsy propped herself on the arm of the sofa, trying to look nonchalant. At first, she'd page Ian only when Gavin was home. Now, it was something she did almost exclusively when he was out, and more frequently than she wanted to admit.

"I'm running low on the Vics, but I've got this killer new stuff called Oxy," he said, unfastening the latch of the box and peeling open its hinged drawers and dividing it into sections with his thumbs like he was separating orange slices. "I think you would be into it. Wanna try? I've also got this crazy good bud from Hawaii. Smells like Christmas."

"It better not be as strong as that other stuff," said Betsy, who lost two or three unaccounted hours last time Ian had something new to share.

"Aw, come on, old lady. What are you, twenty-nine? Thirty, tops."

Betsy clenched her teeth. She hated when people thought she looked older than she was. It was her eyes. The hollows aged her. She watched as he plucked a few large, white pills from one of the middle drawers and slid them into a small Ziploc.

"Ziploc!" announced Betsy. "Aiding and abetting criminal behavior since 1968."

Ian turned to look at her

"That's what you think I am? A criminal. What does that make you? My accomplice?" He shrugged. "Selling it, buying it, we're in the same boat."

They avoided eye contact as he pinched the murky pink weed into an expert joint.

Betsy moved to the sofa to find her water glass and took one of the pills with a single, swift gulp. Ian lit the joint, took a drag, and passed it to Betsy. It still scorched her throat every time. She would start to worry when it didn't.

"I don't think I'm better than you, if that's what you're implying. The way I see it, we are more in the same boat than you realize," she said, as she stifled a cough. "I'm not as innocent as you think I am."

"Oh, so seventy-nine has a past. You and your man, Mr. Decoy, on the run from the law?"

"Not exactly running, I don't know. I guess we're running from something, but we're not wanted in ten states or anything." She motioned with one hand to clear the smoke while she reached for the joint with her other. "I think that what I'm doing could best be described as avoiding, which is like a passive running."

He nodded, silent. The kid wasn't much of a talker, which made Betsy talk even more.

"I had some dark days. I lost my best friend. I let her die."

Four months earlier, in March, Scottie McRae had been tried on five counts of first-degree murder in an Alachua County courthouse, and the details of the student murders in Gainesville once again flooded the news. Betsy thought about calling Caroline at least once a day in the weeks after the verdict was read and he received the death penalty, but she didn't have her number, and was too chicken to call her mom, Viv, at her Miami office to get it. Now that she knew he was behind bars, with no possibility of parole, Betsy was desperate to tell someone what had happened, and thoughts of Caroline kept surfacing. Eventually, she got a recommendation for a therapist from Shana at work and called her instead. It worked for a while. Then she found herself confiding in Ian.

"I knew he looked familiar," said Betsy, wondering how long she'd been talking, how long Ian had been sitting on the chair opposite her, leafing through a year-old issue of *The Atlantic*, listening. "Once I saw his face in the papers, it haunted me for weeks. I said to myself, 'He looks so familiar.' It was eerie as hell."

She heard herself talking, how much she sounded like a stoner, and she hated herself for it, but she couldn't stop. She told him about the dreams, the persistent visions she had of the night Ginny was killed. Warmth radiated from the base of her skull, forward to her hairline, and down her spine. The new mystery pill she swallowed was doing its job.

"I knew I had seen him before, but where? I couldn't figure it out. Then one night, I don't know when, maybe in June, while I was hauling bags of groceries back from Gristedes, I figured it out. It was one of those quiet, warm nights with no sirens wailing, and I felt calm and still even with two heavy bags in my hands. Even that sweet, rotten smell that comes up through the subway grates, you know what I mean when I say sweet? It didn't bother me."

"It's rat poison," said Ian, nodding intently. "That's what my grandma says."

"Oh God, really? That's depressing. Well, even that sweet, rotten smell didn't bother me that night. It was like my brain was turned on to some different frequency, or something."

Betsy had pieced together a profile of her friend's murderer from newspaper clippings and interviews with McRae, which had been published after his conviction the previous year. From what she had read, McRae dropped out of high school and spent his late teens and early twenties in a constellation of prisons across the South, robbing stores and stealing cars. He had been abused as a boy by his father and his grandfather, both mechanics with anger issues, and had his wrists taped to his brothers' and been shoved to the floor more than once, just for sitting on the furniture in muddy jeans. Then, he was the one who started taping wrists, and found the power too delicious to resist.

She knew she'd seen his face before, but she couldn't place him for months.

"So one night I was walking home from the grocery store

after work, like I said, and I got about twenty feet away from our building and I just stopped. I dropped the bags on the sidewalk and I thought, 'Taco Bell.'"

McRae was the loser on the bike at the Taco Bell, the one she saluted, the words echoed in her head. *McRae handed Ginny the marker at Walmart.*

"Aw, man, I could use some Taco Bell right now! Stat!"

"No, you don't get it. I *saw* him, and my friend Ginny did, too, at Taco Bell. She wasn't a random victim. The guy who killed her *chose* her. Or worse. Maybe he chose me and got the wrong girl."

She could picture him standing in the kitchen of Ginny and Caroline's apartment waiting for them, the water dripping from his hair onto the linoleum floor in steady, rhythmic drops as he raided Ginny's fridge. According to the press, it's what he had done in all of the apartments. He came in, searched for snacks, and took his time looking through the rooms. He couldn't have found much. There was rarely more than a couple of bruised apples, a brown banana, a few condiments, and some expired yogurt in the fridge. She imagined his gloved hand moving along to the cabinet, over a jar of popcorn, a bottle of expensive maple syrup, and a box full of flavored instant oatmeal. And he took a shower.

Her vision of him was so vivid that she could smell his stench from sleeping in a tent in ninety-five-degree heat, the camp he set up in the woods off of 34th Street behind Bennigan's. It was secluded enough, hidden from the street by the thick overgrown scrub around it, but easy to get to through a hole in the fence at the far end of the bar parking lot. How many times had Ginny driven by, not knowing what or who was hiding back there? He would find a neglected pool to jump into when he couldn't stand his own filth. When he needed to rinse off the blood, he found a hose for a quick blast over to clean his hands and drench his shirt and filthy jeans. He was almost caught once, by a superintendent of one of the large apartment buildings nearby, who saw the man rinsing clothing from the hose in the back of the building and threatened to call the cops, but never did. But once he was inside the girls' homes, he was concerned that they would notice his foul smell and sense his presence, so he cleaned himself up. In his mind, it was a seduction. He needed to think that the women wanted him, and he was making himself presentable, more desirable. An actual shower, with soap and hot water, had become a rare event, and he likely took his time, and breathed in the scent of Ginny's shampoo, which smelled like the tropics.

She pictured him toweling off, rifling through the medicine cabinet. Caroline had done the same thing dozens of times at parties around town, so it was stocked with prescription bottles written to at least five different names. Maybe he stashed the Percocet in his pocket for later. He needed to stay sharp.

According to police interviews, it had been easy enough to get into the place. One thing about Gainesville was that the doors were rarely locked, and if they were, it was easy to pop them open like a can. Old Florida windows, the ones with the long, narrow panes of glass that opened with a crank, were the easiest to get into. All you needed to do was slide a couple of those narrow panes off of their tracks and pull yourself inside. Betsy had done it herself when she was locked out of her house once. Or a person could hop onto the back balcony and jam a screwdriver into the lock of the sliding door so fast that no one would notice. He could be inside in under a minute and no one was the wiser. She thought of him browsing through the apartment with a small flashlight between his teeth, examining the bookshelf next to the television and its stack of old videotapes—*Purple Rain, Dirty Dancing.* Did he notice that it wasn't like the other apartments he had seen over the last week, all of them mostly the same with a futon, a plastic crate of books, one of those lamps that cast a sickly greenish light on the ceiling? Did he notice it was special? There was a rug that looked worn but expensive, real wood furniture, and a big chintz sofa. Betsy remembered the silver frames that were clustered on top of the tables, showing the girls in various poses: dressed up but cross-eyed drunk at a formal; Ginny glancing over her shoulder on a bike against a background of the bluest water in the world; Ginny and Betsy hanging upside down from a tree, their T-shirts falling down to expose their tan, teenage skin. He would have remembered them from the drive-thru, the way Ginny called him "Sir," like no one ever did. Did he remember the way her ponytail blew in the wind behind her? Did he see Betsy's face and think of the salute? Of course he did. That's why he was there. It was no coincidence.

McRae blamed the murders on a multiple personality disorder, claiming that a thing, a dark force, took over that convinced him to kill. But if he started following them at Taco Bell, he spent days trailing after Ginny. McRae confessed to stalking his victims for a day or two, sometimes trailing after multiple women at once. Then, Betsy wondered again, was it really Ginny he was after? Or Betsy? Could it have been Caroline? When he broke into that apartment, who was he expecting, even hoping, would walk through that door? Once he had Ginny in his grip, in the dark apartment, and was close enough to look directly into her terrified eyes as he wrestled her onto the ground, was he relieved, because she was the one he really wanted?

Ginny's hazel eyes shone through those picture frames, and Betsy hoped they peered through to him, bored into his brain.

Betsy saw Scottie McRae in her dreams, in front of Ginny's car, in the aisle at Walmart, in the shadows at Weird Bobby's party, ordering juice at Bagelville. She would be riding on the handlebars of Gavin's bike, but she'd turn around and see that it was Scottie pedaling hard, his hot breath on her neck.

Did he hear me laughing when the markers dropped near his feet? wondered Betsy. Did her irreverence set him off, and seal her fate as his next victim? Or when he reached out to hand it to Ginny, did he feel her skin brush up against his sleeve and realize his good fortune? Like the gods had intervened and delivered this girl to him. She remembered that Ginny blushed crimson at their exchange. Was there a flash of recognition before she quickly looked away?

She read about the blue duffel that he had strapped across his chest, the tapes, about the knife that was inside. How did he find out where they lived? With the traffic the way it was, and the stoplights, and the thoughtless way Ginny drove her car, it must have been easy for him to follow on a bike. Betsy must have tried to piece together that day after they left Walmart hundreds of times. They dropped Betsy off at the record store, and went back to the house. Did he wait there for Ginny and Caroline after they went inside? He had nothing better to do than watch those pretty girls come and go for hours. It was after midnight by the time she left, and she and Caroline never would have noticed the man across the street as he hopped on a bike and followed the two of them in Caroline's car down the hill to their apartment.

He knew there was a pattern. After a few days of following them, McRae knew no one would be back at that apartment until after midnight. He'd hide behind the bedroom door and grab her, tape her mouth, quickly bind her wrists and ankles like he did his other victims. He would draw his knife out of the bag, put two strips of duct tape together on his left hand, and find a spot in the shadows to wait.

THE GIRLS AT the sorority house didn't remember seeing Ginny leave. She was in the TV room until at least midnight, and someone remembered seeing her in the back with her arms outstretched in an exaggerated yawn. She asked Nan, the house supervisor, for an ice pack and some Excedrin earlier that night, which she washed down with a Diet Coke. She had a headache, everyone remembered her saying, and nothing she tried would dull the pain that crept in after lunch and lingered over her right eye. Even the nap she took after dinner in one of the cool, dark rooms lined with bunk beds upstairs where all the residents of the house slept—the "sleeping porch" system many sororities adopted after Ted Bundy's killing spree at Florida State, designed to keep the girls together in one room, naively thinking there was safety in numbers—didn't help. She and Caroline were sprawled out with at least twenty other students on the floor, half-awake, half-watching a lame thriller on VHS they'd all seen at least twice.

She must have grabbed her bag and her keys from her mail cubby and tiptoed out the back door for fear of being caught. Betsy remembered the air that night, how it felt cool and wild in her ears as she coasted down that same hill on a stolen bike a few hours later. The emptiness of the streets and the dark quiet of the night must have made her feel better almost immediately. She thought of the conversation she and Caroline and Ginny had in the car on the way to Walmart. *What are the odds?* She remembered Caroline saying. *In a town this big?* Ginny needed her migraine pills, to be alone, peace and quiet.

In her visions about that night, Betsy pictured Ginny walking inside the apartment, putting her keys in her bag, and walking down the hall toward the kitchen for a glass of water, which she'd need to take her medication. When she opened the refrigerator to pull out the pitcher, did she notice, in the pizza-slice of light it cast onto the counter and linoleum floor, a puddle of water? A used spoon or a bowl? Anything that would have hinted that she was not alone?

She must have been too tired to think, or to register that anything appeared off or out of place. The days had been endless since murder mayhem began, and Ginny wanted so much for life to get back to normal, to get back to class and a regular schedule, and to figure out whether she and Betsy would have a shared afternoon off for *Oprah* and popcorn for another semester.

Ginny could have been halfway up the stairs before she registered that the hall light was on. Did she peer up at it and notice a few dead moths in the dome of frosted glass, like Betsy had, and realize that she had never seen it illuminated? Did she see how the yellowish light cast strange shadows down the carpeted stairs, showing stains she'd never seen before and odd scuffs and marks on the white paint of the walls? Did she pause at the top of the stairwell, sensing his presence? It would have taken a fraction of a second for the adrenaline to start coursing through her body and send the message to flee. Did the angle of the opening of the bedroom door give her any clues? Did anything inside the apartment, any inanimate object pulsate or quiver, like the door of her bedroom, mute and wooden but wailing like a siren in its eerie stillness?

Everything in Betsy's vision up to that point plays out roughly the same way, no matter how many times she reviewed it in her head. But there were alternate endings, each playing out differently according to Betsy's state of mind. In one version, Ginny makes it two steps down the stairwell before she slips and knocks noisily into the wall. That's when Betsy arrives at the front door and hears the commotion inside. Ginny races down the rest of the stairs and the two friends run down the hill to safety.

In another version, Ginny lands hard on her ass on the fourth stair as the bedroom door flings open and the knob strikes the drywall in her room with a thud. Behind her, she hears the quick, heavy steps of work boots across the creaky floor. To her left, she sees a black blur, an arm swinging around to knock her head against the railing. He, the he she was so certain wouldn't be waiting for her, slaps tape over her mouth and part of one nostril and presses it, hard, against her skin. He hooks his right elbow under her armpit and drags her back up the stairs, into the room, and onto the bed. Her right temple, again, stings from the blow, and her pulse roars in her ears. She strains her eyes to focus on the figure before her, silhouetted by the hall light. Then she sees the knife, and feels him press the weight of his body against hers. That's when Betsy barges into the room with the golf club they keep in the hall closet downstairs, and she swings it hard enough that it makes a fleshy thudding sound as it lands on his skull, and the two of them are free. But in the most persistent version, the one that creeps back into her consciousness again and again, Betsy shows up in time, but she does nothing. Nothing at all. Then Ginny dies.

"I'm going to pull this tape off now if you promise not

to scream. If you scream, you're dead," he growls in her ear. "This knife here," he says, as he cut off her shirt, "would cut through you like warm butter. You hear me? Not a word. You scream, you fight, and that's the end of you."

Ginny nods furiously as he binds her wrists together and forces her arms over her head. Her body shakes uncontrollably.

"You let me do what I want and, honey, you can live," he says, negotiating with her like he claims he did with all of his victims, plying her with lies. "You can go on your way, flipping your hair, laughing at guys like me, teasing guys like me."

Her shorts were off now, and he's at her underpants. She heard him fumble with his buckle. He reaches up to stroke her face and then pulls, hard, ripping the tape from her mouth. Her head reels backward from the pain.

"Somebody's walking through that door any second now," Betsy can hear Ginny saying the words before she spits in his face. *"You'll never get away with this. My friend's going to walk in that door any minute, and you're going to be done, do you understand? You're never going to get away with this. You're going to rot in prison and then in hell and I will* not *see you there."*

Maybe she reaches for his ear, as Caroline said. Thirty pounds of pressure. *I could rip his ear off with my hand.*

Downstairs, a key turns the lock of the front door. He clasps his hand over Ginny's mouth and threatens to slit her throat if she screams. She struggles against his weight, jamming her knees and her elbows in the softest spots she can find.

They hear someone downstairs. McRae shifts his weight

to the edge of the bed and a creaky floorboard gives way. Then they hear the crash of a chair, the clamber of footsteps down the hall, and the slam of the front door.

Then Betsy knows how the story ends. Ginny feels pressure on her chest, a hot sear of pain, a tearing sound coming from deep inside.

This isn't real, she thinks, as she stares at the blank, white expanse of her ceiling. *This can't be real.*

And the room around her starts to fade into what feels like a dream, and Betsy is falling backward.

NO MATTER HOW many scenarios she imagined, Ginny was still gone when she came back to reality. And nothing would bring her back.

WHAT IF MCRAE knew that Betsy was the one who walked in on him? Betsy had had to leave, to get as far away from that place as possible, to become Elizabeth, someone else entirely. After all of those years, even when she didn't know who he was, he haunted her, behind bars and a death sentence.

"I could have . . . ," she said, trailing off. She straightened up, scanned the room to remember exactly where she was, to remember who she was talking to, forgetting that she was talking out loud at all. She rubbed her eyes. She heard a faint vibrating sound from across the room.

"Ah, it's me, my pager." Ian unclipped his beeper from his back pocket. "Hold tight."

He checked the number and then scanned the address list in his phone.

"Hey, Ian," said Betsy.

"Ian?" He laughed. "Who the hell is Ian?"

"Um, I forgot. I'm supposed to see a movie tonight. With a friend. You've got to go."

"Yeah, yeah, I know. I've got to go. I was on my way anyway." He folded up his box of treasures, slid it into his backpack, and skulked toward the door.

"You alright?" he asked, stopping a moment to look back at Betsy.

"Yeah," she croaked a little, her throat suddenly dry. "I'm alright."

And then he was off into the still-warm night.

She kicked off her Birkenstocks, shuffled to the bedroom, and spread herself out on top of the cool, percale sheets, the AC's vents pointed directly at her face, where she would stay, motionless, until morning.

CHAPTER 17

THE BACHELORETTE

August 15, 1997

Five days on, two days off, two weeks' vacation, summer Fridays on the jitney, cardio classes after work, wine-soaked dinners with big groups of acquaintances who haggled over the check, and lazy, queasy hungover mornings—time slid by whether Betsy noticed it or not. Before Betsy realized it, she had been promoted to Senior Cataloguer in the Prints and Multiples department. She had been employed for over six years. And she and Gavin were getting married. Betsy was amazed by how quickly time passed once you accepted your fate and succumbed to a steady rotation of work days and weekends, the almost imperceptible ebb and flow of daily life, as lethargic and uneventful as the tide in the flat waters of the Gulf Coast.

She watched the clock perched on the rickety side table next to the bed burn through the minutes. Its orange-red numbers glowed in the murky dark hotel room. It was 2:45. Betsy, after abandoning hope of sleep, started to sift through the schedule of events in her head. At 11:00 a.m., a small group of friends and family would gather on the lawn at the Gideon Putnam hotel in Saratoga Springs. A string quartet would play "Motion Picture Soundtrack" by Radiohead as she walked down the aisle. By 11:12 a.m., they would be married.

They chose the location both for the New Deal–era park, full of graceful brick archways and shady woods that surrounded it, and for the opportunity to wear big hats and bet on the ponies at the track nearby with twenty of their bourbon-thirsty friends. Her dress, an oyster satin column that hit just below the knee, hung on the back of the door next to Gavin's gray suit. Her flowers, a tiny cluster of lilies of the valley, would be delivered in just a few hours. When she stood in the grass at the rehearsal that afternoon, long fingers of sun reached through the clouds to warm Betsy's shoulders through the thin silk of her sleeves. The smell of damp grass, mixed with the mint in her julep and the gardenia in her hair, was such a dizzying combination of so many good things that it made her want to close her eyes to block out everything else and concentrate on the scents alone. She wanted to lock down the memory in a place where her other senses couldn't reach. But behind her eyelids, despite the warmth on her skin and the fragrant air and the excitement of the day, all she could see was what was missing: Ginny, and even Caroline, and she felt a shot of loneliness and regret that took her breath away.

When she opened her eyes, she saw Gavin, who narrowed his eyes to peer at her more closely, no doubt wondering what she was thinking, as always. Some say the secret to a lasting relationship is a continual element of mystery. Close the bathroom door. Never reveal all of your secrets. Keep them guessing. If that was true, she and Gavin were in it for the long haul. Even though Betsy felt so raw and exposed all of the time, she was beginning to realize that everyone else—including her future husband—perceived her as something of a closed book. Gavin reached out to touch her elbow and Betsy shuddered.

"You OK?" He mouthed the words to her, trying not to interrupt the chatty local clergy that the hotel hired to marry them. Betsy forced a smile and offered a tense little nod.

"Totally fine," she whispered. "Jitters, no big deal."

At the rehearsal dinner, Betsy shifted uncomfortably in her seat when Teddy raised a glass to the happy couple, alluding to the way the two of them met, how he knew them both separately but could hardly remember a time when they weren't a unit, and how tragedy brought them together but they weren't going to dwell on sadness that day. Jay, Gavin's brother who was struggling through business school in Atlanta, was six beers into the evening when he stood up to offer what Betsy thought would be a fairly uninspired toast. And it was, for a while.

"Gavin, you know, we always say that the day you met Betsy, it was like a solar eclipse." He chuckled. "Kind of cool to observe, in some ways, but *dark*." Here, he faked a shiver for added emphasis. "Spooky, even. But I know you've been through a lot together, some hard times, and, I can only assume, some good ones. I can see that she makes you laugh. She makes you happy, I guess? Can you call it happy? If not, we wouldn't be here, right? All the way up here in New York? Or are we in Canada yet? You're happy, I'm happy."

Teddy tried his best to be nonchalant when he wandered over to Jay and patted him on the back with a hearty thwack.

"Alright, Jay," said Teddy. "Thanks for that, that sentimental journey."

The table laughed a bit, in relief no doubt. And Betsy wondered if anyone noticed, or noticed as much as she did, that no one was there to offer quaint or funny stories from her distant past. No one there had seen her climb the kumquat tree in Key West with Ginny, or sat on the back of the sputtering secondhand scooter Betsy had for a single semester before its tiny motor failed, or sat outside Krispy Kreme with her waiting for the hot doughnuts sign to turn on at 4:00 a.m. No one knew about her *Golden Girls* obsession, or kept track of how many bikes she either lost, forgot to lock, or stole, how many dance parties she'd started in the middle of the night. There was no proud father's speech. Kathy thought it inappropriate for the mother of the bride to make a toast, so she sat there silently, shifting in her own brand of discomfort and uncertainty, attempting to deflect all of the attention that was directed her way. Jessica stood up to offer a few early work stories, like the time Betsy was in the warehouse digging a print out of storage and knocked over a hanging metal sculpture, which she then convinced the maintenance men to help her "fix" with spray paint.

Jessica was laughing so hard she snorted, overestimating how entertained her audience would be by such highbrow hijinks. "The paint threw the whole thing off balance," she said, to only muffled laughter. "Trust me, it was a catastrophe."

Later, when their parents and aunts and uncles went to the hotel bar, Teddy pulled out a couple of fat joints from his suit pocket, and she and Gavin, Teddy, Jessica, and a handful of other friends from New York smoked them under the cover of ancient trees and ran through the vast expanse of dewy grass, tossing a Frisbee across the wide-open lawn, until the light turned from dark gray to deep bluish black.

It was foolish to stay up so late the night before her own wedding, but Betsy didn't care. When they were making their way back to the hotel, in the dark, through a little stand of trees, Gavin laced his arm through hers and around her back.

"Hello, Mrs. Davis," he said, leaning down to kiss her.

"You mean, Ms. Young. Or Ms. Davis-Young?"

"Ms. Elizabeth Davis-Young-Sinjin-Smythe, esquire?"

"Sounds about right."

"What were you thinking about earlier, on the lawn during rehearsal? You seemed worried."

"Not worried, exactly. Just, you know."

"I think I know," he said, nodding in an attempt to assure her. "I just wish you would tell me."

"Later. We'll talk about it later."

THEY WENT TO bed at 1:00 and she'd been flopping around on the sagging, old mattress for nearly two hours.

"Gavin," she whispered. "Are you awake?"

"Hmm," he grumbled. "Sort of. What's up?"

"I can't sleep."

"It's got to be nerves," he said, putting his hand on her hip and pulling her close. "I've got 'em, too. Tomorrow's a big day. You know you only get married once. Twice? Three times, max." He leaned in to kiss her neck. Betsy chuckled despite herself. "Any more than that and it's just embarrassing."

"I know. You're right," she said. "But I've got something to tell you. Actually, I have one thing to tell you, and one thing I need to ask you."

"OK," he said, rubbing his eyes. "Should I be worried? You're not calling this off, are you?"

"No, no. Of course not." She paused, debating which would

come first, the question or the confession. She led with the latter. "It's just that I . . . I didn't have a bachelorette party."

Gavin propped himself up on his elbow.

"Wait . . . what do you mean?" he asked. "When I went to Atlantic City, with Teddy and the guys from work, you did the spa thing, and a dinner with Jess and Shana and those guys, right?"

"Well, I went to the spa, which was great. But I was alone," she said.

"And then?"

"And then Jess met me for dinner downtown with Courtney and Shana. We had a drink after and I said I was feeling light-headed from the sauna, and I went home."

That part was true, mostly. They had a drink, but she wasn't feeling light-headed, and she sort of went home. First she stopped at the Silver Swan, a dingy German bar in the East 20s, for a bourbon on the rocks. Then she paged Ian on her walk home. He was waiting in front of their building by the time she got there.

He was thinner than when she first met him, almost gaunt, with deepening hollows under his eyes. It was easy for Betsy to separate from him, to say that the years of itinerant pill popping were harder on him than they were on her, and that the bruised crescents under her own eyes weren't as obvious.

"Well if it isn't the blushing bride," he said, as she approached their door.

"Yeah, yeah, very funny."

Upstairs, he gave her the pills and they smoked the tiny joint he would roll just for her. By then, Ian had heard most of the things Betsy vowed to tell no one. She felt an odd mix of vulnerability and safety around this virtual stranger who knew all of her secrets, but whom she saw only once a month, or every other week, and only very occasionally, when work or life were particularly rough, on a weekly basis. As far as she knew, he still didn't even know her real name, or didn't care to know. That veil of anonymity, and the utter improbability of their social and professional circles intersecting, kept him at a comfortable distance. But his knowing also gave him power.

That night, instead of moping around the apartment alone, she let her curiosity get the best of her and went out with Ian on his "errands." They cut a strange, zigzag path through the East Village as he responded to pages. She'd wait for him out in front of a building after he'd been buzzed in through the intercom and disappeared down a dimly lit hallway with his backpack of wonderment in tow. Once he was out of sight, the minutes she spent waiting for him were oddly endless, and what felt like an hour would pass before he'd return. She was left out on the sidewalk, steadying herself against a bike rack, suddenly paranoid about running into someone she knew, though most of the people walking by barely seemed to notice her. New York was being New York. Dogs on leashes sniffed at anemic little trees. Angular women in dark lipstick and wide sunglasses strode by with haughty grace. Old women in housedresses shuffled along the same sidewalks they'd been treading for five decades. The smell of burned hot pretzels and falafel and exhaust and garbage wafted by in small gusts blown by the breeze. She wondered about the people Ian met inside, all of the people that occupied the warren of boxy rooms stacked in neat Tetris columns in building after building, block after block. How many secrets were contained in those rooms? How many had Ian heard? How many people took confession with him, behind that veil of anonymity?

"So I bet you hear it all," she said, after the door finally opened again and he was back with her on the sidewalk. Betsy felt herself slur and struggled to get her shit together. "Does everyone confide in you? Is it like a *thing* people do, pill-head confessions, like an HBO show or something?"

"Nah, not everyone. But I hear enough," he said. They meandered down the sidewalk a bit and Betsy could see, for the first time since she met him, that he was thinking, choosing his words carefully.

"You know, this thing? With the McRae guy you keep talking about? And your dead friend? It's nothing," he said. "I mean, it's something. But everybody's got something. You didn't kill her. Technically, you didn't even let her die. You were just kind of a kid and you were scared and your timing was off. Forgive me for offering some advice. As they say, you've got to consider the source. But you've got to let that shit go."

Betsy wandered ahead a bit, too self-conscious to turn around and look this kid, this punk nickel-and-dime dealer, in the eye. And then he spoke up again.

"Also, you're getting married. I hope I get married someday, and if I caught my wife hanging out with somebody like me when she was supposed to be excited about getting married and all of that? I would not be happy. So I've got to work. And you should go home. I'll walk you back."

GAVIN WAITED PATIENTLY for her to continue, in the darkness. And then he spoke first.

"Is this about the pills? About Ian?" he asked. "Because I know that you don't think I know, but I do."

Betsy put her face in her hands.

"I'm so embarrassed."

"Come on, now. I've been paying attention. I didn't know what to say. But I promised myself that if I thought it was getting really out of hand, I would speak up."

He didn't know about the blackouts.

"I should have bridesmaids! I should have had some terrible bachelorette party with dick-shaped lollipops, or something. But instead, I trailed after a skateboarding drug dealer all night. It's pathetic."

"Maybe a little." Gavin rubbed his eyes with his thumb and forefinger. "I'm not going to lie to you. But as long as that's where it ends, we can deal with it. You can kick the pills. It hasn't affected your work. At least not much, right? I think you're OK, and I'm OK. We're OK, right? There's nothing more is there?"

Betsy considered fessing up to her sleepovers with strangers, but then thought the better of it. Instead, she went on to the question.

"No, there's nothing more," she said, "but I need to know, the stuff Jay said tonight . . ."

"Oh God, screw Jay. He was wasted, and he's always been spoiled, and he knows that you're smarter than he is and he can't take it. My parents felt so bad about what he said. They know what you've been through."

"But is that how people think of me? As dark and uncaring? You're this sweet, affable guy and I'm the moody one you're saddled to? Because I feel like if I care even a tiny bit more, I'm going to break. I feel like I care so much about not hurting people that I can't even move sometimes. And I end up hurting them anyway. And the worst part is that Ginny's the reason I think I'm afraid to get close to people, and why

I think I need to dull this pain, but I'm starting to forget," she said. "I'm trying to remember her face, her features, the exact shade of her hair, and I can't. All I have are these ancient pictures, which are starting to fade, too. And it makes me so sad."

Gavin reached over to click on the light on the nightstand. He sat up in bed with his hair sticking up in every direction, squinting in the light.

"I know it's hard to take me seriously when I'm not wearing a shirt, but you have to listen to me, Betsy, and listen very carefully," he said. "I have been in love with you since that day on the dock at J.D.'s. You are kind and curious and smart. You are wry and observant and funny as hell. When I watch you look at some work of art that I don't even try to understand, you concentrate so hard that your face contracts into these weird expressions that I have honestly never seen on another human being. You are braver than you think you are. You work so hard to do better, to be good. You always have. I didn't know anybody else who was getting on a bike at 5:00 a.m. to go to work when we were in college, only you. Sometimes you struggle to fit in because, I don't know why, maybe because you take things so seriously? So personally?"

"Gavin, I . . ."

"No, wait, let me finish. I am as surprised as the next guy that I met the woman I was going to marry when I was twenty-one years old. And, I admit, things have not been perfect between us every step of the way. But we are supposed to be together. I know we are. That day you lost Ginny, you found me. I wish like hell you could have had both of us, but that's not how it worked out. And I'm sorry."

She reached out and combed his hair with her fingers.

"I am nervous about so many things. I'm nervous about everything, really. But I am not nervous about you," Betsy said. "You are the one thing I know I got right." Gavin rested his head back on the pillow and pulled her close.

"You know, if you weren't a little sad about the memories of Ginny fading, that's what would make me worry." He moved her hair out of her eyes. "And one thing I know, I really know for sure, is that if Ginny could see you crying about her on the night before your wedding, she'd kick your ass. Hard."

"You definitely have a point there," she said.

"So let's just do this, together, like we've done all of that other crap, OK? Then when the chaos is over, we're going to go back to being just fine. Or even better. I can feel it."

CHAPTER 18

THE TOURIST

February 17, 1998

Six months into marriage, either the novelty had worn off, or February's punishing deep freeze had muted her heady newlywed optimism, but life had gone back to business as usual—minus the blackouts—with impressive speed. Then she got the voice mail.

"Betsy, that's as clean as that shower is ever going to get," said Gavin. She had one toothbrush in her mouth, and another old one in her left hand, working at the graying grout under the showerhead. The mine-cut diamond and simple band on her ring finger was coated with a fine dusting of Comet, which would have bothered her eighteen months ago when he first slipped it on her finger, but didn't anymore. The bathroom wasn't great. No amount of Comet was going to change that.

"I know you're nervous about our houseguest, and she rattled you with that Elizabeth bullshit on her voice mail message," he said as he crouched down to tie the laces of his boot. "But trust me, she's not going to inspect the shower grout."

"Yeah, right, Caroline would never do that," she said. *Then you don't know Caroline.*

Betsy had been in New York for seven years before she heard from Caroline. She had called Betsy's mom to get her phone number, and when she played and replayed Caroline's voice mail, it became clear that Kathy had informed Caroline of her professional name change.

"Why hello there, *Elizabeth,* sophisticated woman in New York. It's Caroline." Betsy stood dumbstruck, holding the receiver as the voice registered in her ear. "I'm looking for my friend *Betsy.* Perhaps you remember her? One time, we wore fake grass skirts and bikinis to a luau-themed fraternity party in January. Of course, *you* would never do something like that, *Elizabeth.* If you see Betsy, tell her to give me a call. I'm coming to New York, or *The City,* as I'm sure you call it now. I'll be there next Friday."

Betsy wrote her number, with a Miami area code, on the palm of her hand and then replayed the message three times. They exchanged a couple more messages and finally connected by email. Caroline's writing style had always been terse, stingy with details, and in this medium especially, it came off as especially cold. The gist of it was that Caroline was now a real estate agent in Miami, working with her mother.

Betsy had seen Caroline only once since she left Gainesville, at Teddy's wedding in 1996. He married Melanie, a serious and quiet sorority sister whom Betsy couldn't remember, even after she saw her photo. As the best man, Gavin flew down to Palm Beach on Thursday and the plan was for Betsy to meet him there Saturday morning. She claimed that she couldn't get the time off of work, but the truth was that she was crippled with anxiety about the wedding, knowing how many ghosts would be lurking there, all of those uncomfortable blasts from the past. Betsy bought her ticket using her coworker Shana's ninety-nine-dollar Delta flight coupon from Amex, and then had a fake I.D. made in some back alley on the Lower East Side with her name on it in case anyone checked, which they didn't. She didn't want to spend money she didn't have on cab fare, so she took a bus to LaGuardia and missed her flight, despite the fact that an airline employee threw her garment bag over his shoulder and sprinted through the airport with her to the gate. She sat waiting for the next flight to Palm Beach International, listening for them to call her alias when they found her a seat. Six hours later, she was changing into a black thrift store cocktail dress in the ladies' room at the airport. She hailed a cab and made it in time to snag the last remaining place card at the Everglades Club. She ordered a martini, dirty but dry with three olives, at the bar, and wove her way to her seat through the maze of tables just in time to hear Gavin's speech. She scanned the crowd of four hundred faces in the dimly lit ballroom looking for Caroline. Word had traveled fast about Caroline's first job out of school as a pharmaceutical sales rep. She'd aced the recruitment process, beating out hundreds of other recent graduates from Southeastern Conference schools like Tennessee, Alabama, Louisiana State that churned out pretty, well-spoken girls with big smiles who could sell Lipitor with their eyes closed. It was a coveted job with a decent starting salary, plus commission, in a part of the world where the average resident—median age in Coral Gables, sixty-two—choked down six prescriptions a day.

"Teddy's a man of unwavering loyalty," said Gavin from

the stage, with a barely perceptible slur of his words, collar unbuttoned, holding a microphone in front of the twenty-piece big band onstage. "Once he commits to something, whether it's the sartorial style of the mid-1980s, or the unbearable music of the, *ahem*, Grateful Dead, if Teddy decides to love something, he will love it a lot, and he will love it forever. So Melanie, you poor thing, it looks like you're stuck with this guy for life."

A wave of "*Awwww*"s rippled through the crowd. Betsy felt someone's breath on the back of her neck and a shock ran down her spine.

"Isn't that cuuure," said a voice in a harsh whisper, just inches from her ear. She knew who it was before she turned around. "He's like a game show host in training, right? Do you like buying his vowels?"

"Every day," Betsy said, cold as ice. She turned to see Caroline crouched beside her seat, wearing a thick pearl choker and a navy silk minidress with tiny cap sleeves. Between the gap in Caroline's knees—her legs were even thinner than she remembered—Betsy saw the line where the control top of her stockings began. Carolyn Bessette-Kennedy had made wearing any kind of tights or pantyhose desperately unchic the year before, and it gave Betsy a quick, competitive pang of delight that Caroline didn't know this. Betsy smoothed the crepe pencil skirt of her 1960s dress and shifted in the gold bamboo rental chair, which was pressing the stiff, metal zipper uncomfortably against her back. She worried that the fabric still carried the faint scent of thrift store dust and decay. "I thought I might see you here."

"You know Melanie was my little sister. I held her hair while she puked off of the balcony at a Chi Phi party. We *bonded*,"

Caroline said, in her signature deadpan. Betsy studied her face in the dim light, noticing the faint lines that framed her mouth like parentheses and a dusting of freckles across her cheeks that she hadn't noticed before. Her eyes were glazed and hollow. Her smile was frozen.

"You're in New York, right?"

"Uh-huh," Betsy answered. Betsy must have missed the rest of Gavin's speech, because the next thing she heard was clapping, and some hoots of approval from Teddy's fraternity brothers who rushed over and lifted him over their shoulders, threatening to take him out back and throw him in the pool.

Gavin left the stage, and the actual bandleader took his place, cuing his musicians to play "The Way You Look Tonight." As the first notes were played, the ceiling of the ballroom slowly retracted, revealing the cloud-flecked night sky and a blazing full moon.

"Well look who it is," said Gavin, nodding to Caroline. She stood up and gave him an awkward hug. Betsy looked at him with pleading eyes.

"Nice speech," Caroline offered. "Who knew you'd become such a softy?"

"Nah, I'm still tough as nails," he said, reaching over to take Betsy's hand. "You made it! Let's dance."

On the dance floor, filled with older couples swaying to the music, Betsy put her hand on his shoulder and leaned in close to his ear.

"What the fuck happened to you?" he said through a clenched-tooth smile.

"I took the bus to the airport. There was an accident on the Triborough Bridge and I missed the plane by, like, three minutes. It was a nightmare. I'm so sorry," she said.

"I know you don't want to be here," he said. "But it's important to me, and to Teddy. Try not to pick a fight with Caroline, OK?"

"Oh, so now I'm picking fights," she said. "I missed a flight, Gavin. I'm not going to burn the place down."

Caroline must have had more catching up to do with the 399 other guests, because Betsy avoided her for most of the night without much effort, until the very end. Gavin went to call a cab back to the Chesterfield Hotel for the after-party, and Betsy ducked into the ladies' room. Caroline was on a tufted bench in the lounge in a gossipy huddle with two women Betsy didn't recognize.

"Well, we're heading back to the hotel," Betsy said as she dried her hands with a small, monogrammed towel. "Maybe you'll get lucky and you won't have to hold anybody's hair tonight."

Caroline's friends stared at her blankly.

"I'm sorry, what did you say?" Caroline asked. She shook her head and squinted her eyes in a pantomime of confusion.

"You know, like at the Chi Phi house," Betsy said. "What you said earlier about Melanie."

"Oh, right," Caroline said, even flatter than before.

There was so much tension between them, Betsy wanted to scream or grab Caroline's shoulders and shake her, anything to break it.

"So I'm going home to New York tomorrow, but I'll see you around," she said.

"Yeah, sure. You're going *home*," Caroline said, mocking her for adopting New York as her native ground, yet another way to reject her and where they came from. "See you around."

Betsy felt her cheeks burn red as she turned to leave.

"What was that all about?" she heard one of them ask.

"Nothing. She's just someone I knew a long time ago."

A FEW MONTHS after the wedding, the gossip about Caroline grew significantly darker. She'd started faking business expenses, going shopping when she claimed to be making the rounds of sales calls. She was missing her sales goals, staying out late, sleeping through appointments, and the slide down the slippery slope ended with a pink slip less than a year into the job. People in Miami said they saw her face on a couple of real estate ads on bus stops around town, and she was selling waterfront condos. In her email, Caroline mentioned that one of her clients, an English banker named Simon, had just closed a deal on a two-bedroom in South Beach. She wanted to keep it professional until the deal closed, but then he called her to say he was coming back to the States for some business in New York and asked her to meet him there.

Betsy had offered her their air mattress for a few nights on their living room floor, though she knew Caroline wouldn't take it, and rattled off some restaurant ideas and tourist alternatives in her usual way, determined to prove that she knew the *real* New York to anyone who might question her place there. She'd suggested meeting for lunch. She could show her around SoHo, maybe go vintage shopping in the East Village, come back to their apartment for a glass of wine (hence the grout excavation).

Betsy kept her phone on her desk all day as she waited for Caroline's call. When she didn't hear from her by seven, Betsy went home, rummaged through the medicine cabinet for something stronger than Pamprin, but came up empty-handed. Then she ordered in Thai food and put on her warmest socks. The phone didn't ring until 4:00 Saturday afternoon, more than twenty-four hours after Caroline's arrival, when she called her from a bar. She was there with the Brit and some of his banker friends. It was the first time they'd spoken live without the filter of voice mail.

"Hey, Bets, it's Caroline."

"Hey, what's up? Where are you?" Betsy noted the slightly scolding tone in her voice and vowed to keep it in check. She could have come to town and not called her, she reminded herself. At least Caroline made a small effort.

"We're at some bar. It's so fucking cold I can't stay outside for more than thirty seconds at a time. But listen, I'm going back to the hotel for a shower and a disco nap. Can you and Gavin meet us for dinner?"

Gavin was standing near her in the kitchen and could hear Caroline shouting into the phone, and was shaking his head violently and mouthing, "No, no, no." He wanted to avoid the drama, and he'd convinced Betsy that she needed to see Caroline alone, without a bodyguard.

"Uh, no, Gavin can't make it. But I'll be there."

Betsy agreed to meet her at Union Square Cafe for dinner at 9:00. It was a freezing night but she decided to walk, thinking the sharp air would help her focus and calm her nerves. At the restaurant, she found Caroline at a long table in the back, wearing a dress far too short and spangly that hung loosely on her now bony frame, surrounded by men in sports coats and Brioni shirts with their own impossibly thin dates. Caroline's once-thick shoulder-length blonde hair now looked more fragile, verging on white at the ends. Wrinkles were starting to grab at the corners of her eyes even when her smile faded.

She had the tan skin of an avid runner in the Sunbelt that looked bizarre in this dark, wintry city, even in dim restaurant light. Betsy waved hello—Caroline was never a hugger—instantly regretting that she'd agreed to see her old, it would be fair to say former, friend in a group situation like this. Caroline waved and extended her index finger, as if to say "Just a minute," and Betsy nodded. It had been seven years. What difference would a minute make? She took a chair at the end of the table between Caroline's friend and a slightly bloated guy named Damien who had two full bottles of Heineken perched next to his untouched rib eye on the starched white tablecloth.

"Simon," said Caroline, grabbing the arm of an only slightly less bloated but much redder in the face man, "This is my long-lost friend, *Elizabeth,* the one I've been telling you about." She looked at Betsy with a raised eyebrow.

"It's Betsy, actually," she said. Caroline rolled her eyes and mouthed "What the fuck?" before she turned to the man on her left, who was in the middle of what he thought was a hilarious story about a mortgage mix-up at work, and didn't bother to pause for an introduction.

"I'm sorry?" Simon shouted over the din at the table, pulling a Marlboro out of the pack and placing it between his lips.

"BETSY. MY NAME. I'M ELIZABETH AT WORK, BUT MY FRIENDS CALL ME BETSY."

Or they would, if I had any friends outside of work.

"Oh, right, right. She told me that, too. Do you smoke, Betsy?"

The answer was no, not anymore, but she took one anyway. Outside on the inch-thick ice covering the sidewalk, they chatted for a while about how awful American cigarettes were and how tiny the hotel rooms were in Manhattan. Simon was staying at the Morgan, where the rooms were dark, *ghastly, really,* but the bar was open til 4:00 a.m. Simon had his priorities. Halfway through their cigarettes, Caroline, who put all of her weight behind the colossal wooden door and just barely budged it open enough for her to slip through, came teetering out, unsteady in stilettos and shivering in a borrowed wool coat. Betsy took a drag of the cigarette with her left, gloveless hand.

"There y'all are," Caroline said. Her eyes darted immediately to Betsy's ring. Her 'y'all' had always been reserved for special occasions, and apparently this was one of them. She linked her arms around fat Simon's waist for warmth. "I had a feeling I'd find you here."

Was this man she was hanging on, deferring to in a way that was so unlike Caroline that she hardly recognized her, really a complete stranger? A client who paid her 15 percent commission?

"Hey, Nanook of the North," she said, eyeing Betsy's Army/Navy store peacoat and extra-thick black tights. "Aren't you bundled up like an Eskimo tonight? I bet you can still feel your toes, though! I know I *cannot* feel mine. Last time I was here was a year ago August. People say Florida is hot, but this place was Hades."

Betsy understood this as the dig Caroline intended. She had been in New York and not bothered to call. Betsy's next move had to be defensive, retaliatory.

"Well I, for one, am surprised that you didn't pull one of your mom's furs out of storage for the occasion," said Betsy, surprised by how angry her voice sounded. "I know how you love the scent of mothballs and Shalimar."

Betsy noted the tiniest wince in Caroline's face as she pretended to wipe a stray ash from her eye.

Back inside, Caroline waved Betsy into the ladies' room, and again into a shared stall to chat about her bar crawl with Simon while she scooped bumps out of a brown vial with the tip of his hotel key. That explained the $600 worth of uneaten food on the table. She offered some to Betsy, which she declined just to prove a point of some kind. She was mad at Caroline for not calling sooner, even though the two were practically strangers now, and drugs weren't going to change anything. Caroline shrugged off the snub and then rattled on about Miami, how South Beach was still totally happening, no matter what people were saying about it being over, about how Hurricane Andrew was, like, *ages* ago. They went back to the table, where the men were settling the check. All of them tossed their credit cards in a pile and asked the long-suffering waiter to choose one at random onto which he'd charge the entire bill. This was the favorite game of a certain young, moneyed population in town, and it made Betsy squirm with discomfort, recognizing that her own card would be swiftly declined under the burden of that one uneaten dinner. Betsy offered to pay for her wine, but the men batted her hand away. *As if,* their eyes said. They piled into cabs to ride the twelve blocks to a forgettable bar in the West Village and she agreed to one more drink with the fancy accent dickheads before calling it a night. Inside, after a single round, she got up to leave.

"Afraid you'll miss something good on TV?" said Caroline as Betsy shoved her arms into the sleeves of her stiff coat. "Don't worry. I'm sure Gavin's keeping your spot on the couch warm."

"Oh, Caroline, it's been a pleasure," said Betsy, tossing down a twenty-dollar bill for her watery vodka tonic, the rage creeping into her shaking hand. "It's nice to see that some things, including your hostility, never change."

"I don't want your money," Caroline said, throwing the twenty back at her.

"No, Caroline, really, you keep it. Buy a scarf. Maybe some blizzard appropriate footwear? You don't want frostbite. You'll need your toes back home in the land of eternal sandal season."

Betsy bolted for the door, blood burning in her cheeks. Caroline came barreling after her.

"Betsy . . ." Caroline shouted. Betsy spun around to confront her.

"So that's it, right? We haven't had a real conversation since Ginny . . . since Ginny . . ." She couldn't get the words out. She stopped and started again. "I haven't spoken to you for more than thirty seconds since Ginny *died*, and this is how it's going to be," said Betsy, refusing to stop until they were outside the door and she could enjoy watching Caroline freeze some more. She'd thought of Caroline so many times when she was back at home in Venice with her mom, and in the early months, even years, in New York, when she felt so alone and nearly ached for Ginny.

"Oh, are you talking about Ginny's funeral? When you hid in the back like a big, fat baby? Please spare me your sanctimonious bullshit, Betsy. Our best friend died and you stood in the back of Nana Jean's dining room propped against the wall like *you* were the corpse. And then you took off," Caroline said. "You just left town! Totally bailed. You couldn't be bothered with the sun-dried idiots back home anymore, right?" said Caroline, eyes flashing, more the Caroline she knew in that moment than at any other during the night. Betsy searched those eyes for recognition, for softness, but they were hard and glassy and cold and filled with years of spite.

"I had to! I had to get out of Gainesville, Caroline. I couldn't deal," she said, fighting her tears. Caroline was not going to see her cry. "Ginny was gone and I didn't know how I was going to go on."

For a split second, Caroline's body looked like it was starting to relax with forgiveness, with understanding. Then her shoulders crept closer to her ears and she steeled herself against the wind.

"It's all about you, right? Ginny's fucking *murder* didn't affect me at all, did it? *I* was the one who found her body. You didn't stop to think that you weren't the only one in pain, did you? You don't even realize what a joke you are. You and Gavin playing house, and now you're married? You married the guy I bought pot from in college. Well played, *Elizabeth*. Even your name is a joke."

"Oh, I'm the joke? It's twenty degrees. You're wearing a fourteen-inch dress, coked out of your head with a fat, old, beet-faced man you don't even know," said Betsy, tears falling despite her efforts. "And the saddest part is that in the morning I'm the only one who will remember the shit you're spewing. Why don't you go back to Miami and get fired a few more times? Prove that you're the one who isn't the joke. Or I guess Mommy can't shit-can her only child, right? How's that for job security?"

"We're done, Betsy," began the last words Caroline shouted while Betsy scrambled across the ice for a cab. "And if it weren't for Ginny defending you and your self-righteous bullshit, we'd have been done a long time ago." Betsy watched through the back window of the cab as Caroline stood there, shaking in the cold, defiant, her hair suddenly wild in a gust of wind as the driver pulled away.

CHAPTER 19
THE FOLDER

February 17, 1998

Gavin was already asleep by the time Betsy came home, tears partially frozen on her eyelashes, angry, buzzed, and miserable from the unholy mix of red wine and vodka she'd consumed with Caroline. She flung her coat on the back of a chair, pried off her boots, and chucked them into a basket near the door. She sat down on the sofa in the dark and replayed the events of the evening in her head. Betsy hadn't expected much from Caroline, but she had considered the idea that calling her before this trip to New York was, at least in part, an olive branch. It had been over seven years since Ginny died, since they'd spoken at any length, and to get her message out of the blue with the news she was coming to town seemed a little like a flare shot from across enemy lines, a call for a truce. They'd had that weird exchange at Teddy's wedding. Betsy and Gavin didn't invite Caroline to their wedding. Ginny, their peacekeeper, was long gone, and though history and experience hadn't erased Betsy's bitter memories of Caroline completely, they'd been blurred around the edges, worn by time, and she was beginning to remember the good in her, or if not the good, exactly, at least the fun parts. Betsy realized, too, that Caroline seemed like an amateur compared to the ice queens she had met at work. While Betsy hadn't endured much hazing herself, per se, the stories of interoffice torture, the chewing up and spitting out of assistants, were legend. Rumor had it that one of her colleagues, a beleaguered assistant to the head of Impressionist Art, was driven to the edge of her sanity so many times that one day she snapped and urinated on a pear before she sliced it and presented it to her boss on Tiffany porcelain. A few times, Betsy had been allowed to stand in an officious-looking line on the side of the room and accept phone bids. Despite her effort to cajole Australian bankers, Hollywood producers, or budding tech entrepreneurs into opening their wallets, she typically came up empty-handed. Jessica, however, was a master. Once, she charmed an eccentric heir and notorious recluse to pay nearly a million dollars for a *stamp*. Betsy's proximity to such major-league manipulators had bolstered her confidence, and Caroline seemed stuck in the minors.

She went to the kitchen to pour herself another vodka, with plenty of ice and a couple of olives, by the light of the refrigerator. Then, almost reflexively, she walked over to the metal desk she and Gavin kept in their "home office," a repurposed dining alcove lined with DIY bookshelves, flicked on the vintage lamp that they had found on the street, and opened the large file drawer to look for the folder.

It was tucked in the back of the drawer, behind her tax records, a few shockingly thin manila folders with the critical mementos of her life—her birth certificate, a handful of letters from her father dating back to 1982, random ticket stubs. It had been two years since she'd searched for it, and even then it was only to stuff in an interview clipping with a screenwriter who claimed Scottie McRae was the inspiration for his popular, cult slasher movie, with a ruthless killer who posed as a sensitive singer/songwriter, like a bloodthirsty Bob Dylan. But she thought of the folder often, daily, for a while, and then not once in the past year.

The newspaper clippings, from *The Tampa Tribune,* the *Orlando Sentinel,* anything Kathy could find in those early days after Ginny's death, were yellowed and crumbling now. There was a flurry of renewed interest in 1995, around the time of McRae's sentencing hearing. From these clippings she'd created a person, a composite character, a face, and a story to associate with the figure who haunted her, even behind bars and with all of that time stacked up against him.

She flipped through the pages, items she'd found on Lexis-Nexis, the arcane legal research platform she used, pre–search engine, at work. There was a copy of his autobiography, co-written with one of those bizarre women who befriend and fall in love with death row murderers. Through this research and reading, she thought she'd find something to soothe her, but it also left her feeling raw and cold, like she did on the sidewalk screaming at Caroline. Betsy was certain that she wouldn't notice any new details on the aging newsprint that night, but the pain was starting to dull and she needed to stoke it to keep Ginny alive.

Betsy closed the folder, drained the last of her drink, and fumbled around under the desk for Gavin's slippers, which she knew would be there. She stood up, went through the front door, and walked down the hall to the service closet. She opened the trash chute and placed the folder inside. She paused for a moment to consider what she was doing, acknowledge that she was drunk and angry and eager to "let go," even just metaphorically. She wanted to will herself to be done with the whole mess, with Caroline, with this psychotic killer, with the haunting memories of Ginny. And then she let go. Betsy closed the door of the chute and its hinge made a metallic squeal as it slammed shut. She paused for a moment to listen to the folder rattle and thump as it fell rapidly down to the trash heap six stories below.

PART 4

CHAPTER 20
EXPECTING

October 26, 2006

Betsy opened her eyes and stared at the flat, white expanse of her bedroom ceiling. The daily purgatory between sleeping and waking was always the hardest part of her day. It was when the certainties of her life weren't so certain. Time wound back and scrambled, and her dreams were still vivid. Inevitably, the images from those nightly visits to her past would blur and fade, and an odd nostalgia would settle in. Reality loomed.

Soon, very soon, this morning struggle to join the land of the living would be interrupted by the cries of the child that was growing inside her, the seven-pound wake-up call that was due to arrive in five weeks. Throughout her pregnancy, she had imagined what kind of cry her baby would have. Would it be high-pitched and nasal, a little raspy, like the sound effect on a television show? Or would it be throaty and low, shouted between jagged gasps? Almost immediately, she'd push the thought away. What kind of mother thought about what her child's cry would sound like? This was supposed to be one of the happiest times of her life. She should be joyful. Blissful. Betsy suspected this pressure to be the beatific expectant mother was all bullshit, a kind of cultural brainwashing designed to mute the fear of childbirth and the uncertainty of early parenthood. If anything, she was shocked when she felt moments of sustained pleasure, verging on joy. Betsy had experienced plenty of joy—the thrill of the first ultrasound image, the rush of adrenaline when she felt her daughter's first movements, like a wriggle of a fish, her squeal of delight when Jessica came into the office with the first itty-bitty onesie—though it hadn't been as simple as all that.

She propped herself up on her elbow, grabbed Gavin's pillow, and shoved it behind her back to help support her girth. Gavin emerged from the bathroom in the hall, showered but unshaven, buttoning his favorite striped shirt. He sat on the edge of the bed opposite her to put on his socks. She stared at the back of his still-wet head and spotted a small cluster of gray near the crown.

"You can tell your mom that those Celtic names are out. Too many extra N's and consonants pretending to be vowels. And Reagan?" Betsy asked, rearranging herself on their bed and adjusting the pillow behind her back. She reached over to the nightstand and took the list of six baby names that Gavin had scrawled on the back of a Vietnamese takeout menu. He opened the window and let in a sudden gust of brisk air, letting the sound of distant honking horns drift into their room. "You can't be serious. Is this just 1980s nostalgia or are you actually turning into a Reaganite on me after all these years?"

"First, uh, how about 'Good morning,'" he said, walking

around to her side of the bed to place his hand on top of her undulating middle. Betsy studied his face. At thirty-seven, he was still as boyish and lanky as he had been when she first met him at twenty, like a kid who'd never fully grown into his limbs, with a slight paunch around the middle. "Second, I like to think of our daughter as an Independent. I guess it just sounded right. I'm feeling an even number of syllables. Reagan Davis. Iambic pentameter and shit."

"Um, iambic pentameter is a ten-syllable line in a poem, dumb ass. My question for you is this: Does Nancy Davis Reagan ring a bell?" she asked. "Or are you just going to say 'No'?"

She'd decided to let Gavin take a shot at choosing the baby's first name. They'd waited so long to decide to have a child, she figured, so he'd had plenty of time to think it over. As soon as the ultrasound technician waved her wand in the right spot and told them they were having a girl, Betsy decided she would present Gavin with the challenge.

"G, will you help me come up with some names for the bump?" she called out from the shower one morning, months before. He looked at her blankly, as though he'd never suspected their child would need a name, or had thought that she would present it upon arrival with a business card, or maybe they'd find it tattooed in looping script on her left inner biceps. Betsy worried that this represented a larger blind spot Gavin had for parenting, and that this was only the first of many times he would drag his feet when she asked him to help.

They'd been together over fifteen years now, more or less, hot and cold. When they first headed north on the interstate from Florida in his ancient Honda Accord, they couldn't have known that all of these years later they'd be buying organic cotton crib sheets and researching lactation consultants.

Could they have imagined, as they wore out Dinosaur Jr.'s *Green Mind* in the tape deck after the CD player broke, and plowed through bag after bag of original flavor Corn Nuts on their drive up the coast, Gavin laughing as Betsy gripped her seat as they skidded across snow-slick asphalt for the first time, that one day they'd be approved by the condo board of a doorman building on 18th Street and 7th Avenue and granted the privilege of paying off a mortgage in $5000 monthly chunks?

For years, the question hung between them: Kids or no kids? Could they raise even a single child in the most exhausting and expensive place imaginable? If yes, when? Finally, Betsy's gynecologist showed her "the chart," the one with the steadily plummeting red line that tracks the average woman's reproductive decline, peaking at twenty, sliding steadily southward until it screeches to a halt and takes an acrobatic cliff dive at thirty-five. They'd reached yet another "now or never" milestone in their relationship, which was what was typically required to get either of them to take any meaningful action, and plunged headlong into *now*. Any doubts she had about their future, their past, and the sad, strange ties that bound them together were tossed in the trash with a half-full blister pack of Ortho-Cept. After eight months of trying and one round of Clomid, she was pregnant.

"I LIKE REMI," she said, calling out to Gavin, who'd left the room to make coffee and find the newspaper. Remi was short, no possible infantilizing nickname. "What do you think of Remi Virginia?" She knew the instant they found out the baby was a girl that she wanted her daughter's first name to be gender neutral, so no one would make knee-jerk assumptions about her when they read it, and that her middle name would be Virginia.

She stayed perfectly still under the covers, waiting to feel a flutter of movement beneath her skin and muscle walls. No movement, no spark of recognition from within. Then, a few moments later, she felt a sensation of pulling from her back and then encircling her abdomen. Betsy held her breath and then exhaled. For the past two days, she'd been having contractions that everyone assured her were harmless Braxton Hicks. But something about the waves of tightness across her belly gave her pause.

Early on, she'd had a scare. Eight weeks into her pregnancy, she'd hemorrhaged in the bathroom at work and she had been terrified that she'd lose the baby ever since. Betsy called Jessica on her cell phone from the stall, panicked. Jess called a car service, ushered her discreetly out of the loading dock in the back of the building, and rushed her to Dr. Kerr's office. She'd clutched Jess's hand until the doctor found a heartbeat. After seventy-two hours of bed rest, she was back to normal, back at work, but determined to be more "relaxed." She had been diligent, and a little tentative, ever since. Gavin thought she was ridiculous whenever she placed headphones across her abdomen to play classical music from her iPod to the incumbent of her uterus, but whenever he stayed late at work, she'd take the headphones out of the top drawer of her nightstand, recline on the couch, and listen to Yo-Yo Ma with her unborn child. It wasn't just for the baby, she told herself. It was for her; the muffled hum of Bach's Cello Suite No. 1 would lull her right to sleep.

Now Betsy rolled onto her side, pushed herself out of bed, and slid her feet into flattened shearling slippers. Her belly slackened again. Her heartbeat regulated. Remi Virginia would be her name. She struggled to keep her mind from wandering, resisting the pull of the warm sheets and the serene blankness of the white ceiling.

"Hey," she said, shuffling through the kitchen. Gavin was standing in the hall, still in his socks, shirt untucked, so engrossed in the paper that he hadn't heard the question.

"So, what do you think?" Betsy asked. He looked up, clearly startled, folded the newspaper, and placed it in his bag, which hung from a hook near the door. He was pale, his eyes looked bloodshot.

"So, what? Sorry. I spaced for a second. Do you want decaf?"

"Sure. What's going on in the *Times*?"

"Oh nothing, you know, same shit." He shoved the paper into his work bag and brushed a stray hair from her eyes. "The Thursday Styles wants me to wear a pocket square."

"Alright. But only if it's purple," Betsy said. "So . . . what do you think of the name? Remi Virginia?"

"Hmm," he said. "I like it, but . . ."

"But what?"

"Well I know how much you like monograms."

"And?"

"And her initials would be R.V.D. R.V.? V.D? One part motor home, one part genital herpes."

"Jesus, Gavin." She rolled her eyes. "You could ruin anything."

He went back into the kitchen to start the coffee. Betsy opened the refrigerator and eyed a selection of plain yogurt, a bowl of hard-boiled eggs, and some dense and grainy brown bread. Given her "advanced maternal age," her gynecologist had suggested a low-glycemic diet, which Betsy had followed to the letter and continued, as much as she could, through her pregnancy for fear of gestational diabetes and ninety-five extra pounds. There were days, and this was one of them, when she wanted nothing more than a salt bagel with chive cream cheese.

"Hey, Gav, do you want to grab a bite with me after my appointment?" Betsy had an ultrasound scheduled at ten. "Just looking at the font on that Greek yogurt is making me queasy."

"Sure, that's a great idea," Gavin said as he watched the coffee drip into the pot. "In fact, I have an even better one. Why don't you take the whole day off?"

"Wait—what? Are you serious?"

"I have to run into work this morning for a minute to take care of a few things, and then I'll be free for the rest of the day." Gavin had vaulted up the ranks in television news to become the executive producer of a cable talk show that aired live at 9:00 p.m. He was rarely home before 11:00 p.m., and they were just delusional enough to think that their reverse schedules would prove to be an advantage once the baby arrived. "I can hook up with you at the doctor's office, then we can have lunch and check out that overpriced Japanese baby store in SoHo that you like before I head back to the office."

"OK, *now* you're freaking me out."

"What? What's the matter? You haven't taken a day off since the summer. You could use the break."

He was right. She was tired, and it was getting harder by the day to cram her feet into heels.

"Um . . . alright," she said, smiling, still with some suspicion. Betsy ate an egg, just to curb the hunger pangs, which came on intensely and often. She showered, slipped into black leggings, which resembled a deflated balloon animal when she pulled them out of the drawer, and a stretchy, heather gray dress that Jessica had passed along in a bag of maternity clothes that were chicer than anything Betsy owned pre-pregnancy. She plopped down on the edge of the bed, already winded from the morning's effort, and slipped on a pair of Converse, grateful for a day that would not require decent shoes. She scraped her shoulder-length, dark blonde hair, which was longer and thicker in her third trimester than it had ever been in her life, into a bun, grabbed a scarf and her handbag, and made her way down to the lobby. She walked the handful of blocks to Murray's, hurrying past her favorite newsstand, and started salivating as her bagel was plastered with cream cheese. She had sworn them off for years once she left Gainesville. Betsy recognized the irony of giving up bagels upon arrival in New York. Still, every time she passed a bagel bakery and the scent of caraway seeds and burned garlic singed her nostrils, she thought of her boss Tom and his vampiric 2:00 a.m to 10:00 a.m. schedule. Betsy never thought that she'd remember those painfully early mornings with any fondness. To her surprise, she often did.

Betsy barely made it onto a stool at the counter before she devoured her bagel, licked her finger to pick up stray salt crystals to devour those, too, and walked to the corner to catch the M20 uptown.

She hoisted herself up on to the bus, slid her MetroCard into the slot, and waddled toward the back. She pushed a discarded *New York Post* off of a blue seat and lowered herself down slowly. Betsy loved riding the bus. To Gavin, it was torture, a shuttle to ferry the elderly and nannies with their tiny charges, only for the very young or the very old who were in no particular rush to get anywhere, up and down the congested streets. When Betsy had the time, she stayed aboveground. She liked to see what was happening around her, the bikes weaving in and out of traffic, the NYPD gathered in suspicious clusters on the sidewalk for reasons unknown, the ambiguous steam that rose up from manholes on chilly fall mornings like this one. Taking the bus was a habit she picked up when she'd first moved to the city, when she felt an urgent need to learn about her surroundings, memorize intersections, master the landmarks that helped her get her bearings, and keep an eye on the people around her. She felt more in control of her life on the bus. She could jump out the back door at any point, if the occasion called for it.

Betsy was always planning her escape.

Once they hit Central Park, Betsy decided to walk. The office was only a block or two away, and she wanted to see if any of the autumn colors remained on the lingering leaves. Years before, she and Gavin used to take the train up to Cold Spring and marvel at the view along the Hudson. Growing up in the oppressive Florida climate had given them both a deep appreciation for the change of seasons. Fall had become Betsy's favorite time of year.

"It looks like a puzzle," she'd say every time she saw the intermittent patches of golden ash and bright red maple leaves along the riverbank. As a kid, she never understood the appeal of autumn, the cool dampness of the air and crunch of decaying leaves on the ground, the last dramatic, spectacular show of nature before the deathly grays of winter. Cold weather made her mother anxious. When her mom learned of Betsy's baby's December due date, Kathy was perturbed, claimed she didn't want to be subjected to the crush of holiday crowds, but Betsy knew it was the cold that frightened her.

The cramped but tidy waiting room at Dr. Kerr's office was empty, except for a woman dressed in a pink nurse's smock rocking a weeks-old infant. She cooed at the baby, reassuring him that his mother would be out shortly. There was a low table piled high with parenting and pregnancy magazines, beaming infant faces looking up at her from their covers, locking on to her gaze. Betsy scanned the stacks for something that wouldn't terrify her, with all of their caustic warnings about runny cheese and caffeine. The sets of massive, searching baby eyes and the crying of the fussy boy—short bursts of volume followed by a snorting inhale—made her tense. On the seat next to her, someone had left behind most of *The New York Times*. And though germy abandoned newspapers also occupied a slot on her list of phobic worries, Gavin had made off with theirs that morning and missing a day of the news would further stoke her anxiety. The headlines were predictable: Bush continued to bungle the situation in North Korea, seventy dead in a Baghdad car bombing.

Then, on page four, Betsy saw it. She drew in a sharp breath and suddenly understood why Gavin had urged Betsy to take a well-earned mental health day.

SERIAL KILLER CONVICTED OF MURDERING
FIVE IN FLORIDA IS EXECUTED

Her eyes darted across the first paragraph.

GAINESVILLE, Fla., Oct. 25—The man convicted of murdering five college students here in 1990 was executed on Wednesday by lethal injection. Scott Charles McRae, 42, was pronounced dead at 6:13 p.m. at Florida

State Prison. Witnesses said he stared toward them and began to sing just before the drugs were administered . . .

Betsy stopped reading. She suppressed the urge to vomit. Everything inside of her churned like a fire. And there was his picture, gazing out past her shoulder. His forehead was furrowed and his right hand covered his open mouth. From his still-warm grave, traveling across state lines and decades, she got one last, long look. Betsy could feel her throat tighten. Her heart flipped suddenly and softly in her chest like a hooked fish. She jerked when the phone in her bag vibrated.

"I'm in a cab, sorry, I got a little sidetracked," said Gavin. Betsy couldn't speak. She breathed heavily into the phone, wincing with the tightening cramp that was now radiating down her left side.

"Bets—are you there? Everything OK?"

"I found the paper." She could barely force the words.

"Christ. Shit. Where are you?"

"At Dr. Kerr's."

"Elizabeth Davis?" A young nurse in purple scrubs with a long dark ponytail stuck her head out from behind the office door, holding Betsy's chart in her hand. Betsy felt the baby kick and a tight pull in her left side.

"I'm so sorry, Betsy, I was going to show you at lunch. I just wanted you to get through this appointment first."

"I can't fucking breathe, Gavin. Gavin, please, I can't breathe . . ."

The nanny glared at her, pulling the boy tight to her chest.

"Ms. Davis? Everything alright?" The nurse was standing in front of her now. "Ms. Davis, just try to breathe."

"I'm on my way, Bets," said Gavin. "Just hold on."

CHAPTER 21

OUT OF THE GAME

September 9, 2010

Each morning in the Davis household played out in roughly the same way: awake by 6:45, stirred by the soft pounding of Remi's feet on the hardwood floor, followed by a couple of perfect minutes in bed. It wasn't the way it used to be, the blank staring at the ceiling and gradual reentry into the land of the living. Now Betsy relished that handful of blissed-out, uncomplicated minutes under the covers with a tiny four-year-old body pressed against her chest. It was taking Betsy an unusually long time to get used to the idea that her daughter was growing, not just growing up, but growing longer and leaner, with expanding hands that were strong and callused from the monkey bars at the park and cheekbones emerging from a once-round face. She'd sprung up like a sunflower that summer, bright, happy, and sturdy in the wind. Betsy could hardly believe that the girl who was sprinting down the beach, the one with the squealing laugh that carried in the breeze for what seemed like miles, belonged to her.

In the beginning, in those first few hours of her daughter's life, Betsy wasn't even sure the baby would live to see her first birthday. When the doctor first held up their tiny daughter, in the briefest minute before she was whisked away to the NICU, Betsy was in such shock that she'd had a baby at all, and so much sooner than she'd expected, that all she could do was marvel at her tiny fingernails and perfect, miniature lips in the way that people admire a scale model of a tall ship.

"How did we make you so small?" Betsy whispered, not understanding enough about what lay before her to cry just yet. The scale read four pounds, three ounces.

"She's going to make it," said Dr. Kerr, or Sara, as Betsy had come to know her obstetrician during the intense hours she spent in the hospital fighting to keep her daughter safe inside her womb a little longer. Sara was sitting on the edge of the hospital bed, where Betsy was propped up, glassy-eyed, trying to grasp what her doctor was saying through the Dilaudid. "But you've got a rough patch ahead. Rest if you can. Remi is in good hands now. She's going to need you to be strong."

Sara had explained that what had happened was called placental abruption.

"Essentially the baby's food source detaches from the uterus, which triggers pre-term labor. The baby's only chance for survival is outside of you," she said. It was rare, and Sara explained that stress and anxiety weren't known risk factors, but no one could say for sure. Betsy had been complaining of abdominal pain, which was the reason she was in Sara's office when the worst of it began, but she avoided any mention of the newspaper article. It wasn't something she talked about. After the contractions started in earnest, there was nothing they could do to stave off labor. So Betsy and Gavin's Christmas present became their Halloween surprise, destined for a lifetime of jack-o'-lantern carving costume parties, birthday cake taking a backseat to sacks full of candy.

While Betsy rested and Remi slept in the NICU, Gavin did the only thing he could think to do: He made a playlist. He started with "I Found a Reason," from the Velvet Underground, Brian Eno's "I'll Come Running," "Little Fat Baby" by Sparklehorse, Radiohead's "Sail to the Moon," Calexico and Iron & Wine's "History of Lovers," Bright Eyes's "First Day of My Life." When they weren't snatching moments of sleep between limited, sterilized visits with their child, Betsy kept her headphones on to drown out the hospital noises and mask the sound of her racing pulse in her ears. After a week passed, Remi's lungs were stronger and things looked less dire, Gavin would slip in a song sung by a female badass, but only terrible ones, as a rallying cry. It made Betsy laugh.

"Thanks to you I have 'Warrior' by Scandal stuck in my head," she said one weary morning, when she was leaving the hospital to go home to shower and he was arriving for the day shift. "I've been shooting at the walls of heartache all night."

Gavin navigated through the sea of insurance paperwork. He made sure Betsy ate a few bites of something. He kept things in order at home, called Betsy's office to inform them of the latest news and asked for their discretion and patience. He did a scathing and dead-on impersonation of the sternest of the NICU nurses, which made Betsy laugh in a deranged, sleep-deprived way. It was hardest in the middle of the night, usually 3:00 or 4:00 a.m., which was when they weighed their tiny girl to see if she managed to eek out a few more ounces. Betsy's body was just catching on to the idea that it had given birth, and nursing her was all but impossible. Gavin was her rock.

"I'm your three a.m. guy, right?" he said, forcing a smile. "That's how this all started, sort of, right? We drove away into the unknown in the middle of the night."

"And lived happily ever after?" she added, delirious from endorphins. "Sort of?"

"Sort of. I promise." He kissed her forehead. "You're still cute when you're crazy."

NEARLY FOUR YEARS later, that promise was proving difficult to keep, and their new morning routine, with Betsy struggling at preschool drop-off, was the latest of many issues. Her obsessive, oppressive impulses would override any hope they had of peace, and it would subvert even the easiest of parenting tasks, like packing their daughter's lunch.

"Gav," Betsy called from the bathroom, "I sliced up some fruit for Remi's lunchbox. It's in the fridge."

On the second shelf, there were two rows of BPA-free containers with organic apples, diced into tiny shards to prevent choking, pears sliced razor-thin and sprinkled with lemon juice. There were carrots, julienned and blanched (uncooked carrots, another silent killer), pan-fried tofu cubes, a viscous dip made with avocado and honey. Remi sat in her Tripp Trapp chair, licking her pointer finger and pressing it onto her Hello Kitty placemat to pick up the last of her toast crumbs. She was funny, too, and rebellious, like Betsy used to be. At the park, ever since she could walk, she'd spin in wild circles, as fast as she could, until she fell down. Then she'd squeal with laughter, her green eyes sparkling.

"Dizzy, it's the gateway drug," Betsy would overhear Gavin say to another father on the bench, shaking his head in mock disgust. "At least she has a designated driver."

Every once in a while, when Betsy would have a second martini, or order nachos instead of the harvest vegetable plate, or when she'd come back from a long, head-clearing run along the Hudson River, she noticed that the clouds parted for a moment, and she would be embarrassed by how Gavin would look at her anew and smile, as though he recognized a long-lost friend. Then the darkness would close in again.

"I found it," he said, pulling out a jar of sunflower seed butter to smear on a hunk of baguette, which he then stuffed in a Ziploc, another item of contraband he picked up on late-night runs to the corner market.

This was how Betsy managed their lives. At work, her hyper-vigilance made her credible, if a bit feared. She was known for her exceedingly thorough research and attention to detail. At home, it wound everything around her as tight as a tourniquet. Betsy's determination not to fuck up her daughter went beyond the typical limits on TV and sugar and battery-operated toys. Betsy was happiest when Remi was inside the house, under the watchful eye of Flavia, their mildly paranoid nanny. Betsy had instantly recognized Flavia's tendencies to anticipate the worst during her first interview, before the police background check, and listed this quality in the "pro" column in the thorough notes she took on everyone who applied for the job.

All this streamed through Betsy's head during her first cup of coffee at home, and again in the shower, as she scrubbed at her aging elbows, and later examined the soft pouches of flesh that were forming below the corners of her mouth in the foggy bathroom mirror. She wondered if her high cheekbones would save her aging face in the end.

Still in her robe, she wandered into her daughter's room, which was pale, sunny, and spare, save for a few pops of muted color and handmade toys, in a studied imitation of the chic Scandinavian nurseries Betsy would ogle online. She shored herself up against the struggles that would play out in front of Remi's closet, as they did most mornings. Would she want to wear a costume again, so their walk to school would be punctuated with glances that implied she was one of *those* kinds of parents? Was she one of the mothers who never brushed her daughter's hair for fear of tears and let her exercise control over her own destiny by wearing a bedazzled Ramones T-shirt over a tattered yellow Snow White dress? Or would she reach for the tidy, tasteful French cotton top with the smocking detail and the Aster Mary Janes, inspiring equally loathsome judgments from passersby convinced of Betsy's need to project good taste and order into the world through her hyper-managed child? She remembered her own delight over clothes as a child, the tidy brown paper packages, shakily addressed to Miss Elizabeth Young that would arrive from her paternal grandmother. She'd met her a handful of times before her father left, before her mother cut off all contact beyond a holiday card. Every year on her birthday, when she was very young, a package arrived that contained a perfectly pressed cotton dress. Betsy remembered being about Remi's age when she opened the box to find a dress adorned with fabric cherries so round and red that her hands shook with excitement as she reached out to touch them. Betsy would sit quietly by while Remi chose her outfit, swallowing all of her memories and opinions and worry, trying to let go.

Remi wasn't as forgiving in front of her mother's closet. Betsy and Gavin were the proud parents of a kale-eating preschooler who chided her mother mercilessly about her chronic under-accessorizing.

"That's red," said Remi, fed and dressed in a Breton striped T-shirt and yellow leggings, topped with a shredded tulle tutu that was snug around her middle. She sat on the bathroom counter watching Betsy get ready for work as she stuffed her index finger into a lipstick cap. "*Red* red. What makes it red?"

Betsy knew there'd come a time when her daughter would start asking questions she'd struggle to answer. Betsy kept a picture of her and Ginny, laughing, jaws agape, dangling from a branch of the kumquat tree in Key West that was close to snapping under the stress of their weight, in a frame on her dresser. When Remi asked about the person who was in the picture, Betsy said, "An old friend," and then changed the subject. She didn't know what to say. She thought she'd have more time to figure it out.

"It's called pigment. It comes from minerals, like rocks, or sometimes plants and flowers," said Betsy, carefully curling her eyelashes, avoiding her daughter's pale blonde head bobbing beneath her elbow. "It's how they make paint, too."

"But, *Mommy,* rocks are dirty," Remi said, pausing a minute to scowl and imagine the process of turning rocks into makeup.

"They clean them, I think. Then they smash them to bits," she explained, twisting her face into a grimace with hopes to raise an eyebrow or induce a giggle. Instead, she was on the other end of that long, steady stare.

"Mommy, why do you wear makeup?"

Betsy wanted to say *Because I feel like death without it.*

Because worry has carved deep lines all over my face. Because I am the oldest forty-year-old in the world.

But instead she smiled at her daughter and said, in the studied tone of nonchalance she was trying to perfect, "Sometimes it just makes me feel pretty." She paused. *Was it working*? "It's one of the things grown-up women do to make themselves feel good."

"Are you wearing that shirt because it makes you look pretty?" asked Remi, studying the shimmering bronzer she'd smeared on the back of her hand and the vaguely boxy, abstract floral Marni top that her mother slid over her head. Remi looked up at Betsy, looking her straight in the eyes.

"I guess so. Do you like it?" Betsy asked.

Remi lay on the floor and kicked her fleshy legs out in front of her. "Umm, not exactly."

How this pattern was established, a mother's attempt to preserve a daughter's ego, protect her innocence, only to have the daughter snap back with a crushing blow to her own, was a mystery. Was this how mean girls were made? Or was it just childhood innocence? Whatever it was, Betsy fell for it every time, fighting the urge to retreat to the closet to change her shirt. "Let's go say bye-bye to Daddy, OK?" Ending sentences with an approval-seeking "OK?" was another habit Betsy found almost impossible to break. Betsy was learning what it meant to be a parent, that even if you want something, desperately, for your child, you can't will it into being. They can't be coerced or molded, only occasionally persuaded—and protected, of course, but Betsy's focus on guarding her daughter from the evils of the world was as hot and precise as a laser. Children are born who they are. The challenge for Betsy was to learn how to get out of Remi's way.

It had been three days since Gavin busted her lurking on the stoop. Out on the street, tiny backpack and lunch in hand, they tromped down the sidewalk, Betsy and her girl—in ladybug galoshes on one of those perfect, blue-sky September mornings—ready to face the world. Just choosing a route for the morning walk to the Montessori school in their neighborhood had been a challenge for Betsy. They'd tried a few paths, sampling them for distance, horn noise, exhaust from idling cars, and the number of street crossings, and Betsy had decided on a slightly longer, less direct path that she timed at seventeen minutes.

She was determined to walk her daughter to school. For starters, if she subtracted the walk to school from their time together, she was spending only three waking hours with her child every day. She also didn't want to give the other mothers at school another reason to criticize her. She had to go.

The division of parental duties was an illusion, Betsy was convinced, which existed so working fathers and mothers could feel like they were pulling equal weight in the contemporary American family. Trading off the rituals of meal preparation, bath time, and dish duty was fine. But the other hidden tasks, including decoding the subtle signals at school, tipped heavily to the maternal side. Gavin had offered to do drop-off, but he was so oblivious to his surroundings, the dynamics between the kids and the school director, the dreaded Elodie, that she knew he'd return with no pertinent information and decided to take on the task herself until she was satisfied that she'd gathered sufficient intel. During her early years in town, Betsy had fought (and lost, mostly) her own social battles before she gave up on the idea of meeting new people. Then she had a baby, and it all started again. When would she be free of the tyranny of the alpha female? The pattern that began in grade school repeated itself again and again, in high school, college, at work, and now in the well-lit hallways of her daughter's preschool, decorated with construction paper cutouts.

BETSY WAS SURE the other parents had heard about her lurking and crying in front of the school. She was so humiliated by Elodie's admonishing leer out of the window, the way she'd been chastised for stalking the school and had to have Gavin swoop in to save her from herself, that she had decided that going back for a college reunion, a hastily organized gathering around a few of her pledge-sisters' fortieth birthdays, might not be a terrible idea. Or it might, in fact, be a terrible idea, but it was her only idea. She was surprised that she had even been invited. Betsy pictured the women she went to college with riffling through old photos and memorabilia and thinking, with blurry and faded memories, "I wonder what ever happened to Betsy Young?" Betsy's memories, on the other hand, were permanently etched, and they stuck to her skin like wax. Going back to Gainesville to reconcile with her past, to see how tiny the buildings looked, how small the town felt, and how hundreds and thousands of students had shuffled sleepily through that campus since she left, might be her only way forward. In the meantime, she repositioned herself on a different stoop, a few doors down and out of Elodie's sight, set her timer for twenty minutes, and accepted that those tortured moments in front of the school were part of her morning routine until she could sort herself out.

By the time she made it to midtown, an hour late to work, and into the austere white marble lobby, she was fully aware of all of the people she was disappointing. When she breezed past the front counter, past the latest crop of fresh-faced Client Services and Catalogue girls, she envied their youth, their utter lack of real responsibility. The more academic of the specialists liked nothing more than to poke fun at them, wondering what kind of "special" client services they really offered behind closed doors. But Betsy remembered enough about being that age to understand that they had more on their minds than waiting to pounce on the next eligible bachelor to walk through the door. Life was never as simple as it seemed. She caught her own distorted reflection on the polished brass doorframe, which looked as twisted and tortured as she felt.

Betsy remembered how she worried at that age, and how she was always concerned about the type of mother she'd become. Back in college, Teddy had given her his dog-eared copy of *Geek Love*, the Katherine Dunn book about circus freaks that college kids flocked to in the early 1990s for its combination of gore and commentary about the damage parents inflict on their children in order to better their lives. When one of the characters, a dwarf-like creature, becomes pregnant in the book, she gives up her daughter to be raised by nuns and watches her blossom into adulthood while posing as a strange but kindhearted neighbor. She didn't want her child to grow up thinking she was a monster, or even the daughter of a monster. At the time, Betsy thought it was pure, twisted fantasy. Now she knew better.

Her potential return to Gainesville, which would be the first time she'd spend more than twenty-four hours away from Remi, was still on her mind when she made it to her corner of the office—not the corner office, just an office near the corner—cutting through a center hall to avoid walking past the regal-looking women in the Jewelry department and the trendy, angular specialists in Asian Contemporary Art, with two nonfat lattes, one for herself and the other for the department assistant, Nina, who thanked her with a woozy smile.

"Rough night?" Betsy asked, marveling at the way last night's mascara and three hours of sleep could look so perfect on her twenty-five-year-old face. "You were here so late! Did you go out after?"

"Is it that obvious?" Nina asked, without the apology that Betsy would have been compelled to offer back when she was in those shoes. Betsy felt that the twenty-five-year-olds owed a world of debt to the forty-year-olds who made showing up at work reeking of last night's tequila shots without retribution possible.

"Sadly, no. But I know you," said Betsy, stashing her bag under her desk, feeling generous, considering that Nina was in early and obviously had been covering for her. *"I used to be you,"* she mumbled, under her breath.

"Oh, Liz, I should tell you, Jessica came by to see if you might be free for lunch," Nina said, eyebrows raised. Nina was the only one who called her Liz, and Betsy was weirdly OK with it. At work, officially, she was still dignified, aloof Elizabeth. Jessica had left to start her own highly lucrative business as an art consultant to aesthetically challenged tech entrepreneurs, but she still breezed down the halls like she ran the place.

"Uh-huh," said Betsy, trying out her best nonplussed expression, turning on her desktop, sorting through the marked-up catalogue copy before her. "What time?"

"She was here to check out the pre-sale. I think she's buying for a new client or something? I don't know. She was here about a half hour ago," said Nina, who straightened up in her chair, shoved the last bite of her bagel into a balled-up napkin, and tossed it into the trash. "And again *now*. She's here now."

"Elizabeth! There you are. The scary preschool saga continues, huh?" Jessica breezed in wearing a black, belted Jil Sander shirtdress that might look plain on anyone with less confidence, or less prominent collarbones, a minimal but substantial gold ring, and towering Saint Laurent platform boots. Her hair, which was once lank and dishwatery, was now icy blonde, nearly platinum, and always pulled back in a sleek ponytail.

Jessica Martin was now Betsy's oldest friend. She had been there from the beginning, helping her navigate the complexities of the environment, letting her tag along to cocktail parties where she'd meet important collectors or potential clients. At first, Betsy could mask her anxiety with as many glasses of free champagne as she could swallow and still remain standing. Eventually, she and Jessica both accepted the fact that Betsy was better off behind the scenes, or dealing privately with loyal clients, gallery owners, and dealers she'd grown to trust. It had been over a year, though, since Betsy had brought in any significant business. Her department's sales were being eclipsed by the competition. Her colleagues in London were starting to grumble that the New York office wasn't pulling its weight. Perhaps her greatest shame was that most of her peers had long since moved on, establishing careers in public relations or consulting or anything more glamorous, and she felt stuck.

SHE AND JESSICA had remained close, as close as Betsy would allow, for almost twenty years. She was a bridesmaid in Jess's wedding, one of eight. She kept a photo of the bridal party in a frame at home and would always manage a laugh when she saw herself among the beaming smiles of Jessica's aggressively highlighted high school friends and cousins. Around Jessica, Betsy would always be the girl in the grungy sweater.

"Lunch at Nougatine?" Jessica asked.

"God I wish," Betsy said. "But I can't, I'm so behind. Here, sit for a second."

Jessica sat in one of Betsy's Sergio Rodrigues leather chairs, which was low slung and pouchy, like an oversized, glamorous baseball mitt, and made her friend seem even more angular and narrow than usual.

"Is it the mom guilt again? Trust me. You'll get over it," said Jessica, who'd married a venture capitalist who was more than pleased to introduce his clients to his art-savvy wife for consultations, and had a six-year-old son, Cash, named without an ounce of self-awareness. She kept the job for the cachet, the occasional media profiles that included her as an "influencer," and the excuse to buy $1,500 shoes. "Who is it serving, really? Remi is being raised by a competent woman, otherwise known as Flavia. Just get over it."

These days, Jessica always twirled her hands around when she talked to Betsy, like she was holding a martini, letting the tiny ice chips make faint clinking sounds against the glass. Frequently, she was.

"Remi asked me why I wear makeup before I left this morning," Betsy said, desperate to change the subject and get to the pile of work before her but unwilling to show it. "And I wanted to tell her that being a mom was like being president. Four years in and everybody looks like shit."

"Ha! So true. Speaking of, I had another Kim Gordon

sighting at a gallery last night. You know that she paints now, right?" she said. Betsy was obsessed with Kim Gordon of Sonic Youth. She was the standard by which all other women were measured. "I know you're desperate for her to get Botox so you can finally paralyze your face, too. But I must say she is still wrinkly and still fabulous."

"Uh-huh." Betsy nodded, distracted, scanning the pages in front of her. "She's always been an artist."

"Elizabeth?" Jessica was annoyed by anyone who didn't grant her their full attention.

"Yes? Oh, Kim Gordon, right. Sonic Youth is going out with Pavement on a reunion tour," Betsy said. She thought of Gainesville. Her chest tightened. *Reunion*. "We should go and seek comfort in the presence of other elderly and infirm music fans."

"Thanks for the offer, but I don't think so. Jesus, are you even listening to me?"

"Of course I am. You just reminded me of something, that's all." Betsy scribbled "reunion?" on a sticky note and tagged it on the bottom of her screen, next to the one from last week that said "Milk: Almond or hemp?"

"Oh, hey, you know that I was over at Phillip's last week, and their Prints department is killing it," said Jessica. She turned and headed for the door.

"Why? What do you mean?" asked Betsy. She looked up from her work, trying to look more inquisitive than defensive.

"Well, they've just got some major stuff coming up."

"I see. More major than what we're doing, obviously," said Betsy.

"I just thought you'd want to know what's happening with

the competition. I never see you out and around anymore. I just don't want people to think you're out of the game."

"Out of the game. Nice, Jess. That's just what I need," she said, coolly.

"Look, I don't know what is going on with you these days, but your head is *not* in the game. And not that it's my business, really, but as a friend I have to tell you that I hear your approval rating around here is at an all-time low. I mean, you were never Miss Popularity, but it's worse than ever."

"Well, I'm a little preoccupied, but I wouldn't say I am *loathed,* exactly," said Betsy, taking a swig of her latte with what seemed, immediately, like too much panache.

"Hmm, actually, I might. I might almost say loathed. If you're not going to do your job, trust me, there are a dozen people here who will. This isn't France, Betsy. You're not grandfathered into permanent semiretirement just because you've worked here for nineteen years," said Jessica. She folded her arms, which were toned from boxing and Pilates and, Betsy often chuckled to herself, pushing away all of that food, across her chest. "I'm just worried you're closing yourself off from the world. Name one actual friend you have in the building, now that I'm gone."

"Nina!" said Betsy. She could see from the corner of her eye that Nina was leaning far forward on her desk trying to hide behind the half wall of her cubicle.

"That doesn't count. You're her boss. She has to pretend to like you."

"Oh, then I guess *your* former assistants didn't get that *memo,* as they say. A couple of years ago, I was grabbing a yogurt out of the fridge one day and I heard one of them say that she was going to take the new Paul Smith shirts you made her order for your husband and have the letters ATM monogrammed on the pocket! That doesn't sound like something a 'friend' would say, does it?"

"Which assistant was it? Alexandra or Sam?"

"Oh, please, why does that matter? They don't even work for you anymore. What are you going to do, have them fired? I was just saying that to . . ."

"Absolutely. I can make one phone call and have them fired by someone else. And by the way, if the assistants find out that you were the one who shared that little story, that wouldn't be the fast track to likability and redemption around here."

"Whoa. Is that a threat?" Betsy asked. "Fine, Jessica, you're right. I have no friends. I have no friends because . . ."

"Because why? What is wrong, Betsy? All these years and sometimes I feel like I hardly know you."

Betsy sighed. "Jessica, the truth is I am a terrible, terrible friend."

Jessica, for once, was speechless.

"Now if you'll excuse me, I have work to do. I don't want to slip even further out of the game, right? Miss the second half? Insert your favorite sports metaphor here."

Betsy stood up to emphasize her point. She watched Jessica walk out of the door and down the hall, listening to the hollow knocking footsteps of her platforms get softer as she strode away. She glanced back at the sticky note again.

"The last thing I need is to go to a reunion," she said to no one in particular, suddenly mystified, remembering her bitter fights with Caroline, the ruthlessness of her sorority. "It's like I never left."

"Have you got a reunion coming up?" asked Nina, desperate to change the subject, as she picked through her garbage to see if she could salvage the remains of her breakfast. "Man, those are tough. But you don't have anything to worry about. I swear, Liz, from some angles you don't look a day over thirty-seven."

CHAPTER 22

KUMQUAT TREE

September 24, 2010

Betsy saw Ginny sitting on the porch, barefoot, in the same beat-up Levi's she'd had since college. Her hair was shorter now. It grazed the tops of her shoulders and was a duller shade of brown with a few grays sprouting up from the top, coarse as electrical wire. She'd heard voices coming from inside the house. Boys, two of them, ran through the open doorway and into the yard with a wiry, black-and-white terrier trailing behind them. The dog came up to inspect Betsy's shoes, barking to announce the presence of a stranger.

"Fletch? Is that you?" said Betsy, crouching to scratch the chin of the tiny stray dog Ginny found in high school and gave to Nana Jean. "How are you still around?" When she got closer, she could see the accordion lines around Ginny's eyes, the same high, angular bone structure, but speckled with a spray of faint age spots the crept up from her cheeks. She was watching the children play and she was laughing, that same,

short, sharp laugh, head thrown back, mouth gaping. Catching flies, as always.

"Come here, you little scruff," she called to the dog, scratching his bony head. Ginny started peeling oranges for the boys' snack, wiping the juice on her T-shirt.

"Remember the time," Betsy said, the words lazy, drawn out, "when we climbed that kumquat tree? It was spring break, right? What year was that?"

Key West. The two of them had rented bikes and circled that tiny, overstuffed island at least five times. They'd made it to the southernmost point. Ninety Miles to Cuba, read the sign, but all they could see in the distance was a couple of catamarans and a few drifting cotton ball clouds. They'd found a tiny hammock shop and climbed into the display, strung between two banana palms, listening to the sound of the birds and loving that they'd managed to sneak away from the crowd of drunks they'd arrived with. Later, they pedaled down to Duval Street for the sunset and a guy who Ginny recognized from her Statistics class offered them a pot brownie, which they split without much hesitation. He wandered off to buy a beer and when he returned to the spot where the three of them had been standing, Betsy and Ginny had slipped away. A few blocks down the road, the two friends met some old queens on Harleys who said they liked their smiles, and then invited them to join in a round of Rum Runners at a sidewalk bar, which they did. And just before the light disappeared completely, they found the biggest kumquat tree either of them had ever seen. Not that they'd seen many kumquat trees. And they climbed to the highest branches that would support their weight. Why the kumquat tree was so hilarious was hard to say. But they stayed up there until Betsy had to pee. It was always Betsy who broke first.

The wind blew Ginny's hair into her mouth and she brushed it away. "I miss you," Betsy said. Ginny looked her in the eye, holding her gaze longer than Betsy could bear. She looked away and thought, "Just say it. Say you're sorry. Say that it should have been you. Say that you should have spoken up before it was too late."

The boys ran back inside the house until their laughter grew faint and Ginny followed them.

"Wait," *Betsy thought.* "It isn't over yet." *In the background, she heard a man's voice, the sound of a radio coming from inside.*

"It's been over for a while now," said Ginny, standing in the doorframe, letting the screen slam loudly behind her.

She shot awake and her knee slammed against the tray, knocking her plastic cup and a single round ice cube onto the royal blue carpet of the plane. She could feel her heart thumping through her shirt, electricity shooting from her spine to the beds of her fingernails. Her mind raced to remember where she was.

"We've begun our descent into the Tampa airport," continued the pilot's voice over the intercom. "Flight attendants, prepare for arrival."

The air was heavy with clouds, of course, since it was September and the Florida fall was still at least a month away, which made for a rough landing. Off the plane, in the pastel-drenched Tampa airport, she stared at the manatee mosaic on the wall as she descended on the escalator to ground transportation. She felt an odd connection to the gentle but doomed creatures, floating along the stream in all of their passive awkwardness, defenseless to the speedboats that sliced their flesh with their angry props.

CHAPTER 23
REUNION

September 25, 2010

In a cracked and weedy parking lot next to a Starbucks, attached to a church or a school or some other unremarkable single-story brick structure identical to hundreds of others that dotted the Tampa landscape, Betsy stood with her coffee in hand. It was 9:15, fifteen minutes before the scheduled meeting time to board the bus and make the two-hour trek to Gainesville, and she stood alone near the center of the lot. She'd forgotten how small the city was and left the hotel with too much time to spare. The taxi driver dropped her in the empty lot, but not before he asked her to check the address twice.

"This is it," she said. "I think. I'm starting to believe this is all a bad dream. I'll call you if it turns out I'm right."

Convinced the others were hiding in their cars, sizing her up through deeply tinted windows, Betsy was feeling self-conscious, which always led to second thoughts about her outfit. She wore a cotton summer dress in a too-cheery plaid and simple leather sandals that later, when her feet were swollen from standing for hours in the heat, she'd regret. Her hair, which had a memory for the humidity and sprang into odd angles when it topped 80 percent, was smoothed back into a stubby ponytail, wrested into order for the moment. Her hair wasn't the only thing that had its recall triggered by the familiar surroundings. She suddenly realized that she might be the only person she'd see that day who didn't have writing on her clothing. Her dress and shoes bore no swoosh or logo, and neither item was made of fiber that employed the word "micro" to describe it. She missed Gavin.

"Gooooo Gators," he said, answering after the first ring.

"Yeah right, go Gators," she said. "I'm standing in some sad parking lot waiting to be ripped limb from limb."

"Hold on," he said. "Hey, Rem, no climbing in the fountain."

"You're off to an early start," she said, wondering where all of this parental energy was coming from.

"Up and at 'em," he said, with a kind of forced brightness. "We had pancakes. We hopped the bus to Central Park. It's not even ten and I've accomplished more today than I did in all of 1994."

That was sixteen years ago, Betsy thought. *I was an adult sixteen years ago.*

"I'm starting to regret this," she said, as her Ray-Bans slowly fogged.

"Which part? There are so many things we could regret, you'll have to be more specific," he said. Betsy paused. She was determined not to let anyone see her cry that day. She didn't have an answer.

"Can you at least remember to laugh?" he said. "If not with

them, then *at* them? It's just a tailgate party at a football game. It's just one day."

She could call a taxi. She could tell the driver to take her to the airport and she could go home, or rent a car and drive to the beach in Venice or Sarasota to spend the day on the long, sandy, empty expanse of shoreline where she'd wasted countless hours in high school, drifting silently in bathtub-warm water, plotting her escape.

"Holy shit, if it isn't Betsy Young," boomed a voice from behind her, causing her to jump and splash the first of many lukewarm beverages on her feet that day. She turned to see a familiar face, at once harder (around the cheekbones) and softer (around the eyes) than it had been twenty years ago.

"Jen?" She remembered there were four Jens, a handful of Stacys, three Kims, and a couple of Hollys. She'd flipped through old party pics like flash cards the night before she left to see how many names she could recall. But standing before her, plain as day, was Jen Haws, with Molly and Brooke and one of the Kims, exiting a Mercedes wagon with the blackest tinted windows she had ever seen.

"Gav, I . . . they're here," she said, trying not to sound so ominous. "I'll call you later?"

"I'll look for you and the face painters on ESPN," he said.

"I love you," she said.

"I know."

"Look what the flippin' cat dragged in," barked Jen. Despite the hour, and the informality of the event, lip gloss had been distributed generously among the pack before her, a sort of suburban, mannered version of *Real Housewives* with Bible study and Reef flip-flops. The hair was straight and excessively tasteful now. Their breasts still perfect after childbirth, their limbs Pilates-toned. Betsy imagined them all in a line at their respective private school drop-offs in a parade of luxury SUVs, hopping out to shuttle their small, bobbed, doppelgängers into fifth grade. *They* were the Lycra pants moms, bearing more discreet swooshes on non-game days. Betsy knew that she had been one of the last of her classmates to get pregnant and expected to be presented with photos of sons and daughters before the high school homecoming dance. She'd seen their offspring on Facebook and realized, not without feeling the looming inevitability of her own mortality, that she was not much older than those kids when she first met their mothers.

A tour bus the length of a city block with an entire swirling, purple galaxy airbrushed on its side panels came wheezing into the parking lot. Then, a woman in knee-length shorts and a blaze orange T-shirt, holding an Ann Taylor Loft shopping bag full of metallic Mardi Gras beads and blue plastic Solo cups appeared from around the corner.

"Oh my God, this thing is hideous," she said, peering into the tinted glass door of the bus after it whined to a halt in front of her.

"Excuse me, sir?" She tapped on the glass with her index finger. "Can you open this thing up so we can load the coolers?"

A cardboard box full of toxic energy drinks and liter jugs of vodka, plus three bags of rapidly melting ice, were unloaded from the back of a Ford Expedition onto the gravelly asphalt by a man who, if she squinted, looked like Phil Portner, a guy she had made out with once after a day spent floating down the Ichetucknee River in an inner tube with a bunch of drunk frat boys. She had erased him, and his awkward groping in her dorm room, from her memory until that moment.

"Betsy, Jesus, it's been a while," he said, slapping her on the shoulder, never removing the sunglasses that were secured across the back of his neck by a neoprene strap.

"Phil, honey, that ice is toast if you don't get it in the cooler, pronto," said the woman with the beads, who Betsy was now realizing was Leslie Richmond, a woman about whom she remembered two facts: she was in the room the night she walked out of the sorority house for the last time; and she kept six bags of peas in the community freezer, which she would eat, almost exclusively, for dinner.

"Stacy was supposed to bring some food, but I told her, what's the point?" she said to no one in particular, chuckling to herself. "Oh hey, Betsy Young! Or I guess it's Davis now, right? Someone told me you go by Elizabeth now, too? Who are you anyway?" She laughed, though Betsy didn't think she was trying to be funny.

"Hey, Leslie. Nice to see you," she said. "You can call me Betsy, or Elizabeth if you want. Just not 'gal' or 'sport.'"

Leslie squinted slightly, no trace of a smile.

"What about you? So you're Leslie Portner now? You and Phil have been together since school?"

"Oh, please. We've been married since 1996," she said, rolling her eyes. "And he's still filling the cooler for me. Who says romance is dead?"

"I do," said a voice from behind her that sent a chill down her spine. Betsy turned to see Caroline, with chin-length hair, almost brown now, grinning slyly behind oversized black oval sunglasses.

"Look who's here to save the day," said Caroline.

"Thank God," said Betsy, louder than she intended.

"Yes, the Lord is certainly to thank for this pleasure," said

Leslie. "What a surprise! I didn't see your name on the list." If she was trying to conceal her disappointment it wasn't working.

"It's not on the list," she said. "But I'm here now."

Betsy couldn't stop staring at her old friend, startled by her sudden fondness for someone she thought she hated.

"But it's full. The bus is at capacity."

"It's a forty-foot bus, Richmond," she said. "There's room for one more. When is the last time everybody showed up who said they were coming to something like this? You're telling me that nobody has a kid puking on them somewhere? You think there isn't a single sitter who canceled in this whole pathetic crew?"

Leslie shot Betsy a rueful look and turned to leave without another word.

"That's my motto," said Caroline, flatly. "Not taking shit for forty years."

"What are we doing?" said Betsy, grabbing Caroline's forearm, shaking her head. "I have no idea why I'm here."

"Because this," said Caroline, making a loop in the air with her index finger, indicating the madness around them, "is going to be fucking hilarious."

By 10:15 a.m., a full forty-five minutes behind schedule, they boarded the party bus, which was already filled with the stench of a urinal cake and Gatorade. In back, the "bar" consisted of two cases of Bud Light, three liters of vodka, two of Jack Daniel's, a single, warm carton of orange juice, a jug of Ocean Spray cranberry juice cocktail, and infinite cans of Red Bull.

Caroline and Betsy opened two more beers.

"I'm sober with more frequency now, especially during the day. Today I will make an exception," said Caroline. "It's like smoking. If I say I'm never having one again, it's all I think about."

They examined their surroundings briefly, taking stock of who was there and who was mysteriously absent. Instead of rows of seats, the bus was lined with two long, velour upholstered benches, so they all sat facing each other. AC/DC was barely audible in the background.

"I was kinda hoping to see Kendra," said Betsy. "You know, the quiet one who was secretly so wild? With the crazy hair?" She shook her free hand around her face to indicate a big, wild mess. Kendra was famous for her studying habits, which were borderline obsessive. Every couple of months, she'd explode like a powder keg and go on wild drinking binges. Once, they found her on a Sunday morning passed out on the front lawn of the house. She was eager to see how that mess organized itself twenty years on.

"Holy shit, Betsy, she died," said one of the Hollys. "Like, in 1994 or 1995. She was an au pair for a family in Europe one summer when she was in graduate school. She died there, in her sleep."

"I heard she choked on her own vomit," said Stacy, sitting hard next to them, taking a swig of her JDC.

"Oh God, I had no idea," said Betsy. "I'm sorry! Jesus, that's really awful."

"You did. You knew. You just forgot," said Caroline. "People were talking about it at Melanie and Teddy's wedding."

Betsy flashed back to the wedding at the Everglades Club. She'd missed her plane. Caroline was mean as a snake.

"All I remember about that wedding," Betsy said, "is what a bitch you were to me in the bathroom."

"Hmm," said Caroline, shaking her head. "Those were

dark times for me. I guess you're not the only one who forgets terrible things."

Betsy looked out the window, hoped no one would notice the sudden shift in her mood, and wondered how long it would take her to walk back to Tampa if she got out right there on the side of the road.

"How many funerals were we supposed to attend before we turned twenty-five?" said Jen, in a clumsy defense. "Give her a break."

"I'm not giving her a hard time," said Caroline. "But I'll be honest, I would have bet you five dollars that she forgot about Melanie's wedding, too."

Betsy could see the landscape turn back to that familiar rural desolation, vast green fields punctuated by the occasional wandering cow, a few gray-tinged clouds that hung absurdly low in the sky.

"They're divorced now anyway, so who cares," Betsy mumbled, willing herself back into the moment. "I do. I block stuff out. I'm sorry. It's how I survive."

Betsy's eyes locked on Caroline's for the briefest second, searching for some connection.

"So how's New York? How's Gavin?" asked Holly, who was now sitting beside her. "You two still together?"

"Yeah, we're hanging in," said Betsy, surprised that Holly knew anything about her life. "We've been there almost twenty years now, if you can believe it."

"You know Cammie?" asked Holly, who, in her pale early forties was almost unrecognizable. Back in school, she was perpetually tan, but in a lifeguard kind of way with wide strap marks on her shoulders and faint, pale lines that extended from the outer corners of her eyes to the tops of her ears. "I heard she's out in L.A. Someone saw her on an episode of *Law & Order* once."

"Oh, great. Good for her," said Betsy, nodding her head, searching for the segue.

"What is it that you do again?"

"I'm a specialist in Prints and Multiples at an auction house in New York," said Betsy.

"Oh, cool. Is it like *The Devil Wears Prada*?" she asked.

"Um, no, not really. That takes place at a magazine, I think, right? Isn't it *Vogue* or something?"

Betsy had long wondered what people from here had thought of her, of her life in New York, of her disappearance after Ginny's funeral. If she'd been wondering what Holly, or anyone else on that party bus, had thought of her in the meantime, she got her answer that day: Not much.

"So what do you do, Holly?" Betsy asked. She struggled to stay focused in the present.

"I work in the state attorney's office," she said. "Thirteenth circuit, back in Tampa."

"Oh, yeah, I think I remember hearing that," she said and hoped the lie wasn't too transparent.

"Alright well, I've got to pee. I've been holding it since Plant City because I'm terrified of that bathroom," Holly said while she made her way through the crowd, swaying with every tip of the bus, in the midstages of a buzz. A small group in the back had started singing loudly and off-key to George Michael's "Freedom '90." One of the Kims checked her reflection in the mirrored surface of the tinted window when she thought no one would notice.

"Well, that one's a firecracker, right?" Caroline said. "She's a regular dynamo. To be honest, I didn't think Holly knew that many words."

"She's smart as hell, Caroline. She's a state attorney," said Betsy. "And come to find out, I'm an asshat."

Caroline tapped the side of her plastic cup to Betsy's.

"Seems like old times, right?" Caroline laughed, and it sent a jolt of joy through Betsy's brain to see her happy.

"Tell me you didn't vanish for twenty years and come back expecting to bond over the glory days," she added in a way that wasn't exactly unkind, but more familiar. Then, like quicksilver, she softened again. "Do I really have to remind you that you never had much in common with them? Unless you were serious about liking soap operas."

"They were on during my lunch break," said Betsy with a smile, swirling the remains of her warm beer. "Jack and Jennifer? What, you didn't watch?"

"It's just a day, just a two-hour ride to a football game," Caroline said, and Betsy noticed she was echoing Gavin's words almost exactly. "The only thing that's wrong about any of this reunion bullshit is that we're forced to stay in touch with, like, everyone we've ever known and look at pictures of their fat husbands on social media. It ruins the element of surprise."

"What about you?" Betsy asked, relieved to be listening to someone say exactly what she thought before she had to think it for herself. "Didn't you ever want a fat husband?"

"I was engaged once," she said. "But that was a long time ago."

Betsy didn't press for details. There was time for that.

They sat listening to the hum of the tires on the highway, which was now clogged with game day traffic, wondering what to say next. One of the Kims was talking to a Dana *(had she been there the whole time?)* about her divorce, which was clearly not amicable and left two damaged tweens in its wake. The bad beer and the bumpy ride had conspired to make Betsy queasy, and the fact that she was speeding down the highway to a place she had tried so hard to forget wasn't helping matters. There she was sitting next to Caroline, who had hurt her so deeply a lifetime ago, but was the only person she needed in that moment.

"So tell me about Remi Virginia," Caroline said, grinning. "I bet she's just like her mom. For better or worse, right?"

CHAPTER 24
GAME TIME

September 25, 2010

Since traffic had slowed to a halt less than a mile away from the freeway on their way into town, Betsy had plenty of time to get used to the idea that she was back in Gainesville twenty years after the fact. As the bus crept along University Boulevard, the most granular memories and details came flooding back. So much of it was the same, the rolling hills of the golf course, the ornate buildings of the original campus wedged in between the hulking, windowless brick mistakes from the late 1970s. The stadium was imposing as ever, the dominant structure on the landscape, metaphorically and otherwise.

The group plan for the day, as Leslie arranged it, was to stop at the sorority house for a brief tour and make it back to the other side of campus with plenty of time for tailgating. Two years earlier, after a massive capital campaign during which they pried open the heavy purses of dowager alumni sisters of a certain age, and nickel-and-dimed the less moneyed alumni for fifty-dollar donations at every turn, the forty-room house Betsy remembered so vividly had been partially razed and entirely renovated to mimic the kind of cartoonishly regal Southern mansion you picture when you think "sorority." There were white columns installed where a sort of angular modernist facade once stood. There were wide stairs leading to a stately white painted door. Once inside, Betsy didn't feel any of the gut-aching dread she'd anticipated. The past had been demo'd, rebuilt, and then finished with dark-stained floors and plush carpets, designed with the kind of neutral and deeply inoffensive style from the Ritz-Carlton school of decorating. Every detail was so strenuously tasteful that it all just kind of disappeared in a not unpleasant way. They had even rebranded rush. It was called "recruitment" now, which sounded vaguely militaristic, and much more accurate.

At first, Betsy tried to linger outside, hesitant to enter the place even though none of the circa-1990 dwelling was intact. After a few minutes on the shadeless, baking sidewalk, it occurred to her that no one on that bus had mentioned how she'd quit the sorority in a huff. It was likely that none of them, save for Caroline, remembered the details. Two decades ago, she struggled to break the rules in a place that didn't value rebellion, or at least that's what she'd told herself, and Dr. Hirsch, in therapy for all of those years.

But what was she rebelling against? She knew it must have had something to do with her missing father. Kathy was so afraid of the world after he left that she cautioned her daughter against being different, acting out, against taking up too much space. When she started college, she was just beginning to realize what that meant: that the people in the world in charge of making decisions weren't capable of or interested in making decisions on her behalf. She just began to realize, like waking up from a dream, that she had other ideas. But there, in that bubble of hair spray and tailgates and white BMWs, everyone embraced the status quo, because that's what allowed privileged kids to screw around on their parents' dime.

Betsy wished she had understood her rebellion of 1990, which amounted to wearing Army surplus boots, cutting her own hair, drinking too much, and fairly run-of-the-mill bad behavior, before she bailed on the sorority and left for New York. She wished that she had known some of the other young women around her in the midst of that same transformation and embraced it. In hindsight, it all seemed so clear. She walked up that sidewalk to the now unrecognizable front door, with a flashy brass knocker and a dramatically different view from adulthood. Betsy wondered why the intensity of her youth never led to a more radical adult life, why she wasted that energy on getting wasted and, more recently, endless web searches for ideas for her kitchen remodel. She vowed to stop making granola bars when she got back home.

The question she asked herself, as she walked into that house and plastered a smile on her face, is how did the girl who wanted to be so different grow up? What if she didn't feel like being vegan, or a subversive crafter, or mastering the art of butchering a pig, or getting a tat sleeve, or doing anything else predictably shocking or edgy? What if she'd rather take a cab than brave traffic on her vintage reproduction bike? What if she now thought secondhand clothes smell terrible, and would rather fill virtual shopping carts on Net-a-Porter, only to abandon them later when she was too lazy to get out of bed to find her credit card?

"I know I've stood in this exact same spot, exactly as buzzed as I am now, but I don't recognize a fucking thing," said Caroline, who found Betsy at the top of the stairs and pulled her aside to whisper conspiratorially.

"This is way too creepy," said Betsy, eyeing oversized frame after oversized frame of house composite photos, each sister's perfect smile frozen in time and shrunken into a stiff, two-inch-by-two-inch mug shot and assembled into a neat grid. "We're so old that our composite pictures have been moved into the basement."

"Don't be so sure," said Holly, calling for them at the end of the hall. "Here. I spotted one from 1988."

Sure enough, the top row of towering bangs gave it away at twenty paces. Betsy was on the second row from the bottom. It was a different photo than the one in the email, just row after row of faces, each with its own imprint and shards of memories attached. She'd forgotten about her own photo from sophomore year, that shiny forehead, a last glimpse of her long hair, and the shirt with the lace collar that should have been pressed. In the row above her were Caroline Finnerty and Ginny, Virginia Harrington, hazel eyes shining, her hair falling past her shoulders in heavy brunette waves. Betsy and Caroline were so lost in that photo they didn't hear Stacy approach them from behind.

"Every time I see the two of you together I expect her to come around the corner at any minute," she said. Stacy was the first one, the only one, brave enough to mention the missing piece. "It's got to be hard to be here without her."

Betsy and Caroline heard what she said, but they were speechless. Their eyes were locked on the photo. Neither one could tear them away.

BACK ON THE bus, it was standing room only in the thick, stifling air, since more people had joined the reunion tour. The part of Betsy's brain that retrieved faces and names from the distant past on demand was on overload. She just nodded and smiled at anyone who looked her way. Once they were parked, the shimmering purple bus door with the celestial scene slid open and spilled forth a clown car's worth of middle-aged women who were off to find their respective visor-wearing mates in Izod shirts. Lacoste had created a staggering variation of orange and blue stripes, wide-wide-narrow, narrow-wide-narrow, all narrow, all wide, which were all on display here. Betsy fought her way through the crowd on Caroline's arm, dazed from the heat and the beer, hobbled by swollen feet in her defiantly non-athletic shoes. Gavin had mentioned that Teddy would be in for the game from Savannah, where he was an architect who designed mammoth beach houses for red-faced, Atlanta businessmen and their grandchildren. They had talked about Gavin coming, too, but in the end she knew this was something she had to do on her own. She made a note in her phone of the parking space where Teddy would be tailgating, thinking how much less fun things would have been back then if you were so easily found, textable, traceable, identified by a pin dropped on a tiny, electronic map. She spotted Teddy through the crowd instantly, same rumpled blue oxford, a red cap pulled low to the top of his glasses, a few graying blonde curls springing around the back of it.

"Betsy Young, in the flesh," he said. "Jesus, it's like seeing a ghost." If any of Gavin's other old buddies in his immediate company was interested in seeing her, they didn't show it. Their wide, dark, black glasses concealed any glimpse of enthusiasm for life they might experience until kickoff, when all of the rage and passion they'd been storing up during the off-season let loose. If they'd always been boring, Betsy hadn't noticed in school. She had interpreted their aloofness as proof that they were special, above it all, but she realized now that it was in fact a kind of smoke screen to conceal that they didn't have much to say, or at least not to her. They had become exactly like their own fathers, the graying men in khaki shorts with the giant RVs, wearing hats to cover beleaguered hair follicles clinging to their scalps like sparse, windswept scrub on the side of a cliff.

Whatever trouble she was having with Gavin, she was sure she'd ended up with the best from the lot and was grateful for the renewed perspective. Teddy was a close second. He had come up north for Betsy and Gavin's wedding with Melanie, and Gavin had seen him a handful of times for fishing trips. Betsy only half remembered his attempts to reach out to her during the blurry days she left Gainesville for good. But she remembered that he tried.

"Teddy, you remember Caroline," she said, stepping aside to let them shake hands.

"How do you forget Caroline?" he said.

"Yeah, right, scary Caroline," she said, looking over her giant sunglasses at Betsy. "I was nothing compared to the bitches who run this place now."

"I'm fully aware that this will make me sound like a Quaker," said Betsy. "But do you think these girls are aware that their butt cheeks are hanging out of their shorts?"

"Sorry, I hadn't noticed," laughed Teddy. "That would make me a sad, divorced, middle-aged man, trying to relive his youth. And I am far from it."

"Hey, Betsy, do you think any of these girls wear giant

T-shirts over their bathing suits when they're in the hot tub like we did?" said Caroline.

"Watch your use of pronouns, Car. There was no 'we' in the hot tub, because, you know . . ."

"Yes, I know that you thought you were going to get the clap from some residue left behind."

"Doesn't the chlorine kill all of that stuff?" asked Teddy.

"Not according to my mother," said Betsy. "Anyway, I don't think any of the girls I've seen today would get in a hot tub. It would ruin their blowout," said Betsy.

"Anybody want a beer?" Caroline nodded hello to the grumpy semicircle of men protecting the cooler, poured one into her cup, and started a roundtable discussion about the Florida quarterback at the time, Tim Tebow, and his alleged virginity.

"So did Remi start that preschool? You know, the labor camp one where they all have 'jobs'?" asked Teddy.

"Oh, yeah. She started this year," said Betsy, surprised that Teddy and Gavin had spoken so recently.

"And Gavin? How's he?"

"Well, it sounds like you could answer that question as well as I could."

"I remember that night I saw you together at Weird Bobby's, before you took off for New Orleans," he said, shaking his head. "I thought, 'They're going to hate each other's guts, or they're going to get married. Nothing in between.'"

"Or both?" added Betsy, with a weak smile, but she quickly regretted it.

They could hear the distant sound of the marching band through the crowd.

"If you ask me, you got lucky. Really lucky," he said. "It

just works that way for some people. But if I talk anymore about feelings, they're going to run me out of town. Maybe even the state."

"It's true," Betsy said. "It's Florida. Men who talk about their feelings would be *happier elsewhere*."

"Speaking of, I'm headed back to Tampa to see my folks before I fly back home tomorrow. You want to skip the recap on the bus ride home and come along?" said Teddy.

"Oh Lord, yes, please," said Caroline, who had given up on trying to sully Tebow's reputation and returned to the conversation. "You've had enough of this by now, right? No need to barrel back down memory lane when the mascara starts to run. Blood, sweat, and tears, am I right?"

After making plans to text Teddy after the game, they made the long ascent to the upper deck. Once inside the stadium, they wound their way through the crowd, up the endless ramp to the very top. By the time they were out into the stadium, the dizzying height, the roar of the crowd, and the heat conspired against her. The two friends sat pressing their shoulders against their sweat-drenched seatmates. At the end of the first quarter, a halting, commercial-interrupted bore of a game, Betsy made her confession.

"Caroline, I just realized, once and for all, that I don't really like football," she said, at almost a whisper.

"Holy shit! Are you serious? Do you seriously hate football?" her voice escalated slowly, and Betsy started to remember why they were friends. She stood up.

"Wow, you hate football?" Caroline was practically yelling.

"You are an ass," said Betsy, trying to suppress her smile, pulling on her arm to get Caroline to sit back down on the hard aluminum bench. The fans around them started to boo, yelling at Caroline to sit down, and Betsy made a run for the exit while the people in the surrounding seats launched trash at her. Caroline followed her out, cackling with laughter over their loud jeers. They sprinted down what seemed like thousands of concrete stairs, like a low-security jailbreak, and burst back into the vast parking lot. They made their way across the street in search of someplace familiar, only to realize that all of the old places had been replaced with slicker, more polished but somehow sadder versions of their predecessors, kind of like Times Square. She was devastated to discover that Bagelville was long gone, replaced by a Schlotzsky's. She wondered what happened to Tom. The old vegetarian restaurant in the Victorian house had been converted into a plantation-style bar with shady outdoor seating, outfitted with fans that sprayed a delicate mist of cool vapor on its inebriated patrons. There was over an hour wait for a table at the hostess stand, but Caroline being Caroline had talked her way into two empty seats at a table in the far corner of the wide patio occupied by a couple of meek grad students who didn't have the balls to tell her she couldn't sit down, directly under a mister with an unencumbered sight line to the TV. By the third quarter, Caroline was giving Charles, the smaller one with the recessed chin, dating advice, and Betsy was showing Albert photos of Remi on her phone.

"Just don't tell her you love her, Charles," said Caroline. "Trust me, she's walking all over you."

Out of some sense of obligation to the past, they ordered a massive plate of chicken nachos and a couple of bourbon and Cokes.

"Ah, bourbon on a hundred-degree day. I feel like I'm twenty again," said Caroline.

"If that means you feel insecure about your thighs and sticky from sweat, so do I," said Betsy. They sat in silence, pretending to watch the game, half listening to the conversations between the people two decades their junior that surrounded them.

"I don't even remember what we were fighting about, you know, before everything went to shit," said Caroline, not meeting Betsy's eyes. She paused for a minute.

"Actually, that's a lie. I remember all of it."

"I do, too," said Betsy. "We pretended that it was about guys and my leaving the sorority and all of that. But there was more."

"I think I probably felt rejected, like you were leaving us behind. Like you thought that we were stupid and you were too wise for all of it. And maybe I thought on some level that you were right. But then you literally disappeared," said Caroline. "You just left me here."

In the two decades she'd been gone, it had never occurred to her that Caroline needed her help.

"I was desperate to leave, even before everything went down," said Betsy. "And then, you know, the drama just expedited things. I couldn't take it. I couldn't do it without Ginny."

"You know, I called you on the day McRae was executed," Caroline said. "But I couldn't leave a message."

Betsy remembered being pregnant with Remi, her walk up Central Park West on that awful morning in Dr. Kerr's office. "It was Remi's birthday. As in, the day she was born," said Betsy. "I was kind of busy anyway."

"Part of the problem was that I was jealous," said Caroline. "*I* was the one who was supposed to get out of here first. I was the one who was on to bigger things. But you and Gavin just sailed into the sunset, like Danny and Sandy in that fucking flying convertible. And all of a sudden I was Frenchy, standing on the ground with some freaked-out hairdo waving a fucking hanky. I was the one who was supposed to get out. You were the one who was supposed to sell real estate in Miami. We got it all wrong."

Betsy stared at the bottom of her empty cup.

"I'm sorry," she said, finally.

"Sorry for what? You didn't stop me from going. I stopped myself. In the end, I just couldn't do it. I don't know . . ." Caroline said.

"I'm sorry, but you got it all wrong," said Betsy, averting her eyes. "You were Rizzo."

"What?"

"Frenchy was way too nice. Rizzo was the mean, slutty one. You were Rizzo."

Caroline took a beat.

"I was totally Rizzo."

And for the second time that day, the two friends laughed so hard that Betsy nearly peed herself, and then had to wait in an endless bathroom line, standing helplessly while a quarter inch of beer slop on the unmopped floor seeped above the soles of her sandals and between her toes.

CHAPTER 25
LONG DRIVE HOME

September 25, 2010

By the end of the fourth quarter, Betsy was all but sober. The beer and nostalgic Jack and Cokes had done nothing but fog her brain and dull her senses, and she was covered with the salty, sticky residue of dried sweat. As Teddy predicted, they were ready to head back without saying goodbyes, so when he texted them the location of his parking spot, they hopped into the first bike cab they could flag down. A sinewy nineteen-year-old with a couple of missing teeth towed them through the crowd to a lot next to the baseball field.

"Should we ask one of these shirtless wankers what the final score was?" asked Caroline, gesturing to a pack of skinny college boys who had their T-shirts tied around their foreheads.

"Nah," said Betsy. "I don't care."

The last time she went down that street, she was sitting on Gavin's handlebars. She wondered if Remi was in her pj's yet. She called Gavin, who picked up after the first ring.

"You survived," he said. She could hear Remi in the tub in the background.

"Yes, but just barely. I'm with Caroline on the back of some guy's bike," she said.

"Of course you are," he said.

"Can you put Remi on speaker?" she asked.

"Hi, Mama!" The sound of her voice sent electricity down her spine.

"Hi, sweetie! Can you say hi to my friend Caroline?" She put the phone on speaker.

"Hi! Daddy says 'Go Gators,'" a small voice squeaked on the other end of the phone.

"Oh yeah? Well don't believe everything your daddy says," said Caroline.

"Nice to hear your voice, Car," he said.

"You, too, Gavin."

"Listen, Teddy's giving us a ride to Tampa and I have to pay attention or we'll ride right by his parking spot.

"Bye guys, I love you," she said. "I'll see you tomorrow, Rem."

"We love you, too."

Caroline put her hand on her friend's knee and gave it a squeeze.

"Well, well," Caroline said, nodding in approval. "He turned out alright, didn't he?"

"Hey, I'm as surprised as you are," said Betsy.

They found Teddy standing next to his mom's Camry.

"Nice wheels, Ted," said Caroline. "Clearly, it's your midlife crisis car."

Caroline took the passenger seat, as usual, and Betsy slid in the back, forgoing the seat belt in favor of perching on the edge of her seat, her head poking over the console that divided

Caroline and Teddy, like a kid. The traffic out of town was stop-and-go for miles, which allowed for plenty of time for a recap of the day's events, who was divorced, who had a lingering drug problem, and to Betsy's horror, who among their peers had negotiated an open marriage to cope with eighteen torturous years of sexual fidelity.

They'd made it to Lake Panasoffkee before anyone mentioned Ginny.

After Betsy hung up the phone at Miss June's bed-and-breakfast, back in New Orleans on the day they found Ginny, she lost track of the details. Gavin went upstairs to pack their things while June tried to console her, though she couldn't understand the extent of her loss. Instead of stopping in Gainesville, they drove to Ocala, to Ginny's Nana Jean's house. Betsy found her on the porch when they pulled into her driveway. She took Betsy into her plump, pale arms and the two of them wept together on the wicker glider.

They returned for the funeral, and then she tried to go back to school, but Betsy didn't remember much about the days she spent back in Gainesville after Ginny's funeral. She packed her clothes and filled a Dumpster with all the things she no longer wanted. She remembered loading a suitcase and book boxes into Kathy's car, and then standing in the Embassy Suites parking lot with Gavin, worried that she'd be left alone with their secret, that she'd never see him again. She drove away and never came back.

"I can't believe this is the first time you've been in Gainesville since Ginny died," said Teddy to Betsy.

"You mean since Ginny was killed," said Caroline, anger building quickly in her voice. "That really pisses me off. When people say she 'passed away' or 'died' like she fell asleep and tiny angels swooped down and flew away with her tidy little soul. Or that she fought some noble battle with a terminal illness. She was murdered. And before she was murdered, she was raped. And the freak that did it ate a lobster dinner the night before he was executed, courtesy of the state of Florida."

Caroline paused. Teddy looked stricken. Betsy inched back into the seat, trying to hide in the corner of Teddy's mom's car.

"I mean, it was sixteen years after the fact," said Caroline. "He got sixteen more years after Ginny was dead. And that's justice?"

"I'm sorry, I . . . " said Teddy, but he couldn't find the words.

"No, it's alright," said Caroline, putting up her hand in defense. "It's not your fault that it's been twenty years and I can't get over it."

Betsy wanted to disappear. She'd read the press about the lobster tail and cheesecake he ate before he was executed. There was no shortage of details. As the story goes, McRae filled endless legal pads with details, page after page of his dense, looping cursive, line after line filled with song lyrics and childish illustrations of the visions that came to him in the night. Sitting cross-legged on a steel locker, in his six-by-nine-foot cell, he'd written his apologies. It would never be enough. She had read and reread all of it, but never found the answers she wanted. It would never bring Ginny back.

When Betsy dreamed of Ginny, she imagined her friend's last moments a dozen different ways. But every time, Ginny bargained for her life, and McRae lied to her, like he did to all of the others. He told her she could live if she would just stop the screeching and cooperate. In fierce whispers, she warned him that one of her roommates was going to show up at any minute and find him there, and that he was going to rot in hell. In Betsy's dreams, moments after the light faded from Ginny's eyes, he heard the door downstairs, footsteps, and he tiptoed across the floor to hide behind the bedroom door. The floorboard creaked under his weight. He heard a fall, the sound of a chair slamming against the floor. He barreled down the stairs to the small hallway and slid on a pile of mail and newspapers. By the time he got back up on his feet and made it to the door, all he saw was a faint figure disappearing into the far edge of the dark parking lot. In her dreams, Betsy looked back and saw him in the doorframe. In her dreams, she tried to force herself to look back. But in reality, she couldn't. She never did. She didn't look back until it was too late.

According to all of the articles written about his execution, the last hours of McRae's life passed without incident. He cooperated with the guards, said please and thank you when he was asked a question or offered the most basic comforts. By 4:00 p.m. he was led to the room next to the death chamber, which had a small bathroom and a couple of chairs. Some men's clothes hung on hangers from a hook. Did he wonder about the person who would seal his fate, plunging the chemicals through a syringe into his veins while hiding behind a mask? At 5:00 p.m., Scottie showered and shaved. He put on a crisp white shirt, and new pants that fit around the waist but had cuffs that skimmed the ground behind his heels.

In the viewing area, which was separated from the chamber by a large window covered with a drawn curtain, prison guards brought in extra chairs to accommodate the forty-six people who had arrived to witness the execution. McRae's brother and his pastor took seats next to the victims' families. Robert Harrington, Ginny's father, walked stoically into the room and took his seat toward the back. Despite his wife

Martha's pleas for him to stay home, to put it all behind them, to not be complicit in even more violence because their daughter Ginny wouldn't have wanted that, he had to go. Betsy sent them a card a couple of weeks later, when she was home with Remi and lucid enough to pull it together. She never received a reply.

As Scottie waited, the prison warden read him the death warrant listing his crimes and the reasons for his execution, cited by the judge who delivered the verdict. Then the guards led him into a small and sterile room, strapped him to a hospital gurney, and secured his arm to the attached splint. A red phone on the wall, a direct line to the governor's office for dramatic, last-minute pardons, did not ring. They rolled up his sleeve and placed the needle in his arm, forgoing the usual sanitary swipe with an alcohol pad. At 5:50 p.m., the brown curtains parted to a couple of short, stifled gasps, and low, muffled sounds of crying.

AT 6:00 P.M., Scottie began to sing.

He flung those stars into the vast heaven above
Created the rivers, the valleys, the fish and the doves
None greater than Thee . . .

Betsy never learned the tune, but the lyrics stuck with her. *The dumbest song I've ever heard,* she thought.

"What was that?" asked Caroline, who craned her neck around to look at Betsy in the backseat, huddled in the dark corner.

"Oh, um, the lyrics." She was shocked that she'd said it out loud. "The shitty hymn that McRae wrote and sang right before he died. It is the worst, most predictably cliché song ever written. The song pissed me off more than the lobster."

Caroline stared at Betsy. She saw the reflected, green glow of the dashboard lights in Caroline's eyes. A minute passed before she looked away.

"It's got to be hard," said Caroline.

"What? I mean, which part?" asked Betsy.

"To send Remi out into a world that creates guys like Scottie McRae," said Caroline. She turned back around to face the road. "I couldn't do it. I just wasn't strong enough to do it."

Betsy nearly gasped with relief, and she saw Teddy reach over and place his hand on Caroline's knee, just for a second or two.

"Oh, Car," Betsy said, "you have no idea. There are days when I just, I can't."

TEDDY WAS PLAYING Explosions in the Sky on his phone, the sad, lush music that Betsy identified with *Friday Night Lights*, the TV show that made her rethink how she felt about nostalgia, how she finally understood its value now that so much of her life was behind her. And even though the characters were Texan, the love and the loss and the beer and the football and the struggle to get out from under it all made her feel nineteen and lost again, driving the streets of Gainesville, the wind filling her ears in the backseat of Ginny's car.

All of those years later, everything looked different, smaller, blurrier, a little desolate, and they finished the drive mostly in silence. When they finally pulled up to the hotel in Tampa, groggy and weak from the drinks, the heat, and the endless day, Betsy and Teddy said their goodbye. He parked the car and waited while Caroline walked her to the door. Betsy had nearly forgotten about the moths, the way they fought to get close to the burning bulb, jostling for position in the murky light.

"You know that I dream about her," said Caroline.

"Me, too," Betsy nearly whispered. "All the time."

One of the waiters from the hotel restaurant was off to the side smoking a cigarette and Caroline bummed two.

"I never do this anymore," she said.

"I know, me neither," said Betsy. "It tastes like shit, but I like it. If I make it to eighty, I'm starting again. At that point, what's to lose?"

Caroline lit their cigarettes and took the first, harsh drag.

"There's one more thing that I have to tell you," Betsy said, her voice shaky, her hands starting to vibrate from exhaustion, maybe from relief, or maybe from the onset of a hangover. It felt a lot like fear.

"Yeah?" Caroline asked. She saw Betsy's hands trembling and took one in hers and gripped it, hard. "There's literally nothing you could say that would surprise me."

"I made Gavin swear never to tell a living soul," said Betsy. "And I've said it only a handful of times since that night, the night Ginny was killed, twice to my shrink, and another couple of times to this kid, this guy who sold me pills for a while back in . . ."

"You were there," said Caroline.

"What?" said Betsy, not hearing, or believing, what she said.

"You were there that night. In the apartment," said Caroline, flatly.

Betsy felt the blood leave her face and rush to her stomach, which was churning wildly.

"How . . . how did you know?" The cigarette dangled in her hand, its ash growing long with neglect.

"When I got to the apartment that morning, the front door was unlocked, but the back door was opened by force. It didn't make sense," Caroline explained. "Scottie had a pattern. He would identify a victim, stalk her for a day or two, force his way into the apartment, and wait for her to come home. Mostly, he would just slide some glass panes of a window off of the track and pull himself in, or jam a screwdriver in the lock of a sliding glass door, like he did at our place. But the police found a loose key on the floor of the front hall."

"Oh God, the key," said Betsy. "Of course."

"When the police were questioning me, they were all over the apartment looking for evidence. Ginny's key was in her bag. Mine was on my keychain. The landlord still had his," she said. "So the cops asked me if anyone had an extra. There was only one other spare when we rented the place. That's when I figured it out. You were the one who unlocked the door and scattered the mail everywhere in a panic, not Ginny."

"You knew that it was mine. You knew I was there."

"I did."

"And you didn't say anything?"

"I told them that you stayed there sometimes and would use the key, but that we kept it under the potted plant on the stoop, and maybe you dropped it a few days before when you were staying with us," she said.

"And they believed you?"

"Might I remind you that I'm a very skilled liar?"

"Why didn't you tell them that I was the one who unlocked the door?" asked Betsy, bewildered, shocked. And something else: a weight lifting. A lightness, returning.

"I figured that if you'd wanted the police, or anyone else, to know that you'd been there, you'd have come forward and said something when they were questioning you, but you never did," said Caroline. "I was still so pissed at you at Teddy's wedding that I wasn't interested in making you feel better. Then that time I saw you in New York, I wanted to talk to you about it. But I was nervous. I know you don't think I have any typically human emotions, but it can happen. You were so mad at me. And I was mad at you for being angry. I guess I just changed my mind. I didn't want to let you off the hook."

Betsy stood shaking in the circle of light from the moth-swarmed bulb.

"I was there, Caroline," said Betsy, hearing the sound the words made as she spoke them, but so shocked by the admission that she couldn't believe it was happening. "I walked into the apartment and I heard a strange noise. The second I walked in, I knew something was off. I saw the light at the top of the stairwell, the overhead light was on, so obviously something was up."

"I still hate it. Overhead lighting."

"And then," Betsy said, replaying her moves in her head, feeling so completely transported, so present in that apartment in 1990 that she could describe the smell of the place, the exact shade of white paint on the wall. "I walked down the hall to the bottom of the stairs and I looked up, but as soon as I heard that creaky floorboard, you know, the one at the end of Ginny's bed, I ran."

She remembered racing through the parking lot, how startled she was by Gavin's headlights.

"It must have been terrifying," Caroline said.

"But all I could think, all I've been able to think almost

every single day since it happened, was 'Maybe I could have scared him off? Maybe I could have saved her?' But I ran. I was too high. I was too afraid of getting in trouble, of what my mom would say. I convinced myself I was being paranoid. I called 911, but the story I wanted to tell the operator didn't make sense, so I hung up. I didn't have any details. I thought I was making it all up, being high and crazy like always, you know. I didn't think they'd believe me anyway."

Betsy started to sob, and Caroline put her arms around her.

"Ginny had a headache," Caroline told Betsy as she stroked the back of her head. "She'd been struggling with it all day. And she was worried about you. But I begged her to stay and made her promise that she'd go upstairs, grab a blanket and a pillow, and find a dark corner to sleep it off. Instead, she grabbed her bag and snuck out the back door. Once she walked into that apartment, nothing could have saved her."

"You ladies OK?" called Teddy from the parking lot.

"Oh Lord, would you just fuck off already?" Caroline said, not loud enough for him to hear.

"Say again?" he asked.

"I said, 'Please, just give us five more minutes!'" Caroline shouted.

"I was convinced I was hearing things, like I was hallucinating and paranoid," Betsy continued. "So I just ran away. I ran through the parking lot, and I saw Gavin, who'd driven there to find me. And we took off. I didn't call 911 until we pulled into the Steak 'n Shake. I could have saved her."

"Oh no, sweetheart, no," she said, shaking her head, grabbing both of her hands now. "It was too late. You couldn't have saved her."

"Wait, how do you know?"

"I was the one who found her the next day, you know that," said Caroline. "I've been over this so many times, sorry if I seem detached. I lashed out in the car at poor Teddy, but this is stuff I've been over and over a thousand times." She took the last drag of her cigarette and flicked it away. "That was disgusting, by the way. So I went to the apartment to check on Ginny, who'd gone home sick from rush the night before. We were watching a movie. I don't know, it was twenty years ago, right? I can't remember what I was doing last week, but I remember everything about that night except for what movie we watched. Anyway, she snuck out without telling anybody, because she knew we wouldn't have let her go. I remember that conversation we had in my car, on the way to Walmart. What were the odds? Like, of all the women in that town, he was coming after us? Early the next morning, I searched the house looking for her. She wasn't at breakfast. I realized she must have taken off. I thought, *That sneaky little bitch,* and I called the apartment. Nobody answered, and I started to worry a little. I borrowed somebody's car. It was a stick shift, I remember that, and I almost left the transmission in the middle of 16th Street four different times on that short drive. All I can remember thinking was that it wasn't the first time she'd slept through the phone ringing, you know, that she was just sleeping it off."

"Oh God, I feel sick," said Betsy. "I always assumed you were the one who found her."

"You know that pattern the investigators mentioned, of stalking his victims? Well, they said that McRae also had a pattern with his method, the way he killed them. He'd assault them first, you know, sexually."

Caroline paused.

"Look, I know this is hard. I know that I seem crazy-detached right now, but I have to be. You have to know the facts."

"No, I get it, Car," said Betsy. "I've been strangling myself with these words for so long, it's a relief just to hear someone say them out loud."

"Alright, well, stop me if it's too much. So he'd force himself on them, and then he'd stab them, repeatedly, and do all sorts of other sick stuff . . . and when he was finished, he'd wash them with dish soap and water to remove all of the evidence before he arranged them in weird poses."

Betsy turned to vomit in the landscaping behind her.

"Oh God, too much, right? I told you. I'm sorry," she said. Caroline rubbed her back. The waiter who was smoking nearby pretended not to notice, but nearly sprinted inside.

"I read all of this stuff a long time ago," Betsy said, "but it's been a rough day, the bourbon, the nicotine."

Caroline offered her water bottle.

"I'm just going to tell you the rest because you have to hear it. The police said that McRae must have left in a rush. The dish soap and the bloody rag were left on the floor in a mess. At the other crime scenes, he hung around after to clean up. Sometimes he would eat food from the kitchen. Can you believe it? But it was clear that he left in a hurry that night, like he got spooked and took off. The way I see it, he heard you come in the door and ran. But it wasn't until *after* she was dead."

"Are you sure? How can you be sure?" said Betsy.

"Well, that's what the police investigators said." Caroline raised her eyebrow at Betsy. "They placed the time of death right around one thirty or two a.m. There's no denying that he left the place in a mess, which was unusual for him. And then Ginny was his last victim. He left town, because of you."

"And you're absolutely sure she was dead by the time I got there?"

"The detectives seemed to know what they were talking about," said Caroline. "And now the sick fuck's just a corpse in a box so, thank God, we'll never get to ask him. Not that Scottie would have told us. He wasn't interested in putting anyone at ease. But listen, there's something I have to tell you, too."

Caroline paused for a minute before her expression turned grave.

"Wait, what?" Betsy said. "You're freaking me out. There's more? How could there possibly be more?"

"It wasn't your fault that Scottie knew where we lived."

Betsy eyed her warily.

"But we saw him at Taco Bell, and again at Walmart," said Betsy. "He must have followed us back."

"Maybe he did," Caroline said, "but he had been there before."

Any part of the landscape that wasn't spinning in Betsy's vision before, the weirdly manicured plants in front of the hotel, the sliding glass doors filled with yellowish light from the lobby, was set in motion.

"Wait, hold on," Betsy said. "What are you saying?"

"That night at the Porpoise, the night I came home from summer break, do you remember it?" asked Caroline, her voice quivering now.

"Yeah, I mean, vaguely. We went to C.J.'s first and then to the Porpoise and we hung out in back by the pool tables. You were in a booth talking to one of Ginny's guy friends from high school, right?"

Betsy remembered leaving Caroline at the bar.

"I was in a booth, but it wasn't with a guy from Ginny's high school," said Caroline. Betsy could feel her heart pounding hard against her sternum. She put her hands up to her ears, reflexively, afraid of the words they would hear.

"You've got to stay with me, Betsy. I have got to tell you. I've been trying to tell you for twenty years," said Caroline.

"Y'all OK?" asked Teddy again, clearly desperate to leave.

"Yep, we're fine. Just give us five more minutes," shouted Caroline in his direction, and then turned back to Betsy and squeezed her hand tightly.

"You and Ginny were doing your thing. You'd been together all summer without me, and I walked into this chummy roommate situation. I mean, you weren't even paying rent. And I felt like a third wheel in my own apartment. So I was being pissy and I bought those shots, and then another round of shots. We had already had so many drinks at C.J.'s. I was feeling angsty and rebellious and, you know, twenty-one fucking years old, so I wandered into the front bar. He was sitting on a stool by himself."

"Who, Caroline? Who was sitting on a stool by himself?"

"Scottie."

Betsy pulled her hand away from Caroline's in shock, but she hung on every word.

"He was sitting on a stool, nursing a whiskey or something, just brooding and you know, dark. He had a guitar case. He said he was a musician and that he was playing for tips. And I believed him. He was a little dirty, kind of scruffy, but interesting. You know, his face was almost handsome, if you didn't stare too deeply into his eyes. The eyes were what gave him away."

"Jesus, Caroline." Betsy's mind was reeling.

"I know. It gets worse," she said, putting her head in her hands. "And I would do literally anything for something to drink right now. My throat is dry as hell. Let's go look for a vending machine."

They walked into the lobby of the hotel, past the front desk and down a long corridor of hotel rooms. The fluorescent lights in the hallway made Caroline's cheeks look hollow, and her skin glowed nearly green.

"So we were talking. I don't remember everything he said, but he told me his name was Michael something. He had a thick accent and he said he was from Louisiana. He said he was making his way down to the Keys to play at a bar where his friend worked. He said he was just passing through."

Caroline scavenged through her pockets for change but came up short. Betsy dug through her bag to find a dollar bill crisp enough to feed into the slot. Everything about her felt limp and soggy—her dress, her hair, her brain. A can of Coke tumbled through the machine and landed with a thump at the bottom.

"I bought us some drinks and we were just bullshitting, you know how it goes. Ginny came in to try to make me leave and she looked at him funny, like maybe she recognized him or something? But I was thinking that couldn't be possible. Ginny doesn't remember anybody, and this guy was just on his way through town. So I stayed. He said he would drive me home later. We had a few more drinks and then he walked me out to his car. I say it was his car, but it was stolen. He stole it from a Piggly Wiggly in Lutz, or something. I think it was like a Caprice Classic, a total beater. We were talking some more in the car, had a cigarette or two. He got out his guitar and starting playing. I mean, he wasn't terrible. Well, he was obviously terrible. But he was a decent guitar player."

She took a long swig from the ice-cold can and passed it to Betsy.

"We should get back out front or Teddy's going to leave me here," said Caroline, and they walked toward the front drive.

"So, by then it's late, at least three, and he drove me back home. I remember he was swerving a little bit, but I wasn't too worried. Then we got to the parking lot and we started making out, and he got right to it. I mean, I was sloppy and drunk and just kind of fumbling, but he just had his hand up my skirt right away. He wasn't a big guy, so I was surprised by how strong he was. He had one hand on my shoulder, pulling at the neck of my T-shirt and pressing me against the seat of the car. And the other one, I mean, this dirty rough hand was all over me, he fingers were inside me, and he started saying stuff."

"Saying stuff? What do you mean saying stuff?" Betsy couldn't believe what she was hearing.

"At first I just thought it was drunk guy stuff, like asking me if I liked it, calling me a slut, telling me not to fight it, just to let it happen. And then he reached over and opened the passenger door and he kind of jumped over me and was trying to lift me out of the car. It was creepy, and I started to catch on, like, wait, this guy isn't just a stupid frat boy. I have no idea who he is. So I just said, 'You know, I can get it from here. I'm tired. I just want to go to bed. Alone.' And he had both of my wrists in his hands."

"How did this happen? Why didn't you tell me before?" asked Betsy.

"I tried! You wouldn't even talk to me. I came in the apartment that night and tried to wake you up, but I was so drunk, and all you could say was how creepy I was. I just wanted to forget about it."

"But how are you still alive?"

"I mean, exactly at that moment, I was twisting my wrists free from his grip and a truck full of these idiot guys pulls up. Do you remember those neighbors, the KAs who used to blast Garth Brooks at their parties? I mean, they pulled up in a giant pickup. There must have been four or five of them in back. It was crazy. What the hell were they doing out at that hour? Cow-tipping? Then they did that whole 'Miss, is this gentleman causing you any trouble?' thing, even though I am sure they were just coming home from a gang rape or something. They were real charmers, right? Anyway, he must have been spooked, because he let me go. Then he watched me walk right up those steps to our front door."

"So what does all of this mean?"

"I guess it means that I'm just as guilty as you are, maybe more. You know, in all of the interviews McRae did, he talked about Ginny and the women he killed, but he followed others, too. He was trying to portray himself as a criminal mastermind possessed by a split personality. He didn't want people to think it was random, that he got the wrong girl. So there was always a part of me that wondered . . ."

"That it should have been you. Or it could have been you," said Betsy. "I know. I feel the same way."

She stared at Caroline, trying to process everything she had told her. They had both been struggling all of those years, alone.

"Of course, I hadn't known it was him until years later when I saw his photo in the paper. It took me a while to connect the dots, but when I did, that's when I really started going off of the rails."

Betsy remembered that night with the grocery bags, when the perfectly formed memory of Scottie McRae on a bike at Taco Bell fluttered gracelessly into her brain like a moth.

"But Betsy, here is my point: I led that guy straight to our front door, but I didn't kill her. Scottie McRae killed her. I couldn't have saved her. You couldn't have saved her. If you'd walked in five minutes before you did, he would have killed both of you. If you'd walked in two hours before, you'd be the dead one. If Ginny had stayed at the sorority house that night, like she said she was going to, like she *promised* me she would, maybe she would have lived for another day. Maybe he would have come back again and again until he got her? Maybe I would have been there that time and I would be gone, too? The unlikely scenario is that he would have just given up and walked away. And I'll say it again. The only thing you maybe should have done differently is to tell the truth after it happened. And the only thing you can do now, going forward, is to keep telling the truth, to yourself, to Gavin, to me, to everybody. And one thing that's true is that you were a really good friend to Ginny."

"Wow, Car," Betsy said, shaking her head in disbelief. She reached out and pulled Caroline toward her, hard. Caroline resisted at first, but she softened in her friend's arms. Teddy's car pulled up in front of them and he rolled down the passenger window.

"I'm glad you two are hugging it out," he said, "but I feel I need to remind you it's been a long-ass day."

Betsy was dazed and drained, and certain she would hurl again. Betsy let go, reluctantly, since she loved the way Caroline's long arms felt wrapped around her neck, after all these years.

"Caroline, I'm so sorry. I'm sorry I made you lie for me. I'm sorry I disappeared. I was a mess. You were always stronger than me."

"I think we both know that's not true," she said, taking Betsy's face in her hands, the way Betsy did with Remi when she wanted to stop time for a minute, remember the little golden flecks in her green eyes. "He'd been watching her for days, after we ran into him when we were out buying poster boards. I didn't recognize him right away when I first saw his picture, but then I put it all together."

Betsy felt a painful jag of what must have been relief deep in her chest. She'd imagined so many scenarios of how this might happen, how she would be absolved, unburdened, and none of them felt anything like this.

"I can't believe you knew all of this. I can't believe you picked up Scottie McRae at a bar," said Betsy in a low whisper, out of Teddy's earshot. "And you never said anything."

"You've got to remember. I hated your fucking guts for years," said Caroline. "The last thing I wanted to do was make you feel better."

Caroline opened the passenger door and slid in. Betsy blew Teddy a kiss.

"See you, T," she said. "Thanks for the ride."

"Tell that deadbeat dad back in NYC to give me a call."

"Will do."

"So how about I come for a visit?" asked Caroline. "I want to meet Remi Virginia. Do I get to call her R.V. for short?"

"We'll set a place for you at Thanksgiving," she said. "Gavin makes a mean fried turkey."

"Thanksgiving, huh? I'll consider it, but only if I get to hold down the Snoopy balloon in the parade."

Betsy realized that she hadn't made a plan more than a month in advance for as long as she could remember, like she'd been waiting for the other shoe to drop. Tonight, she felt different.

"Sure," she said. "We can arrange for that."

UPSTAIRS, THE COOL, dark room with the crisply made bed felt like the Le Meurice hotel. She lay down on top of the sheet and called Gavin.

"Oh, thank God, you're still up."

"It's not even midnight, B. I was waiting for your call. How was the ride home? How's crazy Caroline?"

"I have so much to tell you. I would bet you a thousand bucks that Caroline and Teddy hook up tonight. Plus, I threw up in the bushes."

"You must be in Florida."

SHE SLEPT ON top of the cool, clean sheets, lulled by the steady hum of the overworked air conditioner straining against that muggy night air. Her skin felt sticky from dried sweat and spilled drinks, but she was too tired for a shower. She'd get up early tomorrow and put Florida behind her again for a while. But right then she wanted to let her heavy eyes close, to visit her friend in her dreams, to tell her she was sorry one more time.

CHAPTER 26

COMING HOME

September 27, 2010

"Hi, Mommy."

Betsy opened her eyes to find Remi, blurry at first, then in sharp, beautiful focus, standing beside her bed.

"Good morning, sweet girl," she said, lifting the bedcover with her left hand and pulling her daughter close with her right.

"I missed you," said Remi.

"Oh, I know, I missed you, too. You were asleep when I got home and I didn't want to wake you," said Betsy. "But I tiptoed into your room and gave you a kiss anyway."

Every time Betsy flew home to New York, she felt like she was reentering the earth's atmosphere with a bang and a jolt. Even two days away, two stressful, humid, sweat-soaked days, interrupted her rhythm. The problem with being a transplanted New Yorker was that you no longer felt entirely at home anywhere, not in your adopted city, despite two decades spent trying to perfect it, and not in the place from which you emerged, whether it was a bloodless suburb, a slow beach town, or a dense but less kinetic American city. Each time the plane descended over the water and found, miraculously, the edge of the runway at LaGuardia, Betsy was amazed. She was proud of the life she'd built there, stunned that she had made it that far, and more than a little perplexed by how she would raise her child there.

Remi's childhood was already so unlike her own. They were both only children, but that was the extent of their shared experiences. In Betsy's case, it was due to a faulty marriage and an uncommitted father. Remi wouldn't have a sibling because of Betsy and Gavin's collective indecision. Then there was the trauma of Remi's birth, which was enough to scare both Gavin and Betsy away from baby-making for good. They were so grateful for one, for their sweet and happy little girl, that neither of them had any regrets. Gavin and his brother would ignore each other for most of the year and then happily reunite for Christmas like nothing happened, so the importance of siblings escaped him. It was Betsy who worried.

Would Remi find someone to trust? And then would someone else, someone lurking in the shadows, take her away? Betsy pulled her daughter closer.

"Daddy said that we can have pancakes today," said Remi, wiggling out of her grip and slipping back onto the floor.

"Oh, he did, did he? Well, I for one cannot wait to taste the pancakes Daddy is making this morning, in the next forty minutes, before we have to leave for school."

Gavin was waiting at the door when she came home Sunday

night, and Betsy, embarrassed, worn out, unable to keep it together a minute longer, wept as soon as she spotted him at the end of the hall. Graying at the temples, so much older than the man she first met, still not as lumpy around the middle as Betsy had predicted on their first trip to the lake. Gavin was the one she needed to see. They had arrived in New York with hopes that the constant thrum of life there would drown out their shared sadness, erase the blight on their past. She was slowly starting to understand that the blight was what made them. Without that premature reminder that life was often tragically short, would they have squandered even more precious time? Would they have made it as a couple for a few months and then drifted away after graduation, not feeling the urgency, neither one allowing the other to look at their weaknesses, the ugly parts, head-on?

Post-pancakes (which, to appease Betsy, were made with spelt flour but still drenched with syrup), Remi excused herself and announced that she would be getting dressed on her own. Minutes later, Remi emerged in her favorite purple striped dress, topped with a turquoise cardigan and accented with a fringed vest that was part of last year's failed "cowpoke" costume and gold high-tops.

"Perfect," said Betsy. She dug out a pair of rhinestone earrings, shaped like clusters of leaf-shaped stones, from her jewelry box and slid on her patent leather pumps with hopes that Remi would notice.

"You're so shiny today!" she said, with a clear stamp of approval.

By the time Betsy and Remi rounded the block closest to school, Remi had counted to ten in Mandarin a dozen times.

Betsy drew a deep breath, crossed the threshold to school, and greeted Elodie with a smile.

"Betsy! I'm delighted to see you!" Elodie said. "And Remi. Don't you look happy today?"

Betsy knelt down to give her daughter a hug.

"OK, Rem. Go get 'em."

Remi pecked her mother's cheek before she darted into the classroom.

Before Elodie could speak, Betsy waved goodbye, with the briefest "See you tomorrow," and turned to leave.

Outside on the sidewalk, the air felt crisp on her flushed cheeks. She looked up at the cloudless sky, infinite blue over the tops of the low buildings that lined the street. The clear morning light filtered through the tiny trees and reflected off of the windshields of cars parked along the curb. She wiped away the first tear, then the second. And then she started to laugh. She realized how ridiculous she looked in her sparkly earrings and heels, frozen in front of a preschool, her face wet and red with tears, and hunched over with laughter. People walked past her on the sidewalk, unfazed, expertly dodging the potentially insane woman on the sidewalk with barely a raised brow. Her phone buzzed in her bag. *Gavin,* she thought. She dug for it, but the call had gone to voice mail. For a few seconds, she debated calling him back, but decided it could wait until she got to the office. She texted Caroline instead.

I have a story you are going to love, Betsy tapped with her thumbs.

She looked down the sidewalk in the direction of the subway station. Maybe she'd take the M20 instead? If she needed to, she could hop off of the bus at any time. Once she got to work, she could hail a cab from the office and get back to the school in minutes, if she needed to, she thought. She just had to move her legs, put one foot in front of the other. Betsy took a few deep breaths, relieved she finally knew, instinctively, which way was north, summoning all of the forward momentum she could to move that way.

ACKNOWLEDGMENTS

For her excellent guidance, patience, positivity, and for believing in me and in this story, I'm indebted to Brettne Bloom. For her editorial insight, generosity, and overwhelming kindness, thanks go to Emily Krump. For being early and enthusiastic readers, I am forever grateful to Jen Wang, Heather Fogarty, Anamaria Wilson, Ira Ungerleider, Catherine Elsworth, Suzanne Lennon Portner, Melissa Thomas, Sarah Rafferty, Anna Roth Milner, Deanna Kizis, Eve Epstein, and Whitney Langdon. This wouldn't exist without you. For nearly three decades of friendship, sharing their memories, and their mutual stamp of approval, thank you Liz Bowyer and Kari Olivier. For their unconditional support and overall badassness, I am grateful, again, to Jen Wang, Sara Lamm, Mary Wigmore, and Tuesday night margaritas. For their insight on matters of the mind and the spirit, I am grateful to Deb Stern and Sylvia Hirsch Jones. For some critical intelligence and showing me the ropes all of those years ago, thanks go to Doris Athineos and Dana Wood. For getting me over that last hurdle toward the finish line with some heartfelt high-fives, many, many thanks to Andrew and Catherine Stellin Waller. For being awesome, I send love and thanks to Crystal Meers. For a lifetime of love, I am grateful to my family. For enriching my life and filling my heart in infinite ways, thank you Millie and Louis. For literally everything else, including the best thirteen years of my life, thank you Andrew Reich.

Insights,
Interviews
& More . . .

About the author

About the book

Read on

About the author

Meet Christine Lennon

Darcy Hemley

CHRISTINE LENNON is a Los Angeles based writer. Before she moved to the West Coast and started her freelance career, she was an editor at *W*, *Vogue*, and *Harper's Bazaar*. Since then she has written for publications including *T*, the *New York Times* style magazine; the *Wall Street Journal; Town & Country; W; Vogue; Harper's Bazaar; Martha Stewart Living; Sunset; C California Style; Marie Claire; Self;* Net-a-Porter's Porter and The Edit online magazine, among others. Christine lives in California with her husband, Andrew Reich, and their twins. *The Drifter* is her first book.

Questions for Discussion

1. Betsy sees herself differently than others see her. Do you think that you perceive yourself in the same way that others do? When and why are there discrepancies?
2. *The Drifter* delves into sorority culture of the late 1980s and early 1990s. How does this inform all of the women's relationships throughout the novel?
3. Betsy's friends become like family when she's at school. How do these friendships define her over the course of her life? Is Caroline a true friend? Is Gavin? Is Betsy?
4. What are your impressions of Caroline? What are your impressions of Ginny? Do those change as the novel progresses?
5. Music is a big part of *The Drifter.* How do you think the songs relate to the story? Do they foreshadow events? Do they set a tone for the story? Are there any themes hidden within them?
6. Betsy's adult life is defined by her time in Gainesville—the music, the art, the fashion, the friends. Is there a time or a place in your life that has helped to define you? ▸

Questions for Discussion *(continued)*

7. Betsy often uses unconventional humor to lighten the mood or cast a shadow over a situation. Why do you think she does this? How does this influence her relationship with those around her? Does her humor reveal how she is feeling? Explain why or why not.

8. Gavin and Betsy have a complicated relationship. Do you think it progressed too fast? Was Ginny's death a catalyst for their relationship? Do you think they are ultimately a good match?

9. There are a number of parent–child relationships in the story. How would you describe the relationship between Betsy and Kathy? Does this affect how Betsy interacts with her daughter? Do you think Betsy is a good parent?

10. To what extent do you think that each of the girls could have prevented Ginny's tragic death? Were they in any way guilty? How did their innocence play into the crime?

The Story Behind the Story

At 6:55 a.m. on November 16, 1984, I was standing in front of my bathroom mirror, struggling with my uncooperative bangs, dreading another friendless day of ninth grade at a new school, when the windows of our house in Clearwater, Florida, shook from the force of a sonic boom.

My family had been in the state for less than two weeks. We moved from Kansas City to the Gulf Coast because my father had another new job, and chronic wanderlust, and he dragged us along for the ride.

We hadn't lived there long enough to know that when the space shuttle *Discovery* descended toward the Kennedy Space Center after its three-million-mile mission, it would hurtle through the sky over our single-story, cinder block and stucco rental house at an astounding speed. When it passed overhead, it made more than just a sound. The force of its motion on the atmosphere rattled your bones and your teeth and your organs. It felt fascinating, kind of cool, a little creepy, and generally weird. It was unlike anything I had experienced before. In short, it was very Florida.

To me, *Florida* is an adjective and a proper noun, a feeling *and* a place. ▸

The Story Behind the Story ***(continued)***

It conveys oppressive humidity, the sticky-warm water of the Gulf of Mexico, dirty soles of bare feet, relentless sun, salt-stained visors, sunglasses permanently perched on the tops of heads of the odd characters that populate the place.

I lived in the state for eight years. To everyone's surprise (especially mine) I stayed in state for college at the University of Florida in Gainesville, another peculiar town in the center of the state, which felt like it was being slowly consumed by trees and moss, climbing vines and all manner of growing green things.

The city was small but the school was huge, so I pledged a sorority to feel less anonymous. It's a fact that is constantly amusing to the people who know me now, but should come as no real surprise since I've made my living working among women for fashion magazines. I guess I feel most comfortable in an estrogen fog? My new "sisters" were completely irresistible and terrifying, exotic creatures to be admired, studied, and sometimes feared. It was girl culture at its most extreme. We were young and not exactly stupid, but we said and did ridiculous things in the way that audacious young people who think they run the place often do. When I see the women those girls have become, successful business owners, executives, doctors, lawyers, and excellent mothers—one of them worked in the White House for the first Clinton administration, another was the youngest female to ever make the *Forbes* billionaire list—I'm still impressed. I don't regret the time I spent with them, but I'm glad I got out when I did.

At my first official fraternity party as a freshman, a man fell off of a third-story balcony on to concrete and died. I heard screams over the pounding music. Someone called 911, and everyone at the party, including underage drinkers like me, scurried out in a panic. I remember downing my red Solo cup full of keg beer before I ran up the back steps and out to the parking lot. I remember catching a glimpse of a shoe and part of a leg on the ground through a small crowd of people, though I'm sure it's just a trick my mind plays on me, Photoshopping a detail to embellish a memory. Later, I was told that the guy, who I did not know, died saving his girlfriend, who was about to fall herself. I doubt that it's true, but that's how news traveled back then. It was distorted, exaggerated, passed along in rumors and whispers as if the facts of what actually happened weren't tragic enough. In some ways, that dark beginning set the tone for my entire experience at school. We were wild ▸

and a little reckless, feeling immortal, cooking up ways to spike our adrenaline in an otherwise sleepy place.

Don't get me wrong. Gainesville was, and still is, fun. It delights in its weirdness in the same way Austin, Texas, does, except without the added legitimacy of being the state's capital. It's a town that's obsessed with sports, both playing them and gathering in large crowds to watch them, where drinking also takes on a competitive zeal. College campus culture has changed considerably since then, but back in 1990, the perception was that the greatest threats to students were alcohol and drug-related: Drunk driving, booze-fueled fraternity hazing, overdoses, and alcohol poisoning were justifiable causes of concern.

But in August of that year, there was a more acute danger lurking in the shadows. Danny Rolling, a career criminal, sex offender, armed robber, and murderer from Shreveport, Louisiana, arrived in Gainesville by bus. He checked into a hotel under an alias and started stalking his future victims. He claimed that voices in his head told him to do it. By the time he was finished, he killed five people—four women and a man—and a shockwave traveled through college campuses across the country, places populated with students who were still riding high on the Reagan 1980s, all optimism, John Hughes movie angst, and popped collars. And the world had another serial killer to analyze and mythologize, the Gainesville Ripper. Kevin Williamson, the creator of the *Scream* movies, has said that the first film was inspired by the murders. When I tell people where I went to school, I often see the flicker of recognition in their eyes. People remember the Gainesville murders. It was a time before student deaths and violence were plastered across the news and the headlines stayed with them.

The timing may have been pure coincidence, but the fall of 1990 also ushered in a darker moment in our culture. There was a shift in music from pop anthems to grunge, fashion became darker and more subdued as women my age traded in their white sneakers for Doc Martens, and a generation, X, was born.

The Drifter is inspired by that time and those events. It is not a roman à clef or a memoir or true crime. It's a story that evokes the place and the time as I remember it, with a cast of fictional characters who feel completely, eerily familiar to me. It's a story about the strange and powerful bonds of female friendship. It's a story about Betsy Young who loses the first love of her life—her best friend, Ginny—to a brutal act of violence, and finds the ▸

second love of her life, Gavin, over five long, excruciating days in Gainesville. It's about how losing someone you love and the ensuing grief can shape our lives into adulthood, and how we struggle to manage the guilt we feel when we make terrible choices and others suffer the consequences. It's about building a life in a strange new city, and returning to the place that made us who we are, to make amends, to reconnect, and to say good-bye.

The Playlist

Psychologists refer to our freaky ability to recall fully formed memories from our adolescence and early adulthood as the "reminiscence bump." For reasons we don't completely understand, the friendships, stories, events, and thoughts from the third decade of our lives—our twenties—become our most vivid recollections. It makes perfect sense, then, that the music we hear during that time of our lives plays a big role in our life story, and in many ways, shapes our lives for decades to come.

As a young teenager in Kansas, if I fiddled with the tuner dial on my clock radio late at night, I could tune into Jayhawk Radio (KJHK 90.7 FM), the college station at KU in Lawrence, almost forty miles away. It's when I first fell in love with R.E.M. and the Smiths and the Replacements and all of the other staples of classic alternative radio. By the time I got to school at Florida, I was very excited to be in a college town where I thought that kind of music culture lived. Little did I know that in the late 1980s the South Florida dance music/Vanilla Ice–force in Gainesville was strong, and the scene I was looking for was harder to find than I thought. I did find some kindred spirits, though, and we rarely missed the Wednesday late-night alternative dance parties at Gator Bumpers, a ▸

The Playlist ***(continued)***

bar with bumper cars (really) and a tiny dance floor. Every week, the last song they played at 2:00 a.m. was R.E.M. "Superman," and I remember feeling that as long as I had music, I could, in fact, do anything.

By the time I was a senior, popular music had shifted so completely that you were more likely to hear Nirvana blasting from a dorm room than the 2 Live Crew. And the transformation of the culture was fascinating to watch.

When I began writing *The Drifter*, I started by listening to the music I loved in 1990. Whether you experienced it the first time over twenty years ago, or are discovering it now, I hope that hearing these songs makes you feel twentysomething and equal parts excited and terrified by what your future holds.

Here is a playlist of songs mentioned in and that inspired *The Drifter.* For a complete list of the bands and songs mentioned in the book, and the more contemporary songs that inspired modern-day Betsy, check out The Drifter: The Playlist on Spotify.

"Here's Where The Story Ends" by the Sundays
"Gone Daddy Gone" by Violent Femmes
"Dirty Boots" by Sonic Youth
"Slow Down" by the Feelies
"Makes No Sense at All" by Hüsker Dü
"Freak Scene" by Dinosaur Jr.

"Wichita Lineman" by Urge Overkill
"Psycho Killer" by Talking Heads
"You My Flower" by the Afghan Whigs
"No New Tale to Tell" by Love and Rockets
"The Globe" by Big Audio Dynamite
"Sour Times" by Portishead
"Needle in the Hay" by Elliott Smith
"I Am a Scientist" by Guided by Voices
"Like a Fool" by Superchunk
"Motion Picture Soundtrack" by Radiohead

(Honorable mentions that didn't make it into the book, but were no doubt on Betsy's mixtape: "911 Is a Joke" by Public Enemy, "I'll Be You" by the Replacements, and "Nightswimming" by R.E.M.)

Read on

Narrowing my list of favorite books to just eight was nearly impossible. So many books! And yes, so many years of my life! I didn't start out with a theme, but it occurred to me when I saw the titles I picked—in chronological order—that each of these stories feature characters that could be described as drifters, or at least adrift in the way that Betsy is drifting. For the most part, they all feel rootless and disconnected or on the outside of life looking in, and are considering their past and how it shaped them. With a few exceptions, they're brutally honest (maybe not Tom) and self-critical, but none of them fail to see the humor in their situation—even if it's a bit morbid (yes, I'm talking about you, Esther Greenwood). Below, a few of my favorite stories:

TOM SAWYER BY MARK TWAIN

In fourth grade, I was assigned to a reading group. We were given a list of classics and I picked *Tom Sawyer.* At that age, the thickness of a book was almost as important as its contents. I remember people being impressed by a ten-year-old lugging around a big book and feeling pretty pleased with myself. At the time, I lived in Kansas City and

I roamed our neighborhood with a pack of unruly kids, so despite the century that separated us, Tom was a character who was weirdly familiar to me. I also have a soft spot for troublemakers, and Tom was a badass.

THE BELL JAR BY SYLVIA PLATH

When I read this in high school, I missed the point of it as a cautionary tale about mental illness and treated it more like an aspirational, feminist "Modern Girl's Guide." I was so obsessed with Sylvia Plath that I applied to a bunch of the Seven Sisters colleges (I didn't get in) and was determined to move to New York, write for magazines, and live in a hotel for unmarried women which, I am realizing now, must be a lot like living in a sorority house.

GEEK LOVE BY KATHERINE DUNN

A friend gave me his dog-eared copy of *Geek Love* in college and I devoured it. I didn't realize how popular it was—like a counterculture bible of the Pacific Northwest alternative scene (Kurt and Courtney were fans)—until much later. The Binewskis made every other sick and twisted family look like amateurs, but the raw emotion of the story and the relationship between the siblings was what really got me. ▸

Read on ***(continued)***

HERE IS NEW YORK **BY E. B. WHITE**

As a kid, I read *Stuart Little* and *The Trumpet of the Swan* and *Charlotte's Web* so many times. And as a young journalist, *Elements of Style* saved my ass every day. But *Here Is New York*, which is really a long essay, is my favorite of White's stories. A friend gave it to me during a weird transitional time in my life. I was ending a long, difficult relationship and felt so lonely. When I read this, it struck me that people had been living there and feeling exactly what I was feeling, which was both isolated and somehow connected to the city, for generations. It made me feel less alone.

WHERE I WAS FROM **BY JOAN DIDION**

I've been a Didion fan forever, but I really reconnected with her writing when I moved to Los Angeles. I'd roll down the windows of my Passat and wish I were in her Stingray on my way to a beach house on Portuguese Bend instead of my tiny bungalow in Silver Lake. When I went to hear her read from *The Year of Magical Thinking* at the Hammer Museum, my husband and I were running late so we dashed into the elevator. Just as the doors were closing, I realized that Joan Didion was one of two other people on it with us. I interview celebrities for a living, but I couldn't come up with a single thing to say. I wish I had just remembered to say "Thank you." I love everything she touches, but this one is a favorite.

A VISIT FROM THE GOON SQUAD BY JENNIFER EGAN

I have loved Egan's writing since I read her *New York Times Magazine* profile on model James King back in 1996. I devoured *Look at Me* and *The Keep*. But *Goon Squad* is a masterpiece. From those first lines describing Sasha in a restroom at a bar, fixing her yellow eye shadow, focusing on a handbag that someone left on the counter and trying desperately not to steal it, I was hooked. I love how she weaves music through the story, too. It's amazingly complex and so fun to read.

ST. LUCY'S HOME FOR GIRLS RAISED BY WOLVES BY KAREN RUSSELL

Southern Gothic writers like Carson McCullers and Eudora Welty are among my very favorites. I find all of those dark characters, all of that suffering and booze, and the strange social politics of small-town life really irresistible. Somehow Russell has turned the whole genre on its head with her bizarre stories about Florida, which is clearly a place that fascinates me. The worlds she creates are so unique and, yes, *dark*. And she's so ►

young! I've loved everything she has written and can't wait to see what's next for her.

***DEPT. OF SPECULATION* BY JENNY OFFILL**

So many terrific books have been written about the challenges of being in a modern marriage, but I think it's harder to write about being a modern parent. A mother who is conflicted about raising kids, even a little bit resentful about the sacrifices she has to make to do it, is considered unlikable. And the world just doesn't embrace female assholes the way it does their male counterparts. Anyway, Offill writes about motherhood with such breathtaking skill, marveling at women who "cast ambition off like an expensive coat that no longer fits" when they have children, that it was impossible not to like, or at least admire, her nameless main character, even as her world implodes around her. ~